A POCKETFUL OF DIAMONDS

PAM LECKY

Storm
PUBLISHING

Copyright © Pam Lecky, 2024

The moral right of the author has been asserted.

Ebook ISBN: 978-1-80508-699-4
Paperback ISBN: 978-1-80508-700-7

Cover design: Ghost
Cover images: Shutterstock

Published by Storm Publishing.
For further information, visit:
www.stormpublishing.co

ALSO BY PAM LECKY

The Lucy Lawrence Mysteries

No Stone Unturned

Footprints in the Sand

The Art of Deception

To Olive & Sean Murphy

PART 1

RIPPLES ON THE WATER

ONE

August 1888, a train enroute to Basle, Switzerland

Lucy Stone twirled the wedding band on her finger as she gazed out of the first-class carriage window. To her disappointment, the French countryside was passing in a blur in the rapidly fading dusk. A tiny sigh escaped her lips. It wasn't that she was unhappy; far from it. But changing trains in Paris had been a difficult point in their journey. The urge to stay had been strong, but instead of hailing a cab to take them to their hotel – and a jolly nice one Phineas had chosen, too – they had had to wait over an hour for the next departure to Basle. *It would have been pleasant in the French capital this evening with the weather so fine,* her treacherous mind whispered. *The sights, the smells, the romance...*

'Isn't it strange how waiting for steamers and trains can be so tiring?' she remarked a few moments later.

When there was no response, she turned, only to catch Phin watching her from the opposite seat. He had been unusually quiet since Paris, and she knew the reason. He felt guilty about their change of plans, even though it had been a joint decision.

She flashed him a smile and was rewarded with an answering one, which promised that their second night as man and wife would be just as wonderful as their first. Now, slightly giddy, she looked out of the window once more, this time grinning at her reflection.

It was almost surreal. Their wedding, which had taken place at Thorncroft, the Stone estate in Kent, had only been yesterday. And what a glorious day it had been. As she had fallen asleep in Phin's arms last night, she had thanked God for her good fortune. She had woken, happy and excited to be setting off on their honeymoon. Except, of course, it wasn't to be. If that telegram had arrived even an hour later, they would have missed it. They would now be enjoying Paris, and not on their way to Lake Como, Italy, to find a missing count...

Phineas cleared his throat and patted the seat. 'I'm feeling neglected over here, dear heart. It's almost dark. What could be so interesting out there?'

'Sorry. I was daydreaming. Reliving yesterday,' she replied. She jumped up and pulled down the blind before sitting down beside him and resting her head against his shoulder.

'Happy thoughts, I hope?' he asked, entwining his fingers through hers.

'Very.'

'I wish—'

Lucy straightened up and placed her index finger on his lips, shaking her head. 'Stop! Don't say it. We can visit Paris another time.'

Phin's eyes strayed to the railway map on the wall above the opposite seat. 'We're only a few hours out of Paris. We could turn back.'

'And let Elvira down? Absolutely not!' Lucy squeezed his hand. 'Of course we must go to Como and the sooner we get there, the better.'

'It's a long and tiresome trip if we go straight through. We could break the journey and overnight in Basle at a hotel?' he suggested.

'No, the sleeper is fine. Poor Elvira. She must be going out of her mind with worry. Your sister desperately needs our help.'

'I fear you're right,' Phin replied. 'But let's hope we're in luck and Luca will have turned up by the time we reach Bellagio.'

'And if that is the case, we can spend our honeymoon on the lake. I've heard it's a very beautiful place.'

Lucy had first met Phin's sister Elvira at Thorncroft earlier in the year. They had instantly become friends. Luca had been with Elvira on that trip, but Lucy, in a state of nervous tension due to meeting Phin's family for the first time, had paid him little attention. Now she wished she had. That Elvira and Luca were madly in love, she was certain. They had radiated happiness even after four years of marriage. And Lucy couldn't blame Elvira, for Luca was a handsome man, tall, with expressive dark eyes and an easy manner. In their one brief conversation, he had spoken warmly of his young son and daughter, all the while bestowing loving glances on his wife. All of which made his disappearance odd. Still, you never could judge people based on a few hours' acquaintance. Over the last few years, Lucy had discovered that to her cost.

Elvira's cry for help, although worrying, had fired Lucy's curiosity. Where was Luca? Why had he disappeared? Was there a sinister reason for it? Could Elvira be overreacting? Perhaps they had had a silly row, and he had stormed off in a rage to punish her. Italians were renowned for being emotional and dramatic. Lucy pulled up short. *Now, that's uncharitable. Stereotyping is a lazy form of analysis.* Besides, whatever the cause of his disappearance, there was no point in speculating until they had the facts.

'If only Elvira had given us more information. I wonder how

long he has been missing,' Lucy mused. 'How well do you know him?'

'Not well at all,' Phin said. 'Since their marriage, Elvira and Luca have only been to England a handful of times. But I liked him. He struck me as a decent sort, well-educated and sensible. We have a common interest in art, and I understand there's a fine collection at the villa which I look forward to viewing.'

'I suppose it's not surprising that they haven't visited Kent very often. It's a long journey,' Lucy said, trying not to think about the hours of travel which lay ahead of them for the next twenty hours or more.

'Yes, and the children are very young to undertake such a trip.' Phin sighed. 'However, it's hardest on Father. He can no longer travel and misses seeing Elvira and the grandchildren.'

'I sensed she might be his favourite daughter,' Lucy said.

With a smile, Phineas said, 'Yes, he's not good at hiding it, even after all the predicaments she has landed in over the years.'

Lucy raised a brow. 'Predicaments? Now, that sounds intriguing.'

Phin continued, 'More unfortunate than intriguing. The circumstances around her marriage in the first place are... regrettable.'

'I'm astonished! In what way?' Lucy asked. 'I thought it was a love-match.'

'Eh, partly. I love my sister dearly, but she has always been impetuous and headstrong. Not unlike you, my dearest.' Lucy threw him a dirty look, but he just chuckled and kissed her. 'I wouldn't have you any other way.'

'Hmm. You were saying about Elvira...'

'I may have omitted certain details.'

'Such as?'

'She left England as a companion to our elderly aunt on a trip to Italy. Elvira didn't want to go, protested quite strongly, in fact, but there had been an incident at a ball in London and it was considered best she disappeared for a little. All appeared—'

Lucy sat up straight. 'Whoa! What incident? You can't just leave me in the dark like that!'

'You're incorrigible,' he replied. 'Besides, it's irrelevant.' But his eyes were alight, and she realized he was teasing her.

'Phin! Tell me! Please.'

He pursed his lips, trying not to laugh. 'She slapped Lord Kerridge in the face and left him standing in the middle of the ballroom floor.'

Now, this was interesting. 'Did she indeed? Why?'

'I don't recall,' he replied, not quite meeting her eye.

'Yes, you do. Out with it!' Lucy demanded.

With a sigh, he continued, 'Elvira claimed he made an inappropriate suggestion. Let's just leave it at that.'

'That doesn't surprise me. I met him once at Lady Sarah's and thought him quite an oily individual,' Lucy replied. 'Still, why was she the one being punished? He was the one in the wrong.'

'That's not how society sees it, as well you know, my dear. She embarrassed a peer of the realm in public.'

'Well, I say, good for her!'

'I thought that might be your assessment, but you can guess the consequences. The gossips had a field day. And Andrew—'

'Ah! I might have known he had something to do with her banishment.'

Phin threw her a knowing look. 'It wasn't banishment... Anyway, she saw sense eventually and agreed to the trip. They returned a month later, Elvira as a married woman with a husband in tow and under something of a cloud.'

'Gracious! But why under a cloud? Did your family not approve of Luca?'

'Well, there was more to it than that. Let's just say Elvira gave the family little choice in the matter. While in Milan, my aunt caught the couple *in flagrante delicto*, in an orangery – I know, not very original! Aunt Margaret nearly had a heart seizure. Elvira and Luca had to marry rather quickly before there could be any hint of scandal. From Luca's family's perspective, Elvira was the worst possible choice, being English, Protestant and, in their opinion, of questionable morals.'

'Which is nonsense. It takes two to be naughty.'

'True, but not to a noble Italian family, Lucy. Pure bloodlines are paramount. Religion is even more so. They insisted Elvira converted. Which she did.'

Lucy mulled this over. 'Which suggests she was very much in love.'

'Or perhaps had little say in the matter.'

'Do you think Luca has regrets? That he may have gone off with someone else?'

'Good God, I hope not! No. As I said, I have no concern that he is anything other than a gentleman. Besides, I'm not in the errant husband finding business, even for Elvira.'

Lucy patted his arm. 'Yes, that would be ghastly. But equally, it would be awful if something dreadful has happened to him.'

Phin scowled. 'Either way, my love, I have a bad feeling about this summons.' Then his expression softened. 'But thank goodness you will be with me.'

'You're truly happy for me to help you investigate?'

Phin caressed her cheek. 'I'm relying on you.' His words thrilled her. They meant he was accepting her as an equal. Taking her involvement as a given. Phin continued, 'It would appear the universe has conspired that our marriage is to start as it will probably continue: us chasing shadows and unravelling puzzles.'

A lump formed in Lucy's throat. She turned to him and cupped his face with her hand. 'Thank you. You don't know how much that means to me.'

'I may do, actually. Most women want fine clothes, expensive jewellery. Perhaps a majestic home...'

'I have all of that already, thanks to a certain Maharajah and his stolen sapphires!' she said with a grin.

'Or to be worshipped, up on a pedestal—'

Lucy gurgled with laughter. 'You know I hate heights. I'd only fall off onto my face!'

Smothering a grin, his gaze narrowed. 'But *you* are different. What you desire is as much intrigue as the world can throw at you.'

'No, that's not quite true. It's simply that I want to use this,' she said, tapping her temple. 'I wasn't made for sitting around, indulging in endless gossip and needlework.'

'And I'm grateful that is the case, for I'd be at the bottom of the North Sea if it weren't for your quick wits,' he said, kissing the tip of her nose, which led to a far more intimate interlude.

'And please stop feeling guilty about our honeymoon,' Lucy said, some five minutes later. 'We can return to Paris when this – well, whatever it is we're facing – is sorted out. Once we're together, I don't care where we are.'

'I feel the same, but I'm hopeful it's a storm in a teacup and we can return to Paris in a few days,' he continued with a frown. 'I had... plans.'

Something in the way he said it sent a tingle down Lucy's spine.

TWO

Two days later, 24th August, Como, Lake Como, Italy

It was dawn, and a pink-hued mist was hugging Lake Como, making the first ten minutes of the journey north silent and eerie. But as the steamer travelled towards Bellagio, the haze dispersed, revealing tantalising glimpses of the glorious views. In a matter of moments, Lucy fell in love with the astounding scenery, a perfect blend of glass-smooth lake and towering peaks. As she watched, bands of low cloud, which hugged the dark green flanks of the mountains, crept southwards in the direction of Como.

All along the shoreline were magnificent villas and gardens sweeping down to the water's edge. Many of the estates had private access to the lake, either via stone jetties or wooden piers that snaked out into the water. Lucy soon realised the lake was home to some very wealthy people. She couldn't blame them for wanting to have houses here; there was something magical about the place. Such a shame that their visit was not one of pleasure, and an unhappy thought momentarily broke the spell.

Could such a beautiful place as this prove to be less than the idyll it appeared to be?

It was mid-morning when they disembarked at Bellagio. The town rose steeply before giving way to a dark green forest. As they waited for George, Phin's valet, to organise their transport, Lucy stood beside Phin, taking in the bustling town. Across the road, a covered walkway meandered beneath the first row of houses. From the glimpses Lucy caught of it through the crowds, the lower level was home to shops of various kinds, some with stalls outside, waiting to be explored. But, of course, that would have to wait. Lucy sneaked a peek at Mary, her maid, who was standing off to the side, her bright blue eyes scanning the scene before them. Mary disliked travel and was suspicious of foreign places and those who inhabited them. It sometimes made Lucy's life difficult, but the young Irish-woman made up for her foibles by being loyal, hardworking, and she had an aptitude for rooting out even the darkest of secrets.

George soon procured a carriage, their bags were strapped on, and they were driven south along the lakeshore at a leisurely pace. The town was busy with tourists, many strolling by the water, which sparkled in the morning sun. Already, the air was warm with the promise of heat to come as the sun crept higher above the mountains to the east. And out on the water, the sails of pleasure boats glowed white against the cerulean of the lake. A little envious, Lucy could only think how carefree a scene it was compared to what they might face when they reached Elvira and Luca's home.

Not far out of Bellagio, the carriage swept inland, then through huge ornate gates, before travelling down a long gravel carriageway towards the Villa Carmosino. Lucy gasped, for the house was magnificent. Although it was a square building, and sparsely decorated compared to others they had seen as they had journeyed up the lake, it was, in Lucy's opinion, more beau-tiful for its simplicity. The pale stone exterior, topped with a russet-coloured roof, stood on a rise, and multi-level gardens fanned out from the villa. Shady terraces overlooked the lake below.

The carriage pulled up at the portico, and within seconds, their arrival triggered a flurry of activity. Several footmen streamed out of the house, followed by a tall man with the rigid bearing and formal attire of a butler. He stood, regarding his underlings as they unstrapped the bags. His orders, in rapid Italian, were obeyed without question. Then he stepped down onto the gravel and approached the carriage just as Lucy and Phin alighted.

With a deep bow, he said, 'Welcome to Villas Carmosino. I am Esposito, butler to Conte Carmosino.' He smiled suddenly, which softened his features. 'Am I correct to assume you're Senor Stone, the contessa's brother?'

'Yes, indeed.'

'We have been expecting you, signore. The contessa received your telegram from Basle.'

Phin nodded. 'Tell me, has the conte returned?'

Sadness flickered in the servant's eyes. 'I'm afraid not, signore. There has been no word.' He waved towards the house. 'Please come inside. We have a suite of rooms prepared for your visit.' He frowned at Phin for a moment. 'Perhaps you would like to rest after your journey?'

'Not at all.' Phineas tucked Lucy's arm through his. 'It would be best you lead us to my sister straight away, Esposito.'

'Indeed, signore, she is most eager to see you.' Then he bowed to Lucy. 'Signora.'

Lucy shared a concerned glance with Phin as they followed the butler towards the entrance steps. It appeared their hope of this being an unnecessary trip was in vain.

They followed the butler through a magnificent hallway. Then Esposito stopped in front of decorative double doors and tapped before stepping inside. 'Senor and Senora Stone, ma'am,' he announced.

As they entered the room, Lucy heard a squeal, and no sooner were they across the threshold than a white-faced Elvira was rushing towards them.

'Oh, thank goodness! Phin! Lucy!' Elvira cried, holding out her hands to Phin. Lucy kept back, to give brother and sister space to greet each other. Elvira tried to smile at Lucy, but her chin trembled. 'Forgive me, Lucy. This is no way to welcome you after your long journey, but Luca is still missing and I'm desperate. I don't know what to do.'

As Elvira dissolved into tears, Phin pulled her into an embrace. 'Don't distress yourself. And we're only too happy to come and help.' Once her tears subsided, he held her at arm's length. 'Is there no word at all?'

'Nothing!' she gulped. 'Luca has vanished into thin air.'

A discreet cough came from the other side of the room, and an elderly gentleman rose to his feet.

Elvira took a shaky breath. 'My apologies. Phin, Lucy, this is Giuseppe Carmosino, Luca's uncle,' she said, looking towards the man who stood, his expression solemn, sizing them up. 'Uncle Giuseppe, this is my brother Phineas Stone and his wife Lucy. Here at last.'

Giuseppe was almost as tall as Phin, with greying hair and sideburns which hung down over his collar, giving him, in Lucy's view, a somewhat comical appearance. However, there was no humour in those steely grey eyes, only disdain. As they approached, the man continued to gaze at them. *For all the world like a man assessing horses at a fair*, Lucy thought. Once they all shook hands, he gave a curt nod before sitting back down.

'Your journey wasn't too unpleasant?' Giuseppe asked in heavily accented English.

'No, Senor Carmosino, it was long certainly, but not uncomfortable,' Lucy replied.

Giuseppe's brow twitched. 'I only hope your trip isn't a
wasted one.'

Elvira threw him an irritated glance before turning to Phin.
'You must be exhausted. Did you stop over anywhere?'

'Only briefly at Basle from where I sent you the telegram.
We came straight through because your message alarmed us.
We didn't want to waste any time,' Phin replied, his focus on his
sister. His words were a subtle snub to the uncle, Lucy thought.

'I wouldn't have sent it, only I'm desperate, and it's so unlike
Luca to do anything like this. I fear he has come to harm,' Elvira
said, her voice breaking. 'If anyone can find out where he is, it's you.'

The uncle sniffed and turned his gaze towards the window.

Lucy couldn't help herself. 'Senore, you do not share Elvira's concerns?'

His head snapped round. 'No, I do not. This is a lot of fuss
over nothing. I'm sure Luca has an excellent reason for his
absence.' This was said with a hard stare at Elvira.

Lucy sneaked a look at Phin. If he was as annoyed as she by
the man's attitude, he was hiding it well. She was surprised that
Phin didn't pick up on the suggestion that Luca's disappearance
was deliberate. But she could only suppose it was to spare
Elvira, who looked close to tears once more. How cruel this man
was! Lucy reached across and squeezed Elvira's hand. 'We will
do our best to find out what has happened to him, my dear.'

With a grunt, Giuseppe got to his feet. 'I'll leave you to
entertain your guests, contessa,' he said.

'Oh!' Elvira blinked at him, then jumped to her feet and
rang the bell. 'I thought you would stay for lunch.'

Giuseppe sniffed. 'I think not.'

Elvira's lips tightened. 'That is a shame. Little Salvo will be
upset to have missed you.'

The man flinched, his features softening for a moment before his gaze hardened once more. It happened so quickly Lucy wasn't sure if she had imagined it. 'Then do not tell him I was here,' he growled.

'Very well. Thank you for calling, Uncle,' she said.

'Inform me immediately if there are any developments,' was the brusque reply. Then he threw a glance at Phin. 'However, I expect Luca will turn up soon. Then, hopefully, all these dramatics will come to an end.'

Esposito drifted into the room. 'You rang, ma'am.'

'Yes. Senor Carmosino is leaving,' Elvira said, sounding close to tears.

'Very good, ma'am,' the butler replied as Giuseppe bowed over Elvira's hand, nodded to Phin and Lucy, and strode out the door.

Elvira's gaze lingered on the door as she composed herself. 'I apologize. Giuseppe can be...'

'Abrupt? Rude?' Lucy asked.

'Unfortunately, yes, sometimes,' Elvira said with a sigh which spoke of long suffering. 'But do not pay him any heed. I'm *delighted* you're here.'

Esposito appeared in the doorway once more. 'Luncheon is served, ma'am.'

Once the footmen had cleared the table, Phineas cast his sister a gentle smile. 'Do you feel up to telling us about Luca?'

'Yes, of course,' Elvira replied, taking a deep breath. Lucy swelled with affection and pity for her. Elvira was doing her best to present a calm front. However, the dark circles beneath her eyes spoke of sleepless nights wracked by worry.

'It's so bizarre,' Elvira said, her voice low. 'It was a business trip to Milan. A journey he has undertaken many times. But he has vanished. Not even a telegram, and he knows how much I worry. That I dislike when he is away from us.'

'When did he leave?' Lucy asked.

'Last Thursday. The sixteenth.' Elvira swallowed hard. 'I haven't seen him in eight days.'

'Have you notified the police?' Phin asked.

'Of course! The day after he was expected home. When his valet turned up alone... well, I knew something awful must have happened.'

'Can the valet not shine any light on this?' Phin asked, exchanging a worried glance with Lucy.

'No, that's what's so peculiar. Luca left him behind in Milan. Nor did he take leave of his brother, who he had been staying with.' She paused, her lips pressed together. 'The police are doing nothing. An inspector from Como came asking questions a few days ago.' Elvira twisted her wineglass in her hands. 'But he left me with the impression that he wasn't taking it seriously. Much like Uncle Giuseppe, he implied Luca must have his reasons.' Anger flared in her eyes. 'I'm sure you can guess the nature of their insinuations.'

'Another lady? Is that what they are implying?' Lucy asked.

Elvira nodded, her bottom lip trembling. 'Yes! Which is ridiculous. Luca isn't like that. I insisted as much to the inspector, and it was with some reluctance he promised to investigate, but I've heard nothing since.'

'What's the fellow's name?' Phin asked.

'Commissario Marinelli,' Elvira replied, turning to him. 'Would you talk to him? Convince him this is urgent. He might listen to you. They all think I'm a hysterical female and fob me off with platitudes.'

Phineas' brow creased in anger. 'You're the least neurotic person I've ever known.' With an angry sigh, he continued, 'Of course something is wrong. Eight days is far too long for him to be just missing. I can't understand why that uncle of Luca's hasn't done anything... or his brother, for that matter. They should have been pushing harder on this.' Phin looked across at Lucy. 'But don't worry. Lucy and I will go back to Como as soon as possible and speak to this officer. Impress on him the seriousness of the situation. We will get to the bottom of this.'

Elvira sighed. 'I'd be so grateful if you could talk to him. There should be a proper search carried out, but nothing has been done either here or in Milan.'

'What can you tell us about Luca's trip?' he asked.

'All he said to me was that he was going to Milan on business and would be back on Friday evening. He planned to meet up with his brother Matteo in Milan, which he did, but then Luca left the city on Friday, telling no one. There was a storm that night, so when Luca didn't arrive, I assumed he was waiting in Como until the morning when the steamers would be running again. But he didn't appear. He just... vanished.'

'And you're sure he didn't stay in Milan?' he asked.

'Yes. Matteo was able to confirm that Luca caught the train to Como. Luca doesn't like Milan and goes there only when he must. We have a townhouse there, but since the children were born, we spend most of the year here.'

'I can understand why. It's very beautiful,' Lucy said.

'Yes, it is, but the main reason is that Luca oversees the family businesses, most of which are located here. He could, if he wished, leave them to others to run, but the world of business fascinates him. The Carmosinos have been here for hundreds of years, and Luca takes his responsibilities seriously. Most of the locals are poor, depending on fishing for their livelihood. Luca's father felt it was the family's duty to provide employment if they could.'

'What's the extent of the family business?' Phin asked.

'Well, there's the silk factory in Como and, of course, the

hotels. Luca's favourite, however, is the hotel here in Bellagio. His grandfather built Grand Hotel Bellagio, and it holds a special place in Luca's heart. He has a manager, Francesco Revello, but it's Luca who is always coming up with new ideas and schemes for improvement. He oversees all the major plans.' She smiled proudly. 'It was Luca's stroke of genius to install a lift and then last year, the hotel was wired for electricity. The first on the lake.'

'How modern,' Phin said with a smile.

'Yes. He is determined Grand Hotel Bellagio will be the finest in northern Italy.'

'How many hotels do the family own?' Lucy asked.

'Three. Matteo runs the hotel in Milan and a cousin, the smallest hotel in Turin.'

Phin sat back in his chair. 'And his brother hasn't heard from Luca since he left Milan?'

'No. Matteo was astonished to hear Luca didn't make it home, so much so that he came here to see me earlier this week. He is as mystified as everyone else.'

'Might this chap Revello know anything about Luca's trip?' Phin asked.

'That's just it. He's as baffled by the whole affair as I am. Luca said nothing about the trip to him, which is highly unusual. Revello has offered to search for him, but when I knew you were on your way, I put him off. However, I asked him and his wife to join us for dinner tomorrow evening. He might know something that will help you.'

'That was a good idea, my dear,' Phin said.

'Francesco is a good friend of ours, not just the hotel manager,' Elvira said. 'I know it's a little unusual, but you see, Luca and Francesco were at Cambridge together. Francesco comes from a very well-to-do family from Turin, but he was disinherited when he defied his father and refused to marry the woman his father had chosen. But he was in love with someone else.

Luca's father offered Francesco the management of Grand Hotel Bellagio on hearing of his plight and the couple were able to marry. His wife Maria has been most kind to me. When I first married, I had few acquaintances here and struggled with the language. Maria made a point of befriending me and introducing me to Como society. Francesco's appointment has turned out to be a wise decision. He is perfect for the position, being highly educated, fluent in several languages and has proved to have a flair for the business. The hotel is thriving under him.'

Phin quirked a brow. 'Does he not resent Luca's involvement?'

'No, indeed. They work well together.'

'I see,' Phin said. 'It sounds as if Luca had no business concerns, then.'

'Except for that awful fire and then, of course, the robbery. The fire was a terrible accident and set back Luca's plans for months,' Elvira said.

'What fire was this?' Lucy asked.

'It happened about eighteen months ago. Just after the wiring was installed. A fault of some kind. The blaze destroyed the northern wing. Luckily, the hotel had not reopened, but there was a skeleton staff in place, preparing for the launch. The alarm was raised quickly, and everyone made it out to safety. But it could have been a disaster if it had occurred after the reopening. Luca insisted a different company be used to repair the damage, and that there was to be an inspection before the reopening. The hotel was relaunched about six months ago.'

Phin appeared to hesitate for a moment before he asked gently, 'Can you think of any reason Luca might want to disappear for a while?'

Elvira paled and clenched her hands. 'It has been a stressful few weeks, but...'

Phineas narrowed his gaze. 'How so?'

'Because of the robbery, all the furore over the theft of the Fitzwilliam Diamonds,' Elvira said in a flat voice. 'Surely, you've heard of the incident?'

'Yes, I did,' he said.

'I'm sorry, what diamonds?' Lucy asked.

'They were stolen about a month ago from Lord and Lady Wallace's room at our hotel,' Elvira said. 'Marinelli was leading the investigation, but the diamonds are still missing.'

'As it happens, I was approached to investigate by their insurance company, but I could not take it on as I was heavily involved in another case,' Phin said. 'As far as I recall, there were five cut diamonds taken.'

Elvira nodded. 'A dreadful business.'

'Why would anyone carry loose diamonds with them on holiday?' Lucy asked.

'Lady Wallace purchased them on impulse at an auction in Milan. They are worth a small fortune.' Elvira shrugged. 'But I'm not sure why they are so valuable.'

'If I recall correctly,' Phin replied, 'they are unusually large, each three carats, and cut in the Marquise style.'

Lucy tilted her head. 'Marquise?'

'It's a cutting style named after King Louis XV's mistress, the Marquise de Pompadour. He commissioned a diamond to resemble the shape of her lips,' Phin said. 'The diamonds are an elongated oval shape with pointed ends. Extremely popular with European royalty, I'm told.'

'Yes, well, having met Lady Wallace, I can see how that would have influenced her choice,' Elvira said. 'She intended to bring them back with her to England to have them set into a necklace and earrings. The incident was very damaging to the hotel and Luca was furious. There had been a spate of petty thefts from guests and the culprit had been found and fired months ago, so it was a terrible shock when the diamonds were stolen.' Elvira looked at them both in turn. 'You don't think there could be a connection to Luca's disappearance, do you?'

'I have no wish to upset you further, but I don't like coincidences. I don't like them at all,' Phin replied.

THREE

The next evening, Villa Carmosino

As Phin finished dressing for dinner, Lucy stood on the balcony of their suite, delighting in the view across the lake. On the far side, on the western border, the lights from the towns and villages twinkled in the darkness. The intense heat of the afternoon had dissipated and now the air was still, the scent of roses and lavender drifting up from the garden.

'Will that be all, ma'am?' Mary called out from within the room.

Lucy turned and stepped back inside. 'Yes, Mary. You don't need to wait up for me this evening, I can manage. It's been a fatiguing few days and I'm sure you're as exhausted as I am.'

Mary's mouth twisted into a smile. 'Thank you, but we've survived worse.'

'Indeed, we have! Tell me, have you settled in? Are your Italian counterparts to your liking?' Lucy asked, bracing herself. It wasn't the wisest topic of conversation. The floodgates of complaint would probably spill open.

But to her surprise, Mary smiled. 'They're grand. Treated

me and George very nicely, ma'am. But then, you see, they are good Catholic souls, like meself.'

'Ah! Of course,' Lucy replied, trying not to smile.

'They are awful sad, though, as they are fond of the conte. Most say he is firm but fair and treats them well. His disappearance has them worried.'

'Is there speculation about why he has vanished?' Lucy asked.

'I'm sure there is, but I have heard nothing as yet. I daresay they would be reluctant to pass comment in front of me and George as they don't know us.'

'That's true, Mary,' Lucy replied in frustration. Servants were always a significant source of information, but it took time to gain their trust. 'But what about the language barrier? Or have you been learning Italian in secret?'

Mary grinned and shook her head as she laid out Lucy's nightgown on the bed. 'Ah, now, ma'am, sure the likes of me wouldn't be learning one of them foreign languages! No, Rose, the contessa's lady's maid—she's English, of course, and stayed here to serve her mistress when she married the conte—she's learned the language. She was obliging enough to translate for me. Mind you, all the servants have good English. The conte insists on it for the contessa's sake.'

'I see,' Lucy said. 'And you two have become friendly?'

'Yes, ma'am,' replied Mary. 'We hit it off straight away. I'll be sharing a room with her while we're here, and she's promised to show me around the town.' Then she sighed, but there was a twinkle in her eye. 'So, I suppose you would like to know all the family gossip?'

'Mary, under the circumstances, it might prove useful.' Lucy lowered her voice and stepped closer. 'If you could let *me* know if you hear anything. Don't bother Mr Stone with it.'

Mary gave her a nod. 'Sure, I understand, ma'am. 'Tis his family.'

'Good. We understand each other. I can rely on you to be discreet.'

'I'll do me best. Is there something in particular that concerns you?'

'Almost every aspect of this, but Mr Stone and I are here to help find the conte. Our plan is to retrace the conte's steps tomorrow, if it's possible. In the meantime, perhaps you and George could be our eyes and ears below stairs...'

Mary flashed her a glee-filled smile. 'I'll mention it to George. Nothing easier.'

Fifteen minutes later, Lucy and Phin entered the grand salon. Elvira, still noticeably pale, was talking to a handsome couple who looked up as they approached. This had to be the hotel manager and his wife. Lucy hoped the husband would help solve the puzzle of Luca's disappearance.

The lady sat ramrod straight, her gloved hands clenched in her lap. But as the lady's gaze flickered towards them, she neither smiled nor showed displeasure. Was she socially awkward? Or uncomfortable to be here? Lucy wondered.

'Ah, Lucy, Phin, this is Francesco Revello and his wife, Maria Valetta Revello.'

Francesco stood and shook hands with them both. He was a fine-looking man, Lucy thought. She guessed him to be in his mid-forties, with the most intense gaze she had ever seen, his eyes so dark they almost appeared black.

'Senor. Senora, I'm delighted to meet you. We're only sorry that our first meeting should be under such sad circumstances.'

'Indeed, but we must stay positive,' Phin replied. Lucy caught the undertone of warning. Revello smiled and nodded. He obviously did not.

Elvira turned away as if to compose herself, but it was only for a fraction of a second. 'Lucy, do come and join us,' she said, patting the space beside her. 'I've just been telling Maria about your adventures.'

At last, the lady broke into a smile, but it was a weak effort. Undeterred, Lucy walked over to her and held out her hand. 'Signora, I'm delighted to meet you,' Lucy said.

The woman's handshake was rather limp, but her gaze was penetrating as she scanned Lucy's face. *Ah!* Lucy realised, *she's very short-sighted.*

'And I you, Senora Stone,' Maria answered.

'Please, you must call me Lucy,' she replied, sitting down beside Elvira. 'And I'm sure Elvira has exaggerated my exploits. Most of the time, things just happen to me.' Lucy didn't risk a look at Phin.

A shadow flitted across the woman's face. 'How alarming! And... fatiguing, I would imagine. But I'm sure that now you're a married woman you will cease to... be too busy to...' She trailed off, colour rising in her cheeks. She coughed delicately. 'I understand you are recently married.'

'Yes. On Tuesday, in fact,' Lucy replied with a grin. 'My maid is still finding rice in my hair.'

'Congratulations,' Senora Revello replied in a faltering voice.

'And in the circumstances, I'm grateful that you were prepared to forego your honeymoon to come to my aid, my dear,' Elvira said, touching Lucy's arm. 'Such unfortunate timing.'

Lucy smiled. 'Not in the least. There's no need to be sorry. Our honeymoon can wait. Family concerns must come first.' Elvira nodded her thanks.

'How unconventional,' Maria replied, clearly baffled. 'We honeymooned in Rome. Such a fabulous city. Have you ever visited?'

'Yes, last year, in fact, on my way back from Egypt,' Lucy

replied. And once again Maria's brows shot up, disapproval in her gaze.

'Egypt... how exotic. I have heard they have some terrible diseases there,' she continued with a shudder.

Out of the corner of her eye, Lucy saw that Phin and Revello were talking quietly over at the doors which led out onto the terrace, and she hoped she wasn't missing out on anything important. With a sigh, she turned her attention back to Maria and Elvira, who were comparing notes on the Eternal City. Lucy took the opportunity to study Senora Revello. This was the woman Francesco fell for so badly he walked away from his inheritance. Lucy was a little surprised, for Maria was no striking beauty as she had imagined, though traces of her former charms were still visible. Was she being unkind? But up close, Lucy spied silver wisps of hair amongst the black at Maria's temples and many fine lines around her eyes and mouth. The woman was older than her spouse. By at least ten years, by Lucy's reckoning. Perhaps the lady had other qualities? Money? Connections? Lucy plumbed for money, for Maria's dress was of fine quality midnight blue satin, trimmed in cream lace, exquisite and expensive. Far better than Lucy would have expected on a hotel manager's salary.

FOUR

Lucy was awake, lying in bed, frowning up at the mural of what appeared to be angels cavorting across the ceiling in chariots. It was an extraordinary scene, utterly ridiculous, but beautifully executed. Soon, however, her mind drifted back to more serious matters. Dinner the evening before had been interesting and, despite the circumstances, the Revellos had been good company. For some reason, though, Lucy couldn't quite take to Maria, who clearly disapproved of her. The lady also exuded a world-weary air. Perhaps the Revello marriage was in trouble. Certainly, when her husband spoke, Maria kept her eyes downcast, almost as if he irritated her. Lucy was surprised Elvira considered the woman a friend, for Lucy suspected, based on the ladies' conversation while waiting for the gentlemen to join them after dinner, that Maria was a hypochondriac and a bore.

In the ladies' absence, Phin had questioned Revello over the port and cigars, but had gleaned nothing useful, he claimed, when he had repeated the discussion to Lucy. Luca's disappearance baffled and troubled Revello, and he had kindly offered to help them with their investigation. Phin had thanked him, promising to consult him once his initial enquiries were complete. Phin suspected Revello was relieved, for with Luca absent, and the hotel so busy, it was difficult for him to take time away from his duties.

Lucy stretched out, accidentally touching Phin's leg. He stirred and muttered something. 'Are you awake, Phin?' Lucy asked.

After a deep sigh, he turned over to look at her, his smile drowsy. 'I am now. Can't you sleep?'

Lucy tapped her temple. 'Sorry, no. Too much floating around in here. I'm eager to get started, aren't you?'

'Yes. Elvira is trying to be brave, but she is growing frantic.'

'As I would be in her shoes. We must do our very best for her,' she said.

Phin looked towards the window. 'And we will. But the first steamer isn't until nine o'clock.' Then he stretched over to the bedside table for his half-hunter watch. 'And it's only half past six,' he said with a groan. 'It will be a long day. Try to go back to sleep.'

Phin turned over and Lucy glared at his back. Sleep? Impossible. She wiggled into a sitting position, resting back against the pillows. How could she sleep when her mind was buzzing with possible explanations for Luca's disappearance? His behaviour didn't make sense. Why would a rich young count disappear? Was he in hiding? Was he in trouble and been harmed by an enemy? She didn't know Luca or Elvira as well as Phin but was it possible their marriage wasn't as happy as the family made out? Could another woman be involved? Not that it mattered. The important task was to find him, and quickly. Time enough then to go into the reasons why.

'But what if we can't trace Luca's whereabouts?' Lucy said.

With a sigh, Phineas turned onto his back and looked up at

her. 'Yes, I know. The fact he has been missing for so long is a concern. Let us hope our trip to Como may bear fruit.'

'Should we call on that police inspector?' she asked. 'Marinelli.'

'Most definitely,' Phin replied, sitting up at last. 'Why a proper search has not been conducted is a worry. More than a week has passed. Clues may have been lost; sightings forgotten. By the way, I have arranged to interview Enzo, Luca's valet, before we leave for Como. My hope is that he will have information that might help us fill in the gaps.'

'That's a good idea… may I sit in on that?'

'Of course.'

Lucy beamed back at him, but her smile soon faded. 'You don't think Elvira will want me to remain here and hold her hand while you go off to Como?'

'I doubt it. She knows how… invested you are in my work.'

'If she wanted me to stay, I would.'

Phin reached across and kissed her cheek. 'Thank you, my dear. But two heads are better than one and she would be the first to say it. Now, is there anything else worrying you? This won't be a straightforward case, we both know that, but I don't want you getting upset about it.'

'I'm upset for Elvira's sake. I suppose this is different to the last case we worked on together because it involves family.'

'Indeed. It won't be easy to stay detached,' Phin replied with a sigh.

Over breakfast, Elvira had told Lucy and Phin that Luca held Enzo in high regard and that he had been working for him for the past five years. Tears flowing, Elvira had admitted she had questioned the valet herself several times, but he had nothing to say that shed any light on her husband's actions.

After breakfast, the valet was summoned to the library,

where Lucy and Phin awaited him. The man who entered was small of stature, with a dark complexion and a pleasant countenance.

'*Buongiorno signore,*' Enzo said. He bowed to Lucy. '*Signora.*'

'*Per favore, siediti, Enzo,*' Phin said with a wave towards an armchair. 'How is your English?'

'Very good, sir. The conte insisted I learn,' the valet replied as he sat down.

The tension in Phin's shoulders eased. Although he had learned Italian, he had admitted to Lucy earlier that he was a little rusty. Phineas feared the language barrier would make their investigation difficult.

'I should explain, Enzo. My wife and I are here both to support the contessa but also to help find out what has happened to the conte. His absence is a grave concern.'

'Yes, signore, I understand.'

'Perhaps you could tell us about the trip you undertook with Count Carmosino.' Phin nodded towards Lucy. 'My wife is going to take notes, if you don't mind. Please speak freely.'

Enzo nodded to Lucy, who was sitting at the desk. 'Of course, signore. The first I knew of the proposed trip was about two days beforehand. The conte told me he had urgent business in Milan and that I was to prepare for the journey. I was surprised because the conte rarely visits Milan at this time of year. It's high season, and the hotel is busy. All I knew was that it was to be a short trip; only two days. So, we left here at half past eight on Thursday morning and caught the steamer at nine fifteen. We arrived in Milan just before four o'clock. The conte sent me on to the hotel—'

'Which hotel?' Phin asked.

'We stayed at the Grand Hotel Milano. It belongs to the Carmosino family. The conte's brother, Matteo Carmosino, runs it.'

'My understanding is that the conte owns a townhouse in Milan,' Phin remarked.

'Yes, but if he is travelling without the contessa, he stays at the hotel. There's no point in opening the house for short visits.'

'Yes, of course,' Phin said. 'Did the conte say where he was going that afternoon?'

'Yes, signore. To visit his solicitor,' Enzo said. 'Senor DeBellis.'

'And he followed you to the hotel later?'

'Yes. He arrived about six o'clock. That evening he dined with his brother and his guests.'

'How did he seem to you when he arrived at the hotel?' Lucy asked.

Enzo looked across at her and shrugged. 'Normal, senora. Perhaps tired after travelling, but I noticed nothing unusual. He retired around eleven o'clock.'

'And the next day? Friday?' Phin prompted.

'The conte had breakfast with his brother. About ten o'clock, he summoned me and said he had to go out and that I was to be ready and packed for us to catch the train back to Como in the afternoon.'

'Did he mention where he was going?'

'No. When he didn't return at the appointed time, I became concerned. Eventually, I went to Senor Matteo, his brother. He agreed that something wasn't right, and he sent a servant to the station to make enquiries. The man came back to say that the conte had caught a train for Como about an hour before.'

Lucy exchanged a puzzled glance with Phin. How odd that he would leave without the valet!

'Are you sure he hadn't told you to meet him at the station?' Phin asked.

'No, signore. Definitely not. Senor Matteo sent me to catch the next train to Como, but when I arrived, a storm was raging and the boats were not running. I assumed the conte had caught an earlier steamer and was on his way home. Luckily, my sister lives close by, so I spent the night at her house.' He shrugged. 'I was shocked when I arrived back here the next morning and the conte hadn't arrived home ahead of me.' Enzo threw Lucy a pained look. 'It was very distressing for the contessa.' Then he turned back to Phin. 'But I could not explain it.'

Phin leaned back in his chair. 'I'm sure you're discreet, Enzo, but you must understand how serious this situation is. I must ask you something of a delicate nature.' He caught Lucy's gaze before he continued. 'Does the conte have... might he have a *friend* he visits? Perhaps a lady friend.'

Lucy held her breath. Phin was asking if Luca had a mistress! She kept her head down, her pen poised. If anyone would know, it would be Luca's valet, but would he betray the conte's secret?

'No, signore, not to my knowledge,' Enzo replied, looking embarrassed when Lucy sneaked a look at him.

'Thank you. Tell me, Enzo. How was the conte's mood in the weeks and days before the trip to Milan?' Phin asked.

Enzo frowned. 'Not very good. He was, eh, *stressata*.'

'Stressed?'

'Yes, signore. There was trouble at the hotel. Some diamonds were stolen, and the police were involved. However, I don't know the details.'

Phin smiled. 'That's alright. Thank you, Enzo, you have been most helpful. If you should think of anything else that might be relevant, please don't hesitate to tell me.'

Enzo stood, looking relieved. 'Thank you, signore.'

The door closed after the valet. 'Isn't it odd that Luca left Milan without him?' Lucy asked.

'Extremely.' Phin compressed his lips. 'And I'd dearly love to know why.'

'If Luca was in trouble during that visit to Milan, surely he would have gone to his brother for help?' Lucy posed.

'Again, I can only agree with you. Something was very amiss. It would appear the key to this are those missing hours in the city. Where did Luca go? Who did he meet?'

'And how can we find out?' Lucy asked. 'But we're certain he returned as far as Como. Should we not start there?'

'Are we sure, though? He might have left the train earlier,' Phin replied, standing. 'And of course, we only have the valet's word for any of it. We will need to question Luca's brother to verify what Enzo has told us.'

'Why would Enzo lie?' she asked.

'He may be protecting himself. Don't forget, if anything has happened to Luca, the valet will lose his position or worse, he might be blamed.'

FIVE

Como, Lake Como

Lucy was too tense to enjoy the views as they journeyed south towards Como. Elvira had broken down as she had waved them off from the front steps of the villa, fleeing back into the house in tears. It was dreadful to see her so distressed and the effect it was having on Phin. He had been unusually silent on the journey to the pier at Bellagio. And, for the last half hour, Phin had been lost in thought and Lucy, seated next to him in the first-class salon, could not shake off a growing sense of disquiet. She shared Phin's concern, for she had wondered why the police were not taking Luca's disappearance more seriously. Surely, a nobleman vanishing into thin air would instigate a full-scale search of the area. And yet, no word of such a search had reached them at the villa.

Over breakfast, they had discussed how they would approach their interview with the police officer involved. Knowing how conservative the Italians were, Phin suggested that the policeman might not take kindly to a woman asking questions. Elvira had agreed, her brief encounter with the man in question still fresh in her mind. Lucy agreed to the role of observer with reluctance, but knew they were right.

It was midday when they arrived at Como, and the town was full of activity. The sun was high and the air hot; it was going to be another scorcher of a day. As they walked down the pier, Lucy opened her parasol, grateful for the shade it provided. Out past the ticket office, tourists swarmed the pavements, some promenading at their leisure, others rushing across the road towards Stazione Como-Lago, clutching their luggage.

'It's a lively spot,' Phin remarked, tucking Lucy's arm through his. 'It isn't far. Shall we walk?' he asked. 'Esposito gave me directions.'

'Yes, let's. I'm curious to see more of the town.'

They crossed onto Piazza Cavour and were soon enjoying the blissful coolness of the narrow, cobbled streets, shielded from the blistering sun. But within minutes they were back out in the open in another piazza where a formidable statue of the town's most famous son, Alessandro Volta, had pride of place.

'Do you think the association prompted Luca to install electricity in the hotels?' Lucy asked, as they turned into a street barely wide enough to fit a horse and cart.

'Perhaps. Hopefully, it's something we will discuss over dinner in the not-too-distant future,' Phin replied.

But Lucy detected the doubt in his words and sighed. *If only.*

Minutes later, they spotted a group of police officers standing on the steps of a corner building. As Lucy and Phin approached, the men fell silent, regarding them with open curiosity. A little self-conscious, Lucy closed her parasol, then proceeded Phin up the steps. The officers muttered '*buon pomeriggio*' as they passed through. Once inside, Phin handed his card to the officer at the reception desk and asked for Commissario Marinelli. They were waved to seats across the empty hallway.

'It's a quiet station. Somehow, I was expecting it to be much busier,' Lucy remarked as she sat down.

'I doubt there is much serious crime,' Phin replied. 'In a town such as this, I'd imagine pickpocketing the tourists is the local sport.'

'That doesn't inspire confidence in their abilities,' she whispered. 'No wonder there has been no progress in finding Luca, or those stolen diamonds.'

'Hmm, well, I hope there's some news about Luca, but as for the diamonds, they are not our problem.'

'But you said yourself there could be a link,' she said, puzzled. 'Aren't you a little curious about that incident?'

'Yes, but the priority, for now, is finding Luca. Elvira is my major concern. Besides, the insurance company will have someone looking into the theft.'

'Do you know who?'

Phin shook his head. 'But Revello will. Whoever it is, it would be interesting to get their perspective on the case and what Luca's thoughts are on it. And if in the course of our investigations, we discover a link to the theft, we will look into it at that point.'

Lucy was about to respond when a gaunt individual appeared at the top of the stairs. He descended slowly, clearly in some pain. But his gaze never left them.

When he reached the bottom, he wiped his brow, then held up Phin's card, peering at it. He looked across at them. 'Senor Stone?'

Lucy and Phin stood. 'Yes, I am he,' Phineas said.

'I'm Commissario Marinelli.' Again, he studied the visiting card before fixing a hard stare on Phin. 'Why do you wish to see me?'

'It's in relation to the disappearance of my brother-in-law, Conte Carmosino,' Phin replied, holding out his hand.

Marinelli eyed Lucy as he and Phin shook hands.

'This is my wife,' Phin explained.

'Senora Stone,' Marinelli said, clearly curious about her presence. He gave her a sharp nod.

'I understand you're in charge of his case,' Phin said.

Marinelli's brows shot up. 'Case? Yes,' he said, his tone not particularly encouraging.

'Perhaps we could discuss your progress?' Phin asked.

'Why?' Marinelli snapped, shifting position with a grimace. Lucy guessed his left leg was the issue. He leaned heavily on his right.

'We're deeply concerned about him. As I'm sure you saw for yourself on your visit to Bellagio, commissario, the contessa is in distress. The conte has been missing for over a week.' Phin's response was tinged with impatience. Lucy decided it was time to smooth things along if she could.

'I've no doubt you're an extremely busy man, but could you spare us the time, commissario?' she asked with her sweetest smile. 'As my husband says, the family is desperate for news of the conte, and we would like to offer our help.'

Marinelli glowered at her. 'This is... how do you say in English?'

'Irregular?' Lucy smiled and patted Phin's arm. 'Indeed it is, sir, but my husband has some experience in these matters.' Phin stiffened at her lie, so she squeezed his arm in warning. Feminine charm, her instincts told her, would fare better with this man than Phin taking umbrage and biting his head off. 'I'm sure you have done everything possible to find the conte, but we might be able to offer some suggestions...'

Marinelli smacked his lips, but his eyes glowed with sudden humour. 'I suppose it can't do any harm.' Lucy beamed back at him, and he said, 'Follow me, please.'

As the inspector limped down the hallway, Phin mouthed 'thank you' to Lucy. She couldn't help but respond with a small but smug smile.

The inspector brought them to an interview room and gestured for them to be seated. Then he sat across from them and folded his arms, his gaze flicking between Lucy and Phin.

Phineas cleared his throat. 'Commissario, I'm sure my sister emphasised that this disappearance is out of character for her husband. He has never done anything like this before.'

Marinelli shrugged. 'But it is not unheard of for young men to take flight.' He smirked. 'There could be many reasons the conte has left.' He quirked his mouth. 'It's probably nothing to be concerned about.'

'He's been missing for over a week now. I think there's every reason to be concerned,' Phin ground out.

'And your investigations have yielded no information?' Lucy asked, kicking Phin under the table. She suspected he was close to losing his temper.

Again, a shrug. 'We have heard nothing.'

'Might I ask – forgive me, but I don't know how these affairs are handled in Italy – what form have your enquiries taken?' she asked.

Marinelli rubbed the side of his face and shifted in his chair. His expression was once more dour and discouraging. 'Every station in my district has been notified to look out for him.'

Lucy was tempted to ask, 'And that's all?' but managed to restrain herself.

'I assume the infirmary here in Como has been checked?' Phin cut in.

'Sì,' was Marinelli's curt reply.

'And in Milan?' Lucy asked.

'I have no authority there.'

Phineas stiffened beside her. Lucy quickly continued, 'We understand the conte left Milan on the Friday afternoon, boarding a train for Como. Were you able to confirm this?'

'That he boarded the train? Yes. That he arrived in Como, no.'

Lucy's frustration was growing. It sounded as if the investigation was minimal so far, at best. 'Doesn't that seem odd? That no one saw him arrive.'

'Senora, the train from Milan is always full of tourists. The conte would be just another passenger to them. It's not so strange, I think, that he would not be recognised.'

'But the train company employees would know him, would they not?'

'No one has come forward, senora. As you might say, the trail led to nothing.'

'Then it's possible the conte left the train before it reached Como,' she said.

'*Anything* is possible.' His words hung in the air. Lucy was convinced the man neither cared nor intended to do anything more to find Luca. Faced with such blatant indolence, Lucy felt her own temper stir.

Phin shoved his chair back with some force and stood. Lucy followed suit. 'We won't waste any more of your *valuable* time, commissario,' Phin said. If Marinelli was surprised, he didn't show it, but stood as well. At the door, Phin turned. 'The family will be following your investigation closely, commissario. You will let us know if anything comes to light?'

With a humourless smile, the inspector answered, 'But of course. Good day, senora, senor. It was an absolute pleasure to meet you.'

SIX

Lucy could feel the tension in Phin as they hurried away from the police station. A quick glance at his profile confirmed his jaw was clenched. When they reached Piazza Alessandro Volta, however, he slowed down and eventually came to a stop. When he glanced down at her, his gaze was troubled.

On the other side of the piazza, there was a gelateria with outdoor seating in the shade. Lucy nudged him. 'Why don't we go over there and talk about it?'

Once they were seated and their order taken, Lucy reached across and squeezed his hand where it rested on the table. 'That was awful,' she said. 'Elvira is right; they are doing nothing to find Luca.'

'And I can't figure out whether it's incompetence, laziness or something else entirely.'

Lucy sucked in a breath. Something else? 'Do you suspect a conspiracy of some kind?'

Phin leaned towards her. 'It's possible. A nobleman and the biggest employer in the area goes missing, and all Marinelli does is ask the various police stations to keep an eye out for him? It's farcical. Either he knows what has happened to Luca or has been paid off to do nothing,' he replied.

This threw Lucy. 'What are you thinking?'

The waiter arrived with their ice creams. Phin waited until he was gone before he answered. 'That's just it; I don't know what to think and it won't be easy to sort this out. If Luca has been the victim of foul play, every day that goes by reduces our chances of finding clues. And if the police are involved in some way, they can make it challenging for us to investigate.'

Phin's suggestion made her uneasy, as if a cloud had suddenly blocked out the sun. Lucy twirled her long spoon in the glass dish, mulling this over. 'I have no wish to be blunt and upset you, but do you think Luca is dead? Could he have been murdered?'

She could tell he didn't want to answer, but eventually, he nodded.

'Oh, Phin! That would be too awful. We can't give up hope. Elvira is depending on us to find him.'

'I'll not share my worst fears with her, not yet at least, but neither do I wish to give her false hope,' he said. 'That would only prolong her agony.'

'We must try to discover what has happened,' Lucy said.

'And we will do our best, my dear, of course,' he said.

'I can't stop thinking about those poor children. To lose their father so young is tragic. Little Salvo is only three years old, and Eleanor is only a baby.'

'Perhaps it's a blessing they are so young. They won't understand what's happening,' Phin said.

'I suppose so,' she replied with a heavy heart. 'Should we have demanded that Marinelli do more?'

'You saw his attitude for yourself. No, we must solve this. Besides, any approach we could make would be seen as interference and an attempt to undermine his authority. I've come across men like him before.'

Lucy sighed, knowing he was probably right. 'It's unfortunate he won't help us.'

They sat in silence, eating their ice cream, but Lucy's thoughts were in a whirl. Then an idea struck her. 'Phin, why are we assuming the worst? Luca may not have been murdered. Perhaps he met with an accident or is lying injured somewhere.'

Phin waved his hand, his expression bleak. 'Then where is he? This is the busiest time of year here on the lake. There are tourists everywhere. Besides, the locals know Luca well. Too much time has passed. Someone would have come across him by now.'

'Yes, you're right. Although, what if... could it be a kidnapping?' she asked.

'There has been no demand for money,' he replied.

'So, what do we do?' she asked.

'We need to confirm that he arrived here in Como on the Friday evening. His brother is adamant that he caught the train from Milan, so there's little point in tracing Luca's steps back that far. In fact, we can call into the train station now and make enquiries.'

'Yes, let's. I need to do something. I can't bear to be idle when that poor man's fate is unknown.'

Phin called for the bill and paid.

'Are you ready, my dear?' Phin said, holding out his hand.

'I'm ready. Let's make a start.'

As they climbed the many steps leading up to Stazione Mediterranea, Lucy was struggling with the mid-afternoon heat and envied Phin his linen suit. Beneath her jacket, her blouse was stuck to her back. Despite longing for the cool interior of Villa Carmosino and, even more so, to plunge into a cold bath, her spirits had risen. It felt good to be doing something positive after the disappointment of dealing with the local police inspector.

At the top of the steps, Lucy clutched Phin's arm so he would pause whilst she caught her breath.

'It will be easier going back down,' he said with a smile.

'You're not even out of breath!'

He bent his head close. 'Or trussed up in a corset,' he whispered with a mischievous glint in his eye. 'I'll happily release you when we return to Bellagio.'

'If I survive that long,' Lucy replied with a smile.

She looked across at the station building, in front of which was a line of cabs waiting for the next train to arrive. There was a large central block of two floors, with single floor wings stretching out to either side. Above the main door, the clock read ten past three o'clock.

Phin cocked a brow. 'Shall we?'

While Phin went in search of someone who might answer their questions, Lucy sat on a bench just inside the door, observing the crowds milling about. Almost five minutes later, Phin returned, a gentleman in uniform walking beside him.

'Lucy, this is the stationmaster, Senor Alfredo,' Phin said before turning to the man. 'My wife, Senora Stone.'

Lucy held out her hand. 'Delighted to meet you.'

Alfredo bobbed his head and returned her handshake. 'If you would like to come to my office, senora?' The stationmaster led them up a flight of stairs and along a metal balcony which overlooked the platforms. Alfredo waved Lucy to the only chair.

'How can I help, senore?' Alfredo asked Phin.

'Would you and your employees recognise Conte Carmosino?' Phin asked.

'Of course. Everyone knows the conte. It is... sad to learn that he is missing,' he replied.

'How did you hear of it? Did the police come here to question you?'

'No, senore. But everyone in Como is talking about it.'

Lucy and Phin exchanged exasperated glances. Marinelli hadn't even sent someone to the station to enquire after Luca. No wonder he couldn't confirm if Luca had arrived in Como.

'Would you or anyone else have seen the conte on Friday the seventeenth? His train arrived from Milan around five o'clock.'

'Yes, indeed, signore. I saw him myself and nodded to him as he passed. At the time, I was surprised to see him alone. He usually travels with a servant.'

'Did you, by any chance, see what direction he took when he left the station?' Lucy asked.

The stationmaster shrugged. 'I saw him pass out through the main entrance. I assume he took a cab down to the pier to catch a steamer.'

'And you're absolutely sure it was the conte?' Phin asked.

'Oh, yes, signore. There can be no mistake; he was as close to me as you are now.'

SEVEN

A short cab ride brought Lucy and Phin back to Como harbour, where they went straight to the steamer ticket office. This time, however, Phin couldn't find anyone with sufficient English and had to question the employees in halting Italian. Lucy stood by, frustrated, hoping his language skills were up to the task. Elvira had warned them that many of the locals spoke *comasco*, the local dialect. Although Phineas appeared to struggle a little, at last he was back at her side, their return tickets to Bellagio in his hand.

'Well?' she asked, as they walked along the pier towards the steamer.

'Let us find a quiet place on board and I shall tell you what I have learned,' he replied.

'Is it good or bad?'

'Mixed.'

Impatient to hear what he had to say, Lucy made for the first-class deck at the stern.

'Like Alfredo at the station, the boat crews know all about Luca's disappearance. It's the subject of much local gossip,' Phin said as he joined her at the handrail.

'Was he able to tell you something useful? Did someone see Luca that evening?'

Phin nodded. 'Yes. One of the steamer crew spoke to him. Unfortunately, he is on a steamer somewhere up north now, so I can't speak to him directly. The man in the ticket office could give me some details, but I'd like to verify it with the source when I get the chance—'

'But what did he say?' Lucy cut in with rising impatience. 'Did Luca board a steamer?'

'No. Unfortunately, the storm was coming in fast and the steamers for the rest of the evening were cancelled. Luca missed the last one, which had left about half an hour before.'

'Oh, no!'

Phin sighed. 'The problem is the men were so busy locking everything down no one saw what direction Luca took when he left the pier.'

'That's a pity. What would his options have been if there was no steamer?' she asked.

'I asked that very question,' he said. 'He reckoned Luca went to a hotel to wait out the storm.'

'That would be the sensible option, but did he catch a steamer on Saturday morning instead?'

Phin shook his head. 'That's just it. He didn't.'

'Perhaps he was reluctant to wait here in Como that night for some reason.'

'That's a possibility. There is a road to Bellagio, but I'm informed it's little better than a dirt track through the hills and would be treacherous in the dark.' Phin waved towards the disappearing pier. 'There are small boats for hire, but again, the storm meant none of them were available. I can only conclude that if he didn't stay in a hotel here at Como, he journeyed up the western shore by road.'

Lucy gazed down into the water, considering this. 'Then we need to check all the hotels and inns.'

'We will. When we get back to Bellagio, I'll talk to Revello and Esposito. We can pull a group together from the villa and hotel staff and have them systematically make enquiries at all the hostelries. I would hope to start the search tomorrow.'

'Yes, the quicker, the better. I suppose we have made some progress, but I wish it was better news for Elvira,' Lucy said with a sigh.

'Don't be discouraged. We have only begun.'

Bellagio

Phin and Lucy went straight to Grand Hotel Bellagio. At the entrance gates, they paused for a moment to take in the splendour of the place. Lucy realised it was on a par with, if not finer than, many of the private villas they had already seen on their travels around the lake. One's eyes were drawn to the main door through ornamental gardens, bursting with colour and scent, and a border of tall palm trees, which gave the courtyard area an exotic feel. The hotel building was huge and stretched outwards from a central five-storey block in two wings. White awnings were pulled down over the many balconies to shade the interiors from the late afternoon sun, and Lucy surmised the views from those upper floors must be amazing. Lucy could understand why Luca was so proud of the hotel.

'It's quite a statement,' Phin remarked as they strolled down the path. 'It must have cost a fortune to install electricity.'

'And to repair the building after the fire,' Lucy said. 'Thank goodness it only damaged one wing.'

A liveried man waved them inside and straight into a large reception area. While Phin went to enquire after Revello, Lucy stood to the side, happy to take it all in. The area was vast and bustling with staff and guests. A sweeping staircase dominated the entire space, inviting one's gaze upwards. However, the steps split in two about halfway up, with a run of steps reaching the ground floor on either side of a small courtyard garden. Quite the novelty, Lucy thought. Of more interest, however, were the hotel clientele. They suited their opulent surroundings to perfection, being ostentatiously well-turned-out. Lucy could only conclude the hotel rates were exorbitant.

A few minutes later, a porter showed them into Francesco Revello's office to the rear of the ground floor, behind the reception area.

'Ah, Senor and Senora Stone, this is a great pleasure. Please sit down. Shall I order some coffee?' Revello asked.

'Yes, please, that would be lovely,' Lucy replied.

Revello looked at them both, then smiled. 'Is there something I can help you with?'

'I hope so,' Phin said, before filling him in on their afternoon visit to Commissario Marinelli and what they had subsequently found out in Como.

'This is not good news. If the police have no hope...' Revello commented, before letting out a long sigh and shaking his head.

'But they are not even trying,' Lucy said.

'Oh, no. I'm sure they are. Perhaps you misunderstood? Marinelli is very experienced.' Then he sighed deeply. 'I don't wish to distress the contessa, but I'm troubled.' He shrugged. 'A day or two, perhaps, is nothing to worry about, but Luca has been gone so long.' He glanced at Lucy. 'I'm sorry. I have no wish to upset you either.'

'No, no, Revello. I quite understand and we must be realistic,' Lucy replied just as the refreshments arrived.

'Thank you,' Revello said to the waiter. 'I can manage.' He poured the coffee and handed out the cups and saucers. Then he sat back down, his expression gloomy. 'So, what can we do now?'

'We have confirmation that Luca reached Como, but missed

the steamer that would have taken him home. The logical conclusion is that he waited out the storm overnight, probably in the area. I'd guess his plan was to catch the first steamer the next day. However, the men at the pier are adamant he didn't show up on the Saturday morning. Therefore, we must check all the hostelries around the lake. Yes, I know it will be a massive undertaking, but Luca was too well known for someone not to have recognised him... perhaps even put him up for the night. I hoped that between hotel and villa staff, we might pull a team together for the job.'

Revello rubbed at his beard. 'I think it may be an impossible task... but we should try. For the contessa's sake.' He sipped from his cup, deep in thought.

Lucy's irritation grew. It was as if he had given up hope. She fixed him with a hard stare, but he didn't meet her eye.

'If Luca did stay somewhere that night,' Revello continued after a moment, 'I can't imagine it was far from Como. The night was bad with heavy rain and strong wind. He would have sought shelter immediately. It would make sense to concentrate our efforts within, say, a mile or two of the town.'

'Yes. And not just the hotels, Revello, small inns, too. A check of all the cabmen working out of Como might also be useful.' Phin finished his coffee and stood. 'Send a message to me at the villa when you have made your decision on who you can spare. Let us aim to take the first steamer to Como in the morning. The sooner a proper search begins, the better.'

Revello nodded in agreement and showed them back out to the reception area. 'Until the morning, Senor Stone,' he said. Then he shook hands with Phin and bowed over Lucy's hand.

It was some hours later, and Lucy and Phin were dressing for dinner. As they had expected, Elvira had been deeply upset at their news, and it had taken quite some time to calm her down.

Once Phin explained what he and Revello planned, she pulled herself together, insisting, then and there, that they speak to Esposito to see how many men he could spare to take part.

Lucy sat at the dressing table, waiting for Mary. In the room next door, she could hear Phin and George discussing the plans for the search the following day, but she didn't join them, suddenly giving way to despondency. Surely anyone looking at the problem dispassionately would realise Luca's fate looked hopeless. The only conclusion that made sense was that Luca had come to harm and was dead. It was now a matter of recovering his body for his poor widow to mourn over. Revello's reaction earlier that afternoon only confirmed this. He had been upset by their news, but not surprised.

Lucy grimaced at her reflection as she pulled pins out of her hair. What was keeping Mary? Lucy had no wish to be late for dinner. Just as she picked up her watch to check the time, the door opened, and Mary burst in.

'So sorry, ma'am. I was in Bellagio with Rose, and we lost track of time,' Mary said, rushing across the room to her. 'But you will never guess who I saw there, about an hour ago.'

Phineas and George emerged from the dressing area as Lucy twisted around on the stool. Mary's colour was high, and she was clearly het up and dying to reveal her news.

'Who?' Lucy asked.

'Only that good-for-nothing Jabber Kincaid!'

'Kincaid!' Phin exclaimed. 'Are you certain, Mary?'

With a satisfied grin, Mary answered, 'Sure, I'd know that scoundrel anywhere!'

Phineas turned back into the dressing room with a groan. 'The diamonds. Of course, it would have to be him.'

EIGHT

Villa Carmosino, Bellagio

If the mood in the villa had been gloomy before, it was now worse. To add to the melancholy mood, Uncle Giuseppe had turned up, uninvited, according to Elvira, in a whispered aside to Lucy. Seemingly, it was a regular occurrence. Even so, Elvira welcomed him with as cheery a smile as she could manage and was repaid for her kindness with a grunt and an abrupt question regarding Luca. The man was abominably rude, in Lucy's opinion, and she was coming to the conclusion that Elvira was nothing short of a saint to put up with him in her home.

Over dinner, Giuseppe questioned Phin about their trip to Como, but what he felt about their discoveries he kept to himself. Overall, Lucy sensed Giuseppe resented their activities, viewing them as intrusions and a personal affront. In some ways, the man reminded Lucy of her mother, a snob who only cared about the family name. Justice or lack of it didn't bother them much.

For most of the dinner, Phin appeared to be preoccupied. He spoke little, and Lucy filled in the awkward silences. She knew the reason, of course. The news regarding Kincaid had thrown Phin. The Irish police inspector, turned private investigator, was the last person either of them expected to find at Lake Como. They had not parted on the best of terms on the last occasion they had spoken in Lucy's London home. Phin had employed him to help on a case, but Kincaid had turned out to be, as Mary put it, a complete scoundrel intent on lining his own pockets. When it had come to the more dangerous part of the investigation, Kincaid had bailed out once Phin had assured him that he would get his share of the rewards. The man made no secret of the fact that he wished to replace Phin as the premier investigator employed by insurance companies.

Elvira rose from the table, Lucy's cue to do likewise, and excused herself to leave Phin and Giuseppe alone over the port.

As soon as they reached the salon, Elvira gripped Lucy's arm. 'What is it that you're not telling me? What did Phin find out? I've never seen him so morose. I know you're keeping something from me!'

'No, no, not at all. Phin is out of sorts because we received some startling news just before dinner,' Lucy replied, drawing Elvira over to the sofa. 'Don't be alarmed, please. We will always tell you the truth about Luca and our investigation.'

Elvira looked a little relieved. 'Was the news related to Luca in some way?'

'In a roundabout fashion, it might be. An old... acquaintance, for want of a better word, has shown up in Bellagio. He is an investigator, like Phin.'

'Who is he?' Elvira asked as she accepted a cup of coffee from a footman.

'Kincaid helped Phin on a recent case but turned out to be a bit of a rogue. He withheld information for his own ends and made our investigation more challenging.'

'A rival then?' Elvira asked.

'He thinks he is,' huffed Lucy. 'Not a trustworthy man.'

'What's he doing in Bellagio?'

'My guess is that he is working for the Wallaces' insurance company and is investigating the stolen diamonds.'

Elvira's brow shot up. 'Oh, the Fitzwilliam Diamonds.'

'The insurers approached Phin, but he couldn't take the case. Kincaid must have stepped in. It's the only reason I can think of for his presence.' Lucy sipped her coffee. 'Besides, it doesn't matter. Our focus is on finding Luca.' She smiled, doing her best to reassure Elvira. 'An unfortunate occurrence that he is here, but little we can do about it. Phin can ask Revello about him in the morning. I wonder how long he has been here. Did Luca mention him to you?'

'No, I don't believe so,' Elvira replied with a frown. 'But then he didn't discuss the robbery with me much. Luca was upset over it.' Elvira made a face. 'And to make matters worse, it was in all the newspapers.'

'You mentioned there had been other thefts.'

Elvira set down her cup. 'Yes, but on a much smaller scale. Money and trinkets taken from guests' rooms or, if left lying around, in the public areas. Luca was concerned it would damage the reputation of the hotel, so he was determined to find out who was responsible. It turned out to be one of the housekeepers, Fiorella Armano. Her family is not quite respectable. When Revello searched her room, stolen items were discovered hidden under the mattress.'

'What happened then?' Lucy asked, thinking it wasn't a clever place to hide the loot.

'Luca dismissed her without a reference. Of course, she protested her innocence, but the evidence was damning. The hotel attracts some very wealthy clients. I suppose she couldn't help herself.'

'I see.' Might this woman hold a grudge against Luca? she wondered. 'Did she go to prison?'

'Oh, no. Luca wanted to avoid any hint of scandal. The

police were never involved. She had an excellent job. Luca pays the hotel staff well. It was punishment enough that she would never work in a hotel on Lake Como again.'

Lucy thought it odd. No matter what, the woman had deserved a proper investigation, but perhaps Luca had his reasons. Maybe a witness had seen her take something. Why else would the management have searched the housekeeper's room?

The door opened and Phin entered, alone.

Elvira frowned at him as he approached them. 'Where is Giuseppe?'

'He left and asked me to make his apologies.'

'I'm sure we will bear the loss of his company,' Lucy said as Phin sat down opposite.

'Be kind, my dear,' Phin said. 'I know he has an unfortunate manner, but I think our news about Luca upset him this evening. Perhaps, up to now, he hasn't taken the situation seriously.'

'I agree, Phin. You must understand, Lucy, he is a proud man,' Elvira said with a sigh. 'He is fond of Luca and Matteo in his own way, and he dotes on Salvo, but he finds his position difficult.'

'How so?' Lucy asked, struggling to have much sympathy for the man.

'Well, it's my belief that he always felt that when his brother, Luca's father, died, he should have become conte. But of course, the rules of succession meant he had to accept his young nephew Luca as the heir.'

'So, Giuseppe sees himself as the rightful head of the House of Carmosino?' Lucy asked.

'In a way, yes, poor man, I think he does,' Elvira replied. 'Luca tries to involve him in the businesses and Giuseppe has substantial shareholdings in most of the family companies. But his ideas are often old-fashioned. For instance, he fought against installing electricity. When the fire happened, he wasn't slow to say, "*I told you so*".'

'Their relationship is fraught with difficulty, then?' Phin asked with a sympathetic smile.

'Yes, at times.'

'Is Giuseppe a wealthy man in his own right?' Lucy asked.

'I believe so,' Elvira replied. 'Though...'

'Though?' Lucy asked.

'I don't like to gossip, but there have been rumours he might be in financial trouble.'

'Indeed. Do you know the details?'

'No,' Elvira replied. 'But it can't be anything to do with the family businesses. I know he invested in a horse stud. Horse racing is a passion of his. My guess is that the problem relates to that.'

Lucy waited for the footman to refill her cup. 'Is that why he lives at the hotel? Could he not afford his own home?'

'He could, of course, but does not wish to. He owned a villa in Laglio, but after his wife died, he sold it. That was about twenty years ago. Luca's father was happy for him to take up residence in the hotel as he himself had little interest in the business and was content for Giuseppe to run things and to keep him informed.'

'Ah!' Lucy said. 'It's understandable that he would resent Luca a little for stepping into what he may have seen as his role, yet again.'

'Yes, he has struggled with the changes Luca has introduced.' Elvira smothered a yawn as she smiled. 'And hasn't always been able to hide the fact. Now, you must both forgive me. I must retire,' she said, rising. Lucy jumped to her feet and hugged her.

Phin kissed Elvira's cheek and walked her to the door. 'Let us hope for better news tomorrow, my dear,' he said. 'Sleep well.'

NINE

Villa Carmosino, Bellagio, Lake Como

It was early morning. Lucy stood at the top of the steps with her arm tucked through Elvira's, and watched as Phin, George and several footmen climbed into the waiting carriage which would take them to the pier. It was a horrible feeling, but Lucy feared the search the men were about to embark on at Como was their last chance of finding Luca alive. He had been missing for ten days. If he were alive, surely, he would have turned up by now? Whether Elvira shared her concern, she didn't know, but Lucy was reluctant to voice it. Hope was all that was left.

Halfway across the hallway, however, Elvira came to a sudden stop and burst into sobs. Lucy steered her to the nearest room and closed the door, away from the prying eyes of Esposito and the other servants. Gently, she guided her sister-in-law to a sofa.

'I'm... I'm so terribly sor-ry, Lucy,' Elvira managed to say between her heaving tears.

'No, my dear; it's perfectly understandable,' Lucy replied. 'Please don't lose hope. Phin will do his very best. They have enough men. They are bound to discover something useful. Luca reached Como, we're sure of that now. Someone must have seen him. Might know where he is.'

'But what if... there is no trace? I shall go mad. Indeed, I think I am already!'

'We must be strong,' Lucy said.

But Elvira shrugged. 'I am trying to be, but what do I tell the children? Salvo was asking about his father last night when I went in to say goodnight. He is old enough to realise something is wrong.'

'Then we must keep him occupied,' Lucy replied, looking out at the sunlit garden. 'Why don't we take the children out for the morning? I have yet to explore Bellagio. Dry your eyes now,' Lucy finished, rising to ring the bell to summon the nanny. 'A few hours away from the house will do us all good.'

An hour later, the ladies set out with baby Eleanor in her perambulator and little Salvo holding Lucy's hand. Elvira was less pale, and Lucy hoped the distraction of their little outing would help. As they strolled along the lakeshore, Elvira pointed out the various villas and told Lucy about the residents.

'Please, Aunty Lucy,' Salvo suddenly piped up. 'I would like some ice cream.'

'Well, little man, I'm sure we can find some when we reach the town,' Lucy said, smiling down at him. He beamed back at her.

'Salvo has taken to you straight away, Lucy. He doesn't always,' Elvira remarked with a knowing look. 'Perhaps soon you will have a child of your own.'

'Oh!' Lucy exclaimed. 'I don't think that would be possible.' She glanced down at the little boy to see if he was listening, but he was standing looking out over the water, intrigued by a large sailing boat whisking past. 'I had problems before.'

Elvira's face fell. 'I'm sorry. I didn't mean to pry or upset you.'

'No, no. I don't mind talking about it. Phin knows and accepts it. Well, we don't have a choice.'

Elvira squeezed her arm. 'Still, it must be difficult.'

'It caused a lot of problems with my first husband, Charlie. He found it difficult to accept. The doctor was adamant the problem lay with me.' Lucy sighed. 'Charlie didn't have Phin's generosity of spirit.' She smiled and tugged Salvo's hand. 'But now I have lots of nieces and nephews to dote on. Isn't that right, Salvo?'

The little boy grinned, slipped from her grasp, and skipped ahead.

'Be careful, Salvo. Don't go near the edge,' Elvira called after him. Then she turned to Lucy. 'Would you like to push Eleanor?'

'Yes, please!'

A few minutes later, they had reached the entrance of the hotel. Elvira nodded towards it. 'Shall we go in and get your ice cream, Salvo?' The child ran ahead of them, skipping down the path with glee.

Just as Lucy made to follow Elvira with the perambulator, a young woman caught her attention. She was further along the path, pacing up and down outside the boundary railings. Their eyes met, but the young woman's gaze slid away as if she were embarrassed. She wore the traditional dress of the locals and Lucy guessed she was waiting to meet someone. A romantic rendezvous, Lucy guessed, and smiled.

At the entrance, the concierge bowed and opened the door. 'Contessa! You're very welcome.'

But as Lucy pushed the perambulator through the door, a familiar figure, tall and fair, was walking towards her. Lucy froze, irritated. It would have to be that worthless rogue. Kincaid! She set her features to frosty and was determined to greet him in such a manner that he knew she hadn't forgiven him.

'Mrs Lawrence!' exclaimed Malcolm Kincaid. He scanned the outside path as if looking for someone, before turning back to her. Then a frown shadowed his features as he stared at the baby carriage. 'Good Lord! What on earth are you doing here?'

Miffed at his tone, Lucy gave him a hard stare. 'It's Mrs *Stone*, now, Kincaid.'

The man smirked. 'I see. You went through with it then.'

Lucy, determined not to lose her temper, pursed her lips and nodded.

The investigator sidled up to her and held out his hand. With some reluctance, Lucy returned his handshake. 'My congratulations, Mrs Stone. Phineas is a lucky man,' he said with some of his old bonhomie. 'I hope he appreciates your unique talents.'

Despite his suave tone, Lucy wasn't fooled. Her presence had rattled him for some reason. Elvira stood close by, holding Salvo by the hand, one fine brow arched, clearly curious.

'This is my sister-in-law, Contessa Carmosino,' Lucy said, beckoning Elvira closer. 'Mr Kincaid, Elvira. He *used* to work for Phineas.'

'Ah!' he replied, bowing to Elvira. 'I'm delighted to meet you at last, contessa. I was very sorry to hear about the conte. Such a tragedy.'

Elvira stared at him in horror.

'The conte is *missing*, Kincaid. That is all,' Lucy cut in, raging that Kincaid had upset Elvira after all her efforts to soothe her.

'Of course! My apologies. My misunderstanding,' Kincaid replied smoothly, though he looked confused.

'Thank you,' Elvira replied in a clipped tone before turning to Lucy. 'Follow us into the salon.' And with that, she walked away, dragging Salvo with her.

Kincaid didn't look contrite at all, ignoring the snub. 'Strange situation,' he muttered. Then he glared down at her. 'I do hope that Phineas hasn't changed his mind. The Fitzwilliam Diamond case is mine. He need not think he can swoop in and take it from me. I'm close to solving it.'

'Are you indeed! Well, trust me, Phineas has no interest in the case. In fact, he turned it down,' Lucy ground out. 'We're here to support the contessa. Now, if you will excuse me?' She was about to walk away but stalled. Something troubled her. Phin's words regarding coincidences coming to mind. 'Do you know anything about the conte's disappearance? Anything that might help us?'

Kincaid sniffed. 'An exchange of information?'

'Yes!'

'I don't think so!' Kincaid gave her one of his cheeky grins, bowed and headed out the door. Lucy stared after him. To think she had liked the man when she had first met him! But he had turned out to be devious and untrustworthy. It was unfortunate that he should be here, she thought. Could it be a bad omen? Why had he assumed Luca was dead? Now that was worrying. What did he know? However, it wasn't something she could discuss with Elvira. She'd have to wait until Phin was home later that evening.

Lucy moved over to the window. Kincaid strode down the path towards the gate. To her astonishment, he paused at the entrance and spoke to the woman Lucy had spotted outside. Whatever was going on, the young woman was extremely agitated and even from a distance, Lucy could see Kincaid was not reacting well to what she had to say. At last, he dismissed her with a jerk of his hand and turned abruptly, striding away in the direction of the town centre. The woman remained standing, watching him leave. After a few moments, she slowly walked away.

TEN

Villa Carmosino, the next afternoon

A footman had just removed the afternoon tea tray for Elvira when Esposito entered the salon and announced Matteo Carmosino. Lucy looked up, curious to meet Luca's younger brother at last. She studied him with interest as Matteo strode in on Esposito's heels. He wore his curly hair a little longer than Luca, and his dark expressive eyes were fixed on Elvira as he crossed the room. Lucy was struck by his strong resemblance to his elder brother. Something that must be extremely difficult for Elvira, his presence in her home now a sharp reminder of her missing husband.

Elvira jumped to her feet, her face flushed. As Matteo drew close, she gnawed at her lip and Lucy noticed the sparkle of unshed tears.

'No news?' Matteo asked, reaching for her hands.

Elvira looked at Lucy, unable to speak.

Matteo's dark gaze fell on Lucy. He dropped Elvira's hands. 'Ah, you must be Lucy. I'm delighted to meet you at last,' he said, crossing to her and bowing over her hand.

'And I, you,' Lucy replied.

'It's so kind of you and your husband to travel here to help us.' He looked at Elvira, who was now sitting down. 'We're growing desperate.'

'Please sit, Matteo,' Elvira said softly, and Lucy was relieved to see she appeared calmer. 'Esposito knows you well. Your coffee will be here soon.'

Matteo beamed back at her. 'Always, you spoil me.' Then his expression changed as he must have realised the inappropriateness of his words in the circumstances. Colour rushed into his cheeks.

Elvira cast him a troubled glance, concern etched deep on her brow. 'You're always welcome here, Matteo. Luca is very fond of you.'

Lucy held her breath as she watched the young man recover his sangfroid.

'Please. Is there any news?' he asked.

'Phineas and Revello have taken a team of men to Como to conduct a search,' Elvira told him.

Matteo nodded slowly. 'Thank goodness! Something positive is being done at last.' A ghost of a smile flitted across his face. 'I had to come, Elvira. I was going mad in Milan.' He gave a helpless gesture. 'I can't concentrate on anything. Even Angelica has been complaining that I'm neglecting her.'

'Angelica is Matteo's fiancée,' Elvira explained, in answer to Lucy's quizzical look. Then she turned back to Matteo. 'I'm sure she understands. She is a kind-hearted young lady.'

'Hmm.' Matteo stared down at the floor. Lucy guessed it was only her presence that was preventing him from saying something not quite complimentary about his betrothed.

After a moment, Matteo looked up. 'Has your husband learned anything new? Is that why they have gone to Como?'

'We did a little investigating in Como the day before yesterday. Luckily, we were able to confirm that Luca reached there by train. However, he missed the last steamer that ran because of the storm. It seems likely he would have waited for the weather to turn at a hotel or inn. They are searching them as we speak,' Lucy said.

'That is excellent news. I assume the police are helping?' Matteo asked.

'I'm afraid not. When Phin and I spoke to the inspector, we were very concerned about the lack of progress or, indeed, interest.'

'You're right, they have been useless,' he replied. 'That buffoon Marinelli had some strange notions when I conferred with him a few days ago.'

'We weren't impressed by him, either,' Lucy said with some emphasis. 'He made it blatantly clear that he didn't wish us to interfere in his investigation. An investigation which appears to us to be non-existent.'

Elvira dropped her head into her hands and moaned.

Lucy hurried to the seat beside her and put her arm around her shoulders. 'Do not despair, my dear. If it's humanly possible, Phin will find Luca.' Lucy looked across at Matteo for support. 'Perhaps he has been injured or fallen ill.'

'But we would have heard. Everyone in the region knows who he is, and that he is missing,' Matteo said. And it took a great deal of effort for Lucy not to scold him. Did he not see he was only adding to Elvira's distress?

Something in her expression must have registered. 'Let us hope they are successful,' he said with a sheepish look.

A footman entered with a tray, which he set down beside Matteo. Elvira made to get up and Matteo waved her back down. 'I can manage, thank you.'

Once the footman had left, Elvira asked him, 'Will you stay the night?'

'Yes, of course.' Then he looked at Lucy. 'I'm eager to speak to your husband and to offer what help I can.'

'That would be wonderful,' Lucy replied. 'Thank you.'

Elvira rose and Matteo jumped to his feet. 'I need to check on the children. I'll see you both at dinner,' she said, as she turned to leave. Matteo stepped up to her, calling her name. When she turned, he embraced her briefly, much to Lucy's astonishment and Elvira's by the look on her face. Elvira stepped back, attempted to smile and failed before turning on her heel and leaving the room.

'I hate to see her so upset,' Matteo said with a frown as he sat back down. 'Where the devil could Luca be? This disappearance doesn't make any sense.'

Lucy was taken aback by the passion in his voice. However, this was an excellent opportunity to ask some of the hard questions. 'Do you have a theory?' she asked. 'You were the last person in the family to see or speak to him. Did he seem upset or troubled in Milan?'

'No! He was his normal self. We breakfasted together that morning.' Matteo hesitated. 'He was a little preoccupied but when Luca is planning something new, he tends to become... distracted. Yes, distracted is how I would describe it.'

'Did you ask him what was on his mind?'

'Yes, but he brushed me off.' Matteo ran a hand through his hair. 'The manner of his leaving Milan is what's most strange, as if...'

'He was running away?' Lucy prompted.

'Yes. But from what?'

'Did he have any enemies that you're aware of?' she asked.

But before he could respond, the door opened, and Esposito entered carrying a silver platter. He walked up to Lucy and held it out. 'Ma'am.'

There was a telegram addressed to her on it. 'Thank you.' Once the butler left the room, she opened it and scanned it. 'It's from Phineas. Hopefully, it's good news. Oh dear!'

'What is it?' Matteo asked.

'They have found nothing so far, and Phin and Revello have decided to stay in Como until the morning so the search can continue this evening.' With a sigh, Lucy sat back. 'This is disappointing. I had hoped there would be a sighting at least.'

Matteo was staring out the window, his mouth a grim line. 'How could he do this to Elvira?'

'I'm sorry!'

'No! Not your husband. I mean Luca. To disappear without a word' – his gaze was tortured – 'he is breaking her heart.'

It was early evening the next day by the time Phineas arrived back at the villa. Lucy had been anxious since the afternoon when there was no sign of the search party coming back. However, she took one look at Phin's face as he entered the salon and knew something was wrong. Unfortunately, Elvira also noticed and sprang up from her seat, the little colour she had in her face disappearing rapidly. Matteo also stood, but his gaze was fixed on Elvira.

'What is it? What have you found out?' Elvira cried, wringing her hands.

Phin shook his head as he approached her. 'Do not distress yourself; there's still hope. We did not find him, unfortunately, but we have one possible sighting of him heading west out of Como.' Elvira sat down with a sigh, her look of defeat all too plain to see. After a concerned glance at his sister, Phin turned to the young man hanging on his every word and held out his hand. 'You must be Matteo. I'm delighted to meet you.'

'Thank you, and I you, Phineas. Though, I'm sorry to hear your news. We hoped someone in Como might know where he is.' Matteo quirked his mouth and huffed. 'The puzzle grows more and more complex.'

Phin gave Lucy a meaningful look before he replied, 'It certainly does. But we will not give up. We have left two hotel staff to follow up on the sighting. We may receive better news tomorrow. My apologies for being late, Elvira, I'll update you over dinner. Now I must freshen up.'

Lucy stood and made her excuses on catching Phin's eye as he headed for the door.

'What is it you can't or won't say in front of the others?' Lucy demanded as soon as they reached their suite. Phineas sighed and let George shrug him out of his jacket. Both men looked exhausted, but Lucy's antennae were twitching wildly. 'Well?'

'It's nothing to do with the search for Luca, but something bewildering occurred whilst we were in Como. I'll fill you in while I dress for dinner,' he replied, heading towards his dressing room. Lucy followed and sat down on the chair just inside the door. Phineas threw her a disgruntled look. 'Tapping your foot like that will not speed matters up, you know.'

George did his best to smother his grin and wouldn't meet her eye.

'Hmm,' Lucy said, as she did her best not to scowl. She had to wait patiently as Phineas washed and then changed his clothes. She then had to watch while George fixed the wings of the shirt in place before tying a fresh white bowtie in place.

'That will be all for now, George,' Phin said at last, taking his jacket from the valet's hands.

'Very good, sir,' George replied before nodding to Lucy and heading out the door.

'Is George alright?' she asked. 'He's quite pale.'

'I don't think the heat agrees with him. But he was a godsend. Even Revello was impressed by his organisational skills. Unfortunately, as regards Luca, our efforts yielded little.'

'But *something* happened.'

Phineas blew out his cheeks and sat down. 'Indeed, it did. Kincaid.'

'What? What about him? Was he in Como? I met him at the hotel. Very full of himself, as ever. Boasting about solving the diamond case and warning you off. I put him straight on that.'

'I'm sure you did, dear heart.'

'Did you quarrel? Is that it?' she asked. 'He looked like a man itching for a fight.'

'No, my dear. I didn't see him at all. Kincaid was attacked last night and left for dead in a back street in Como. Luckily, he was found and taken to the infirmary, but he remains unconscious. It was sheer chance George came across the incident while checking out a guesthouse on the same street, otherwise I might not have known about it.'

'And you went to see him when you heard?'

Phin grimaced. 'I tried, but our friend Marinelli was there and refused to tell me anything. George worked his charm on a nurse, however, and that was how we discovered Kincaid's condition.'

Lucy mulled this over. 'When I saw Kincaid, he was heading for Bellagio. He must have taken a steamer to Como shortly after.' Phin nodded. 'I wonder why he travelled there. Could it have been something to do with the diamond case? Could there be a connection?' she asked. 'I mean, if the thief thought they were about to be exposed...'

'I would hazard that is likely, but neither can we rule out the possibility that he was merely in the wrong place at the wrong time.'

'A robbery, perhaps? That would confirm that theory.'

Phineas shrugged. 'Impossible to know, and Marinelli has no intention of taking me into his confidence. However, I like your theory more. We both know how much Kincaid likes to brag about his prowess. If he did so in the wrong company and they thought he was going to the police...'

'They would have followed him,' Lucy concluded.

'It's all supposition, however. But what we do know is that whoever attacked him botched it, or they might have been disturbed. Kincaid may yet recover.'

'Obviously, I hope he does.' Lucy mulled it over for a few seconds. 'But could this have anything to do with Luca's disappearance?'

'That, my dear, is the pertinent question.'

ELEVEN

It was a misty dawn. Lucy shivered and pulled her shawl tightly to her body. Elvira was next to her on the steps, ashen-faced in her anguish, her fingers digging into Lucy's arm. To their left, Phineas stood with his eyes fixed on the water below, his face tight with anxiety. Did he expect the worst? Lucy wondered. It was difficult not to despair. Phin caught Lucy's gaze and his expression softened, and despite the dreadful circumstances, it brought her some comfort.

A little apart were the rest of Luca's family. Matteo's eyes were constantly moving between the lake and Elvira, deep concern in his eyes. Giuseppe, in contrast, stood stiff and indignant, having been summoned from his suite at the hotel, as the awful news had spread. There had been no words of comfort for Elvira when he had arrived.

This waiting and not knowing was the worst part. Lucy took a deep breath, but still her heart raced. She wanted to cry but knew she must stay strong for Elvira's sake. To see her so cast down was difficult. Each day since their arrival, the hope in her sister-in-law's eyes had diminished. Despite everything, Lucy still clung to the notion that it was a case of mistaken identity. That the body about to arrive at the stone jetty was not Luca. But the conte had been missing for two weeks now.

Suddenly, the water lapped against the stone jetty as ripples of silver and black appeared on the surface of the lake. Something was approaching. Lucy braced herself, but it was Elvira who gasped as one of the traditional lake boats, a *gondole lariane*, emerged ghost-like from the haze, making its way towards them. A sob escaped Elvira, her trembling hand flying up to her mouth. Lucy reached over and hugged her tightly. This was a tragedy not only for Elvira, and her young children, but for all the family.

The boat crept ever nearer to the jetty, and Lucy could see a fisherman and a Carabinieri officer standing to attention, sombre, their hats in their hands. A third man, who Lucy guessed was another fisherman, was guiding the boat to the shore. He, too, wore a troubled expression.

It was only fitting: their cargo was, indeed, a body.

Lucy glanced across at Phin, his brow now creased with concern. Was Phin reproaching himself? Lucy wondered. And yet she knew Phin had done his best to trace Luca.

Then at four this morning, Elvira had banged on their bedroom door, distraught. When Phin had answered, she had fallen into his arms, sobbing. It took a good ten minutes to decipher what she had to say. It transpired that a message had just arrived. Some children playing at the water's edge near Musso, earlier that evening, had raised the alarm. An hour later, a body had been pulled from the water by the local fishermen.

Now, that same boat drifted alongside the jetty. Several of the villa servants rushed to help secure it with ropes. All the while, not a word was spoken. Lucy shivered. As the boat was finally secured, Elvira moaned and clutched Lucy's arm once more. Lucy knew her sister-in-law's heart was breaking but had no words of comfort to offer that didn't sound trite in the circumstances. Phineas stepped forward, put his arm around his sister's shaking shoulders, while sharing a helpless glance with Lucy. Luca's uncle and brother remained silent and motionless.

'It's best we stand back and let them do their work,' Phin murmured to Elvira, nodding towards the boat.

Lucy bobbed her head in agreement and gently directed Elvira back up the steps, past Giuseppe and Matteo, whose horrified expression shifted to Elvira, then back down again to the boat. Giuseppe, however, ignored them, and Lucy's dislike of the man grew. *A cold fish* was how she had described him in a letter to her friend, Lady Sarah. It looked as though her assessment of the man had been accurate. How could he stand there, with not a flicker of emotion, when Elvira's world was falling apart?

Elvira stumbled as Lucy guided her towards the lawn, away from the men. Lucy whispered comforting words and held on to her, fearing Elvira might faint. All Elvira could manage in response was a nod of her head. The next few days would be hell, Lucy thought. How would they support Elvira through this?

From their vantage point above the jetty, Lucy could see down into the boat. The unmistakable outline of a body lay on the deck, covered by a rough blanket, an ominous pool of water spread outwards from the corpse. Lucy shivered again, but this time it was not from the cold. Lucy had a dread of deep water and a fear of drowning. A fear made even worse by witnessing the near drowning of Phin in the North Sea only a few months before.

As they waited, the body was moved onto a makeshift stretcher, gently, and with respect. One or two of the servants standing on the jetty wiped their tears. Esposito's cheeks were deadly pale, and although he didn't cry, his chin quivered. It was clear the conte was held in high regard by his servants.

Lucy could feel a lump rise in her own throat as the men manoeuvred the stretcher out of the boat and up the steps.

If the body was indeed Luca, he was home at last.

Then, as the stretcher bearers walked past with their heads bent, Elvira trembled again. She made to reach out and pull back the blanket.

'No, don't; not here, my dear,' Lucy said, tightening her grip on her. 'Come along. We must follow them into the house.'

Phineas came alongside and took Elvira's other arm and slowly they steered the poor woman up towards the terrace. Suddenly, up ahead, one of the men stumbled where the paving stones met the lawn and the stretcher tipped to the side for a moment before the men recovered their balance and continued into the house. But in that instant, Lucy noticed something small and black fall to the ground from under the blanket.

'Phin, what's that?' Lucy pointed at the bundle now lying on the dewy grass.

Phin released his sister's arm and stooped down. It appeared to be a drawstring cloth pouch. Phin frowned at Lucy as he felt the contents through the bag.

Lucy's mind was racing. It couldn't possibly be, could it?

'There's something inside,' he confirmed, and Lucy's heart pounded. He flicked a glance of concern at Elvira, who now seemed to be in a shock-induced trance, staring at the pouch in his hand.

Lucy scanned ahead and saw that the others had disappeared into the villa. 'Open it, quickly while we are alone,' Lucy urged. 'This could be an important clue to what happened to Luca.'

Phineas flinched, looking at Elvira's pale face, then threw Lucy a warning look. 'Lucy!'

'No, Phin. She's right. If that is... Luca, we need to know everything,' Elvira said, so softly it was almost a whisper.

'Very well,' he said, before loosening the drawstrings

securing the pouch and tipping the contents out into the palm of his hand. Lucy couldn't believe her eyes. Even Elvira gasped.

Five oval-shaped diamonds glittered in the early morning sun. They were magnificent.

'Oh my God!' Lucy exclaimed. 'The Fitzwilliam Diamonds – they have to be.'

'I believe so, my dear,' Phin replied with a grim expression.

What on earth were stolen diamonds doing on the body of a dead man? Lucy swallowed hard. And if that was Luca under that blanket, the implications were profound.

Could Luca Carmosino have stolen the Fitzwilliam Diamonds?

TWELVE

Esposito directed the stretcher bearers to a room at the back of the house, and by the time Lucy, Phin and Elvira entered, the shutters had been closed and the remains, still covered by the blanket, had been placed on a table, drawn into the centre. The Carabinieri officer stood to attention beside the body. Next to him, Giuseppe and Matteo remained close to the head of the corpse. The two fishermen remained by the door, with their caps in their hands. One was surreptitiously taking in the room's splendour in wide-eyed amazement; his companion, however, looked like he wanted to escape out the door. Esposito went up to them and quietly asked them to leave, but Elvira stepped forward.

'No, wait, please,' she said, holding out her hand. '*Grazie!*' she managed to say as she shook their hands. Both men looked uncomfortable, but grateful for her courtesy. Then Elvira turned to the police officer and shook his hand, too. Lucy swelled with pride. Despite the awfulness of the situation, Elvira still had time to be kind to them for bringing her Luca home.

Giuseppe harrumphed his displeasure and rolled his eyes at Matteo, who scowled back at him. Lucy flashed Giuseppe a warning glance; the man was obnoxious. But then she felt pressure on her arm from Phin. With reluctance, Lucy had to admit Phineas was probably right. Now was not the time for unpleasantness or hasty words. But it was yet another black mark against the man, in Lucy's opinion.

Meanwhile, Esposito ushered the fishermen out the door. Then he addressed Elvira. 'Ma'am, do you wish me to send a message to Commissario Marinelli in Como?'

Giuseppe drew himself up and snapped, 'Nonsense! There's no need to involve the police.'

Elvira gasped, 'But—' and focused on Phin in confusion.

Phin cleared his throat, and Lucy knew he was doing his best to control his temper. 'On the contrary, Signor Carmosino, there's every reason to inform him. He was in charge of the investigation when Luca went missing.' Phineas turned to the now deeply embarrassed Carabinieri officer and said, '*Si prega di avvisare il Commissario Marinelli che è stato ritrovato un cadavere.*'

The policeman nodded and headed out the door.

'But it was an accident,' spluttered Giuseppe. 'Anyone can see that. A tragic accident.' Then he took a long, deep breath and fixed his gaze on Elvira. 'Must we drag the family name through even more scandal?'

Lucy fumed. How dare he!

'Uncle, please. Phineas is correct,' Matteo piped up. 'A full investigation is needed. Family honour demands it, if nothing else.' He gazed down at the body. 'However, perhaps first... we should find out if this is indeed Luca.'

Everyone's eyes fell upon the covered corpse. Lucy allowed herself a moment of hope, but it quickly died. Who else *could* it be?

'But that is easily confirmed,' Giuseppe said with an angry shake of his head, reaching out to pull back the blanket.

'Please stop!' Phineas stepped forward. Even in the dimness of the room, Lucy could see the angry stain on his cheeks. 'My sister does not need to be here for this. Elvira is distressed enough.'

'But she must confirm it's Luca,' Giuseppe replied. 'No arrangements can be made until it's certain.'

'Sir, any of the family would suffice for legal purposes. But I must warn you: I have been unfortunate enough to have seen bodies pulled from the water. After this length of time, identification will be... problematic,' Phineas replied in an icy tone. 'It may not even be possible.' Giuseppe snatched back his hand while Matteo grimaced and turned away to compose himself.

Lucy grasped what Phin was trying to say delicately so as not to upset Elvira. But hearing Elvira's sharp intake of breath, she knew it was in vain. If it were Luca under that blanket, it was best Elvira remember her husband as he had been.

Lucy moved closer to Elvira and put her arm around her waist. 'Phin is right, dearest. Come upstairs with me. There's no need for you to witness this. Phin and Matteo will take care of it.'

Phineas turned to them and nodded his agreement. 'I'll join you shortly,' he said, his eyes full of sympathy, and if Lucy wasn't mistaken, dread for what was to come.

At the door, Elvira stalled beside Matteo, who reached out and squeezed her hand. She gave him a grateful smile before turning to look once more across the room towards the covered remains. Then her shoulders slumped, and she let Lucy lead her away.

They waited up in Elvira's suite. On entering the room, Elvira had taken one look at the marital bed and rushed past her maid and into her adjoining dressing room, where she curled up on the window seat and gazed down towards the lake. Elvira's hand shook as she pushed her hastily tied-back raven hair out of her eyes. She was deadly pale. Lucy's heart went out to her, trying to imagine what she was going through. In a few minutes, the corpse's identity might be confirmed. In the circumstances, she realised it was best to let Elvira grieve. Anything she might say would hardly give Elvira any comfort.

But Lucy could not relax. Instead, she paced the floor between the bedroom and the dressing room, every so often stopping to check on Elvira. But her sister-in-law stayed silent, lost in her sorrow, staring at the slowly emerging lake view. Lucy stopped at the other window and looked out. The water was now visible as the rays of the sun burnt off the mist. But it was still an eerie sight, and her thoughts dwelled on poor Luca. How many days had he been in the water? She shivered and was suddenly glad she wouldn't have to witness the unveiling of the body. But the burning question remained: was it Luca or someone else lying on that table down below? At least they might now have an answer, for they were all at breaking point.

Ten minutes later, there was a tap on the bedroom door. Lucy steeled herself as Rose, Elvira's maid, opened it. Phineas and Matteo were out in the hallway. To Lucy's relief, there was no sign of Giuseppe. However, from Matteo's expression and Phineas' pallor, she knew it was the news they had feared. Lucy drew in a breath, fighting back her tears, all the while her gaze fixed on Phin. The men stepped inside, Matteo leading the way.

Elvira rose and came into the bedroom. She, too, didn't need to hear the words: it was enough to see the men's faces. With a cry, she rushed towards them, and into Phin's arms, sobbing.

Once she had composed herself, Lucy followed Matteo across the room, where he was staring down into the empty grate of the fireplace. She touched his arm gently and said, 'I'm so sorry. There can be no mistake?'

'None,' he replied, holding out his hand. Nestled in his palm was a signet ring, which bore the same crest that graced the archway above the main door of the villa. The Carmosino crest. 'It's Luca's ring.'

'Perhaps it was stolen?' Lucy asked, more in hope than conviction. Matteo placed the ring on the mantelpiece, shaking his head.

'There's little room for doubt, Lucy,' Phin said. He gently guided Elvira back to the window seat and sat down beside her, taking her hand in his. Elvira leaned her head against his shoulder, silently weeping.

'I'm so sorry, Elvira,' Matteo said, his voice breaking. 'You must be devastated.' Elvira held out her hand to him and he took it between both of his. Matteo swallowed hard and paused as if to gain control. 'However, I do not understand how this could have happened. How could he have fallen into the lake? He was an experienced yachtsman, and he was a strong swimmer, too.'

With an almost imperceptible movement of his head towards Elvira, Phineas spoke up. 'Time enough for speculation, my friend. Right now, we must inform the rest of the family and take care of Elvira and the children.'

Elvira suddenly straightened up, her features set in a fierce expression. 'No! Matteo is right, Phineas. Luca and his entire family have spent every summer here at the lake. He knew the area and was well aware of the lake's dangers. He would never take an unnecessary risk.' She paused, gulping through fresh tears. 'Because of the children... Someone is responsible for his death, I am certain, and I want you to find out who.'

'My dear—' Phineas objected.

'Only recently you found out who murdered Edward Vaughan, did you not? Lucy told me all about it.'

'Yes, I did, with Lucy's help,' he replied, throwing Lucy a rueful glance.

'Well then, surely you can do the same for your sister?' Elvira demanded with some of her old spirit.

Phin's expression softened. 'I promise you I'll do what I can. Let us see what the commissario has to say when he arrives, Elvira, but he may not take kindly to my interference.'

THIRTEEN

Later that afternoon

The house was eerily quiet. As Lucy walked along the hallways, she was struck by the fact that every servant she encountered wore their grief like a badge of honour. Their usual friendly smiles were missing and even their footsteps were muted. What greater tribute to Luca, Lucy thought, than this? He had been well loved by everyone, and would be sadly missed.

Elvira had eventually agreed to go to bed to get some much-needed rest, and Giuseppe had declared over lunch he would return to Grand Hotel Bellagio. *Good riddance,* Lucy had thought as he departed. Phin accompanied him, but he was bound for Bellagio and the post and telegraph office, which was further along the shore. Many telegrams had to be sent, and Lucy knew Phin was determined to check at the police station that Commissario Marinelli had been informed, whether Giuseppe agreed or not.

Lucy longed to discuss Luca's death and the discovery of the diamonds with Phin but could hardly do so while the family was around. But now Phin had gone off on his errand, so she would have to be patient and keep busy until his return. Perhaps Salvo would like to play in the garden, she thought, and climbed to the upper floor only to find him and baby Eleanor fast asleep in their beds. It was heart-breaking to observe them sleeping so peacefully, unaware of the fate of their father. How sad that the little girl would never know Luca. Salvo at least would have some memories, though no doubt these would be faint. Lucy wondered how Elvira would break the news to him and how he might react. How could he understand what was happening at only three years of age? Similar thoughts appeared to be going through the head of the nursery maid, who sat forlorn and red-eyed in the corner, watching over her charges. Lucy gently closed the door behind her and made her way back downstairs, now glummer than ever.

If only there was something practical she could do, but she found she could not put her mind to anything. If she sat down in one of the many beautiful rooms, all now with shutters pulled across the windows, all she could think of was Luca's death or Elvira's distress. Overwhelmed by helplessness, Lucy wandered out into the garden. But the intense heat soon drove her back indoors. Perhaps it was time to change into mourning, a task she had been trying to avoid all day. How she dreaded donning black once more, nor was it ideal attire in such a climate, but it had to be done. Still, it was something to do while she waited for Phin's return.

Lucy set off to find Mary, her maid. Eventually, she found her in the dressing room of their suite. She should have known that Mary, efficient as ever, would anticipate her needs. There she stood, shaking out a black silk dress.

The maid turned and gave her a sympathetic smile. 'I'm afraid it's a wee bit creased, ma'am,' she said. 'But don't you worry, I'll have it as good as new in no time. I'll just run down-stairs and iron it.'

'Thank you, Mary, but there's no need; those creases will

fall out. I really should change into it now.' Lucy peered into Phin's dressing room, but there was no sign of his valet. 'Where is George?'

'He's downstairs, ma'am, helping to lay out the conte.' Mary gave an exaggerated shiver. 'Not that it's a valet's job and him not even of this household. Awful kind of him, but all them Italians are so upset I don't think they can put their hand to anything.'

'Yes, the conte was a popular man. And I'm not surprised George is helping. He is a very kind man.'

'Just like his master,' Mary said with pride. Mary's increasing esteem for Phin amused Lucy, for Mary was usually suspicious of everyone. And much to Lucy's delight, Mary and George appeared to be getting on famously. It boded well for a smoothly run household when they eventually returned to England.

With reluctance, Lucy slipped out of her summer dress and handed it to Mary. 'I won't see that again for some months,' she commented with a sigh.

'No, ma'am. And I would suggest some new mourning should be ordered. We only have that one dress with us.'

'Wonderful!' Lucy replied and made a face. 'You know how much I adore black.'

Mary's reply was a sympathetic chuckle.

'Perhaps you could speak to the contessa's lady's maid,' Lucy continued, eyeing up the black dress. 'I'm sure Rose can recommend someone local. I have no wish to travel to Milan.'

'Yes, ma'am. Don't worry, sure I have your measurements in my wee notebook.' Mary held out the black silk for Lucy to step into, then gave her one of her looks in the mirror as she buttoned up the back of the dress. 'Apparently...' Then she bit her lip and stopped.

'Ye-es, Mary, do go on.'

'I don't want to upset you, ma'am, and you know well I'm no gossip,' Mary said with a doe-eyed glance.

Don't laugh! She really believes that.

'Of course not, Mary, but if it's important... you must tell me, for the conte's death may not have been an accident.'

Mary's hands stilled and her eyes popped. 'Oh! No, it wasn't anything sinister, ma'am. Just there was a bit of a to-do in the servants' hall earlier.'

Lucy prized Mary's observations. 'Yes?' she prompted.

'Normally, they have a wake when someone dies here, like they do at home in Ireland,' Mary said. 'I'm glad to say they are all good Catholics in *this* country.' Again, Lucy tried not to smile. Mary's prejudices, both racial and religious, were deeply entrenched. Their stint in Egypt had done nothing to diminish them.

Mary continued, 'But sure, in this heat, they've had to put the poor man down in the cellar where it's coolest. Until the doctor comes to examine him, at any rate.'

Lucy nodded. 'The doctor has been sent for?'

'Oh, aye, ma'am. Seemingly, the policeman who was here mentioned it to the butler. He's due to arrive soon. From Bellagio, I understand.'

'Is that what's upsetting the servants?' Lucy asked.

'Not exactly. No, it was one of the younger footmen. He helped moved the body and saw the state of it. Unfortunately, he felt the need to share the gruesome details at lunch.'

'Oh dear! I'm sure that was distressing for everyone,' Lucy said.

'Yes, ma'am. I've never heard such wailing and cryin', and I've seen my share of funerals. Anyway, what upset those craturs most was that the coffin will have to be closed due to the condition of...' Mary gulped.

'Yes, yes, I'm sure it will. But they understand the reason?'

'Aye, but they are very aggrieved about it, as it breaks their tradition, so to speak. They like to kiss the dead farewell.'

Lucy's stomach did a little somersault of queasiness. 'I see! That is unfortunate, but unavoidable, Mary, due to the nature of Conte Carmosino's death.'

'They mean no harm. They are good people, ma'am. Sure, already they have a rota set up as to who will sit with the poor man.'

'What?'

'It's their way. Someone must stay with the body until it leaves the house for burial. To pray and keep vigil, ma'am. The contessa can't do it on her own, poor woman, and her so struck down with grief.'

'That is kind of them. However, once all the family has gathered here, I'm sure they'll share the burden.'

'Mr Stone's family, ma'am?'

'I hope so, though the contessa's father is too ill to travel.'

Mary's eyes lit up. 'That nice Captain Stone, perhaps? I'm sure if anyone can cheer up the poor contessa, it will be him.'

Lucy shared a sad smile with her. 'Yes, indeed. However, the captain's state of health may prevent him from travelling. I fear the best we can hope for my sister-in-law just now is acceptance. Her husband's death has devastated her. She loved him very much.'

'Yes, I know, ma'am. All the servants say it. It has always been a happy house.'

Lucy smoothed down her skirt as a lump rose in her throat. 'Those poor children, too. We will have to rally round, Mary, and support them through the difficult time ahead.' Lucy turned and watched Mary put her summer dress away in the wardrobe. 'And, of course, Mr Stone and I will investigate the conte's death.'

Mary turned to her, a brow raised. 'It wasn't an accident, then?'

'We do not know for sure yet, but all I can tell you is I have a bad feeling about what has happened, and I know Mr Stone isn't happy about the circumstances.'

'Ah! So, I should keep my ears open below stairs, even more so now?'

'Yes, please. In particular, if you should hear anything about the conte's uncle, I'd appreciate if you'd pass it on. He is a strange man and there are rumours he is in debt. His attitude and behaviour bother me, though why he would hurt his nephew I'm not sure. What would he have to gain?'

'Nothing as queer as folk, ma'am, as me mother always says. Don't you worry; I'll root out any secrets. Nothing easier.' Mary cleared her throat. 'There *was* something I heard that might be of interest. Rose mentioned an incident that gave rise to a lot of talk below stairs,' she said.

'Go on, Mary!'

'About a week before the conte disappeared, he had a flaming row with his brother in the library. A footman over-heard it as he passed through the hallway. It was something of note, for everyone thought they got on awfully well.'

Lucy perked up. This was intriguing. 'Did Rose have any idea what this argument was about?'

By the look on Mary's face, Lucy was sure she was disap-pointed not to divulge more. 'I'm afraid not, but it was an unusual occurrence, which is why she remembered it. They were normally as thick as thieves, if you'll pardon the expression.'

'That is odd, certainly.' The impression Lucy had formed while talking to Elvira was that the two brothers had a strong, almost unbreakable bond. 'And the servants were sure it was Matteo Carmosino he was arguing with?'

'Aye, ma'am. The footman had served them coffee only ten minutes before,' answered the maid with a touch of triumph.

FOURTEEN

An hour later, it had cooled down sufficiently for Lucy to make her way down to the pavilion at the lake's edge. A marble bench ran around the inside of the ornate interior, a shaded vantage point from which the fabulous views out over the water could be enjoyed. The air was clear enough to see over to the far side of the lake to Menaggio, and the towering mountain peaks beyond. Lucy had only settled down when she heard footsteps on the gravel. Shortly after, Phineas appeared in the doorway, looking hot and out of sorts.

However, when he spotted her, his expression eased into a smile. 'Ah! I thought I'd find you out here,' he said, sitting down beside her and taking her hand. He took off his hat, closed his eyes, and leaned his head back. 'What a dreadful day.'

'Did you send off all those telegrams?' she asked.

'Yes. I'll leave it to Andrew to inform the rest of the family. However, I don't imagine many of them will travel here for the funeral.'

'It will be a terrible shock for your father. I'm sure he is too unwell to travel.'

'Hopefully, Andrew will persuade him not to attempt it.

Andrew will come, I'm sure, and if Seb is well enough, he'll insist on coming.'

'I hope they do. Elvira needs their support more than ever. I'm sorry, Phin. I know how difficult this is for you. It can't be easy seeing your sister in this situation.'

'It isn't. She adored Luca. It's a huge blow. How is she since we left?'

'Miserable and exhausted. She swings between grief, shock and frustration at all the unanswered questions. I suspect she has barely slept since Luca disappeared. However, I persuaded her to retire to her room to get some rest.'

'Thank you. God help her,' he replied. 'It's difficult enough to lose one's husband, but the circumstances are so bizarre. And Giuseppe isn't helping with his snide remarks.'

'I don't understand why he is like that. Elvira is adorable.'

'He can't get over the circumstances of their marriage.'

'Indeed. Poor Elvira.'

'I don't believe she cares what he thinks,' he replied with a sad smile. 'She is used to him. Though I imagine he tempered his outbursts while Luca was alive.'

'Why should she care what he thinks? Good for her!' Lucy said. 'They were in love and could have had a wonderful future together. Giuseppe was probably jealous. He has been a widower for twenty years or so.'

'Yes. His wife died in childbirth, as far as I know,' Phin replied.

'That's very sad, but it doesn't excuse his behaviour.'

'Certainly not, and now that Luca is gone, Elvira is vulnerable. Don't underestimate Giuseppe's power. He may not be conte or ever hope to be, but he has control of some of the family businesses and could make life difficult for Elvira. Let us hope Luca made a sensible will and left her independent, at least.'

'How dreadful.'

'And I fear it will only get worse,' Phin said, much to her dismay.

'From that remark I take it you believe Luca was murdered?'

'I do.'

'And those diamonds?' Lucy asked.

Phineas blew out his cheeks. 'Quite a mystery, my dear! And I've been giving it some thought all day. Two plausible reasons for Luca having them come to mind. The first is that Luca was the thief.'

'Surely not!'

'I agree, but we must consider it.'

Lucy tilted her head as she looked back at him, letting the suggestion sink in. 'What if he was looking for excitement, not monetary gain?'

'But why would he endanger his own business and reputation?' Phin sighed. 'It makes little sense.'

'That's a good point. So, what's your other hypothesis?' she asked.

'That he was investigating the disappearance of the diamonds himself, had found the culprit and retrieved the stones and hoped to return them to their rightful owner. Perhaps that was why he really went to Milan. I never believed his solicitor's story about contracts. No business is transacted in Italy in August.'

Lucy had to admit this seemed the most plausible explanation and came to the inevitable conclusion. 'If he did find them and threatened to expose the thief, it would give that person a reason to kill him. But why would they leave the diamonds on the body? That doesn't make much sense.'

'They might have been disturbed disposing of the body and had to abandon them, hoping neither the body nor the diamonds would ever be found. Or they intended to retrieve them when it was safer. It's possible they might not have realised that dead bodies eventually float.'

Lucy shuddered. 'But why would Luca investigate, Phin? Surely, he would leave it to the police or even Kincaid.'

'Perhaps not. So far, my own dealings with Commissario Marinelli have left me underwhelmed and we both know Kincaid would never put himself in danger if he could help it. Luca probably felt he had no choice but to make his own enquiries.'

Lucy nodded slowly. 'Yes, that sounds plausible. He must have been deeply frustrated by the lack of progress of the local police.'

'As are we, God knows, and it makes me more determined than ever to find out who is responsible. The police's reluctance to carry out even the simplest of investigations beggars belief. Marinelli suggested to Matteo that Luca had gone off with another woman and would return in due course!'

'Ridiculous!'

'Well, perhaps not. I can understand his assertion to some degree. Fidelity in arranged marriages is rare in high society, fidelity in Italian marriages even more so. Marinelli wasn't to know it was a love match.'

'But they are... were madly in love,' Lucy replied.

'Exactly, which is why I dismissed that notion immediately. My belief is that Luca was deeply concerned about the reputation of the hotel. News of the burglaries was bound to have spread. The hotel caters for the well-to-do, who do not take kindly to being robbed of their valuables. I'd imagine it would put them off staying there. Reports of that nature would spread like wildfire. In Luca's shoes, I would have wanted to clear the matter up as quickly as possible.'

'Could the diamond robbery be linked to those previous incidents at the hotel?' she asked.

'Perhaps, but the earlier incidences were mostly petty thefts. When all the fuss has died down, I'll have a long chat with Matteo.'

'Ah! Yes. Strange that you should mention him,' Lucy said and quickly filled him in on Mary's servants' hall gossip.

Phin looked off into the distance. 'I don't like the sound of that.'

'Nor I,' she replied. 'I wish we knew what they had argued about. Was it something so bad that Matteo would contemplate harming his brother?'

Phin patted her hand. 'There may be nothing sinister about it. We can't jump to any conclusion based on hearsay. Besides, siblings argue all the time.'

'That's true. But in the meantime, what do we do about those diamonds?' she asked. 'Will you give them to Marinelli?'

'Yes, I have no choice, though I have informed the insurance company they have been found. Kincaid is not in a position to do so.'

'Poor Kincaid. If he wakes and hears you found them and handed them over, he will be devastated.'

'I won't claim the reward. He's welcome to it after all he's been through. Besides, he may not recover.'

'You're too kind-hearted, Phin,' she replied. 'He'd claim it if your roles were reversed.' But Phin just shrugged. Lucy continued, 'Is Marinelli trustworthy, though? Perhaps you should send the diamonds directly to London.'

'I can't do that. I must follow the procedure. Mind you, it would be a shame if they were to disappear again. For now, however, they are secure in the safe in Luca's library.'

'Do you think the police will reopen the diamond case?'

'I hope so, but I'm certain now that Luca's death is linked,' Phin said. 'In which case, we may well stumble on the answer ourselves.'

'I hope we do, and quickly, for Elvira's sake. Do you think the funeral will be soon?'

'That will be down to Marinelli,' Phin replied. 'He will insist on a post-mortem, so we will have to wait for the outcome of that. As far as I know, there's a family vault in a cemetery in Milan. I imagine that is where Luca will be buried.'

They sat in silence for several minutes, as the cooling influence of the late afternoon *Breva* brought some relief from the dead heat. A yacht glided past, the occupants clearly enjoying themselves as their laughter floated across the water. It seemed discordant, somehow.

'Was it very unpleasant trying to identify him?' Lucy asked at last.

'Yes.' Phin stared out over the lake for several moments. 'I'm not knowledgeable enough on the subject, but it looked to me as if Luca sustained a blow to the side of his head. And yes, I know, it might have happened in the water after death. But the shape of the wound was long and narrow. I don't think a rock would cause that, more likely a metal rod or stout stick; something like that.'

'That's awful. If you are right, that suggests he was dead before he went into the water. If the post-mortem is inconclusive, what then?'

'If there's any doubt whatsoever, Marinelli will have to investigate further.'

'But he was little or no help when we thought it was just a disappearance,' Lucy said.

'Very true, my love, but a missing conte is one thing; a dead and possibly murdered one, quite another.'

FIFTEEN

Much to Lucy's disgust, Giuseppe had returned to the villa before dinner. Instead of greeting Elvira, he had gone straight to the nursery. When there was no sign of him joining them for drinks before the second gong, Lucy had volunteered to fetch him. Her intent was to admonish him for his behaviour, considering Elvira's distressed state. However, when she entered the children's room, she was astonished to find him sitting on the floor playing with Salvo.

Giuseppe looked up and scowled at her in the doorway, clearly irritated to be disturbed. Grumbling under his breath, he had struggled to his feet, refusing her offer of help. Lucy was very surprised, however, when he stooped down and ruffled Salvo's dark curls and the child beamed back up at him. His affection for the young boy did look genuine, and she had to admit that perhaps he wasn't as black a character as she had previously supposed. Then, with a grunt, Giuseppe ushered Lucy ahead of him and down the stairs just as the second gong sounded down in the hallway. The journey to the dining room was made in silence.

When Giuseppe reached out for Luca's seat at the head of

the table, Phin's discreet cough gave him pause. Giuseppe pushed the chair back in with little grace and huffed his way around the table to sit beside Lucy. She treated him to a chilly stare, determined to ignore him as best she could for the rest of the meal.

Dinner was a solemn affair, with Elvira barely touching the food on her plate. Lucy's appetite was poor, too, but she was growing concerned about her sister-in-law's mental state. Elvira was listless and struggling to make even cursory conversation. Lucy looked across at Phin, but he shrugged, his eyes flicking over to Elvira and back again to Lucy. It was to be expected, of course, but it didn't make it any easier to witness. Confirmation of Luca's death was a tremendous blow. Whilst there had been no word, there had still been hope.

Matteo also watched Elvira with concern and Lucy's growing suspicion that the young man cared for Elvira grew. This was unfortunate, for it threw up the possibility that the row overheard between the brothers might have been about Elvira. And to follow that to its logical conclusion, if Luca's death was down to foul play, his brother had a motive. The idea made the food in Lucy's stomach lie cold and hard.

What little conversation there was, was desultory at best, so when Esposito entered the room once more, all eyes turned to him with something akin to relief. He stepped up to Elvira and informed her, in a low voice, 'Ma'am, Commissario Marinelli and Dr Spina have arrived and wish to speak to you. *Anche il prete.*' Esposito grew flustered. 'Excuse me, ma'am, Monsignor Loria, as well.'

'Thank you, Esposito.' Elvira sighed and rose from her seat. Lucy flashed a concerned glance at Phin. Elvira was in no state to engage with officials.

But it was Matteo who jumped up and pressed her back down into her chair. 'Don't worry, Elvira, I'll take care of this. It will just be formalities.'

The butler expressed the relief Lucy felt at his words. 'Very good, sir. If you would follow me, please.'

'I shall join you, Matteo,' Phin said after a quizzical glance at Giuseppe. It was clear the man would not offer *his* services. As Phin passed Elvira's chair, he touched her shoulder. 'All will be well, sister.'

'I don't see how,' Elvira whispered as the men left the room.

Giuseppe muttered a comment in Italian. A derogatory one, Lucy was sure on seeing the flash of anger cross Elvira's face.

It took a great deal of effort for Lucy to control her temper. Willing herself to stay calm, she reached across and touched Elvira's hand. 'Did I tell you that Phineas believes Andrew and Sebastian will come to Italy as soon as they can?' she said, hoping to distract her. 'Hopefully, we will see them by the day after tomorrow.'

Elvira nodded and tried to smile, but failed. She picked up her fork, pushed the piece of venison around the plate once more, then gave up.

Lucy was acutely aware of Giuseppe's hostile gaze on her sister-in-law and bristled. 'Come, Elvira, you're finished. Let us await the others in the drawing room.'

Manners dictated Giuseppe had to stand as the ladies rose. He bowed as they passed. A curt bob of his head, more insult than civility.

Lucy paused at the door when she realised he wouldn't follow them. He seemed remarkably unconcerned about what was happening in the house. In fact, it puzzled Lucy that he had not insisted on meeting with the officials, along with Phin and Matteo. 'Will you not join us for coffee, Signor Carmosino?' she asked.

'No, thank you,' he said with a smug smile before sitting back down and reaching for the decanter of port a servant had just set down.

His attitude made Lucy fume, but she linked Elvira's arm as

they headed out the door. 'Good. Let him stay here out of our way,' she said, not caring if he heard or not.

The beautiful grand drawing room was at the back of the villa. But this evening, the view of the large terrace and the lake beyond were blocked out by the shutters. Elvira sat down in an armchair by the fireplace, her sorrowful expression illuminated by a lamp on a table next to her. Lucy's heart went out to her.

'Have you spoken to little Salvo yet?' Lucy asked as a maid handed Elvira her coffee.

'Yes, briefly, this afternoon.'

'Does he comprehend...?'

Elvira put down her cup. 'At first I thought he did, but then he said he wanted to show papa the toy train Uncle Phin had brought him.' Elvira looked across at her, her eyes bright with tears. 'I didn't know what to say.'

'Nor would I!' Suddenly, Lucy found the room claustrophobic. She jumped to her feet, her own coffee untouched. 'My dear, would you mind if I open the doors out onto the terrace? The room is oppressively warm.'

Elvira sat, twisting her hands in her lap. A tiny shrug was the only sign she had been listening.

Lucy pushed open the doors, gulping the fresh cool air. In the distance, lights from the villages on the far side of the lake were just visible, twinkling in the darkness.

'Come with me, Elvira,' Lucy coaxed. 'Let's take a stroll on the terrace. It's a lovely evening and it will do you good to get some fresh air. You have been cooped up all day.' Lucy walked back over to Elvira and stretched out her hand. 'Please.'

At last, a smile. Elvira got to her feet. 'You are a tyrant, Lucy.'

'Ha! That's what Phin says. But it's for your own good,' Lucy replied. 'It will be pleasantly cool outside.'

The evening was still and the air heavy with rose scent from the flowerbeds that bordered the terrace. They strolled along the length of the house in silence several times. As they walked, Lucy felt some of the tension in Elvira ease.

As they reached the end of the terrace once more, Elvira sighed and pulled away from Lucy to sit on the balustrade. 'I'm so grateful that you both came. I don't think I could have coped this past week without you. Phineas is always so strong and clever, and you have been so kind to me.'

Lucy bit her lip and smiled.

'And now I must implore you both to find out who murdered Luca,' Elvira said, her voice quiet but firm.

'But it isn't certain that it *is* murder.'

'No. But it's the only explanation that makes sense. Not for one moment did I imagine he would return home in the manner he did. At first, I thought Luca had had a mishap of some sort, and that he would turn up embarrassed, but with an excellent excuse. But as the days crept past and there was no word, deep down I knew all hope was lost.' Elvira threw Lucy an anguished look. 'I knew he wouldn't abandon me and the children like that.' Elvira looked out over the lake, for a moment lost in her thoughts. 'So, you see. It must have been foul play.'

'Don't! You will only upset yourself,' Lucy replied.

Elvira's answering look was fierce. 'But I must face the facts. That is why you and Phin must find out what happened. I don't believe it was an accident. I will not rest until I know the truth, but I'm not strong enough to deal with this... situation on my own. You, of all people, must understand; you lost a husband, too. Grief is clouding my brain.'

Lucy sat down beside her. 'There was one essential difference. Charlie and I had fallen out of love by the time he died. His death was a terrible shock and yes, it took me a while to come to terms with it, but Phin's investigations into Charlie's activities revealed deceit and dishonour on a scale that left me reeling.'

'I'm sorry. I didn't know about that,' Elvira replied.

'No matter, it's all in the past. Be easy in your mind. You can rely on us. We will find out what happened to Luca.'

Elvira squeezed her eyes shut and nodded. 'I trust you implicitly. The next few months will be difficult. Matteo is a fine young man and will help as much as he can, but Giuseppe...'

'Don't worry – I have his measure, as does Phin!'

'I don't doubt it. He is so very adept at showing his contempt.'

'A masterly performance at every turn,' Lucy answered with a grim smile.

'I think you misunderstand him, Lucy. He doesn't mean to be nasty.' Lucy stared at her defence of Giuseppe in disbelief. Elvira sighed and then continued, 'You see, for him, the Carmosino family is everything and I'm a blot on his landscape. The family has links all the way back to the House of Sforza. When Luca announced we were to be married, his relatives were horrified. I was the wrong nationality, and the wrong religion, too.'

'But Elvira, you did marry him. You gave up your old life to come and live here, even converted. Did that mean nothing to them?'

Elvira shrugged. 'This is Italy, not England. Honour, religion and family are everything.'

'But you're the contessa and have every right to expect the respect of the family. Giuseppe is so rude to you at every opportunity. You can't excuse his behaviour. I'm sure he didn't behave in such a way in front of Luca.'

'No, but he can't help it. He is a product of the Italian aristocracy, and I thwarted his grand plan.'

'And what was that?' Lucy asked, deeply curious.

'Giuseppe always hoped that the daughter of a distant cousin would be the new contessa. The lady's father was under his financial control.'

'And through the marriage, he hoped to control Luca?'

'Probably. Luca suspected as much,' Elvira replied. 'But Luca was determined to resist his machinations.'

'Good Lord! Quite like the Medicis!' Lucy exclaimed.

Elvira managed a sad smile. 'Yes, I suppose so. When I arrived in Milan with my aunt, Luca had only just become the conte. He was very low in spirits and was still grieving for his father. It was pure fluke that he was at the dinner that night. He had not meant to attend, but a friend had convinced him it would do him good.' Elvira shook her head, her eyes shining in memory. 'He took my breath away. Luca was so handsome, and I loved him quite madly from that very moment,' she said with a fierceness that melted Lucy's heart.

'No one could doubt that, Elvira. I'm so sorry you have lost him so soon.'

'It was like a beautiful dream, Lucy, and now it has vanished in a puff of smoke. But I'm not ready to let him go.'

'I understand, Elvira, truly I do, but your focus must be on the children now. They will need you.'

'It will be, of course.' Elvira scanned the terrace before answering. 'But I must tread carefully where Giuseppe is concerned. He could make life tiresome.'

'You don't think...' Lucy trailed off, reluctant to accuse him with no evidence.

'That he had something to do with Luca's death? No. But he will take advantage of the situation. I only hope that Matteo can restrain his worst inclinations. Oh, Lucy! I have always considered myself a strong person, but I can't think straight. Is it awful that I could not deal with the police or the coroner? Isn't that ridiculous?' She squeezed her eyes shut for a moment. 'Or even worse, the monsignor. He must think me dreadfully rude.

But I can't bear to think of Luca being buried. It's a living nightmare.'

'No, no, not at all. You've had a terrible shock. No one could expect you to talk to those men. You know Phin is happy to be of service, for he is extremely fond of you. I'm sure Matteo will want to help as much as possible, too.'

'He will. All he has ever shown me is kindness.' After some moments of silence, Elvira spoke once more. 'I may take the children back to England for a while. If Andrew comes, I'll ask him if it would be agreeable to him.'

'Why would he object? Andrew is not head of the family yet, though he might act as if he were.' This made Elvira smile. 'Besides, I'm sure your father would be delighted to see you, Elvira, and that is all that matters. Needless to say, you and the children will always be welcome in our home. You can stay as long as you wish, and I'll spoil your children to the point of ruination.'

Elvira's eyes shimmered with tears yet again. 'You are funny, Lucy. Thank you.' She kissed her cheek.

They sat for several minutes, Elvira's head resting on Lucy's shoulder. At last, Elvira sighed. 'I don't understand any of this. Who could have hated Luca enough to harm him?'

Lucy decided to push her a little. 'Can you think of anyone who might have wanted to hurt him? Someone he might have crossed? Someone with a grudge?'

'No! If anything, he was well-loved. The hotel and the silk factory in Como provide employment. He treated his tenants fairly – in fact, better than most. Life is hard for the locals here on the lake. That is why many of them turn to smuggling. Luca hoped that by providing jobs, he could entice them away from that life.'

'What do they smuggle?'

'Tobacco and salt, mainly. We're close to the border with Switzerland, where these items are much cheaper.'

'I can see how it would be tempting,' Lucy said. 'But I'm sure the police try to put a stop to it.'

'They do try, but it's rampant, and it's all done under the cover of darkness.'

'I see.' Lucy gathered her thoughts. Elvira was as determined to find out what had happened as they were. So perhaps it was time to probe about Matteo. 'I hate to bring this up at such a time, but the servants overheard Luca and Matteo arguing not long before Luca disappeared. Did Luca tell you about it?'

Elvira frowned at her. 'Yes. It was over the contractor who installed the electricity in the hotel here in Bellagio. It was Matteo who had recommended him. Luca suspected the man had used inferior materials to cut costs – I know nothing about these things, but Luca was sure that caused the fire. Matteo wouldn't take responsibility, blaming Revello, who had made the final decision. What annoyed Luca was that Matteo then hired someone else to do the electrical work in his hotel in Milan. It was a business matter and Luca was cross about it.' Elvira's eyes widened. 'But you can't seriously think that Matteo could have had anything to do with Luca's death? Over something like that? No! Never, Lucy. I can't even consider such a notion. They had such a strong bond; thought as one on almost everything.'

Lucy suspected that was the problem: their shared interest included Elvira. However, as the carefully thought-out response was on the tip of Lucy's tongue, movement at the front of the villa caught her attention. 'Look!' she exclaimed, touching Elvira's arm, then pointing. 'Isn't that Giuseppe and Marinelli out in the carriageway?' A third man, who Lucy assumed was the doctor, stood to the side. The men shook hands, greeting each other as if old friends. Marinelli and the doctor then walked away towards the jetty. Giuseppe turned back into the house.

'Yes, I think so,' Elvira said.

'They have a conspiratorial air to me. What could they be up to?' Lucy said, squinting into the darkness.

'What does it matter? Listen! I hear voices; the others must be back in the drawing room,' Elvira said, tugging Lucy's sleeve.

But when they entered the room once more, Lucy could tell it was bad news. Phin's jaw was clenched, and Matteo looked as though he might cry as he headed straight for the decanters on the sideboard.

'I just saw Marinelli outside. Have they all gone?' Lucy asked.

'Yes, all but the priest,' Phin said. 'He is leading some prayers at the moment.'

'Phin, I should be there, too,' Elvira said. 'Perhaps you would take me down to where Luca is laid out. I'd like to sit with him until morning and pray.'

Phineas exchanged a glance with Lucy before stepping forward and taking Elvira's hands. 'Of course, but you will only have about an hour. Marinelli and the doctor have ordered that Luca be taken to Como straight away so that a full post-mortem can be carried out. Marinelli is arranging for one of the estate boats to be prepared, as we speak. They'll depart shortly, once the prayers are concluded.'

What little colour there was in Elvira's face drained away. 'They are taking him so soon? But why, Phin? No, no, he should be here with me until...'

'It's because the cause of death is not clear, Elvira,' Matteo said, downing a glass of whisky in one gulp. 'We have no choice.'

'We have no choice in what?' Giuseppe barked as he entered the room.

'The conte is being taken to the hospital in Como for a post-mortem,' Phin informed him.

'Well, that is hardly surprising. You did insist on involving the police,' Giuseppe said. Then he swung around, staring at

Elvira. 'I suppose you thought you'd get away with it.' Then he glared at Matteo. 'Did you think no one knew of your affair? Poor, poor Luca.'

In the stunned silence that followed, Lucy held her breath. Who would react first? Elvira was rigid with shock and Phin looked as if he could murder the man.

But it was Matteo who walked up to his uncle, swung his right fist, and knocked him out cold.

SIXTEEN

Lucy lay snuggled up in Phin's arms, sleepily content. Whether it was an official honeymoon or not, she was enjoying their intimate moments more and more. How pleasant it was to be herself, without inhibitions. With Charlie, Lucy had often been left dissatisfied, particularly in the latter years of their marriage. Their lovemaking had been almost perfunctory. With Phin, it was completely different.

However, as she gradually woke up, the dramatics of the previous evening encroached on her happy state of mind. What a disaster it had been! Once he had picked himself up off the floor, Giuseppe had left the house in a rage, his tirade in Italian lingering like a ghost in the air. A distraught Matteo had apologised profusely to Elvira, but she was so distressed, Lucy reckoned his words went unheard. Lucy's heart went out to Elvira, for it was too much for her fragile emotional state. There was a strangled 'goodnight' from Matteo before he slunk out the door. Once she regained her equilibrium, Elvira begged Lucy to accompany her upstairs. Lucy delivered her into the arms of her beloved lady's maid, heartbroken to see Elvira so brought down by Giuseppe's awful behaviour. But anger soon replaced that feeling on Elvira's behalf. Anger at the man who was making the woman's life so utterly miserable. Her earlier softening towards him had been misguided. The nagging question was, why was Giuseppe being so horrible?

'Why the sudden frown, my love?' Phin asked, breaking into Lucy's thoughts as she lay there reliving it all. He pulled her closer. 'I mustn't be doing my job properly.'

Lucy chuckled. 'Don't be silly. I have no complaints. I couldn't be happier. No, I was thinking about last night. I'm only glad Matteo didn't have a horsewhip to hand. He was so enraged he might have killed his uncle. And poor Elvira; it was the last thing she needed to hear or witness. It's pure nastiness, Phin,' Lucy said. 'And I daresay Giuseppe will keep insinuating there was something going on, purely for mischief's sake. What's worse, some people will believe him.'

'Unfortunately, you may be right. But Giuseppe deserved it; he crossed a line last night. Elvira will never forgive him, and I don't blame her.'

'Nor I! Not very ladylike of me, I admit, but I wanted to cheer when Matteo hit him,' Lucy admitted.

Phin grinned back at her. 'So did I. Though if he hadn't got to him first, it might have been me you were cheering on.'

'Really?'

'Yes. I've run out of patience with the man. No matter what his prejudices may be, that was beyond the pale. But my fear is that it isn't just family pride that is motivating this campaign of his.'

'Oh!' Lucy shuffled into a sitting position, fully alert. 'Do you think he was involved in Luca's death?'

'I have absolutely no evidence, but it's a possibility. He was very quick to dismiss Luca's death as an accident, didn't want the police involved, and then last night implied that Elvira and

Matteo were having an affair, which led to Luca doing away with himself.'

'Yes, he is very anxious Luca's death is not considered murder. But why? To deflect?'

Phin's expression was grim. 'That's possible. He has my measure by now and knows I will not rest until I find out what happened to Luca.'

'What do you think Giuseppe's motive could be?'

'There's the possibility that he had something to do with the theft of the diamonds. After all, he lives in the hotel and must be aware of the various guests and their situations. Might he have overheard Lady Wallace talking about her diamonds?' Phin then shrugged. 'This is merely supposition on my part, however.'

'Could there be another reason? Does Giuseppe gain financially by Luca's death?' Lucy asked.

'Perhaps. I suspect with little Salvo underage, his father's shares will either be re-distributed or held in trust until he is of age. We will know more when the will is read, of course. The rest of Luca's estate will have to be administered by the trust until Salvo is twenty-one. I would imagine Luca will have stipulated who that trustee would be in the case of his premature death.'

'It wouldn't be Elvira then?'

'No. Not in such a patriarchal society as this. My guess is that it will be Matteo or Giuseppe.'

Lucy shuddered. 'Oh no, I hope it isn't Giuseppe. How could Elvira be expected to deal with him after all that has transpired? But Phin, is he not a wealthy man in his own right?'

'I assumed he was, but I'm beginning to wonder. And don't forget what Elvira said about him being in debt. I asked George to make some enquiries. It turns out Giuseppe has sold his townhouse in Milan.'

'Recently?' Lucy asked.

'About six months ago. Strange, don't you think? I would have thought he would enjoy swanning around an elegant villa and entertaining in style.'

'Which suggests his financial affairs are worth scrutinising. I suppose, as family, the suite he uses at the hotel would be free of charge,' she said.

'I'd imagine so. Very convenient if one were short of funds. And don't forget, it also places him at the heart of the Carmosino businesses and privy to everything that goes on in the hotel.'

'And if Elvira is right, he didn't like Luca's plans for the place. Living at the hotel, he was ideally placed to monitor what Luca was doing.'

'I can't argue with that,' Phin replied.

'Oh Lord! The most awful thought just occurred to me,' Lucy said. 'What if that fire hadn't been due to a fault? What if someone had started it deliberately?'

'As in someone who didn't agree with the idea? My God, Lucy. I hope you're wrong.'

'How would we prove it?' she asked.

'Unfortunately, I don't think that would be possible at this stage unless a witness came forward. We can keep it in mind, but I can't see how to connect it to Luca's murder.'

'Yes,' Lucy sighed. 'All indications point to murder.'

'And we should stay until this is investigated fully. But I'd understand if you wish to go home.'

'Absolutely not! Besides, I gave Elvira my word again last night that we would solve this.' He looked relieved. 'And I shall help you in any way I can.'

Phin kissed her nose. 'I wouldn't have it any other way.'

'But...' Lucy gnawed at her lip.

'What troubles you, my dear?'

'You don't think... I hate to say it, and I don't believe it for a moment, but we must discuss the possibility that there's some foundation for Giuseppe's allegation.'

It was several moments before Phin answered and Lucy hoped she hadn't offended him. 'Have you any grounds to think so?' he asked.

'Not really, but... I could be wrong. It's just a hunch, really. But I suspect Matteo *is* in love with Elvira. I mean, how could he not be? She is so beautiful. However, I don't for a minute believe she reciprocates. I imagine she is fond of him, and they appear to get along well. But he is so like Luca in appearance.' Phineas frowned at her, and she rushed on, 'Of course it's clear she adored Luca... But what if Matteo was jealous of his brother?'

'And wants Elvira for himself? That opens up a world of possibilities, Lucy, possibilities I'd rather not contemplate.'

'Sorry. I know,' she replied. 'It's horrible. If I'm honest, I couldn't picture him as a killer.'

'But you are right. We must consider it, no matter how distasteful, after we witnessed his temper last night and how he lashed out at Giuseppe. People are capable of anything for love. And money. If Matteo gains control of the estate...' Phineas grimaced. 'Damn!'

'Why not let me probe it a little with Elvira when the time is right? I think she would be more likely to confide in me than you. Don't worry, I'll be tactful.'

Phin's brows shot up.

'And you can wipe that look of disbelief off your face, sir! Do you not trust me?'

With a chuckle, Phin pulled her back into his arms. 'I do! Utterly.'

Much to her surprise, when Lucy came down to breakfast that morning, Elvira was sitting at the table alone. Evidence of little sleep, dark shadows beneath her eyes, told its own tale. Lucy pressed her shoulder before taking the seat beside her.

'Phin has gone for a walk while it's still cool. Did you manage to sleep?' Lucy asked, nodding her thanks to the footman who poured her coffee.

'An hour or two.' Elvira shrugged. 'My mind won't stop churning.'

'That's understandable, my dear,' Lucy answered. 'Yesterday was horrible.'

'And I thought things couldn't get much worse!'

Lucy set down her cup. 'Why do you think Giuseppe made such a ridiculous accusation?'

Elvira rubbed at her temples with the heels of her hands. 'Nastiness?' she said with a humourless laugh. Then she sighed. 'Of course, I know Matteo has feelings for me. I'm not a fool... Luca used to joke about it, that I had both brothers eating out of my hand. Perhaps he said something to his uncle in jest, but Giuseppe would happily misinterpret. He would always be willing to believe nasty gossip about me.' After a few moments, Elvira looked up from the table from where she had been twisting a napkin in her hands. 'I don't return Matteo's feelings and never have, Lucy,' she said, her voice low.

'Of course! You do not need to tell me that,' Lucy replied.

'Besides,' Elvira continued, 'Matteo is engaged to Angelica, a lovely young woman. You will agree when you meet her. Giuseppe is just being vicious; he can't resist making trouble.'

'You must not let that awful man upset you. And let me tell you, neither Phin nor I give any credence to his nonsense.'

This coaxed a sad smile from Elvira. 'Thank you. It would be comical if it wasn't so horrid.' Slowly, she exhaled. 'Matteo has left for Como. He thought it best that someone was there... with the post-mortem taking place... and he has promised to let me know immediately what the outcome is.' Elvira choked but quickly recovered. 'The poor boy. He was embarrassed about losing control last night. But I assured him I understood. I think that is part of the reason he was so eager to leave.'

'Well, for what it's worth, I thought it was about time someone hit Uncle Giuseppe.'

'Oh, Lucy!'

'And I hope the man has the sense to not darken the door again.'

Elvira agreed just as Esposito entered the room.

'Contessa, Signor Revello is here and wishes to see you. Are you at home, or shall I send him away?'

Elvira mulled it over for a few seconds. 'Are you sure it isn't my brother he wishes to speak to?'

'No, ma'am.'

'It's fine, Esposito,' Elvira said with a sigh. 'Send him in.'

As Esposito left the room, Lucy asked, 'Do you wish me or Phin to deal with him? What could be so urgent that he would bother you today?'

'No, thank you. I must get used to dealing with these matters.'

Lucy rose, but Elvira caught her sleeve and tugged. 'No, please stay. It shouldn't take long.'

Moments later, Esposito announced Francesco. Lucy observed him closely. Now, everyone had taken on a different hue. Murder, unfortunately, did that. But just as quickly, she had to dismiss such notions. Francesco had been Luca's friend, and the man's pallor indicated his feelings on the subject. With a flicker of a smile, he bowed over Elvira's outstretched hand.

'Francesco, it's good to see you again,' Elvira greeted him. 'You remember my sister-in-law, Lucy?'

Francesco bowed to Lucy, then turned his attention back to Elvira. 'Contessa,' he murmured, before straightening up. 'My deepest condolences yet again. Both Maria and I are devastated. And may I add those of all the staff at the hotel? I'm sorry to intrude at such a time. However, there are some matters that require... the attention of the family. As you know, it's high season, and the hotel is almost at full capacity.'

'Thank you, Francesco, I understand perfectly. The business must run as normal. Luca held you in high regard, both as his manager and as his friend. I'm happy to help if I can. Please, won't you join us for coffee?'

Revello nodded his thanks, struggling to regain his composure. Elvira continued, 'I have received many notes of condolence and messages of support from the senior members of staff. Please pass on my thanks to them.' Then she smiled up at him and waved to a chair.

'You're most gracious, contessa. Thank you,' Revello replied, pulling out a chair opposite and sitting down. At a nod from Elvira, the footman served the hotel manager his coffee.

Elvira waited while he drained his cup, then quirked a brow. 'And how is dear Maria? I hope she is feeling better,' she enquired.

'Yes. It was only a tiresome cold. She is much better and will call on you in the coming days... if that is permissible?' he asked.

'Of course. I would be happy to receive her, Francesco. Do encourage her to come. Now, tell me, what's the matter?'

Revello gave them both an apologetic look. 'I'm reluctant to upset you, however, several members of staff have come to me in distress. It's awful that we have lost the conte, but it would appear there are rumours abroad that the hotel is to be sold. Everyone fears they'll lose their positions, me included. The conte didn't discuss any such sale with me, so I'm at a loss to understand or to assuage their fears.'

Elvira frowned across at him. 'This is the first I have heard of it, Francesco. Obviously, I was not privy to all my husband's decisions, but, frankly, this sounds ridiculous. The conte, as you know, loved the hotel and I do know that he had great plans for it.' She shrugged. 'You must ignore the rumour mill. For now, please continue as best you can. My husband's will—' Elvira gasped, her voice cracking with emotion, 'will be read after the funeral.' Lucy stretched across and patted her hand. She, too, had a lump in her throat. How brave Elvira was!

Revello had the good grace to look embarrassed, and he cleared his throat. 'Of course, I understand. I'm only sorry to have distressed you.'

Elvira tried to smile. 'There's no need to apologise. I understand such a rumour would upset everyone. However, I have every faith in you. Your professionalism and care for the staff has always impressed us. All I can do is promise. Unfortunately, Matteo has left for Como. I'm sure he could have calmed your fears. However, when the time is right, I shall discuss your concerns with the family.'

'Thank you,' he replied. But instead of taking his leave, as Lucy expected, he shifted in his seat.

'Was there something else?' Elvira asked.

Lucy could detect the strain in her voice, and shot Revello a warning look, however, his gaze was fixed upon Elvira.

'A small staff matter. We're short staffed at present, as I am sure you are aware. With Luca's unfortunate passing, I was wondering if you still had need of his valet.'

'Well, no, as a matter of fact, my butler broached the subject with me only yesterday. We're hoping to find another position for Enzo. Luca always spoke highly of him, and I'm only too happy to offer references to a future employer.'

'Well, I might be able to help with that. He would fit in well with the hotel staff. Sometimes guests travel without a valet. We're often asked to provide the service...'

'That sounds like the perfect solution. I'll ask Esposito to send him to you later today.'

'Excellent, thank you, contessa. Again, my deepest sympathy for your loss,' he said at last as he rose.

As the door closed behind him, Lucy turned to her sister-in-law. 'That was odd. Why did he come here to you about those matters? I would have thought it would be more appropriate to discuss such things with Matteo or even Giuseppe.'

Elvira shrugged. 'I don't know. Does it matter?'

'What have I missed?' Phin asked, striding into the room as Elvira spoke. 'I passed Revello on my way in.'

'We just had a very interesting conversation with him,' Lucy replied.

'Indeed. You should have referred him to me. He shouldn't have bothered you, Elvira.' Phin kissed his sister's cheek, then sat down where Revello had been only moments before. 'And don't let Lucy badger you. You look as though you haven't slept a wink. Perhaps you should rest for a few hours. Lucy and I can manage anything that comes up.'

Elvira struggled to smile. 'No, truly, I'm fine. I'll rest later.' She reached across and squeezed Lucy's hand. 'And Lucy has been a great comfort to me.'

Lucy threw a so-there look at Phin, who merely grinned back at her. 'So, what did Revello want?' he asked.

'He claims there are widespread rumours that the hotel is up for sale,' Lucy replied. 'Strange timing, don't you think?'

Phin tilted his head as he looked at Elvira. 'Well, sis, do you know anything about this?'

Elvira took a moment to respond. 'No. It sounds like nonsense. Luca turned down several offers because he loved the place. He couldn't bear to part with it.'

'Do you know who actually owns it? Do any other family members have an interest in the hotel?' Phin asked.

Elvira nodded. 'I don't know all the details, but as far as I'm aware, Giuseppe owns about thirty percent of the shares. Luca held the balance.'

'Matteo has no financial interest?' Phin asked.

'Not in Grand Hotel Bellagio, no. He owns the sister hotel in Milan outright. Luca sold him his shares when he was raising funds to install electricity here in the villa and at the hotel in Bellagio. Luca wanted it to be the best hotel on the lake. No other hotel on Como has a lift installed, or such luxurious rooms.'

'Does Revello hold any shares? Would he gain financially if the hotel were sold?' he asked.

'No, on the contrary. He has everything to lose,' Elvira replied, then turned to Lucy. 'My impression was that he was worried about his position, don't you think?'

'Yes, but needlessly if it's just rumour, unless...' Both Elvira and Phin looked at her with raised brows. '...he knows something we don't.'

SEVENTEEN

As had become her habit, Lucy had taken a turn around the gardens while it was still cool, and was walking back along the terrace, lost in her thoughts, when she heard Phineas. It sounded as if he was in the library, the doors of which stood open onto the veranda. However, as she turned to enter through the open doorway, another voice spoke, an agitated one. Lucy hesitated, reluctant to intrude, and backtracked. However, her curiosity was too strong to resist eavesdropping. She backed away as far as a window before taking a quick peep inside. It was Commissario Marinelli in there with Phin; she'd recognise his skeletal figure and lop-sided stance anywhere. Luckily, he had his back to the window and could not see her. By the far wall, Esposito was closing a wall safe. Phineas was standing behind the desk, and she knew by the twitch of his mouth that he had spotted her as she did her best to secrete herself behind a convenient urn. He wouldn't give her away, but she pulled back slightly, determined to hear what was going on. Lucy guessed the inspector was here to collect the diamonds. *He hadn't wasted much time*, she thought.

'Commisario, I must insist you sign this document, stating that you're taking charge of these diamonds, and that you will ensure they are safely passed on to their rightful owners.' Phin indicated the black cloth pouch sitting on the desk. Then he pushed a pen and a page across the desk towards the policeman. 'Due to the circumstances of the conte's death, and the diamonds being discovered on his body, you will appreciate that the family is determined that everything is done properly. There must be a record of this handover.'

Even from outside, Lucy saw the stain of anger creeping into Marinelli's cheeks. The implied mistrust hadn't escaped him, despite any language difficulties. Marinelli snatched up the pen and scrawled his signature at the bottom. 'This is most irregular, Signor Stone,' he muttered as Esposito left the room.

'I assume a thorough investigation into the theft will now... recommence,' Phin said, his gaze sending a chill down Lucy's spine. Her husband was quite a force of nature, she thought, remembering all too well when that steely gaze and abounding suspicions had been directed at her all those years ago.

Marinelli responded with a sharp intake of breath. 'A full investigation was carried out by me at the time of the robbery. I see little point in opening up the case once more since the diamonds are now found.'

Phin stared hard at the policeman. 'An investigation that was inconclusive, I think you will agree. And we still don't know who stole them.'

The inspector shrugged. 'That is unfortunate, but I see little hope of discovering the culprit now.'

'Even though they turned up on the body of a dead man? And not just any corpse, but the owner of the hotel from where the gems were stolen. Someone wants the world to believe the conte was implicated. We trust that your *new* investigation will exonerate the deceased and bring the real culprits to justice. My sister, the contessa, would be much obliged if you keep me updated on your progress.'

Marinelli stiffened. 'If the case is reopened, any progress will be reported to Signor Carmosino, as the senior member of the family.'

Phin's answering smile was decidedly wintry. 'You may tell Giuseppe Carmosino whatever you wish, but it would appear you will have to duplicate your reports.'

The inspector went rigid but didn't respond.

'How is Mr Kincaid? Has he regained consciousness?' Phin asked, arms folded.

'Yes.'

'And?' Phin snapped.

'He is incoherent. Can't tell us anything,' Marinelli muttered.

Or won't, Lucy thought. *Kincaid would be wise enough not to reveal anything to Marinelli.*

Phin glanced meaningfully at the door. 'Then I bid you good day, sir!'

Lucy did her best to hide her disappointment when only Andrew, Phin's eldest brother, arrived at the villa that afternoon. Any hope of Phin's younger brother, Sebastian, coming were soon dashed with the news that he had had a relapse of malaria and was bedridden yet again. This news worsened the overwhelming gloom of the household, for they had just received word from Como that Luca's post-mortem was complete and his body had been released back into Matteo's care. To the surprise of all, the doctor's conclusion was accidental death. When Phin had read out the telegram from Matteo, Elvira had fled the room, rejecting Lucy's offer of accompaniment. Phin stood before the fireplace, staring in disbelief at the telegram in his hand.

Andrew gently removed the telegram from Phin's fingers and placed his hand on his brother's shoulder. 'Do what you must, Phineas. Clearly, there are dark forces at work here.'

Lucy was astonished. Andrew, who was always scathing about Phin's chosen line of work, urging him to investigate. What a turn-up!

Phin turned to Andrew. 'I saw the wound to his head. He was assaulted before he went into the water. I'd swear to it, though I'm no doctor.'

'And Luca's uncle is trying to convince everyone that he committed suicide,' Lucy said.

Andrew's eyes popped. 'Good grief! Why on earth would Luca have done that?'

'Giuseppe has accused Elvira of having an affair with Matteo, which is utterly ridiculous!' Lucy answered with a snarl. 'He is a nasty man, out for mischief. Elvira adored Luca; everyone knows that.'

Andrew smiled across at her. 'Your championing of my sister is appreciated, Lucy. But he must have some grounds—'

'Andrew!' Lucy exclaimed, feeling the heat bloom in her cheeks, her hackles rising in defence of Elvira.

'Giuseppe's motivation to blacken his nephew's name eludes us at present, Andrew,' Phin said. 'Suicide would bring great dishonour to the family.'

'So, he must be desperate to suggest it,' Andrew said, frowning. 'To cover up a murder?'

Phin shrugged. 'He is up to something, and I suspect he has paid off the officials to get that accidental verdict.'

'I saw him the other evening talking to the commissario and the doctor just before the body was taken away,' Lucy interjected. 'That's probably when he told them what he wanted.'

'Has he that kind of power?' Andrew asked.

'We shall see soon enough,' Phin replied. 'Luca's will may hold the key to that. Don't worry, I have every intention of getting to the bottom of this whole business.'

'For the honour of the family, you must,' Andrew replied. 'And quickly, too.'

'When will the funeral take place, Phin?' she asked.

Phin nodded at the telegram, now scrunched up in Andrew's hand. 'Wednesday. We will have to set out for Milan early on Tuesday morning. However, I think a chat with the good doctor who carried out the post-mortem might be in order. What say you, Lucy?'

'An excellent idea,' Lucy replied.

Despite their destination and the likely horrible conversation to come, Lucy enjoyed the walk along the lakeside path into Bellagio with Phin. Just on the outskirts of the town, they passed the entrance to the Grand Hotel Bellagio.

'Wasn't it lucky it wasn't destroyed in the fire, and no one was injured?' she said.

'Revello told me it was a close-run thing,' replied Phin.

'A high price to pay for progress.'

'Indeed.' Phin tugged at the chain of his half-hunter watch and glanced at it. 'We must hurry, my dear. Dr Spina is expecting us at three o'clock.'

A steamer was docking at the pier just as they walked into Bellagio and although it was early September, the town was bustling, with plenty of tourists still milling around the quaint cobbled streets. Lucy held onto Phin's arm as they climbed upwards through the town's endless run of stone steps until they reached the doctor's house on Piazza della Chiesa. A brass plaque beside the door indicated that another doctor and a land agent shared the building. As they waited for their knock to be answered, Lucy looked across the piazza to the beautiful old church. In the shade of its ancient walls, a woman was selling posies of flowers, another, vegetables.

A maid brought them through to the back of the house on the first floor. Spina rose as they entered, barely hiding his surprise as his eyes fell on Lucy. They all shook hands, but the doctor's wary gaze was concentrated on Lucy.

'Forgive me, but I understood from your note, Signor Stone, that you wished to discuss the post-mortem of the conte.' Again, he glanced at Lucy, then frowned. 'Or perhaps I misunderstood? Do you wish to consult me on a personal medical matter?'

Lucy held her peace. After all, it wasn't every lady who wanted to sit in on a discussion about a dead body. If she were honest, she didn't really want to hear too many gruesome details, but she wouldn't pass up an opportunity to be at Phin's side on an investigation.

'There's no misunderstanding, doctor. You need not be concerned by my wife's presence.' Phin's chin twitched ever so slightly. 'You may speak freely.'

Spina threw Phin an anguished look, before sitting back and folding his arms. 'As you wish, sir. However, before we begin, I'd like to offer my deepest condolences. The conte's accident is a great tragedy for the family.'

'Thank you, doctor, however... perhaps the events surrounding the conte's death are not as clear-cut.'

Spina's cheek twitched. 'I can assure you, the post-mortem was conclusive. The conte drowned, there is no doubt.' Then Spina leaned forward, lacing his fingers on the desk. 'I have been practising in Bellagio for twenty years. In that time, I have seen many drownings. The symptoms... the condition of the body was typical of such cases.'

'I don't doubt your experience,' Phin replied, 'but perhaps, just to ease my mind and that of my sister, the contessa, you might outline the basis for your conclusion.'

A flash of annoyance ignited in Spina's eyes. 'I doubt it's something your good wife would wish to hear.'

'Please, doctor. I thank you for your concern, however, it's perfectly fine. We have already discussed the condition of the conte's body,' Lucy piped up.

The doctor's brow shot up. 'Most irregular!'

'We are!' Lucy answered, not daring to look at Phin. 'And, as my husband has just said, the family wishes to be sure the verdict is correct.'

Spina turned to Phin with a shake of his head. 'My estimate would be that the conte was in the water for about two weeks. This time of year, the water is warm, and gas builds up in a submerged body' – he threw a challenging glance at Lucy – 'more quickly than if it were winter. The discolouration and bloating of the corpse all point to submersion, of course.'

'I would concur,' Phin replied. 'However—'

'—there was water in the lungs, which indicates – strongly indicates – the conte drowned,' Spina interrupted, with a defiant stare.

Phineas returned his gaze for several moments before he spoke next, and Lucy was glad that she wasn't on the receiving end of that particular gambit. She knew it of old. Phin had employed it on her the first time they met in London.

'Doctor Spina, that there was water in the conte's lungs is not a definitive sign of drowning. A dead body, thrown into the water, will gradually take water into the lungs. Furthermore, the injury to the conte's head was long and narrow; more akin to a wound inflicted by an object than a gash sustained in the water by hitting a rock or even a boat.'

'There I disagree. The injury must have happened in the water. A rock or a boat could easily have done the damage.' The doctor shook his head. 'As I said, I have seen these types of injuries before. What's more, my colleague, Dr Bianchi, who assisted at the post-mortem at the hospital in Como, agreed with my findings. I can understand the contessa is struggling to accept the verdict of accidental drowning, but I would urge you to persuade her to accept it.' His tone hardened as he continued, 'You do a disservice to your sister in continuing to speculate on this matter. If rumours of foul play become common knowledge, it will cause a scandal for the family. Something I'm sure you're eager to avoid.'

Lucy could sense Phin's anger. He went rigid beside her. She, too, knew that Spina was firmly in Giuseppe's corner now.

'Were there any other injuries?' Phin ground out.

'Such as?'

'Defensive wounds, or signs of restraint on the wrists or ankles?'

The doctor gave him a look laced with disdain. 'You are clutching at straws. There were no such injuries visible, sir.'

'Would such injuries still be visible with the body being in the water for such a long period?' Lucy asked.

'Unlikely,' the doctor replied grudgingly. 'When a body is in water for that long, the skin on the hands and feet... starts to peel off. There's also the interaction with creatures of the lake.'

An image of fish nibbling fingers flashed into Lucy's mind and she shuddered.

Spina sniffed and looked away towards Phin. 'If that is all, Signor Stone, I'll bid you a good day. I have patients to see.'

He couldn't wait to get rid of us and our awkward questions, Lucy thought as they climbed down the stairs and went out onto the sunlit piazza.

'He didn't take kindly to your probing,' she said, linking Phin's arm as they crossed the piazza towards the church.

'Yes, but is that because he felt I was questioning his expertise or because I was getting close to the facts?'

'I would hazard the latter, which suggests he is in league

with Giuseppe. Don't forget I saw them together the other
evening, and they looked to be on friendly terms. But at least
Spina hasn't suggested suicide,' Lucy replied.

'Hmm,' Phin responded. 'Only because there's no evidence
to support that claim. It's all very well for Giuseppe to spout it
in the heat of the moment, but a doctor? No. If Giuseppe was
involved in Luca's death, he will be perfectly content with an
accidental death verdict. Throwing out the idea of a potential
suicide is most likely his fall-back position.'

'So, what have we gained by visiting the good doctor?' Lucy
asked, her mood suddenly dropping in frustration.

'All we do know for certain is that Luca entered the water
around the time he disappeared. Which brings us back to foul
play as the only explanation that makes sense. Luca was an
experienced sailor and swimmer. He wouldn't have risked
either in a storm.'

'But the only potential evidence of foul play is that gash on
Luca's head. Time in the water has destroyed any other clues
such as signs of restraint or, say, bruising sustained in a fight.
Spina seemed to be suggesting any other signs of injury would
be down to submersion.'

Phineas answered with a sigh. 'That, unfortunately, is the
problem. He could be right. But I can't ignore that injury on
Luca's head. No fish or boat is responsible for that, I'm sure
of it.'

'A rock, perhaps? As the doctor suggested,' Lucy said.

Phin closed his eyes briefly, his shoulders slumping. 'Yes, I
suppose it's possible.'

'But you don't really believe that, do you?' she asked.

'No, I don't. His disappearance speaks for itself. Uncharac-
teristic. Why would he do that to Elvira? He was as besotted as
she was.'

'Agreed!' Lucy said.

'It's that trip to Milan that puzzles me, my dear. I think we need to go back to the beginning. Trace Luca's steps again and check where our suspects were the second day Luca was in Milan and the evening he returned and then disappeared from Como.'

'That is a good idea. Who do we tackle? Who are our suspects? My belief is that it's either Giuseppe or Matteo.' Lucy stopped at the church's shady porch and pointed to a posy of mixed blooms. The flower seller smiled, holding out her hand. Phin dropped some coins into her palm, almost absent-mindedly.

Lucy sniffed the perfume of the flowers as Phin gave her a quizzical look. 'For Elvira. I thought they might cheer her up a little,' she said.

Phineas squeezed her hand. 'Thank you, my dear.'

They walked around the corner and started down the steps towards the pier. 'You didn't answer my question,' Lucy said.

'Ah! Giuseppe or Matteo? If it *is* murder, they appear to be the ones who have the most to gain,' he replied.

EIGHTEEN

The funeral of Conte Carmosino would be spoken of for years
to come, Lucy guessed, as the carriage pulled up outside the
Carmosino townhouse. Such a spectacle. From the procession
of thousands of people on foot to the cathedral and, hence, to
the cemetery, it was almost as if Luca had been royalty. In the
eyes of the Milanese, and in particular the city's dignitaries, he
had been.

No one had spoken for the entire journey back from
Cimitero Monumentale di Milano. Everyone was exhausted.
The temperature in Milan was intolerable, and even though
Lucy and Elvira had driven at the head of the procession to the
cemetery in the carriage, Lucy had feared they might both
expire from heat exhaustion. Shrouded in black, Elvira had
wavered only once. As Luca's coffin had been placed inside the
family mausoleum, she had clung to Lucy's arm with a vice-like
grip, one solitary sob escaping her lips. Lucy marvelled at her
stamina.

Now, however, Elvira sat slumped on the seat opposite, resting her head on Andrew's shoulder. Lucy had to look away. She reached for Phin's hand and felt the comforting pressure in return. As awful as the day had been, deep down Lucy knew far worse was to come.

Murder.

Lucy knew what the consequences would be. It would change their lives forever. Hadn't it already ruined Elvira's? Even if she and Phin could solve this, they could not bring Luca back to his wife and children. The task ahead was fraught with difficulty. Would they put themselves in danger as they attempted to unravel Luca's last days on this earth? Lucy shivered. And Phin threw her a concerned glance. Lucy tried to reassure him with a smile; a smile she knew to be brittle.

Matteo sat on the other side of Andrew, his gaze fixed on his hands clenched in his lap. Lucy's heart went out to him. The poor man was struggling with his grief. But at least they had all been spared Giuseppe's company. He had travelled in a different carriage with some of the other Carmosino relatives.

A footman approached and the steps were lowered. Andrew jumped down to hand Elvira and Lucy from the carriage. Elvira linked Lucy's arm, and they approached the ornate entrance gate of the townhouse. But Lucy heard the men's voices and hesitated. Reluctant to miss out on anything of interest, she turned back towards Phin, Matteo and Andrew, who were conversing beside the carriage. It was then she spotted, on the opposite pavement, a small group of people standing, heads bowed in respect. One figure, however, stood out. It was a young woman, dressed in black, staring at the house. She must have been aware of Lucy's scrutiny, for she turned and walked away. There was something familiar about her. But the next carriage pulled up and obscured Lucy's view of the woman's retreat.

'What's the matter?' Elvira asked, her voice little above a whisper.

'Nothing, my dear. Let's get you inside,' Lucy replied. 'You must be worn out.'

'I am weary, I have to admit,' Elvira murmured.

Esposito greeted them at the front door. 'Everything is prepared, contessa, in the Green Salon.'

Elvira hesitated. 'Oh yes, the guests. Thank you, Esposito.'

Once they had handed over their shawls and hats, the ladies made their way along the hallway to the rear of the house. Refreshments were laid out on the tables and the footmen stood ready with glasses of wine and spirits.

'I don't think I'm up to this, Lucy,' Elvira whispered in her ear.

'Just one hour, Elvira, then you can make your excuses. You have done so wonderfully today. I know you can do this,' Lucy replied. 'Come; sit over here by the open window where it's cool.'

Lucy took a glass of wine from a nearby footman and followed Elvira. Once she was settled, Lucy handed her the wine. Elvira gave her a grateful smile. Soon, however, the room was full, and a stream of guests were coming over to speak to Elvira. It was expected she would be a gracious hostess even on such a day, and Lucy felt sorry for her. The strain was visible in Elvira's drawn features and the dark circles beneath her eyes.

Just then, a large, well-dressed man materialised before them, and Elvira greeted him as a grand-duke. His Highness took the vacant seat beside Elvira and drew her into conversation.

With relief, Lucy spotted Phin heading in their direction, Andrew close behind. 'How is she?' Phin asked as he drew level, his concerned gaze fixed on his sister.

Lucy stepped away into the next window bay before she

replied. 'She's exhausted, Phin. I wish she didn't have to go through this as well.'

'Is that who I think it is?' Andrew asked, taking in the magnificence of the duke. 'Young Luca must have been held in high regard indeed.'

'Yes, he was, but it's little consolation to his widow,' Lucy said.

'Oh, yes, of course,' mumbled Andrew, slightly flushed. They stood in silence for several moments before Andrew piped up, 'Who is that young lady with Matteo?'

Lucy strained her neck to see across the room. 'That's his fiancée, Angelica Scaletta.'

'Well, that has put paid to the uncle's theory, hasn't it?' Andrew said. 'Matteo can't be interested in Elvira if she is his future bride.'

Lucy hoped he was right. Angelica was a beautiful young woman, dark-eyed and petite. They had spoken at length at the cemetery. Although her English was only rudimentary, Angelica had come across as charming.

Phin and Lucy exchanged looks. 'You'd do well to dismiss anything Giuseppe says,' Phin remarked, taking a sip of his wine.

Andrew gave him a knowing look. 'On your list of suspects, eh?'

'I haven't ruled him out,' Phin replied.

'Well, I hope you will keep me informed of progress. I'll have to leave in a day or two. Once the will is read in the morning, matters should be clearer,' Andrew replied. 'It's my duty to ensure Elvira is properly looked after.'

Lucy and Phin exchanged an amused glance while Andrew looked about the room.

'Must you leave so soon?' Lucy asked him, not daring to meet Phin's eye.

'Yes, indeed. Seb wasn't at all well when I left. He hated

that he couldn't come with me. Straining at the leash, don't you know? I wouldn't put it past him to attempt the journey, despite the doctor's warnings.'

'Typical Seb,' Phin said with a smile. 'And Father?'

'Heartbroken for Elvira's sake, of course, but he knew it would have been foolish to travel so far. Hopefully, once things have quietened down, Elvira will come home with the children for a while. Father longs to see her.'

About an hour later, Elvira rose from her seat. Lucy spotted her and came across to join her. 'Do you wish to retire?' she asked.

'Yes, I think it would be best,' Elvira said. 'I'm sure I have spoken to all the guests at this point.'

'Would you like me to come with you?'

Elvira gave her a sweet smile. 'No, thank you. Rose will look after me. I'll see you in the morning for breakfast.'

Lucy kissed her cheek and watched her walk away, the crowd parting for Elvira as she headed for the door.

'Lucy?'

She turned to find Angelica at her side. 'Were you looking for Elvira? You've just missed her; she has gone to her room. It has been a long day.'

'No, Lucy. I look for Matteo. My father and I leave now.'

'Esposito will know where he is, I'm sure. Let's see if we can find him.' Lucy led the way out into the hallway. The butler was supervising the footmen, who were handing out coats and hats to the departing guests. Lucy caught his eye.

'Madam?'

'Esposito, do you know where Signor Carmosino might be? Senorita Scaletta wishes to bid him farewell.'

Esposito glanced at Angelica. 'Signor Matteo?'

'Yes.'

'He is in the library. If you would like to follow me, Senorita Scaletta?'

'Goodbye, Lucy. I like meet you,' the young woman said in her halting English.

'And I you, Angelica.'

They shook hands, then Angelica followed Esposito towards the library.

Lucy sauntered back to the Green Salon. Thankfully, most of the guests had now departed but with Elvira absent, they could not seek the sanctuary of their rooms just yet. Lucy scanned the room. Andrew had cornered the duke and appeared to be regaling him with anecdotes. She had no wish to join that particular party. Lucy moved past with a nod, seeking Phin. She was thinking he had escaped the tedium when she spotted him close to a doorway, engaged in conversation with one of Luca's many elderly aunts. The lady was a vision in black bombazine and lace, dripping with pearls and diamonds. Unfortunately, Lucy couldn't remember which one she was.

'There you are, Lucy. Senora Tasca was just asking about you,' Phin said as she approached.

'I'm delighted to meet you again, senora,' Lucy said with a respectful bob of her head, grateful that Phin had guessed she had no clue as to the woman's name.

'Ah! You have pretty manners for an Englishwoman,' Senora Tasca said, grinning. After an open appraisal of Lucy, she looked up at Phin. 'You chose well, young man.'

'Thank you. Lucy has many good points,' Phin replied, trying to keep a straight face which earned him a pinch on the arm from Lucy.

'And I'm told, a taste for adventure.' The lady's lips twitched with amusement. 'Bravo, young woman! Too many women are like sheep. It puts me out of humour.' Her eyes narrowed as her gaze flicked between them. 'I hope you will put your skills to work. This talk of an accident is nonsense. Pooh!

Luca was a fine fellow and an experienced sailor. He was my favourite nephew. Had a good head on him, but I fear he may have ruffled too many feathers – isn't that the expression in English?'

Lucy was intrigued. Was she referring to her own brother, Giuseppe?

'Perhaps,' Phin replied. A very non-committal response, Lucy thought. But he was treading carefully. In such a large family, it was difficult to know who was in which faction. The woman could be fishing on behalf of Giuseppe.

'And you have experience in these matters, I'm told,' Senora Tasca continued. 'Elvira told me all about your work. Fascinating! But I'm not surprised. I met your mother once, young man, many years ago.' She frowned. 'Paris, I believe. A stunning woman with a mischievous smile and a taste for adventure, as I recall. It was before she married your father, of course—'

A commotion out in the hallway interrupted Senora Tasca. Lucy glanced out to see Angelica, in some distress, being helped into her coat by a footman. Lucy excused herself and approached the young woman. Tears were streaming down Angelica's face.

'What's the matter, Angelica? Are you unwell?' Lucy asked, taking her hands in her own. 'My dear, you can't leave like this.'

But the poor girl was so upset that she could only answer in rapid-fire Italian. Just then, Signor Scaletta came out of the Green Salon and rushed up to his daughter. Angelica pulled away from Lucy and collapsed, crying, into his arms. As he listened, Signor Scaletta stiffened with anger, his face suffused with colour.

'Please, let me help,' Lucy said. 'Won't you tell me what's wrong?'

But the man looked at her askance. 'We leave this house of dishonour!'

A hush fell over the guests within earshot, all eyes on Signor Scaletta and his distraught daughter.

Lucy watched in confusion as the Scalettas headed out the door. Slowly, the murmur of conversation rose once more. Lucy stepped over to the window and saw the Scalettas get into their carriage. Angelica was so distressed that her father had to half lift her inside. What on earth had happened? Matteo must have upset Angelica in some way. A lover's tiff? Just then, Matteo, flushed with anger, his eyes glowering, walked past her into the Green Salon.

Curiosity raging, Lucy followed, only to be waylaid by Senora Tasca. 'Well, what's all the fuss?' she demanded. She touched her ear. 'My hearing is not what it should be.'

'I have no idea,' Lucy replied. 'Were you able to understand what was said?' she asked Phin.

'Not easily, but the gist of it appears to be that Matteo has broken off their engagement.'

'Good grief!' Senora Tasca cried out.

'Oh, no!' Lucy exclaimed. 'This is dreadful. It will just add to the gossip.'

Senora Tasca pursed her thin lips. 'I always thought that boy was an idiot. Of all the days to do it!'

'I know,' was Phin's grim reply.

'Shouldn't we warn Elvira?' Lucy said. 'Why don't I go up to her? I wanted to check on her, anyway.'

'Do, my dear, but break it to her gently, please,' Phin replied. His worried expression did nothing to quieten her own fears. It was as if Matteo was playing into Uncle Giuseppe's hands.

NINETEEN

Lucy tapped on Elvira's door, but there was no response. She put her ear to the door. Silence. Undecided, she remained outside, pondering her options. Was Elvira asleep? God knows she needed some rest, but already Lucy knew that there was uproar below as the news of Matteo and Angelica's broken engagement spread amongst the remaining guests. Lucy wanted to break it to Elvira gently, instead of her hearing about it in the morning as servant gossip.

Luckily, at that moment, Elvira's maid, Rose, appeared from the servants' door at the end of the corridor, carrying a tray. Lucy smiled at her as she approached and stood back as the petite blonde maid nodded to her. 'Is your mistress awake?'

'Yes, ma'am. She could not settle and asked me to fetch her some tea.' Rose shifted the tray onto her arm so that she could open Elvira's door. 'Shall I check if she will see you?'

'Yes, please.'

'Oh!' exclaimed Rose on entering the room. Lucy sprang forward. The interior was in semi-darkness, and it took a few moments for her eyes to adjust to the gloom as she stepped inside.

'Ma'am?' Rose called out, then turned around. 'Where is she?' she asked, her face pinched with concern. She set the tea tray down on a table.

'Perhaps she is in her dressing room,' Lucy said. 'Elvira?'

But the door to the dressing room stood open. Rose peeped inside, then shook her head. 'I don't understand. She was here fifteen minutes ago.'

'Your mistress can't have gone far, Rose. Perhaps she wanted some air and has gone down into the garden. If you wait here, I'll check.'

'Thank you, ma'am,' Rose replied.

Lucy slipped down the stairs and made her way to one of the salons at the rear of the townhouse. The courtyard garden it overlooked was empty, however. Now baffled, Lucy retraced her steps only to bump into George, coming out of her suite, which was a few doors down from Elvira's room.

'Is everything alright, ma'am?' he asked.

'Yes, George. You haven't seen the contessa by any chance?'

'She left the house a few minutes ago.'

'Left?'

'Yes. Her coachman was in the middle of his dinner when the request came through downstairs.'

'I see! You wouldn't happen to know where she was going?'

'Unfortunately, no,' George replied. 'Is there anything I can do?'

'You might tell the contessa's maid she has gone out, that she is not to worry, and that I'm going to follow.'

'Certainly, ma'am,' he replied with a bob of his head.

There was probably only one place Elvira would want to be, Lucy guessed, as she went into her own room. It might not be a dangerous place, but she couldn't bear the thought of her sister-in-law being there alone.

Mary looked up as she entered. 'Good afternoon, ma'am,'

the maid said, rising and setting down her sewing on the window seat.

'Good afternoon, Mary. Could you fetch my hat and coat? Quickly, please,' Lucy said, as she sat down at the desk and scribbled a note for Phin. 'And see that Mr Stone receives this.'

When she stood, Mary helped her into her coat. 'Hold still, ma'am, while I put this pin in your hat.'

'Don't fuss, Mary. I'm in a hurry! Here, take this. I shouldn't be too long.'

Mary gave her a knowing look. 'Will he shoot the messenger?' she asked gloomily, staring at the note Lucy had just handed her.

Lucy grinned. 'Not this time, Mary, not this time.'

Lucy hadn't paid a lot of attention to the architecture of Cimitero Monumentale di Milano earlier that morning, as all her focus had been on her sister-in-law. Now, as she stepped down from the carriage Esposito had arranged for her, Lucy was impressed by the large Famedio, a neo-medieval style building of marble and stone at the main entrance. She made her way through an archway and out into the courtyard beyond. But she didn't stop to admire the well-kept grounds. The Carmosino mausoleum lay almost at the end of a long avenue, which faded away into the distance. If she was right, that was where she would find Elvira.

Thankfully, the worst of the day's heat had faded, and it was almost pleasant to walk down the wide gravel path. Bird-song filtered down through the border of rustling trees, but beneath the spread of the branches, monuments to the dead loomed, as shadowy and forbidding as ghosts. Some were of classical design, some more Gothic, but it was uncomfortable to think of their inhabitants, most long dead. With a shiver, Lucy looked away and increased her pace.

With a sinking heart, when she reached the mausoleum with the Carmosino crest above the doorway, Lucy could see one of the metal gates stood open. Elvira must be inside. Shaking off her unease, Lucy made her way past the head-stones, which framed the path, and up to the door. She squinted into the darkness, but bar one shaft of sunlight coming through a window high in the wall, she could make nothing out.

'Elvira?' she called out.

There was movement inside. 'Lucy?' an astonished voice replied. Moments later, Elvira appeared in the doorway. 'There was no—'

'I was worried about you,' Lucy said, holding out her hands. 'You had only to ask. I would have come with you.'

'I know,' Elvira replied, letting Lucy guide her back along the path. 'It was an impulse. I needed to say a private goodbye.'

Doing her best to ignore the lump which had suddenly formed in her throat, Lucy said, 'Look, there's a seat along here. Why don't we sit down?' Before Elvira could respond, Lucy tucked her arm through hers. 'We can sit in silence, or we can talk. It's entirely up to you.'

They sat down and after many minutes of silence, Elvira turned to her. 'Do you think me foolish?'

'No! I can only marvel at how well you're handling all of this.'

Elvira gave her a lop-sided grin. 'I'm not. Inside... I am frozen. I still can't take it in. Luca gone. And now he is laid to rest here in Milan. I pleaded with Giuseppe and Matteo. I wanted him buried in Bellagio. Then I could visit his grave every day, but they insisted it was against the Carmosino tradi-tion.' She paused and sucked in a breath. 'I'll organise a memor-ial, perhaps on the grounds of the villa. Somewhere the children and I can grieve in private.' She squeezed her eyes shut. 'The children... oh, Lucy, the worst thing is that I never had a chance to tell Luca. I was waiting until he returned from Milan.'

'Tell him what?'

'That we are to have another child.' Elvira sobbed, her hand on her stomach.

'Oh, my dear!' Lucy said, pulling her close and hugging her. 'I'm so very sorry.'

'I don't think I can do this on my own,' Elvira whispered.

'You won't be! I promise you will always have us. You know that. Why don't you come back to England when we leave and stay with us for a while? Or Kent. You know your father and Seb would love to have you.'

'Thank you, but I can't take the children away from Italy, not now with so much uncertainty around Luca's death. Also, I know Luca wouldn't have wanted them to leave. The family traditions were very important to him.'

'But his family is not the most affectionate, you must admit, and you need looking after.' Lucy glanced down at her sister-in-law's stomach. 'Even more so now.'

'They are a proud family, Lucy, so they will treat me with due respect, but they have always looked down on me.'

'Which is utter nonsense. You come from an excellent family.'

'I'm sure Phin has told you about... how Luca and I...'

Lucy gave her a sympathetic look. 'The orangery? Yes, he did.'

'So, you see why they feel as they do. They can't help it. It's all about bloodlines here. There was a plan for Luca to marry a distant cousin, and I came along and ruined it all by falling madly in love. They can never accept me, but they must accept the children. And I will do everything in my power to ensure Salvo, Eleanor and this little one claim their birthright.'

'Yes, I sympathise with how you feel, even though I don't have children of my own. You must fight for their rights.'

'Thank you. I knew you would understand. But, Lucy. You must pray for a miracle; for a child of your own.'

'Don't worry, Phin and I are happy with our lot. We have each other. Besides, if we had children, Phin would be reluctant to let me help him with his work. I'm not sure how I'd feel about that. Do you think that is selfish of me?'

'No. These things are in the lap of the gods.' Elvira sighed. 'And I desperately need your help, for I'm relying on you both to find out what happened to Luca.' Her expression hardened. 'It was not suicide or an accident.'

'Absolutely, and now that the formalities are over, we will redouble our efforts.'

'Good. I'd like to return to Bellagio as soon as possible, after the will is read, as I don't wish to be away from the children any longer than necessary. You will come back with me, won't you? And you wouldn't leave me alone with Giuseppe?'

'Certainly not! Though he has been relatively well behaved since we have been here. In fact, suspiciously so.' Lucy gave an exaggerated shudder. 'It makes me wonder if he is planning something.'

'Don't say that! My only hope is that Matteo can exert some control over him. Once Luca's will is read, we will have a better idea of how the estate stands.'

'Ah!' Lucy had almost forgotten. 'Matteo. There's something you need to hear.'

Elvira eyed her with dread. 'What is it?'

'Earlier this afternoon, he broke off his engagement with Angelica.'

'He did what!' exclaimed Elvira, her eyes wide. 'Why on earth would he do that? The wedding is only months away.'

Lucy shrugged. 'I don't know the reason. She was incoherent and upset, as you can imagine. Her father was furious. There was quite a commotion before they left your house.'

Elvira stared down at the ground. 'The boy is an idiot and now Giuseppe will use this against me.'

'Just let him try! He hasn't seen Lucy Stone in full flight yet.'

TWENTY

Lucy looked on as Elvira paced the room. Every so often, she would come to a stop at the door, tilt her head, straining to hear, then resume her restless walking once more. 'They should be finished by now. Why are they taking so long?' Elvira muttered.

Lucy checked her watch. 'It *is* over an hour. Perhaps clarification on some legal point is required.'

'It's a straightforward will, Lucy. Luca showed it to me just after we were married. There shouldn't be any surprises. Matteo is to be Salvo's trustee. He will manage the estate until Salvo is twenty-one.' Heaving a heartfelt sigh, she crossed the room once more, wringing her hands.

'We should have insisted on being present,' Lucy said.

Elvira stalled and stared back at her. 'Yes, indeed. But after my conversation with Matteo this morning, I just wasn't up to it.'

'Ah!'

'Well you may say *ah* in that manner. The stupid boy! I left him in no doubt; I do not return his feelings and never will. In fact, I may have told him his regard was an affront to his brother's memory.'

'Oh dear, did you? I thought he was looking crushed when I ran into him in the hallway earlier.'

Elvira raised a brow. 'Do you think I should've been kinder to him?'

'No, no. You had to be firm. He can't go on cherishing such foolish notions.'

'I was so angry with him. Luca would have laughed it off as ludicrous, but I could not and I don't understand it, frankly. Angelica is a delightful young woman from an excellent family, too.'

'Can you not? Are you not aware of your own power?'

Elvira's eyes popped. 'You don't think I have encouraged him?'

'No, no, of course you haven't, but you're beautiful and charming. He was bound to fall under your spell. Did you not suspect how he felt?' Lucy asked.

'Not the depth of it, no! It never crossed my mind that he would consider Luca's death as an opportunity...' Elvira grimaced. 'You must think me naïve.'

'Not at all. Why would such a notion enter your head? You were in love with Luca. I assume Matteo admitted you're the reason he broke off his engagement?'

Elvira groaned. 'Yes. Though, if he doesn't love Angelica, it was the correct thing to do. A marriage based on falsehood would be doomed.'

'I agree. But his timing could not have been worse!' Lucy exclaimed.

'Yes, indeed. And the poor young woman didn't deserve to be humiliated in front of a house full of our guests. This will be all over Milan by now. It could not have been more ill-judged on his part. However, right now, my concern is that Giuseppe will use this against me. And in the eyes of many, it gives credence to his assertions. He will say we plotted together...' As her voice broke, Elvira clutched the back of a chair, her knuckles blanched of all colour. 'He has already insinuated... How could anyone think such a dreadful thing? But I fear him, Lucy. Giuseppe will make endless trouble for me and the children.'

'Not while Phin and I are around. That solicitor who is here – is he trustworthy? Will he not act in your best interests?'

'He should do, of course, but you don't know how much power Giuseppe wields. In the end, the best interests will be seen to be those of the estate. I'm powerless as a widow. This title I hold means nothing now Luca is gone. And, as far as I'm aware, the same firm of solicitors represents Giuseppe. Who do you think they will favour? An old client family or a foreigner who has wormed her way into the Carmosino family. You need not look so doubtful, Lucy. It's what they all accept as true. They haven't forgiven me for marrying Luca. His death will be laid at my door, have no doubt. Some superstitious nonsense will be spouted.'

'All you can do is rise above it, my dear,' replied Lucy. 'It might not be a bad idea to engage someone else to act for you and the children. I could ask Phineas to look into it for you.'

As Elvira nodded, the door opened and Phineas entered, closely followed by Andrew.

'Well?' Elvira cried, rushing up to them.

Phineas exchanged a worried expression with Lucy before he replied. 'Luca altered his will. It isn't exactly how you described it to me.'

All colour drained from Elvira's face. 'In what wa-ay?'

'Matteo and Giuseppe are joint trustees of the estate until Salvo comes of age.'

'Good God!' Elvira collapsed down onto the nearest sofa. 'What was Luca thinking?'

'When was it changed?' Lucy asked.

'Last year,' Andrew said, sitting down beside his sister and taking her hand. 'Did he not tell you his intentions?' Elvira whispered no and Andrew threw a concerned glance at Phineas, who stood behind them. 'Don't be anxious about it. You're still well provided for, my dear, but they must approve all decisions regarding the children and their welfare.'

'It is intolerable,' Elvira said. 'I don't understand why Luca changed it.'

'I asked that solicitor chap, but he said he didn't know,' Andrew said.

'My guess is that Giuseppe bullied him into it,' Phineas said.

Elvira looked up at him. 'I'm sure he tried, but Luca always stood up to him. This doesn't make any sense to me.'

'Does it really make such a great difference, Phin?' Lucy asked.

'That depends on whether Giuseppe wants to play nicely. It's more the business end of things that will change. Giuseppe will now have far more influence in that sphere. Matteo will have to have his consent for any decisions relating to the Carmosino businesses. However, I understand that the hotel here in Milan he holds in sole ownership.'

'Oh dear. And Giuseppe isn't likely to forget that Matteo hit him the other evening either. I have a feeling Matteo will pay for that for years to come,' Lucy said.

'I wish I had witnessed that,' Andrew said with a grin. 'Not that I condone violence,' he continued with a frown that didn't fool anyone present.

There he goes again, saying things that make me like him a little bit, Lucy thought, and smiled back. Andrew returned her smile before putting his arm around his sister's shoulder and speaking softly to her.

Lucy hoped that smile was another olive branch from her brother-in-law. Was he finally accepting her into the family?

There had been hints of it at their wedding. He might be pompous and overbearing in manner, but he was Phin's brother. Being estranged from her own mother, and her brother still in prison for fraud, Lucy longed to fit into the Stone family. Since Charlie's death, she had been lonely, despite the freedom his demise had granted. Meeting Phin had been fortuitous; a second chance to build a happier family life.

As Lucy pondered this unforeseen melting on Andrew's part, Phineas joined her by the window.

'Why did it take so long?' she asked.

'It was a long and convoluted document. Giuseppe insisted on going into every little detail. The man's a nasty piece of work.'

'Do you think he knew Luca had changed the will?'

'I'd say no. Hence the litany of questions,' Phin replied.

'Why do *you* think Luca changed it?' Lucy asked, sotto voce. 'It seems an odd thing to do.'

He took a moment before answering, his voice low. 'I suspect he may have guessed what Matteo's feelings were for Elvira. In a way, he was trying to protect her.'

'Matteo would never hurt her. He loves her.'

'Yes, but if he couldn't handle rejection, which is what Luca might have guessed might happen, Matteo would have enough power over Elvira to make her life a misery. At least if Giuseppe has an equal say, he can do her no harm.'

'But Phin. Giuseppe is even more of a threat to her!'

Phineas acknowledged this with a pained expression. 'That is how it seems, certainly. But Luca wasn't to know that Giuseppe would react the way he has. Luca could not have foreseen his murder or that his uncle would make those accusations against Elvira and Matteo.'

'It's a very messy business,' Lucy replied with feeling. Phineas stared out of the window. Lucy touched his arm. 'What else is bothering you? You have been preoccupied this morning.'

When he turned back to her, he sighed. 'I'm frustrated. I know we had to go through the formalities of all this' – he waved his hands in frustration – 'but I fear the lost time may result in clues being lost. Witness memories become unreliable over time, too.'

'Then let us form a plan right now. I'm as keen as you to continue our investigation. What do you want to do?' she asked.

'We must retrace Luca's steps here in Milan in detail. I fear I have missed something vital. Also, there would be no harm before we leave to pay Luca's solicitor a visit. I'd like to know the real reason Luca visited him that day before he disappeared.'

'And ask about the will change?'

'Yes, that too. He may be more amenable to discussing it in private,' he answered. 'It might be a good idea to check Matteo's movements around the time of Luca's disappearance as well, while we are still here.'

Lucy's stomach dropped. But he was right. Matteo had shown them through his recent behaviour that he would have had a motive for killing his brother. 'I don't want to believe Matteo guilty, though.'

'Neither do I. Honestly, I like the man, but we can't ignore facts,' Phineas replied.

The door opened and Lucy turned to see Giuseppe enter. He stood in the doorway, his gaze sweeping the room. A more overbearing, hateful man, Lucy had never seen, and her hands clenched automatically at the very sight of him.

'Ah! I see all the Stone family are present. Keeping guard, are we?' Giuseppe drawled.

Andrew stood, his demeanour flint-like. 'Signor Carmosino.' The words were polite. Andrew's tone, however, held nothing but contempt.

Giuseppe glared at Elvira, who remained seated, her back to him. 'You may tell the *contessa* I'll call on her in a few days to discuss personal matters. The will we were just subjected to was a travesty, and I intend to contest it. I should be the sole trustee as the senior member of the family.' He sniggered. 'I suppose you thought you could get away with it, eh? But then you English don't know the true meaning of honour.'

All colour drained from Andrew's face as Elvira stiffened and slowly rose to her feet and turned. Lucy was amazed that Giuseppe didn't turn to stone on the spot, for Elvira's stare was icy-cold. Then, she turned her back on Giuseppe. 'And you may inform my husband's uncle he is no longer welcome in my home and if I do receive him ever again, it will be when, and only when, it suits me.'

'You cannot deny me access to the children,' Giuseppe cried.

'I am their mother. Yes, I can!' Elvira said.

Lucy could have cheered.

Giuseppe went white with rage, clearly struggling not to explode. His mouth twitched once more. He turned on his heel and slammed the door behind him.

'Good riddance!' muttered Andrew, a wish shared by everyone in the room.

TWENTY-ONE

That afternoon, Milan city centre

After a luncheon no one was in spirits to enjoy, Phineas and Lucy made their excuses and took the Carmosino coach to Luca's solicitor's office. Signor DeBellis, a wiry man with round spectacles and a halo of fluffy white hair, greeted them effusively as they were shown into his office. As she sat down, Lucy spied the fabulous view of the piazza below. She reckoned the location and scale of the offices reflected the prestige and nobility of their clientele. However, the solicitor's welcome surprised her. Lucy had expected a cold snub at the very least. Perhaps when DeBellis learned why they were here, his attitude might change. Phin had speculated on the journey through the busy streets that the solicitor would be extremely cagey about what he would reveal. But it was worth a try. Nevertheless, they were not clients and surely Giuseppe would have warned the man not to engage with Phineas.

After an exchange of pleasantries, Phineas wasted little time. 'Signor DeBellis, my sister is at a loss as to why the conte changed his will last year. Can you shed any light on that?'

With folded arms, DeBellis gave him a weary smile. 'Your brother asked me the same thing at the villa this morning, after the reading of the will. As I told him, the conte didn't give me a reason and it would have been highly impertinent of me to enquire... unless, of course, there was something in the new will that was legally unsound. Then... yes, then I would have advised against it. However, the new terms protect the young conte and the future of the estate and the Carmosino businesses. I'm sure if the contessa gives it some *thought*, she will see that is the case.'

Lucy wondered if he was affirming what they had thought; that Luca was trying to protect Elvira from Matteo's sole guardianship. But why was that the case? Could there have been another reason Luca didn't want Elvira at Matteo's mercy? If only he had confided in someone besides the solicitor. Lucy was sure the man knew exactly why Luca had done it. The solicitor would hardly admit it outright, though.

'I see,' Phin replied with a glance at Lucy. 'As you may be aware, I'm currently looking into the circumstances of the conte's death. I'm curious as to why my brother-in-law paid you that visit the afternoon of the day before he disappeared.'

'There is no mystery, Senor Stone. It was a trifling business matter, but the conte was conscientious when it came to his responsibilities.' DeBellis' sigh was deep. 'If only all young men were as careful. And such a sad state of affairs now the poor young man is dead.' The solicitor continued, wagging his head. 'It's a great tragedy.'

'Yes, sir, it is,' Phin said. 'However, it would be helpful to know what drew him to Milan that was so urgent, for it's a tiresome journey and the conte usually stayed in Bellagio for the entire summer. Surely a "trifling matter", as you put it, could have waited?'

DeBellis didn't like that, Lucy thought, as the man stiffened and his lips compressed. 'I assure you, it was merely signatures required on some contracts. As I said already, the conte was diligent in these matters. Signor Stone, business can't be ignored just because the sun is shining.'

What a fatuous comment to make, Lucy thought. She could almost sense Phin's frustration.

'Was it to do with the hotel in Bellagio?' Phineas shot at him.

DeBellis' mouth hardened ever so slightly. 'Yes.'

'Could you be more specific?' Phin ground out.

'No, Signor Stone. The family's affairs are private, as I'm sure you must realise.'

'If the conte was the victim of foul play, any information about his business, and in particular his meetings on that fateful trip here to Milan, is more than relevant.'

The solicitor's thin brows snapped up. 'On whose authority are you pursuing this ludicrous idea?' DeBellis sucked in an outraged breath, staring hard at Phin. 'The post-mortem conclusion was accidental death. The police and the family have accepted this. You can do nothing but harm spreading such rumours.'

'It's not just a rumour. I helped identify the conte. Based on the state of the conte's remains, and his strange behaviour around the time he disappeared, I disagree with the post-mortem result, as does the contessa. She has asked me to continue my investigations. The conte was an experienced sailor and swimmer—'

DeBellis cut across Phin. 'But accidents happen all the time. Perhaps he attempted to cross the lake when it was too hazardous... well, he may have had a drink or two. If I recall, there was mention of a thunderstorm the night he arrived back in Como. The lake is a treacherous place at night, even more so during a storm.'

'The conte missed the last steamer from Como, and no other boats were running because of the storm. There's no record of the conte hiring a boat to cross over, nor did he approach anyone to take him across. He simply disappeared. He was a well-known figure. It makes no sense that no one saw him once he left the steamer pier at Como,' Phin said.

The solicitor tapped his fingers on the desk. 'I can't explain it, Signor Stone, but neither can I agree with your hypothesis. It was an accident. Eager to get home to Bellagio, he took a risk. An unfortunate risk.' DeBellis' expression softened. 'Your sister is distressed. This is understandable, but I can't discuss Carmosino business affairs with you, young man.'

'Was Luca here about the diamonds?' Lucy piped up, hoping to shake his composure.

She hit her target. DeBellis blanched, coughed, and straightened up. 'Diamonds? I have no idea what you're talking about, Signora Stone!' Blinking rapidly behind his spectacles, he rose to his feet and gestured towards the door. 'You will have to excuse me; I have a client waiting. I bid you a good day.'

Although it was pleasant to sit outside the cafe, as the world went by, there was a hard knot of tension in Lucy's stomach. She sipped her coffee, watching the play of emotions cross her husband's face. DeBellis' lack of cooperation was deeply frustrating.

'He was prevaricating, Phin,' she said.

'Prevaricating? My dear, he was lying,' Phin replied, setting down his cup. 'Well done, by the way – bringing up the diamonds was inspired. It certainly shook his composure.'

Lucy smiled her thanks for the compliment. 'But his reaction – what does it mean? Do you think he knows the diamonds have some connection to Luca's death?' she asked.

With a shrug, Phin traced the pattern on his empty plate. 'I wish I knew. If he has information, he should share it with us or the police, if he feels he can't trust us.'

'Unless he has been asked to keep quiet by Giuseppe. He made it clear he doesn't like you pursuing this, Phin.'

'Just like Dr Spina. Could he be involved?' remarked Phin with a cheerless quirk of his mouth.

'Oh, Lord! We're seeing the enemy everywhere!' Lucy exclaimed.

'Murder tends to have that effect, my love,' Phin replied.

His words increased her unease. 'Yes, I can't argue with that. It's quite unsettling.' He gave her a quizzical look as she continued, 'Perhaps we should stick to simple insurance fraud.'

Phineas threw back his head and laughed. 'Lucy! You don't mean that. I know you too well. Why, you have done nothing but badger me to let you be involved in my cases, no matter what they involve. Are you telling me you're scared?'

Lucy grabbed his hand from where it rested on the table. 'Yes, but it's not what you think. It's different now we are married. If someone has murdered Luca, they won't have any compunction in hurting you, too, if you get too close to the truth. I couldn't bear it if anything were to happen to you.'

He looked up at the sky as if seeking divine intervention. 'At last, she sees my point of view!'

'Don't be rotten! You know what I mean,' Lucy muttered.

'I do, only too well, dear heart. However, we're committed to this case. We won't abandon Elvira, no matter what Luca's family thinks, and no matter how many obstacles are thrown into our path.'

'I agree, absolutely!'

'Good,' he replied.

'But you must promise me to be careful.'

'I'd like to believe I'm caution personified. Now that is settled' – he waggled a brow at her and she swatted his hand – 'let us try to think about Luca's trip here in a logical way. We are agreed they discussed the diamonds because of the solicitor's reaction. But were those diamonds in Luca's possession when he visited DeBellis? Perhaps he wanted the solicitor to keep them safe until he decided what to do.'

'Then DeBellis must have refused.'

'Yes. There are other possibilities, however. Luca may have recovered those diamonds here in Milan the following day or came across them later, on his return to Como.'

'Too many variables, Phin. And does it really matter how they came into his possession? The important thing is that he died with them *in* his pocket.'

'True. But we are back to... why?'

'I have no idea. How can we find out if no one is willing to cooperate? But returning to your original theory, why would Luca have brought them to De Bellis?' she asked. 'Would he not have taken them to the police?'

'Would you trust Marinelli with stolen diamonds?'

'No. But you just did,' she pointed out.

'In the company of a witness and I made him sign a statement, taking responsibility for them,' he replied.

'Hmm, good point.'

'Perhaps Luca trusted the solicitor to act as a go-between, knowing he could not show his hand.'

'Which suggests Luca knew he was in danger... which would explain his hasty exit from the city.'

'Perhaps, but I think it more likely Luca would take them to the police here in Milan, not Como, so they would be returned to the Wallaces.' Phin rubbed at his chin. 'Which might explain those missing hours on the Friday afternoon.'

'That's an intriguing idea.'

'Hmm. What baffles me is that he never went back to the hotel. Perhaps something went awry during those missing hours. If only we could find out where he went. Who he met?'

'Perhaps the police, then?' she said.

'Ye-es, perhaps, but which station, which police officer? It's a large city; it would take time to check all of them.'

'Matteo might help with that. I'm sure he could suggest the most likely,' Lucy said. 'But can we trust him to tell us the truth?' Phin shrugged. After a moment or two, she continued, 'Whatever happened during those missing hours led him to – for want of a better word – run. Why else would he leave his valet and luggage behind?'

'Oh, I agree. His behaviour suggests he was trying to make an escape,' Phin replied.

'Perhaps he didn't go to the police but met someone, the person he suspected of the theft and fell foul of them over the diamonds?' Lucy said.

'Yes, that's possible, but who? It can't have been Giuseppe. We know he was in Bellagio.' Then he frowned across at her. 'Or perhaps Luca knew the hotel was being watched, or he had spotted he was being followed.'

'Oh! I don't like the sound of that,' Lucy said.

Phineas tapped his index finger against his mouth. 'Neither do I! But we're making assumptions. All we do know is that something urgent brought him here to Milan. Can we trust DeBellis' assertion that they discussed a contract and nothing else?'

'I'm not sure I can. If it had been about the hotel, surely Revello or Matteo would have known about it and Luca would not have been acting so furtively. Why did DeBellis react as he did to my question? No, I think they talked about those diamonds at the very least,' Lucy said.

'But why won't the solicitor admit that? I am coming to the conclusion that Luca used the time he was stuck in Como to search out and confront the thief.'

Lucy groaned. 'And his murder suggests he found them.' And despite the warmth of the afternoon sun, Lucy shivered. 'The sooner we get back there, the better.'

TWENTY-TWO

Grand Hotel Milano, the next day, Milan city centre

After some discussion, Lucy and Phin decided it was best that Lucy tackle Matteo alone. The awkwardness of Matteo's termination of his engagement, and his declaration to Elvira, were the major considerations. Matteo was bound to be reticent in Phin's presence. Lucy was delighted that Phin trusted her to glean as much information as possible, and therefore entered the foyer of Matteo's Milan hotel with a strong desire to prove her husband's confidence in her abilities.

Through an ornate doorway, Lucy then crossed the entrance hall of the hotel. It was breathtakingly beautiful, and Lucy had to pause and take in her surroundings. A reception desk took up the entire right-hand side of the foyer. As she headed towards it, one of the hotel concierges sidled up to her, enquiring politely if she required assistance. If he was surprised when she requested to see Matteo, it was well disguised.

'Of course. Please take a seat, signora, and I will return directly,' he said, waving to a salon off the foyer.

Five minutes later, Matteo appeared in the salon's doorway,

his eyes scanning the room. Lucy put down the magazine she had been flicking through and gave him a wave. His returning gaze was wary. Did he think she was here to scold him? Lucy put on her most charming smile in return. Matteo visibly relaxed, but not before he had cleared his throat and run his hand through his hair as he approached where she was sitting in the window bay. A slight flush, she noticed when he was up close, told its own tale. He was embarrassed; as well he should be, she thought, as Giuseppe's accusations floated into her mind.

'My dear Lucy, welcome to my hotel. This is a great pleasure,' Matteo said with a bow over her hand before glancing around. 'Is—?'

'No. Phineas is not with me, Matteo. I hope I'm not disturbing you, for I'm sure you're extremely busy, but I wondered if we might have a word in private?'

Again, the wary look. 'Certainly. Did Elvira send you?' he asked.

'No.'

Matteo barely hid the flash of disappointment that crossed his features before he held out his arm. 'We can have tea in my office if you wish.'

'Thank you. That would be lovely,' she replied.

Minutes later, they walked along a carpeted hallway and Matteo ushered her into a large office at the back of the building. The twin-aspect room was bathed in afternoon sunlight and Lucy could make out the distinctive spires of Duomo di Milano glowing golden on the horizon.

'Please, take a seat. Our tea should be here shortly,' Matteo said, pulling out a chair for her.

'Thank you,' she replied, settling down and gathering her thoughts. She would have to be careful, for she didn't wish to antagonise him, at least until she was sure he had nothing useful to impart to help their investigation.

Matteo gave her a nervous smile as he sat opposite. 'Was there something in particular...'

'This is awkward, Matteo, I have to admit,' Lucy began. 'Luca's death is still very painful for all the family, I'm sure, but Phineas and I are anxious to uncover as much as we can while everyone's memories are still fresh. We intend to find out the truth.'

'How can I help?' Matteo asked. 'The rumours and scandal are so harmful, especially to Elvira.'

'Thank you. Firstly, and I'm sorry if you find this upsetting, but what's your opinion of the coroner's verdict?'

All colour drained from Matteo's cheeks. 'That is easy to answer: it's wrong.'

Lucy felt awful seeing his distress. She had surprised him. Had he expected her to admonish him about Elvira, or had she opened the rawest of wounds? After all, the brothers had been close. 'I'm sorry,' she said softly. 'I'm sure this is difficult for you to talk about.'

'No, it's fine. It's a relief to speak of it.' He took a deep breath. 'I was shocked by the verdict, for the circumstances of Luca's death are so strange.' He shrugged. 'Giuseppe... you know his opinion, but I can't agree with him. It was not suicide. Nor an accident. Luca had everything to live for. My firm belief is that he was murdered.'

Lucy was relieved. 'As is ours, Matteo. Your uncle's accusation is ridiculous,' she said in what she hoped was the firmest of tones. 'You need not think that Phineas or I give it credence. Or Elvira, for that matter.'

'Thank you,' he said with a grateful look. 'But I do not know what to do about it. The police appear to be more than happy to accept the verdict and investigate no further.'

'Would you have any difficulty in Phin and I—?'

'Absolutely not! I'd welcome it,' he said, leaning towards

her. 'Nothing about his death makes sense to me. Is there anything I can do to help? Only tell me, please.'

'This may not be easy, Matteo,' she replied. 'But I do have some questions.'

Matteo stretched out both hands, as if pleading. 'No, ask, please.'

'I know we discussed this before, but think carefully. To your knowledge, did Luca have any enemies?' she asked.

Matteo sat back, his gaze unfocused for a moment, his brow creased in concentration. 'Not to my knowledge. He mentioned no threat to me.'

'Was there someone he might have crossed in business, perhaps?'

'Again, I would say no.' Matteo's shoulders slumped. 'Luca had charm and used it effectively. Disagreements always arise in business, but he was adept at handling such matters. We used to joke about it. He could defuse any situation. Even when Uncle Giuseppe was trying to interfere. As you may have guessed, Luca had a much calmer temperament than me.' This was said with an uncomfortable grimace.

Lucy couldn't help but smile back in sympathy. 'I, too, am very different from my sibling. What about your uncle?' she asked. 'Did they get along?'

Matteo rolled his eyes towards the ceiling. 'As well as can be expected. My uncle is... a proud man. Not only did he find it difficult when Luca took over the running of the hotel, he found it difficult to accept Luca being conte, which is ridiculous, of course. Giuseppe was never in line once Luca was born. But I suspect this coloured their relationship. Giuseppe was always coming to Luca with suggestions and would be highly offended if Luca didn't take them up. Sometimes they were excellent ideas, in which case Luca welcomed them. He wasn't a fool. Unfortunately, my uncle tends to gloat. It's not an attractive quality.' Matteo sighed and leaned back.

'And he doesn't hide his dislike of Elvira,' she commented, waiting for his reaction.

And the colour rose in his cheeks. He leaned forward once more and picked up a fountain pen from the desk, running his hand up and down the barrel. 'My uncle wanted Luca to marry someone else and could not forgive Luca for choosing with his heart. This is crude, forgive me, but he saw their marriage as a dilution of the bloodline.'

'Don't worry, I understand. There's a similar view held in English society,' she replied.

Matteo frowned across at her. 'Family feuds aside, my uncle could not have harmed Luca. I'm certain of that. Even if you look at the situation dispassionately, what motive could he have?'

Some form of revenge, power, money, she thought, but she didn't voice it. 'We must consider all possibilities, Matteo. Which brings me to a rather delicate question,' she said. 'I understand that you and Luca had a disagreement at Villa Carmosino about a week before he disappeared. Would you mind telling me what that was about?'

'The row at Bellagio?' he asked. 'A ridiculous argument, which was my fault. Luca was annoyed that I had used a different company to install electricity in this hotel.' He paused, taking a deep breath. 'The truth of the matter is that I was on the defensive that day. I had recommended the company which did the work in Bellagio... we later found out that they had rushed the job and may have used the wrong cables or something.'

'Which led to the fire,' she said.

'Exactly. Naturally, Luca was angry about it.' Matteo gave her a quizzical look. 'We made up before I left, however, if that is what you're wondering about.'

'Good. I'm glad to hear it,' she said, noting his high colour. 'Could you tell me about the last time you saw Luca here in

Milan? I know you have already spoken to Phineas about it when we first arrived, but perhaps there might be some minor detail you overlooked. Something that might have struck you since as odd.'

Matteo frowned in memory. 'It all began with a telegram he sent me here at the hotel, about two days before he arrived. I'll admit to being surprised by his visit. It's high season and both of our hotels are extremely busy.'

'Therefore, you assumed it was an urgent matter that brought him to Milan?'

Matteo nodded. 'Yes, indeed. His servant arrived first and told me Luca was going to see our solicitor and would arrive later. I assumed he would tell me what it was all about when he'd arrive. But it was about half past five when he appeared. Luca joined me and Angelica and her father for dinner that evening. He was in good form and retired to bed about eleven o'clock. As we had guests, we didn't discuss business over dinner but, naturally enough, I was still curious.'

'I see. And the next morning you had breakfast together. Did you ask him the reason for his visit?' she asked.

'Yes. He said it was about a new contract and he needed the solicitor to check it for him,' Matteo replied.

'Was that unusual?'

'No, except... when I asked about the details, he fobbed me off and changed the subject. And that was odd. Frankly, I was put out – he is... *was* normally very open.'

'When we spoke before, you described him as distracted that morning.'

'Yes, and he complained he hadn't slept well.' Matteo shrugged. 'I put it down to the heat. May I be candid with you?'

'Of course,' she replied.

'We were close. Between us, we have a great deal of responsibility. We've always worked together, and it has brought us success. It's not only the hotels, but there are other business interests as well. Normally, we discussed everything.'

'Which suggests whatever was bothering him might have been more personal?'

Matteo shrugged. 'I don't know. I have given it a great deal of thought, but I'm at a loss.'

'Did he tell you what his plans for the day were?' she asked.

'All he told me was that he had a few errands to run for Elvira and he would catch the train for Como mid-afternoon.' Matteo quirked his mouth. 'But I didn't question it; I was still smarting about his visit to DeBellis and his refusal to tell me what it was about.' With a glance out of the window, he continued, 'Luca never returned. Enzo sent me a message around four o'clock and I sent for him. He expressed his concern, saying that Luca had said he would return to the hotel and they would travel to the station together. He didn't know what to do. At first, I assumed Luca had met a friend and been delayed. But an hour later, there was still no sign of him, so I sent a messenger to the station. You can imagine my surprise when I learned Luca had taken the train to Como alone.'

'Very odd indeed. Have you any idea why he didn't come back here?' she asked.

'I can't explain it. Nor could Enzo.'

'And you have no idea where he went between breakfast with you and catching that train?'

'None, whatsoever. If you must know, his behaviour irritated me, so I sent Enzo after him on the next train and dispatched a blistering telegram to Bellagio asking for an explanation.'

'That is understandable. There's one other worrying aspect to the case: the Fitzwilliam Diamonds.'

'Worrying? I found that bizarre. It makes no sense.' He tilted his head. 'Do you know why he had them?'

'No, but we do have a few theories. Unfortunately, we don't

know if he had them here in Milan or came across them in Como, or even if they were placed in his pocket after he had been murdered.'

'Of course, there's no way to know for certain,' Matteo said, nodding his head. 'The theft was an enormous embarrassment to the family, as you can imagine. Luca was furious about it so it wouldn't surprise me to learn he had investigated the affair.'

'Why not leave it to the police or the insurance investigator?' she asked.

Matteo gave a derisive laugh. 'Have you met Marinelli?' He made a dismissive gesture. 'I wouldn't have trusted him, either. His investigation was a joke. As soon as that insurance chap turned up—'

'Kincaid?'

'Yes, as soon as he appeared, Marinelli closed the case. Luca told me that Kincaid complained to him that Marinelli was uncooperative. Luca spoke to Marinelli about it, but nothing changed.'

'So Luca wouldn't have placed much trust in the Como police?' Matteo nodded. 'We wondered if he might have gone to the police here in Milan that afternoon?'

'The idea never occurred to me.'

'But if he had, which police station would he have gone to? Did he know any of the senior officers here in Milan, perhaps?'

'He may have done... My guess would be that he would have gone to police headquarters.' Matteo picked up the pen once more. 'But if matters were that serious, why did he not tell me? I thought he trusted me.' The hurt in his voice was all too clear.

Now, Lucy knew she had to ask another awkward question he would not like, but it had to be done. 'The day Luca left Milan, on the Friday, were you here all day?'

The corners of his mouth went down. 'I see; I must account for my whereabouts,' Matteo muttered. All Lucy could do was give him an apologetic smile. 'It's fine. I understand. Giuseppe has put doubts about me in your head.'

Lucy felt the colour rush into her cheeks. 'I'm sorry, but we need to double-check where everyone was, not just you.'

Matteo picked up a leather-bound book and handed it across the desk. 'Here is my diary. You may check it for the days in question. If you need to ask the people I met, I have no problem with that; my assistant can give you the details. However, if I recall, most of my meetings that day were with hotel staff. Angelica called' – he paused with a stricken look, then quickly recovered – 'and we had tea together around half past three. I was with her when I received the message from Enzo. I'm sure—' Then he paused and grimaced. 'Hopefully, she will confirm that.' He blushed. 'However, I understand her father has taken her away from Milan for a few days.'

'She must be upset—'

'Devastated, I'm made to understand.' He dropped his head in his hands. 'I deeply regret hurting her,' he said, peering up momentarily, 'but at the cemetery earlier, all I could think of was how brief life is, so fleeting. That we deserve to be happy... perhaps I could make Elvira happy. She looked so lost, so devastated.'

'Oh, Matteo!' Lucy exclaimed. 'Elvira was devoted to Luca.'

'I know,' he whispered. 'I know. But perhaps with time... is it so wrong to hope?'

It was heart-breaking to see his distress, but she could not give him false hope. 'You must be like a brother to her. Help her. Guide the children. Be her ally. Look after the interests of the estate, but I think it's unlikely that she will ever return your feelings. I'm sorry if it hurts to hear this, but she needs time to grieve.'

Matteo drew a deep breath and straightened, a look of defeat in his eyes. 'Was there anything else you wished to ask?'

'There was. When Luca didn't respond to your telegram, were you not concerned?'

'At that stage, I was regretting the tone of what I had sent. Then I assumed he was annoyed with me and that was why he had not responded. Then, on the Sunday afternoon, I received a telegram from Elvira, saying he was missing. Naturally, I was alarmed and travelled to Bellagio first thing on Monday. I fully expected to find him home and well. Instead, there was no sign of him, and all was in an uproar. Elvira had notified the police.' He continued, his expression grim, 'Of course, now we know it was probably too late.'

TWENTY-THREE

Lucy made her excuses, and left Elvira, Andrew, and Phin
chatting below in the first-class salon on the steamer. Much to
everyone's relief, Giuseppe had left Milan the day before and
travelled back to Bellagio alone. Lucy didn't think she could
stand one more day in the vile man's company. However, the
awning-covered first-class deck was at the stern, and now and
then a blast of steam from the boat's funnel flowed in beneath
the canopy. Desperate for fresh air, Lucy made her way out
onto the bow deck and immediately congratulated herself on an
excellent decision. The second-class deck was teeming with
much more interesting-looking passengers, enjoying the breeze
coming off the water, and much better views. On one side of the
deck stood a musician, twanging his guitar and warbling away in
a pleasant baritone, while opposite was a bird-seller, with tiny
birds of many hues in a cage. A crowd was gathered around
him. And overseeing all stood a cassocked priest in a wide-

brimmed beaver hat, studying his fellow passengers with a paternal gaze.

This was a journey to and from Como Lucy had undertaken several times now, but one she would never tire of. It was slow certainly – at almost two and a half hours – as the steamer meandered across the lake to call at the different small village piers, but the sights varied according to the weather and time of day, the high peaks creating a unique climate and affecting the quality of the light.

Taking great gulps of fresh air, Lucy rested her hands on the wooden handrail and kept her gaze firmly on the passing scenery. They steamed along at a steady rate, the paddle wheel churning through the water with a great whooshing sound. It was a typical afternoon, the lake busy, and Lucy couldn't help but think about Luca. This scene would have been so familiar to him, perhaps so familiar that it would hardly register. And now, someone had snatched away his life without a second thought. Ruined the happiness of his wife and children, and for what? The afternoon *Breva* wind was dancing along the water from the south, refreshingly cool. Lucy turned her face to take advantage of it, then glanced over the handrail into the depths. Out here, the lake kept her secrets shrouded in the darkness below. And for a moment it was as if the sun had gone behind a cloud, for the thought that she was looking into Luca's real grave crept into her mind. How grim her thoughts were, but the injustice of it all made her angry. Luca was being denied the justice he deserved. There didn't appear to be any way to instigate a police investigation.

All of a sudden, Lucy grew uneasy, as though she was under surveillance. Trying not to draw attention, she ambled along the rail, scanning the other passengers from under the wide brim of her hat. Nothing appeared untoward until her eyes fell on a young woman, leaning back against the wheelhouse wall, her gaze fixed on the musician. Dressed modestly in the dark clothes and style of attire typical of the local women, there was something familiar about her face. Then Lucy realized; it was the same woman who had stood opposite the Carmosino town-house in Milan the day of the funeral; the same woman she had seen outside the Grand Hotel Bellagio. The woman who had argued with Kincaid!

Lucy glanced over once more. Yes! It was definitely her, and now she was looking directly back at her, her eyes wide. With what? Surprise, fear? For a moment, Lucy thought the young woman was going to come over to her, but just as suddenly, the wary expression descended once more. The woman grabbed her bag from where it lay at her feet and moved swiftly out of sight. The moment was lost.

Her curiosity now raging, Lucy tried to push through the throng of passengers, but a sailor was calling out that the next stop was Argegno and the passengers shuffled into line, ready to disembark, blocking Lucy's way. The boat was slowing down and manoeuvring into the pier. She could no longer see the young woman. A wave of panic made Lucy perspire. She had to speak to that woman. In desperation, Lucy went to the port-side rail and scanned the crowd. Too late! The woman had disem-barked. She couldn't follow. There wasn't time to push through to where the others were; to tell them she was following the young woman ashore.

Then, for one brief moment, the woman hesitated halfway up the ramp, and turned. Their eyes met, but the stranger broke eye contact first before resuming her slow progress up the walk-way. Mystified, Lucy followed her progress as long as she could, but soon the steamer was moving away from the pier, the great paddle wheel turning once more. Who on earth was she? Lucy wondered, as she moved back up to the front of the bow. It was hardly a coincidence. Had the woman followed them onto the boat? But then why had she not made herself known if she had wanted to talk to her? Perhaps she knew something about

Luca's disappearance and murder. Which would explain why she acted so strangely. She was frightened, too – of that Lucy was sure – but if she returned to Argegno tomorrow, she might be able to track her down and speak to her.

'I hope that frown is not down to something I have done,' a familiar voice said at her elbow.

Lucy turned to Phin. 'Don't be silly! If you must know, the most frustrating thing just happened. I think I have made an important discovery.'

'Oh? Do tell!'

Lucy quickly explained about the young woman.

'Interesting, and it's hardly a coincidence, my dear,' he said. 'You may be right.'

'And definitely worth investigating? Don't forget I saw her talking – well, arguing would be a better description – with Kincaid outside the hotel.'

'Yes, it's important we talk to her.'

'I could return tomorrow and seek her out,' Lucy said.

'Only on the condition you take Mary with you.'

'Of course,' she said. Phin squeezed her hand, and they stood side by side for several minutes, watching the passing scenery. 'It is such a beautiful place, is it not? And yet, all I can think about is poor Luca.'

Phin answered after a moment or two, his tone subdued: 'It's difficult not to when out here on the water.'

'His death has upset you greatly,' she said.

'It has, even though I didn't know him well, but the few times I did meet him, I liked him.' Phin gave a sad smile. 'If I'm honest, I envied him a little.'

Lucy was surprised. 'Why?'

'Because of what he and Elvira had together. They radiated happiness. Mind you, that was before you stormed into my life and upended it completely.'

'Why, you old romantic!' she said with a grin.

Phin winked. 'Don't tell anyone, I implore you. My reputation would be in tatters, and I'd never be engaged on a case again.'

Lucy treated him to a wry look as the steamer slowed once more. 'Thank goodness. Lezzeno, at last.'

They watched the passengers disembark while the local children played at the water's edge. As the *Vittoria* pulled away from the pier, there was a hoot of steam from the funnel and the children cheered and waved.

'The worst part of all this is the thought of Luca drowning,' Lucy said as they strolled down the deck. 'I have always considered it a horrible way to meet your end. Could he have been dead before he went in?'

'I imagine so. No matter what anyone says, he was experienced enough as a sailor not to attempt sailing across during a storm. It would be madness. He was either forced into a boat or taken out on the water already unconscious or dead.'

'Or he risked going out himself, trying to escape someone,' she said.

Phin waved his hand towards the shore. 'But there are better places to hide than out on the water. Storms pass. All he would have to do is find somewhere to sleep for the night until the steamers were back running in the morning.'

'Such speculation does not help us figure out who murdered him.'

'But it does help us work out who had the opportunity, for we know Luca made it as far as Como,' he replied.

'Which brings us back to our two main suspects: Giuseppe and Matteo. Are you sure we can rule out Matteo? Especially since they argued so violently so soon before he disappeared. Not to mention his apparent and unfortunate interest in Elvira,' she said.

'He is a man of strong feeling, impetuous perhaps, and quick to anger; however, he has produced evidence of where he was and what he was doing for the crucial two days, which, might I remind you, you have proved. He couldn't have done it,' Phin said.

'But Phin, consider; he might not have been involved directly, but he may have instigated it.'

'A horrible notion, but possible. Proving something like that will be extremely difficult, however. Where do you look for that kind of evidence? Unless someone came forward...'

'I agree. It would be impossible for us. We are at such a disadvantage, unless that young woman has something significant to reveal.' A sailing yacht passed them, two young ladies, waving up at the steamer. Lucy waved back, then turned back to Phin. 'What about Giuseppe? He has refused to give an alibi, but we know he was here on the lake when Luca went missing, so he had the opportunity. Though, I admit I'm struggling to find a motive. He acts and speaks as though Luca was his favourite nephew and he wants to defend his honour, yet he constantly maligns Elvira.'

'But he suggested it was suicide; that's hardly defending the poor man's honour, now, is it?' Phin said with a raised brow.

'I suppose not unless it's a red herring. He is duplicitous, for he tried to make trouble for Luca while he was alive. Does he gain financially in any way? It's the only reason I can see for him being involved.'

'Not that I can figure out. He does gain influence, however, which I think would appeal to him even more. As joint trustee, he can make decisions about the businesses if he can keep Matteo under his thumb.'

'Power can be a strong motivator,' Lucy said.

'Power or revenge, perhaps.'

'What do you wish to do next? The longer this goes unsolved, the worse it is for all the family.'

To her surprise, Phin pulled out a piece of newspaper from

his pocket and unfolded it. 'We need to find out who provided the newspaper with this scurrilous article,' he said.

Lucy knew from the torn edges that Phin had hastily removed the page from the paper. There was a photograph of Luca, but the article was in Italian. Lucy frowned up at Phin. 'What does it say?'

'It implies that the diamonds found on Luca's body prove that he was involved in their theft.'

'Good grief!' Lucy exclaimed. 'You said something along those lines at the beginning, did you not? That you suspected the gems had been planted on him to create a scandal?'

Phin nodded, with an expression somewhat gloomy. 'Whoever provided this article has questions to answer. They are determined the world learns Luca had those stolen gems.'

'Then it's progress at last! It might be their first mistake. Which newspaper was it in?'

'*Corriere della Sera*. It's a Milan based paper. I fancy Matteo has had dealings with them regarding the hotel, so I was going to send him a telegram to ask him to investigate the article.'

'That's a good idea. I only hope Elvira didn't read it,' Lucy said.

'No. I spotted it and removed the page before she had a chance.'

'Thank goodness, Phin. That's the last thing she needs to see. If you're trusting Matteo to follow up on that,' she said, indicating the torn page, 'what shall we do next?'

'My intention is to pay Giuseppe a call at the hotel in the morning. He has managed to evade me up to now. It's about time he answered some questions directly.'

Lucy blinked up at him, trying to keep her tone even. 'You're excluding me from this visit? Why?'

Phin's lips twitched in amusement. 'You and Giuseppe are not the best of friends. He has made it abundantly clear that he—'

'—doesn't like me?' Lucy had to laugh. 'Indeed, he has. Oddly enough, I suppose I must admire his honesty. Very well, you may go alone,' she continued airily. 'I shall be busy anyway, for I shall return to Argegno in search of our mystery woman.'

'Thank you!' Phin replied with a grin and Lucy suspected some relief, too.

TWENTY-FOUR

Argegno, the next day

Esposito arranged everything for the trip and at eleven o'clock, Lucy and Mary headed down the stone jetty steps to where the villa's *inglesina* awaited them. Lucy and Phin had used the boat several times and, as ever, the craft was crewed by a young *barcaiolo* who looked no more than seventeen. But she had no concerns, for he had proven to be an experienced sailor. Lucy was delighted to see him, for he was a cheerful youth, who sang as he rowed. Dressed in a white shirt, a colourful waistcoat, and dark trousers, his wide-brimmed hat shaded his face as he took up the oars. 'Argegno, signora?' he asked.

'*Si, grazie,*' Lucy replied, before sitting back to enjoy the journey.

The voyage across the lake was uneventful, but as they slowly approached the harbour at Argegno, Lucy's stomach clenched. Was this a foolish endeavour? Phin had encouraged her, but was that so she would be out of the way for the interview with Giuseppe? No! That was unkind. Phin wasn't mean spirited. Besides, he was correct; Giuseppe didn't like her. If anything, Phin's encouragement for this venture showed he trusted her. Hopefully, she would find the young woman and she would be willing to speak. Lord knows, they desperately needed a hint or a clue of some kind to unravel the myriad of puzzles they were faced with.

The town of Argegno hugged the lakeshore, its houses rising in tiers, clinging to the steep incline of the mountain peak behind. All was bathed in the glow of the hot sun, forming a pretty picture from the water. As they approached the shore, Lucy spotted the steamer pier and ticket office, which was situated on the piazza. However, their boat was headed for the smaller harbour, off to the right. The quays curved out into the water like protective arms, defending the fishermen's livelihoods against the worst of the winter storms. Adjacent to the harbour was an ancient church, its spire and bell tower dominating the skyline.

Within the harbour were many small fishing vessels moored up, along with several *inglesina* indistinguishable from the one in which they were travelling. Some fishermen were working on their boats, fixing nets or unloading their catch; others were standing on the quayside chatting. There could be no doubt as to the occupation of most of the town's inhabitants, for there was an overwhelming odour of fish.

Their boat was deftly manoeuvred up to the quay and secured next to carved stone steps. Much to Lucy's relief, the *barcaiolo* handed them up the slippery steps, with a warning to be careful, for there was no handrail.

At the top of the steps, Lucy turned to the boatman. 'We should only be about an hour.'

He grunted, grinned, and then nodded.

'Not particularly talkative, is he?' Lucy said to Mary as they walked away.

'I've always preferred an ould song to chatter, meself,' Mary replied with a smile.

Once out of the harbour area, Lucy paused. Now that she was here, Lucy's doubts flooded in. How she was to go about this search, she wasn't sure. If the young woman lived here, where might she be found? Not to mention the possibility that she didn't live here at all. Still, they were here now, and a walk about the town seemed a logical way to start. Mary agreed, and they set off towards the church, which was only a short distance away. But although some local women stood close to the front steps, selling fruit and vegetables, they were much older than the woman Lucy wanted to find. The only other people to be seen were some English tourists who came out of the church and paused on the top step, taking in the views.

'This doesn't seem promising. Which way, do you think?' Lucy asked Mary.

The maid's gaze roamed the immediate area. Then she pointed across the street to where a small stone bridge crossed a river. 'That looks like the way into the older part of the town, ma'am,' she replied. 'We may have a better chance of finding her there.'

A path led along the bank of the river where the sluggish waters flowed down from the mountainside and over the stony riverbed. Once across the bridge, they were immediately in the shade of the tall buildings which framed the narrow laneways. The ancient houses, with their closed shutters, loomed towards each other, with barely enough room below for even a horse to navigate the shadowy path of cobbles. But the sudden shade was welcome, for the way was steep and Lucy was uncomfortably hot just walking the short distance from the harbour. Their footsteps echoed off the walls into the silence, making it feel as though they were invading a private space. They climbed steadily upwards, but not a soul met them, and Lucy grew despondent.

All of a sudden, Mary came to a stop, turned, and gave her a quizzical look.

'I know!' Lucy puffed, catching up. 'This is disappointing.'

'Do you wish to go on at all, ma'am?' Mary asked. 'Or should we head back to the harbour?'

'Let's keep going. At least until we reach the highest point.'

Five minutes later, they emerged out of the medieval town centre and into the sunshine. The path ran behind the rooftops of the first row of houses in the town. Down below, over the terracotta roofs, Lucy spotted the main piazza and beyond was the dazzling blue of the lake. The perspective from this height was spectacular, and she was happy to stop and take it all in before they had to continue. Lucy was feeling light-headed as they paused, ostensibly to take in the view, but they were both breathing hard. Exchanging smiles, they leaned against a stone wall to rest.

'Where do you think all the women are?' Lucy asked, nodding back towards the way they had come. 'It's like a ghost town in there.'

With a pointed look, Mary answered, 'Perhaps the problem is the time of day. It's far too hot. Anyone sensible would stay indoors.'

Lucy smiled. 'Oh dear! You may be right. And I apologise for dragging you about in this infernal heat. Perhaps we shouldn't have come here until later in the day. I assumed it was only the upper classes who indulged in midday naps.'

Mary fanned herself with her hand. 'Servants do not have that luxury, but Rose was tellin' me the locals start work very early, rest for a few hours in the middle of the day, then work well into the evening. It's the pattern of things.'

'Which is eminently sensible. Shall we continue? Those steps further along should take us back down to the piazza and, hopefully, some shade. Then we can decide what to do and where to go next.'

A short walk along the road that skirted the lakeside brought them to the small but handsome piazza, bordered by shops and even a cafe with some tables and chairs outside, shaded by an awning. Cafè Armano was the name above the door, and Lucy made a beeline for one of the outside tables. A coarse-faced, grey-haired man, dressed in waiter garb, came out to greet them and smiled in welcome.

Mary muttered something about waiting for Lucy at the harbour. 'No, Mary, please join me. The least I can do is offer you a drink after dragging you around in this heat,' Lucy said. Although Mary gave the hovering waiter a sidelong glance and a nervous smile, she took the seat opposite. 'Would you like some coffee?' Lucy asked her. Mary nodded.

'*Due caffè, per favore*,' Lucy managed when the waiter came up to the table.

'*Certamente, signora*,' he replied and headed back inside.

'Well done, ma'am,' Mary said with a grin.

'That's about the total of my vocabulary, I have to admit,' Lucy replied. 'I'm sorry. This trip was a waste of time.'

'That is a shame, ma'am. I know how much you want to help the contessa.' The young maid wrinkled her nose. 'So strange that anyone would want to harm the conte. By all accounts, he was a decent man.'

'I assume there is a lot of talk below stairs. Anything I should know?'

Mary grimaced down at the table. 'There are some wild theories, ma'am. Most of which I have dismissed. Foolish talk, most of it. However—'

'However?' Lucy asked as the waiter arrived with their coffee.

Mary sipped her coffee before she spoke. 'There is one theory that sounded plausible to me. People here are poor, ma'am. They must turn to... well' – she leaned forward and lowered her voice – 'most are involved in the smuggling trade. It was well known that the conte was trying to put a stop to it. I imagine that would have made some people furious.'

Lucy sat up straight. 'Angry enough to kill him? My goodness, that is an interesting theory. Is the smuggling that widespread?'

'As far as I can tell, yes. However, it's only spoken of in hushed tones. The other servants never speak of it in front of me, but I have overheard some conversations. We're close to the border with Switzerland, where certain items are much cheaper. The men go up into the mountains at night, cross over the border, and are back again the next morning.'

From the inside of the cafe came the sound of glass shattering. Lucy glanced inside as she replied, 'That sounds very organised—' She gasped. 'Oh my, that's her! That's the woman I was looking for – that young waitress.' With a surge of excitement, Lucy nodded towards the interior of the cafe where her mystery woman was now sweeping up the shards of glass. The older waiter who had served them was remonstrating with her. 'Mary, go in and ask her to come out to me, please.'

Mary glanced inside as she rose. 'The young woman in the black shawl?'

'Yes, that's her! Quickly now, before she disappears,' Lucy answered.

She watched anxiously as Mary spoke to the waitress, who darted a look at Lucy, and shrank back. But whatever Mary said next, the woman's shoulders slumped. With a wary glance outside, she gestured for Mary to go ahead of her. The young woman followed slowly.

Lucy judged the waitress to be in her mid-twenties. She was an attractive young woman with a dainty nose and beautiful brown eyes. However, her pallor was alarming, her eyes darting about as she shifted from one foot to another.

'*Grazie*,' Lucy said with a smile before waving to the vacant seat at the table.

The woman's anxiety grew. '*No!*' She tilted her head and darted a glance into the cafe. '*Non posso!*'

Lucy kept her voice low and calm. 'I saw you in Milan and again on the steamer yesterday. You looked as though you wished to speak to me. What's your connection to the conte? Do you have information about his death?'

If it were possible for the young woman to pale even more, she did. Breathing rapidly, she muttered, 'Not here. Very dangerous.'

Better and better – her instincts about the woman had been correct. Pushing down her frustration, Lucy said, 'Who are you afraid of? Why won't you speak?'

The waitress shook her head, but Lucy spotted the furtive glance into the cafe's interior. Lucy followed her gaze only to see the older waiter who had served them staring out.

'Are you playing games with me? Is it money you want?' Lucy asked.

The waitress glowered at Lucy. '*No!*'

Lucy sat back, irritated now, and running out of patience. 'What's your name?'

With a sudden lunge, the waitress grabbed Lucy's empty cup. 'Fiorella Armano,' she whispered. Then she made to escape, but she wasn't quick enough, and Lucy grabbed her arm.

'Tell me what you know of the conte's death, or I'll have the police speak to you.'

The poor woman now looked terrified. Her lip trembling, she whispered, 'The answer lies at the hotel.' With that, she pulled herself free of Lucy's grasp and half stumbled inside. Lucy watched her go, puzzled by her behaviour. But she noticed the gaze of the waiter at the counter flicked between the waitress in distress and Lucy's table. Even from outside, Lucy could see the telltale flush of anger on his face. His voice was harsh when he spoke to Fiorella as she reached the counter. With an angry jerk of his arm, he pushed Fiorella towards a

room at the back. Then he turned and stomped across the floor
towards the door.

'I think it's time we left, Mary,' Lucy said, leaving money on
the table. 'We may have outstayed our welcome.'

Mary nodded her agreement, and they walked away at
speed, back towards the harbour. Lucy dared to glance back.
The man was following them.

Lucy linked Mary's arm and whispered, 'Faster!'

They increased their pace as the harbour came into view.
Then Lucy sighed with relief. The *barcaiolo* was sitting in the
boat, waiting for them. Another look back. The irate waiter was
gaining on them. Lucy waved frantically to the boatman, who
waved back. They hurried along the quay and down the steps,
where he helped them on board.

Once back in the estate boat, Lucy allowed herself to relax.
The *barcaiolo* took up the oars, and they slowly navigated
towards the harbour entrance. On impulse, Lucy looked back
over her shoulder only to see the waiter standing on the quay,
hands on hips, staring after them. *Well, my questions have
stirred up something,* Lucy thought. *Now, where have I heard
the name Fiorella Armano before?* Then she gasped. How
stupid! Of course. She was the housekeeper dismissed from the
hotel for thieving.

TWENTY-FIVE

Villa Carmosino, Bellagio

With the help of the afternoon *Breva*, allowing them to sail as opposed to having to row back to Bellagio, they arrived at the villa just after four o'clock. For the entire voyage, Lucy had been deep in thought. What had Fiorella meant by '*The answer lies at the hotel*'? Was this a meaningful piece of information, or had she said it just to get rid of them? Had she witnessed something strange while working at the hotel? However, the woman's fear had been genuine, Lucy was sure of it. Who or what was she afraid of? Perhaps someone had been keeping her under surveillance at the cafe. The waiter? He had certainly been angry with the poor woman, and it seemed to have been caused by the fact that Lucy had engaged with her. More worrying was the fact that the man had followed them to the harbour. The cafe had been busy. It was hardly idle curiosity for him to leave his post. It suggested they might, at last, be getting close to the truth. There were so many new possibilities, and she couldn't wait to share them with Phineas.

As they waited for the *barcaiolo* to secure the boat, Lucy

glanced up at the villa. All the shutters were fastened shut against the glare and heat of the afternoon sun, and Lucy suddenly longed for the cool of the house. She thanked the boatman as he handed her, and then Mary, over onto the steps at the jetty. Without warning, fatigue crept up on Lucy and her legs felt lead-like as they walked up the path to the villa. It was the heat and their exertions earlier in Argegno, no doubt. Would she ever acclimatise? Still, they were back now and with a bit of luck, she might lie down for an hour or two before dinner.

Just as they arrived on the terrace, Lucy spotted Andrew strolling along the lawn in the shade of some fir trees. He acknowledged her with a wave and turned towards her. But he had only stepped out onto the path when a gunshot rang out. With a cry of dismay, Mary grabbed Lucy's arm. Lucy watched in horror as Andrew fell to the ground. Lucy froze momentarily before shaking off Mary's hand and breaking into a run towards Andrew. As she rounded the corner of the house, she saw someone sprinting away in the direction of the main gate. All she could tell was that it was a man in dark clothes. For a second, she considered giving chase, but Andrew lay motionless, face down with his hands covering his head.

'Get help!' Lucy yelled at Mary as she covered the remaining distance before dropping to her knees beside her brother-in-law. Frantically, she searched for a wound. But to her profound relief, there was no sign of injury. With a grunt, Andrew turned over, his eyes wide open in shock but he appeared to be unharmed. Behind her, Lucy heard a commotion. She turned to see Phineas rush out into the garden from the house.

'What the devil?' Phin asked, the colour draining from his face as he spotted Andrew on the ground.

'Someone just tried to shoot him,' Lucy said, pointing towards the entrance. 'He ran that way towards the gate.'

Andrew sat up, his expression bewildered. '*Did* someone just take a shot at me?' he asked Lucy.

'I'm afraid so,' she replied as she watched Phin sprint off. 'Phin, don't! It's too dangerous,' she cried, springing to her feet, her heart pounding. But he was too far away to hear.

Half an hour later, an ashen-faced Andrew sat on a chair by the window, nursing a large goblet of brandy in his hands. Elvira sat opposite him, her features set. Lucy suspected she was barely holding it together. Lucy continued to pace the room, terrified Phin had been shot. How foolish of him to chase an armed man.

'Do you think he has come to harm?' Elvira asked.

Lucy cast her an agitated look and resumed her pacing.

'What on earth is going on?' Elvira muttered.

'I wish I knew,' Andrew replied. 'I say, Lucy, would you mind sitting down? My nerves are pretty shattered as it is.'

'Sorry,' Lucy answered, taking the seat beside Elvira. No one spoke for a few minutes.

'Why hasn't he returned?' Lucy cried as she jumped to her feet once more. 'I can't stand this. I'll have to follow...'

But there were voices out in the hallway, and seconds later, Phineas walked in. Lucy rushed up to him and threw her arms around his neck, promptly bursting into tears.

'Lucy! Don't, please. I'm fine,' he said at last, as he hugged her back.

'You should not have given chase unarmed.'

Phin patted his pocket. 'But I wasn't, my dear. Not that it did me any good.' Phin handed her a handkerchief. 'Dry your eyes,' he whispered.

'Did you recognise the scoundrel?' Andrew asked.

'No. He was too far ahead of me. I caught sight of a gig headed for Bellagio. I suspect he got away in that. I followed as

best I could on foot, but I soon lost him.' Phineas walked up to
Andrew, putting his hand on his shoulder. 'Are you injured?'

'Only my pride. What the devil is going on, Phin?' Andrew
asked. 'What did I do?'

Phineas sat down. 'Nothing. I suspect *I* was the real target.'

Lucy gasped. 'Oh, Lord. That would make more sense. And
you have a similar build and colouring.'

'And both of us in mourning attire. It's an alarming development, but it means we are getting close to discovering something,' Phin said.

Elvira burst into tears. 'Will this never end? This gets worse
and worse,' she sobbed.

Lucy sat down and put her arm around her shoulders.
'Hush, Elvira, don't cry.' Then she turned back to Phin. 'Could
your lunch with Giuseppe have triggered this? Was he hostile?'

Phineas rubbed his chin. 'Actually, no, quite the opposite.
We parted company around half past two and I made my way
back here. Strangely enough, I had a notion that I was being
followed.' Phin turned to Elvira. 'Could we be wrong about
Giuseppe? From our conversation, I formed the impression that
he's very fond of the children and concerned for their well-
being, Salvo in particular. I know we were all anxious about the
level of authority Luca's will gave him, but I believe he will
always have their best interests at heart.'

Elvira shared a sceptical look with Lucy. 'I hope you're
right.'

'As do I!' Andrew piped up. 'But don't worry. You're not on
your own, Elvira. If you have any concerns in the future, you
must contact me immediately. I'll happily put him straight.'

Elvira gave him a watery smile. 'Thank you. But this
attempt on your life... or Phin's life, whatever it was meant to be,
has me concerned for the children's safety. On top of everything
else...'

'Oh, my dear, try not to worry,' Lucy said. But her words

sounded feeble in the circumstances. This attempted assassination was a sinister development.

They sat in silence for several moments, but Lucy's focus was on Phin, whose features were granite-like. She had a horrible feeling that he would use this to send her home.

'It seems to me that the situation here is complex and dangerous,' Andrew remarked, his eyes on Elvira. 'Would you not consider taking the children back to England for a little while? I don't like the thought of you being here and unprotected. Phineas can't be everywhere at once. In fact, you could all travel back with me tomorrow, Elvira. Lucy?'

Lucy almost groaned aloud, avoiding her husband's gaze.

'For once, Andrew, I'm in perfect agreement with you,' Phin said, and her heart sank.

Elvira stared down at her hands, her mouth clenched momentarily, then she nodded. 'Yes, I think it might be for the best. But what about Phin? We can't just leave him on his own to deal with this.'

'He won't *be* on his own. I have no intention of leaving,' piped up Lucy.

There was a chorus of protests, the loudest coming from Phineas, which didn't surprise her at all. Lucy stood and raised her voice above the din. 'The fact that someone tried to hurt Andrew, albeit thinking he was Phin, suggests we're close to finding out the truth. The murderer or conspirators, whichever it might be, feel threatened. We promised we would find Luca's killer, Elvira, and that's exactly what we're going to do.'

'But—' Elvira protested.

'No.' Lucy shot a glance at Phin, brooking no argument. 'This is even more personal now.'

PART 2
SECRETS & LIES

TWENTY-SIX

Villa Carmosino, pre-dawn the next morning

Lucy awoke, heart pounding, clutching the bedsheet with damp fingers. As she sucked in trembling breaths, the awful images faded, splitting into spectral fragments. A nightmare. She stared into the darkness as she struggled to recall what had triggered her fear, the need to flee. Hadn't she been running, skidding over the cobbles at the harbour in Argegno? Escape had been paramount. She had to get away from that man... Then, to her horror, when she reached the quayside, the harbour lay empty. No boats. No fishermen. Where was the estate boat and the singing boatman? Where was Mary, and why had the maid left her behind?

Slowly, Lucy forced herself to concentrate on reality. As she recognised her surroundings, her fear melted away. All was well, and she was safe. The room was dark, save for a faint chink of light around the window shutters. She was at Villa Carmosino, and in bed with Phin. But how odd! She couldn't remember the last time she had had a nightmare like that. The day before had been eventful both in Argegno and here in Bellagio; perhaps that explained her troubled subconscious.

Lucy's breathing slowed. She yawned and turned over, stretching out her hand, intending to snuggle up to Phin's comforting presence. But the sheet was cold, and the cover thrown back. He wasn't there. Where could he be? Softly, she called his name. There was no response.

Lucy sat up and called out once more, loudly this time. Still no reply. She slipped out of the bed and padded across to the window to open a shutter. It didn't help much. It was still dark outside, with barely enough light to make out the garden features below. The only movement was the silvery ripples on the surface of the lake. Lucy knew it still had to be very early. She turned back into the room, not sure whether to be concerned. There was a dent in the pillow where Phin's head had rested, but no other sign of him. His dressing gown, however, was draped over a chair. He couldn't have gone far. Not too worried, she peeped into the adjoining dressing room.

'Phin?'

Silence.

After slipping on her peignoir and her slippers, Lucy eased the bedroom door open and peered out, on the alert for the slightest sound. But again, only the stillness of a sleeping house.

There's no need to worry; he can't have gone far, she thought as she crept down the stairs. Doing her best not to make a noise, she checked the reception rooms first. All were empty. Exasperated, she was about to give up when she noticed the French doors in the library, which led out onto the terrace, were ajar. As she approached the doorway, she felt the cool air on her skin and shivered. Should she go out? But what if he was unwell or in danger? Might whoever have shot at Andrew be lying in wait, hoping for another opportunity? Had Phin seen or heard something and gone to investigate? She hesitated for a moment on the threshold. The formal gardens were just about visible, some of the statuary taking on a more sinister aspect in the gloom, making her even more reluctant to leave the safety of the house. More worryingly, however, there was no sign of Phin's tall frame striding about, which was what she had half-expected to see. She scurried over to the fireplace and grabbed the poker. *Better to be safe than sorry*, she muttered under her breath, as she headed out the door.

Lucy felt ridiculous, skulking around the grounds, clutching a poker. So it was with some relief, ten minutes later, that she finally spotted Phin. She had almost missed him as he was down at the stone jetty, sitting on the lowest step, his feet dangling in the water.

'There you are!' she cried as she skipped down towards him. 'I've been looking for you for ages.'

Phin looked up and smiled. 'Sorry, my dear. I didn't mean to cause alarm.' He reached up for her hand, which she gladly gave.

'Make room for me,' she said, kicking off her slippers. Then she hitched up her nightdress and peignoir and sat down beside him, plunging her feet into the lake. The water was cool on her skin, and it made her tremble.

'You mustn't get cold,' Phin said.

'No, I like it. It was very warm up in the room. Is that why you couldn't sleep?'

He tapped his temple. 'The problem is up here. My mind was churning. I just couldn't settle, and I didn't want to disturb you.'

'Don't be silly. You should have woken me. I wouldn't have minded in the least. Always happy to discuss a case.'

When Phin didn't respond, she glanced at him. He was frowning at the poker she had laid on the ground. 'Were you cross with me, or do you usually wander around at night with a weapon?'

'No, silly. Just a precaution,' she said with a grin. 'After what happened to Andrew.'

Phin wrapped his arm around her shoulders and hugged her close before planting a kiss on her nose. 'Did you fear I had come to harm? No one would be foolish enough to assault y— *me*, here. Esposito assured me that the gates would be locked after dark and that he would personally check all the doors and windows before retiring.'

'That's very thoughtful of him,' Lucy replied.

'Yes, he's a good sort. Now don't fret. I don't expect you to act as a bodyguard,' Phin said. 'I have plenty to contend with as it is, with George. Since the incident yesterday, he is hovering.' Phin sighed. 'I think he sees himself more as my protector than a valet much of the time.'

'Well, you do get into scrapes,' Lucy replied with a cheeky look.

'As do you, madam. What about your little adventure in Argegno?'

'That's not fair! Nothing actually happened. There's no need to look so uneasy. With all those people around, no one would have dared attack us.' Phin didn't answer. If she didn't know better, she would guess he was biting his tongue. 'Phin, you knew I wasn't a sit-at-home wife when you took me on, so don't go scolding me now. Besides, you encouraged me to go, and in the end, you were the assassin's target, not me.'

'Yet!'

'You just said no one would be foolish enough to come here again and try anything.' Phin turned away with a grimace, his gaze directed out over the water. She knew what was coming. 'Please don't ask me again to go home with Andrew and Elvira. I couldn't bear it,' she said.

'God help me, I know it would be pointless. But you must see, it would be the most sensible course of action. I'd never forgive myself if you should come to harm.'

'That's my point, Phin! I feel the same. How could I even sleep back in England if I knew you were here, alone, facing God knows what.'

'I'd have George.' Lucy just stared him down. With a sigh, he captured her hand. 'Very well. If you stay, it will have to be under certain conditions.'

Lucy smarted. 'Such as?' she asked, her tone as icy as she could manage. But at that moment, something brushed past her foot in the water. With a yelp, she pulled her feet out. 'Ooh! What was that?'

Phineas broke into laughter. 'It's a fish. Look!'

Lucy's heart was hammering in her chest as she peered down into the lake. She could just make out a dark shadow swimming below. 'That's not funny; it gave me a terrible fright. Why didn't you warn me about them?'

Phin glanced at the poker and chuckled once more. 'So much for your weapon.'

'So much for your concern for my welfare!'

'Touché! However, there is a difference between harmless fish and assassins, albeit unsuccessful ones.'

Lucy huffed. 'I hate it when you're right! Go on. What are these conditions of yours?' she asked.

'That from now on, you only leave the villa in the company of me or George. We discuss *everything* no matter how insignificant you may think it, and if I consider the situation is becoming unsafe, that you agree to go home.' Lucy protested. 'No, Lucy. We don't know who we're dealing with here, but between us, we have rattled some cages. You in Argegno and me by visiting the hotel.'

'Do you think whoever it was will try to hurt you again?' she asked.

With a shrug, Phin answered, 'Honestly? I don't know, but I think it would be safer to assume it's a possibility and take the necessary precautions.'

'Good. But what have we learned other than the hotel appears to be at the centre of it all?' Lucy sighed. 'If only Fiorella had been more specific. Could she have been referring to Giuseppe? Did he tell you anything useful?'

'No, he was as slippery as an eel, as usual,' Phin replied. 'He wouldn't tell me where he was on that Friday that Luca went missing.'

'Then he must be hiding something, and he strikes me as the type of person who would react in a negative way to being questioned.'

Phin's chuckle held little humour. 'He didn't like it one bit, but as you know, I'm not easily put off. However, I can't picture him following me and taking a potshot.' Phin rubbed at his chin. 'I did glean some insight from him. From things he said, it appears he and Luca had a strange relationship. It was full of contradictions. I can't fathom it out.'

'What do you mean?'

'There are such conflicting views. Elvira claims Giuseppe was always trying to undermine Luca at every turn, but Giuseppe speaks of his nephew with affection. My instincts tell me he was fond of Luca and admired the fact that Luca stood up to him.'

'Pooh! I find that difficult to believe. He hasn't a kind bone in his body. Look how he treats Elvira.'

'Perhaps, but that is understandable, to a degree. She thwarted his great plan by marrying Luca. There may not be anything sinister behind his words.'

Lucy stared at Phin in disbelief. 'Oh no, I'm not having that. He insinuated that Luca had committed suicide. Probably the worst possible crime in the eyes of the Catholic church. He knew such an act would bring dishonour to the family, and yet he is the one always bleating about honour and family. I'm mystified.'

'Exactly. He's a complicated man, Lucy,' Phin replied. 'And

we know from experience it's dangerous to make assumptions. We still don't have a scrap of evidence against him or anyone else.'

With a sigh, Lucy answered, 'And now we have that awful article in the Milan newspaper. I reckon he was behind that.'

'I'm not so sure. What would he gain from it?'

'Upset Elvira and the rest of the family, for one,' she replied.

'We will know soon enough. Matteo will discover the culprit.'

'Well, I'd wager it was Giuseppe. His actions tell me all I need to know. Maligning his nephew is hardly genuine affection,' Lucy answered. 'Don't forget, Giuseppe was here on Lake Como when Luca arrived back from Milan. He had the opportunity.'

'So, your theory is that Giuseppe, an elderly man, overpowered his young nephew and disposed of his body in the lake?'

Lucy sniffed. 'He might have paid the local criminals to do it for him.'

A smile tugged at Phin's lips. 'You really are determined to blame him.'

'You're the one who always says to trust your instincts,' she said.

'But also, logic.'

'Hmm. Did George find out anything further about his finances?'

'Yes. Giuseppe is part owner of a stud farm. Last year, he bought a retired racehorse and had it transported here from Ireland. Unfortunately, the animal didn't survive long after the journey. As a result, the stud lost a lot of business.'

'Did he lose money then?'

'Yes. But that was a private investment. His Carmosino income wasn't affected. From what George discovered, he has a very healthy income. Besides, all he has gained from Luca's death is the joint trusteeship of little Salvo. There's no financial gain. Influence perhaps, but that is all. Another motive might be at play, of course.'

'We can only hope it will emerge in due course,' Lucy said. 'If only I'd had more time to question Fiorella about the connection with the hotel. She was one of the senior housekeepers at the time she was dismissed. Of course, she could just be making mischief. Misdirecting us. Good jobs are likely scarce, and she wouldn't have been given a reference in the circumstances. Doesn't that give her a motive? To make trouble or revenge for her dismissal? And don't forget, she is part of the Armano family.'

'The best person to consult would be Revello,' Phin said.

'And the sooner, the better,' Lucy replied, getting to her feet.

Phin looked up at her. 'I can't call on Revello at this hour. It's only about six o'clock. Could it not wait until later in the morning?'

'Of course, silly. I didn't mean right now.' Lucy tucked her arm through Phin's when he stood, and they made their way back up the steps towards the house. 'Besides, you must be tired.'

He looked down at her with a wicked gleam in his eye. 'I am a little, but you shouldn't be wandering around in such sheer clothing. Now, sleep is the last thing on my mind.'

TWENTY-SEVEN

Villa Carmosino

Some hours later, Lucy joined Mary, who was waiting for her in the dressing room, one of Lucy's new mourning dresses over her arm. It was one of three new gowns which had been delivered as part of a special commission. The contessa's name, dropped in the modiste's ear, had secured the rush order. While they stayed in Italy, Lucy would wear full mourning, for she was anxious not to offend local society. With Luca's death and the emerging scandal, she knew the house of Carmosino would be under scrutiny. As much as Lucy disliked wearing the weeds, she had to admit the workmanship of the gown was superb. The modiste was extremely popular with the local ladies, and she could see why.

'I don't understand it,' Mary muttered, as she buttoned up the back of the dress.

'Whatever is the matter?'

'This is a tight fit. I'm sure I gave them the right measurements,' Mary replied. With a frown, she did the last button. 'I hope it ain't uncomfortable, ma'am.'

Lucy slid her hands down the bodice, pursing her lips. 'It's a little snug, but don't worry. I've been overindulging. Don't you think Italian food is rather lovely? We will have to ask Monsieur Lacroix to try out some new recipes. I wonder if Elvira's cook would share them with me before we leave.'

Mary quirked her lips but didn't respond. Lucy could almost hear the maid's disgruntled thoughts on all things foreign. 'What is it, Mary? Is there something on your mind?'

'I was wondering if we oughtn't to go home today, ma'am, along with the others. After what happened yesterday, I'm thinking we'll all be murdered in our beds.'

'Mary! Don't be so dramatic. That will not happen.' Lucy gave her what she hoped was an encouraging look. 'And Mary?'

'Yes, ma'am,' the maid replied with narrowed eyes.

The last thing Lucy needed was for Mary to give Phin an excuse to send her back to London. 'Don't repeat that wish in front of Mr Stone. I've had quite a job getting him to agree to my staying behind. He'd jump on it and send me packing. Rest assured, if I thought we were in mortal danger, I would leave.' Mary's answering look held doubt and if Lucy were honest, she shared that view, but they couldn't abandon the case now. If anything, the attack on Andrew only made Lucy more determined to stay and find the culprit.

'It isn't necessary for the contessa to be here. She and the children need to grieve in peace. That's difficult here at present, what with the attempt on her brother's life and the scurrilous rumours that are flying around. The best thing is for her to go home to be with her family for a while. However, Mr Stone and I can't leave while matters are as they stand.'

'I know that only too well,' Mary muttered. 'You can never leave well enough alone!'

Lucy lifted a brow with what she hoped was a quelling expression. 'Is that so? Have you ever come to harm, Mary?'

The maid took an age to answer, undoubtedly recalling

some best forgotten incidents. 'Suppose not, ma'am, but it wasn't for your want of trying.'

'I beg your pardon!'

Mary stared back at her, hands on hips, and Lucy knew she was in trouble. 'What about that night at Somerville when we broke into the house and nearly got caught?' Lucy grimaced at the memory. 'Or that time in Egypt! That was one disaster after another, with you getting yourself blown to pieces and chasing down murderers in tombs and the like. And then—'

Lucy put up her hands. 'Yes, yes... very well, you've made your point.'

'I ain't being impertinent, ma'am, honest. I'm worried about you. If anything happened to you, what would I do? I don't want to work for no one else... And how would I get home?'

Lucy couldn't really argue with her. Everything she said was true. 'If... if something bad were to happen to me or Mr Stone, George would look after you and see you safely back to England.'

This appeared to mollify the maid a little. 'I suppose he would and all. George is a good sort, for sure. But don't be mad, ma'am. Like I said, it's just you attract trouble. Like one of them magnets.'

Lucy spluttered. 'You're far too free with your opinion... but I'll concede that I have dragged you into some *mild* scrapes' – Mary's jaw dropped – 'and had my share of adventures.'

'*Your* share and half the women in the country, too!' Her long-suffering maid sniffed and turned away with a self-satisfied smile. Then she picked up a delicate black lace shawl and draped it over Lucy's shoulders. 'I speak as I find.'

'As always, Mary! However, I promise as soon as we have solved the conte's case, we will return home to London. It shouldn't be long. We are keen to solve this as quickly as possible.'

'Very good, ma'am. I shall note that down in my diary,' Mary replied.

'You keep a diary?'

'Oh, yes, ma'am. How else would I remember all the things you get up to?'

Lucy had no words.

'There, you're all set,' the maid said, standing back to admire her work.

'Tha—'

There was a knock at the bedroom door. Lucy shook out her skirts, as Mary went to answer the door, then Lucy strolled out into the bedroom. It was a housemaid.

'Please, ma'am,' the young girl said in halting English as she stepped into the room, 'the contessa wanting you come to the salon. Please.'

'Certainly,' Lucy answered, and with a quick smile and a nod to Mary, she followed the housemaid downstairs.

Elvira was not alone. Her friend Maria, Revello's wife, was sitting on the sofa opposite. Lucy pasted a smile on her face, for she was sure she was in for half an hour of tedium.

'I've just been telling Maria about what happened to Andrew yesterday,' Elvira said.

'Quite shocking!' Maria exclaimed with a shake of her head. 'I'm sure Francesco will be greatly distressed to hear of it.' Maria treated them both to an apologetic smile and cleared her throat. 'This visit of condolence is unforgivably late, Signora Stone, and I have been explaining to your sister-in-law that I have been ill. It's a feeble reason, but necessary to explain. I'm sadly afflicted with poor health.' Again, a shortsighted smile. Then she turned to Elvira. 'My husband was most anxious that I come on hearing of your plans to return to England, my dear. I'd never forgive myself if I didn't express my condolences before your departure.'

Lucy gulped. *Don't smile! She has no idea how insincere she sounds.*

'You are very kind, Maria. I only hope you haven't jeopardised your health by visiting me today.' Elvira smiled kindly at her guest.

How tolerant she is, Lucy thought. *In Elvira's position, I would not have been at home to receive this tedious woman.*

Maria drew out a handkerchief and coughed. 'Not at all. Though I admit I find it fatiguing to travel around when it's so hot.'

'Isn't it lucky that it's only a short journey here by carriage from the town, Maria?' Elvira said, but the dig appeared to go above the lady's head.

Lucy didn't dare catch Elvira's eye as Maria launched into the minutiae of her recent malady. Once she had exhausted the topic, she asked, catching both Lucy and Elvira off-guard, 'And how is your brother faring after his ordeal?'

'Oh, fine. A little shaken, perhaps. Thank you for asking,' Lucy replied. Was that the reason for her visit? Nosiness? News of the incident would have spread like wildfire around the town.

'I assume you have called in the police?' Maria asked.

'We're waiting to hear from them, signora,' Lucy replied. It seemed the easiest answer to give. Phin, in fact, had refused to involve them despite Lucy's protests. Though, she had to admit, he was probably right. After all, they had not proven themselves terribly effective up to this point where Luca had been concerned.

'Francesco will be very relieved to hear it,' the lady replied. After a moment or two of silence, she turned her myopic gaze on Elvira. 'And you depart for England today?'

'Yes. The change will do me good. There are too many painful memories here,' Elvira replied. 'But Phin and Lucy are staying on for now. You might tell Francesco if he has any problems at the hotel, he may consult Phineas or Luca's brother, Matteo.' It was a dismissal of sorts. Would the lady realise and take her leave? Lucy wondered.

Maria's smile was icy. 'Or Giuseppe?'

'Or Giuseppe. Of course,' Elvira replied.

Maria blinked at her hostess, then nodded. 'I'll pass that on.' Then the lady rose. 'I wish you bon voyage, my dear. I must leave you to prepare for the tiresome journey.' Lucy and Elvira also stood. Maria embraced Elvira. 'Look after yourself. Let me know when you return.'

'Thank you, Maria,' Elvira said as she pulled the bell.

Esposito glided into the room and bowed out the guest.

Once the door was closed, Elvira relaxed and sat back in her chair. Lucy strolled over to the window and watched Maria climb into her carriage. The timing of her visit was odd. Had she been fishing for information? And if so, for whom?

Once the carriage had disappeared from view, Lucy sat down in Maria's vacated chair. 'What a vacuous excuse for a lady.'

'You are being severe, Lucy, though I admit her visits are often tiresome,' Elvira quickly responded, puffing out her cheeks. 'She is a little self-obsessed these days. Unfortunately, the great romance didn't last long. And, of course, there's the age difference.'

'Ah! I thought as much. Ten, fifteen years?'

'About nine years. But Lucy, she has been very kind to me, and I hold her in affection.'

'That's good enough for me,' Lucy said with a smile. 'However, she gives the impression of a woman who has been disappointed in life.'

'Today, she did appear unhappy. But as I said, she has become self-absorbed, and ill much of the time. They never had children, which I suspect could be another reason for her melancholy.'

'Is their marriage in trouble?' Lucy asked.

Elvira wrinkled her nose. 'I do not think so. Luca never alluded to any difficulties, and she has never said anything to me.'

'Would Luca have noticed?' Lucy asked, somewhat surprised.

'Yes, because he and Francesco were very close. Almost like brothers. But Lucy, don't forget you're still in the first flush of happiness. It doesn't always last.'

'I'm aware of that! Charlie grew bored with me after a couple of years. Then he strayed,' Lucy replied.

'I'm sorry. I didn't know.'

Lucy shrugged. 'That was the least of his crimes, my dear. I'll fill you in another time.'

Elvira looked intrigued, then glanced at the clock on the mantel. 'Look at the time! Now, I must check that Rose has everything ready. We must catch the steamer from Bellagio at one o'clock.' Elvira jumped to her feet, then hesitated. 'Do you hate me for leaving?'

Lucy stood and grabbed her hand. 'Goodness, no. It's absolutely the right thing to do. For you and the children. Time away will help you all come to terms with your loss.'

'I don't think a lifetime will be enough, my dear. But you are very kind,' Elvira said with a sad smile. 'Promise me one thing. Be careful!'

'Certainly,' Lucy replied.

'I must admit, I feel so bad leaving you both here. You will stay in touch? Please keep me informed about how the investigation is going,' Elvira said, clutching her sleeve.

'I promise.'

'And you will notify me straightaway if you find out what happened to Luca?'

'Of course we will.'

'I have briefed Esposito. The house and the staff are at your disposal,' Elvira said as they fell into step.

'Actually, that won't be necessary, my dear,' Lucy replied. 'You see, all the clues at present point to the hotel being at the centre of this puzzle.'

Elvira stalled and looked at her askance. 'Our hotel? Oh no!'

'Yes, I'm afraid so. We intend to move there tomorrow. It will be far easier to investigate if we're based there.'

'Will you not be putting yourselves in danger? I don't like it.' With a frown she continued, 'Is it because Giuseppe lives there? Do you suspect he is behind it all?'

'I suspect him, but Phin is less convinced. We have no evidence against anyone yet.'

Elvira drew in a deep breath. 'Oh dear! I hope you're wrong. He isn't my favourite person in the world, but I'm struggling to believe he would have harmed Luca.'

Lucy wasn't so sure.

TWENTY-EIGHT

Grand Hotel Bellagio, the next day

As Phin checked them in at the reception desk, Lucy's gaze roamed about the hotel foyer. In truth, she was searching for any sign of Giuseppe. Despite Phin's warning to leave Luca's uncle to him, Lucy was determined to pin the man down and get some answers from him if she got the chance. If she could only catch him off-guard, he might let something slip. Phin was being overprotective in this instance. How dangerous could it be? Giuseppe would hardly shoot her in the middle of the hotel.

A porter arrived to take their bags just as a familiar voice hailed them from across the hall. 'Welcome! Welcome!' It was Francesco Revello. 'I'm delighted to see you both looking so well. I was shocked to hear of the attempt on your brother's life, Senor Stone. What a dreadful business.' Revello's face was full of concern as they shook hands.

'Don't worry, my brother is not easily cowed,' Phin replied. 'But in the circumstances, we thought it best if my sister and the children return to England with him.'

Revello nodded, still frowning. 'Absolutely, but you must be more careful. I hope you have notified the police.' He lowered his voice. 'Your investigation into the conte's accident appears to have angered someone. And, unfortunately, all these questions are giving credence to the rumours and scandal. I fear it's very damaging to the hotel.' Then Revello flashed them both a smile. 'But what am I thinking? This is no way to welcome such special guests. You're in luck, for our bridal suite is unoccupied at present. We insist you use it for as long as you wish.'

'Thank you, Revello,' replied Phin.

'And Signora Stone. It's delightful to see you again. I hope you will find the hotel to your liking.'

'I'm sure I will. Thank you,' Lucy said, returning his handshake.

The manager turned back to Phin. 'Rest assured, we will take extra care of you, Signor Stone. The contessa would never forgive me if your stay was not perfect.' Francesco waved them towards the stairs. 'We all hope that she will return to Bellagio soon.'

They fell into step with him. 'Perhaps in a month or so – she needs some time away. There are too many memories here for her at present,' Phin replied. They paused at the bottom of the grand staircase.

'I understand. The conte's death has affected us all deeply. Very sad. However, I hope it's possible for you to enjoy your stay with us, no matter how short it may be. Your suite is on the first floor. Please follow me,' Revello continued.

Francesco started up the stairs, and Phin smiled at Lucy, holding out his arm. 'Special treatment, eh?' he whispered to her with a quirk of his brow.

They followed the manager along a corridor for a short distance before he came to a stop. There were two doors opposite each other. One was marked 'Private' and closed; the other stood open.

'Ah,' Revello said with a sad smile as he followed Lucy's

gaze. 'That was Luca's office.' Then he shrugged as if shaking off
an unhappy memory and waved them through the open door.

Lucy stepped through and gasped. The sitting room was
magnificent, filled with light from sets of floor-to-ceiling
windows affording views of the sparkling lake below. Through
one set of doors, she glimpsed a large balcony. The décor was
pale blue and cream, with interconnecting doors through to a
bedroom on one side and dressing rooms on the other.

'What a beautiful suite of rooms,' she said.

Francesco bowed and smiled. 'It is our best.'

'Thank you. I'm surprised it's free this time of year,' she
said.

'Ah! Yes... unfortunately, we have had cancellations.' He
shrugged. 'The circumstances of the conte's death and the
recent robberies have caused...' He stared down at the floor.
'Forgive me. I can't think of the right word in English.'

'Gossip?' Phin said.

Revello's head snapped up. 'Yes, that's it. As I said downstairs, the scandal is harming the hotel. The staff are worried. I,
too, fear what may happen. This should be our busiest month,
but we have empty rooms.'

'Perhaps you should discuss the matter with Matteo
Carmosino,' Phin said. 'Or Giuseppe?'

'I may have no choice but to do that. But they are grieving,
and I do not wish to worry them about business problems.'

'I appreciate that, Revello, but if you're that concerned, you
should speak to them, and soon.'

Francesco nodded and attempted a smile.

'That newspaper article was unfortunate,' Lucy said, 'and
not very helpful.'

Francesco flashed her a worried glance. 'It was very damaging. When I read it, I was horrified. I'm convinced one of our
competitors fed that to them. They circle like vultures. But
please, do not concern yourselves.' Slowly, his face cleared.

'Now, I'll trouble you no longer. I wish you a pleasant stay, and please let us know if there's anything you require.' He waved towards a console table. 'Our compliments.' A bottle of champagne peeped out from a cooler.

Phin tipped the porter and smiled at Francesco. 'Thank you, Revello, that is most kind. I'm sure we will be very comfortable.'

Revello bowed and followed the porter out of the room.

'Well, well, my dear, how interesting,' Phin said, stepping over to the champagne. 'Shall we?'

'Yes, please.'

Phin lifted the bottle out and opened it with a pop of the cork. 'Let's take this out onto the balcony.'

Lucy followed with the glasses, mulling over the encounter with Revello. 'His behaviour is... odd. Forced. Yes, forced is the right word.'

'A little over-enthusiastic for sure,' Phin replied as he poured. 'And very keen to make a good impression on us.'

'He's anxious, isn't he? But I can't shake off the impression that it's his own job he's worried about and not the welfare of the staff, the hotel or the family,' Lucy commented, after a few minutes of taking in the glorious views. 'And it's not very circumspect of him to talk about the business to us.' When Phin didn't reply, she glanced up at him. 'What's the matter?'

'It struck me that he has a lot to lose if the hotel fails,' Phin replied.

'Could he be right about a competitor being up to mischief? Feeding the newspaper that information?'

'It's possible,' Phin said. 'If the hotel runs into trouble, the family may end up selling it off. Someone will swoop in and buy it at a low price.'

'And put their own staff in place,' Lucy said.

'Exactly. But we should know who placed that article soon enough. Matteo will get to the bottom of it.'

'Strange, though, that Revello would mention the present difficulties to us. Though perhaps he sees you as Elvira's representative.'

'He may do, but she has little say in the business. Matteo and Giuseppe will make all the decisions going forward. He knows that very well. Luca's will, the pertinent details at least, will be common knowledge by now. I'm sure Matteo, if not Giuseppe, has already informed him of how things stand. No, he was making a point and not a very subtle one. My investigation is inconvenient if it keeps the rumour mill churning. He wants me to stop.'

'But we can't just cease investigating to save his job!'

'Indeed, but for now, the future of the hotel is in question. You can hardly blame him for being worried.'

'I suppose not,' she admitted. 'This case is so frustrating. Sometimes I think we will never solve this.'

'I couldn't agree more. Frankly, it's driving me to distraction. All we know for certain is that the answer lies within these walls.'

'But Phin, what if Fiorella meant a different hotel? She didn't name it. We've just assumed it was here. Could she have been referring to the hotel in Milan?'

With a quirk of his mouth, Phineas considered this. 'On balance, there are too many connections for it not to be here; Luca, the diamonds, the fact she worked here, and the reaction to my visit. The latter provoked the attack at the villa. Don't forget that. Either Giuseppe, or someone who observed us, felt threatened by my presence that day.'

'And yet we have no clues. Giuseppe must be involved. Perhaps there's another way to get the information we need.'

'Then tell me what it is for we're getting nowhere. I must speak to Giuseppe again. Push harder for answers.'

'I'm willing to try,' she suggested. 'Much as I dislike him.'

'And therein lies the problem. I don't think he would trust you enough to reveal anything.'

Lucy couldn't help but pout. 'You're probably right. Very well, you can tackle him.'

With a smile, Phineas replied, 'Thanks very much!' Then his gaze intensified into a frown. 'What's wrong?'

She took a deep breath before answering. 'I feel vulnerable, and I don't like it. Is it because we're married? There's a terrible fear in my heart that something bad might happen. Above all, I don't want to lose you.'

Phin kissed her cheek. 'Nor I, you.' For a moment, he appeared to be struggling. 'My dear, if you really wish it, we will leave. Right now.'

Lucy knew how much it cost him to say it and for the first time in her life, she was tempted, very tempted, to run away. But she would never forgive herself and deep down she realised he wouldn't either. 'No. We're committed to seeing this through to the end, no matter what.'

'Of course, I would be far happier if you left this to me,' he said.

Lucy pulled back and glared at him. 'Don't ask me to go home!'

His answer was a lop-sided grin. 'I won't. I might want to, badly, but you'd never forgive me.'

'Very true!' But his sad expression made her regret her words. 'I'm sorry, but I *am* worried. It feels as though evil is closing in on us.'

Phin's brow shot up. 'This isn't like you. You're usually the one straining at the leash, eager for action.'

'I know! It's silly.' She waved her hand out towards the water. 'It's such a beautiful place and yet there have been so many terrible incidents. Do you understand what I mean?'

He pulled her into an embrace. 'Unfortunately, I do. And I'm sorry. This is not turning out to be much of a honeymoon.'

'I don't care about that,' she replied.

'Is that so, madam?' he said, before picking her up and carrying her towards the bedroom.

'Stop!' she cried out, laughing. 'Put me down!'

But her protests were in vain.

A few hours later, Lucy left their suite intending to explore the hotel, leaving Phin reading the London newspapers George had procured for him. Poor Phin. The stress of their situation was wearing him down. But foremost in her mind was their safety. Was it foolish to set up camp here? At least Elvira was safely out of the country with the children. It was natural that Phin wanted her to leave, too. And a part of Lucy felt guilty. Should she go home? Was she a liability? But the thought of travelling home and not knowing what was happening would drive her wild with anxiety. No. Her place was here, by his side, no matter what. And two heads were better than one. Their previous collaborations had proven that. They made an excellent team.

As she stepped out into the hallway, Lucy spotted the door of Luca's office was ajar. Too good an opportunity to miss? A quick scan of the corridor confirmed she was alone. Chewing on her bottom lip, she sidled up to the door and tipped it with her fingers. The opening widened enough for her to peer inside. However, the shutters were closed. Squinting, she could make out a large desk near the window. For a moment, she hesitated on the threshold. But what if Luca had left some clue behind?

Decision made, she stepped inside and closed the door, plunging the room into almost total darkness. Feeling along the wall beside the door, she found and flicked on the light switch. It was a soulless room, sparsely furnished, which surprised her. Perhaps Revello had ordered the room to be cleared of Luca's effects, she thought with a sinking sensation. Anything useful might have been removed already. After a quick look around, however, she focused on the desk. Its surface was free of clutter, other than an inkwell and blotter. She skirted the desk and sat on the chair, eyeing up the banks of drawers beneath. She tried the topmost drawer. It slid open. Empty. As were the next few. But the bottom drawer on the right-hand side held a large leather-bound book. Lucy smiled. This was much better. The gold lettering of '1888' stood out against the burgundy leather. It looked like an appointment book. She manoeuvred it out of the drawer and onto the desk. There seemed little point in looking through the entire year, so Lucy skimmed through the pages until she reached the week of Luca's disappearance. It had been a busy week for Luca with every day filled with meet-ings. Lucy ran her finger down each page, hoping something might pop out, something significant.

And then on Tuesday, an entry caught her eye.

Midday—Kincaid.

Now that was interesting. They met two days before Luca left for Milan. The day Luca had informed Enzo about the trip. Was there a connection? What had Kincaid told him? Had Luca taken matters into his own hands based on something Kincaid had found out? Was that why he went to Milan?

Lucy sat back. Of course, Luca would have been monitoring the investigation. It made sense. Quickly, she flicked back through the previous weeks. Kincaid appeared three more times. So, they had been working together, perhaps? But was it a stretch to assume that Kincaid had come to him with evidence regarding the diamond theft, knowing how cagey Kincaid was? So fearful that anyone else would swoop in and claim the reward he would have seen as his alone. The day she met Kincaid, he had... how had he put it? 'I'm close to solving it,' Lucy said out loud. Those had been his words. Was it signifi-cant that he hadn't said 'I'm close to finding the diamonds'? There was only one man who knew the answer to that.

With everything that had happened in the last few days, she had almost forgotten about the attack on Kincaid. It seemed the man might be the key to their investigation. Lucy put the appointment book back in the drawer and left the office to share her findings with Phin. It was about time they checked for an update on Kincaid.

TWENTY-NINE

That evening, Lucy and Phineas were just about to leave their suite to dine in the hotel restaurant when George caught their attention with a discreet cough.

'I noticed something today which may be of interest to you, sir,' he said.

Phin's eyes lit up. 'Yes?'

'Enzo, the late conte's valet, is now working here at the hotel,' George replied.

'Well, now, George, that *is* interesting,' Phin replied.

'Sorry, I forgot to mention it,' Lucy said. 'Elvira and Revello agreed it. Elvira was relieved as he had been a faithful servant, but of course, she has no need of him. I'm sure the man is delighted with the new arrangement. After all, valet positions may be difficult to find locally.'

'Hmm,' said Phin.

'What are you thinking?' Lucy asked. 'Is there some significance to this, for I don't see it?'

Phin shrugged. 'Just noting it, my dear.' He glanced at George. 'It may not be important, but the fact Luca left Milan without him has always troubled me.'

'Oh!' exclaimed Lucy, annoyed she hadn't taken note herself. 'I put it down to Luca's erratic behaviour on the day.'

'Yes, you could be right, but when the opportunity arises, I'll have another chat with the young man. You might organise that for me, George.'

'Very good, sir.' George bobbed his head. 'If that will be all, I shall inveigle myself with the staff below stairs.'

'Good man, George. Off with you!' Phin said.

But as the valet opened the door, there was a hotel servant frozen on the spot, hand in mid-air, about to knock. He was holding a letter. He recovered quickly. 'For Signor Stone,' he said, with a bob of his head, handing it over. George gave him a tip and waved him away.

'Thank you, George,' Phin said, taking it from him. 'By hand. I wonder who could be writing to me here.' As Lucy looked on, he tore open the envelope, then scanned the page. 'Good Lord! It's from Kincaid.'

'Don't keep me in suspense! Read it out,' Lucy cried.

'*Stone, I'm leaving Como for Bellagio. It's urgent that we meet and discuss our respective cases. Meet me at the Armano boathouse. Just follow Via Eugenio Vitali until you reach the lake. Seven o'clock tomorrow evening. Do not involve the police.*' Phin looked up. 'That last sentence is underlined. Twice.'

Lucy's heart skipped a beat. 'Which implies they can't be trusted. But what if it's a trap? Can we be sure that Kincaid even wrote this?'

'It looks like his writing, but we will go prepared for the worst, in any case,' he replied. But she could not mistake the excitement in his voice. After weeks of little progress, at last matters were moving forward.

The following evening

At a quarter to seven, Lucy and Phin joined George outside the hotel, just as Giuseppe strode through the entrance gates. He doffed his hat to them, without a word, and his expression was sour. Phin, however, greeted him cheerfully. Lucy managed a nod.

'I wonder where he has been all day,' Phin said, watching Guiseppe stroll towards the main door. 'If I didn't know better, he is doing his best to avoid me. He never replied to my request to meet him earlier. Hopefully, I can pin him down tomorrow.'

'He may refuse to see you again,' she said.

'Hmm, we shall see. Now, we don't want to be late for Kincaid.'

Tucking her arm through Phin's, they set off for the town.

A cooling and gentle wind came off the water as they followed the road towards the town. Many were taking advantage of the drop in temperature. Out on the water, small sailing boats lazily made their way along. It looked idyllic. Not for the first time, Lucy wished they were here under different circumstances. How pleasant it would be to go sailing with Phin, just the two of them. Maybe, someday, they could come back and enjoy the place as ordinary tourists.

Just as they reached the outskirts of Bellagio, they had to slow down, for there were queues of tourists waiting for steamers at the Piazzale Imbarcadero. As they waited for a parting in the crowd, Lucy looked around. For a second, she could have sworn she saw a familiar figure striding along beneath the arcade which stretched along the roadside. She squeezed Phin's arm.

'I think I just saw Revello,' she said.

Phin strained to see. 'I can't see him. Are you sure?'

'I only caught a glimpse. I may have been mistaken,' she replied. Whoever she had seen was now lost in the crowd.

'Which way was he going?' Phin asked.

Lucy waved her hand back towards the way they had come. 'The direction of the hotel.'

'His lodging is just off this main street, ma'am,' George said, indicating a narrow flight of steps which led up from the piazzale into the maze of tall buildings which formed the heart of the town.

'Very diligent of him. He certainly works long hours,' Phin remarked, just as a gap in the queue appeared and they could carry on.

Once out along the other side of the town centre, they followed Via Eugenio Vitali towards the Bellagio headland. The road was narrow, sweeping past Hotel Villa Serbelloni and climbing steadily for a while. As they continued into a more residential area, there were fewer people around. The roadway was flanked by the high walls of villas, and here and there were hints of lush green gardens, their foliage spilling over the walls as if to tempt them inside.

'How much further, do you think?' Lucy asked as they rounded yet another corner. Her anxiety was growing.

'I can't imagine it's far. We're almost at the end of the promontory,' Phin replied. 'Ah! This must be it.' A narrow laneway between two houses led down towards the water's edge. George volunteered to walk down first. They waited for him to give the all-clear. Lucy gnawed at her bottom lip. What awaited them down at the shore? At last, George reappeared at the bottom of the laneway and nodded. Lucy, much relieved and with a firm grip on Phin's arm, let him lead her down the lane.

They came out onto a tiny rocky shore. It was deserted, with just a solitary *Lucia* pulled up onto the beach. Lucy quickly scanned the area, but there was no sign of Kincaid. The high walls of the houses bordering the beach meant it was not overlooked. *A fine place for a rendezvous*, Lucy thought with unease. *Nicely secluded.*

Phin pointed to a small hut at the back of the beach. 'That must be the Armano boathouse.' It was a ramshackle structure, its wood rotting, and its paint long peeled off and blown away. On the door was a notice. *Tenere fuori!*

'Keep out!' Phin said, following her gaze before checking his watch. 'We are late, but only by a few minutes.' Then he waved towards an outcrop of rock further along. 'Shall we sit and wait?'

Phin took out his handkerchief and brushed off the top surface of the outcrop so that she could sit down. Once she was settled, instead of joining her, Phin walked down to the shore. He was restless. Of course, her presence was an additional worry for him. She was amazed he had agreed that she be one of the party for this meeting. But now she was here, she was beginning to regret her request.

All the while, George paced up and down, ever vigilant.

Lucy did her best to be patient. Could this have been a ruse to get them out of the hotel? Might they be attacked on their return journey as dusk fell? Only Mary knew where they were and could raise the alarm if they did not return. Suddenly, this seemed a foolish idea.

'Perhaps he couldn't come,' Lucy called out to Phin after a few minutes. 'He may not be fully recovered.'

'Or feared to,' Phin said with a sigh.

'Or was prevented,' Lucy said, as her unease grew.

After a few more minutes, Phin walked past her and up to the old boathouse. He tried the door, but it was locked. Lucy watched as he walked around the dilapidated structure, knocking on the panels. Then he disappeared round the corner, out of sight.

Suddenly, George yelled out: 'Sir!'

Phin reappeared and hurried across the slippery stones to

join George at the water's edge at the furthest end of the beach. Lucy slid off her rocky perch and joined them.

'Look!' George said, pointing out into the water. 'There! Do you see? Must be about ten yards out. Something is floating. Something white and black.'

Lucy's heart filled with dread. Phin's thoughts must have been similar, for he threw her a frowning glance. 'Could it be a body?' she asked, suddenly sick to her stomach.

'It could be, for it's the right size,' George said, his voice wobbling.

Phin scanned the beach and the laneway they had come down. 'Stand up there, Lucy, close to the boathouse and keep watch. Draw your pistol. George and I will retrieve whatever it is. While we're in the water, we're vulnerable.' He glanced up towards the high wall that bordered the beach. 'Someone could be watching from up there.'

'Perhaps you shouldn't risk it, Phin,' she said. But he was already wiggling out of his jacket with George's help. George followed suit. 'Do be careful, both of you!' she cried.

But Phin, now stern-faced, just pointed up to the back of the beach. Both men slipped off their shoes and waded into the lake. Lucy retreated up the shore, her pistol in her hand. With growing trepidation, Lucy watched as they reached the floating object. Both men were now chest high in the lake. Luckily, in this cove the water was calm, its surface almost mirror-like. Phin stretched out and pulled at the object. George also grabbed it and between them, they turned it over. Even from where she stood, Lucy saw the horror cross Phin's face as both men recoiled.

Her worst fears were confirmed. It had to be a body.

Male or female? She couldn't tell from this distance.

Lucy could not hear what they said, but they took hold of the body and pulled it back towards shore. When they reached the beach, they gently floated the corpse up onto the shingle.

Then Phin knelt beside the body and pushed the strands of hair off the man's face. Afraid of what she would see but compelled, Lucy walked down to the men.

Her stomach lurched. There could be no mistake: it was Malcolm Kincaid. And there was a nasty gash to the side of his face.

THIRTY

Lucy and Phin stayed with Kincaid's body while George scurried off to the police station to report the incident. They sat on the shingle, beside the dead man, both silent, watching the sun set behind the opposite shore. Lucy shivered, and she was swamped by guilt. She hadn't been particularly friendly when they had last met. She regretted it now. Suddenly uneasy, that sense of vulnerability that had been haunting her for days seemed to increase. Kincaid had paid a heavy price for doing his job. Would they meet the same fate? She was aware of Phin's concerned gaze and soon her emotions bubbled up and she was sobbing in his arms. Luckily, she had recovered by the time the police arrived. After some initial questioning by the Carabinieri officer, and their reassurance to him they wouldn't leave the area, he had given them permission to go back to the hotel.

On arrival at Grand Hotel Bellagio, however, they caused a sensation, as the foyer was full of guests en route to the dining room for their evening meal. Guests and staff alike treated their party to curious glances. One lady tittered behind her fan, another openly stared, most likely due to the state of Phin and George's wet clothes. Revello emerged from his office and stared, assessing the situation rapidly. He ushered them into his office, anxious, Lucy guessed, to remove them from the view of the guests. Phin explained what had occurred in a clipped voice Lucy had rarely heard. Revello's attempt to interrogate them met with icy one syllable answers from Phin. Much to her relief, within minutes, they were traipsing up the stairs to their suite.

It was almost eleven o'clock when George announced Commissario Marinelli's arrival with two officers. Revello had accompanied the policeman to their door. But to Lucy's satisfaction, Marinelli thanked and dismissed him most efficiently. All that man worries about is the reputation of the hotel, Lucy thought as she dismissed him from her thoughts. She needed her wits about her for what was to come. Marinelli looked far from happy as he limped over to a chair. No doubt the two-and-a-half-hour journey from Como on the police boat accounted for it.

The questioning which followed was intense, making for an unpleasant experience as reliving the discovery of Kincaid's body made Lucy slightly nauseous. She couldn't shake the image of the poor young man on the shingle, his life so cruelly cut short. And now, of course, they would never know what information he might have shared with them.

But even more uncomfortable was the feeling that the inspector thought they had had something to do with his death.

'How is it that policemen can make you think you're actually guilty?' Lucy asked Phin as soon as the door closed behind Marinelli. 'Do you think it's a skill they acquire during training?'

Phin tried to smile. 'I'll ask McQuillan the next time I see him.'

'If only it was Oliver we were dealing with,' Lucy sighed. 'But do you think Marinelli believed us? His questions were rather pointed.'

'Eventually,' her husband said. 'Having Kincaid's letter

helped, I suppose. George, pour out three brandies. I know I need one and you still look ghastly.'

George hesitated, looking like he might object. Then his shoulders slumped, and he sighed. 'Very good, sir. Thank you.' The valet went to the sideboard and poured out the brandy. Lucy noticed his hands shook. She didn't feel much steadier herself.

'It was hardly an accident, though,' Lucy said.

'But difficult to prove with no witnesses,' Phin replied. 'It was the perfect spot for a murder. Someone may have planned it very well indeed.'

Lucy gasped. 'Do you think his body could have been planted there to make us look guilty? He could have been killed somewhere else.'

'It's not beyond the bounds of possibility,' Phin replied. 'It would make sense, as it would remove us with our annoying questions quite beautifully.'

'What a terrible notion,' Lucy said with a shiver, taking the glass from George with a sympathetic nod. She touched the arm of the chair closest to her. 'Sit down beside me, George.' Again, he began to object. 'Sit!'

Phin waited until George was settled. 'The other possibilities are that either Kincaid was followed from Como, where he was likely under surveillance, or he was seen arriving in Bellagio and someone guessed he would try to meet me, or his letter to me was intercepted. Where in Bellagio was he staying, George, do you know?'

'In a small hotel.'

Phin's glance shifted between them. 'Unfortunately, Marinelli is unlikely to share any information he might find there with us.'

'You're assuming he will bother to investigate,' Lucy said.

'Indeed. His record in these matters is woeful,' Phin replied. 'Obviously, Kincaid's room will be out of bounds for us, but we can still try to find out if the letter was intercepted here at the hotel,' she said.

George jumped in. 'From what I have seen, messages and letters left at reception are usually delivered immediately. But it would be possible to divert something. Someone could intervene, if senior enough, and it would not be questioned by the young lads who do the deliveries.'

'True. And I imagine any correspondence I might receive would be of great interest to our thief-cum-murderer,' Phin replied. 'It would be useful to know if Kincaid hand-delivered the letter or sent a messenger with it.'

'I can make enquiries with the lad who brought it,' George said.

'Thanks, George.'

Lucy's stomach twisted. 'Do you believe we're under surveillance?'

Phin exchanged a wary look with George. 'Unfortunately, yes.'

'Are we safe staying here, do you think? Should we go back to the villa?'

'I'd rather not, as this does appear to be the centre of things, but if you're uneasy, my dear...'

'No, no. Don't mind me. It's the tiredness talking.' Lucy quickly changed the subject, afraid his next suggestion might be her removal home. 'Are we agreed he was murdered? Marinelli's assertion that it was an accident is preposterous.'

'Yes. And then there was that nasty gash on the side of Kincaid's face...' Phin said, his tone weary.

'Which the inspector insists was caused by a rock in the water,' Lucy snapped. 'How can the stupid man believe he slipped at the water's edge, hit his head, and drowned? It's like Luca's post-mortem all over again.'

'It saves him a lot of paperwork if he can convince everyone it was an accident,' George remarked.

'Unfortunately, I think you're correct, George. Once he could not implicate us, he switched to that theory rather quickly,' Phin said, swirling the brandy in his glass. 'We didn't need a second murder to investigate with so little headway on Luca's death. The only good thing is that I'm sure there's a link. The only reason someone would want Kincaid out of the way is that he knew who stole the diamonds or who killed Luca.'

'Most likely the same person, sir,' George said.

'I believe so. If we solve one crime, we may solve the other.'

'Then my theory could be right,' Lucy said. 'Kincaid passed on his information or suspicions to Luca, who then dashed off to Milan. In effect, Kincaid's investigation triggered both their deaths.'

'Yes. Why else would someone kill Kincaid?' Phin replied. 'The poor man knew too much.'

Lucy suddenly sat up straight. 'Oh, no! Fiorella. She could be in danger, too. I saw her with Kincaid, remember? What if she was helping him with the diamond case?'

Phin frowned across at her. 'You said they were arguing, if I recall correctly.'

'Yes. It looked heated, but does that matter? They knew each other. I'm certain of it. It would make sense. She worked here at the hotel. Would know the people and what they might be up to. She may even suspect who was involved in the robbery of the diamonds,' Lucy answered.

'But she was a thief, Lucy,' Phin said.

'Was she? Perhaps she was set up by someone. The real thief. Who then went on to steal the diamonds.'

'You think she is an informer?' Phin slowly nodded. 'An interesting theory. It fits.'

'We should warn her,' she said.

'How, Lucy?' Phin asked. 'By doing so, we might trigger the very thing we are warning her against. We must trust she is clever enough to avoid arousing suspicion.'

'Well, she was certainly agitated when I spoke to her in Argegno. She couldn't wait for us to leave.'

'Might I make a suggestion?' George piped up. 'Mary has become quite friendly with some of the female staff. Perhaps she could ask about the young woman, and her history here at the hotel.'

'Yes, that's an excellent idea. Mary has a knack for getting people to talk to her,' Lucy said. 'It's quite a skill. People tell her their darkest secrets.'

'Luckily for us!' Phin said, going to the sideboard and topping up his glass. 'Anyone else?' he asked, holding up the decanter.

Lucy declined whilst George drained his glass and did the same. Lucy was glad to see some colour back in the valet's cheeks. Despite his calm demeanour, she suspected the evening's adventure had shaken him to his core.

'You may retire, George. I won't need you until the morning,' Phin said, as if reading her thoughts.

George's eyes widened. 'As you wish, sir,' he replied. With a bow to them both, George departed.

'The poor man,' Lucy said. 'That was quite a shock for him. For you both.'

Phin was frowning at the closed door. 'It was, and he isn't getting any younger. I only hope I do not lose him. I fear our investigations are a physical strain on him.'

'You will never lose him. He's devoted to you,' Lucy said, rising from her chair and joining him on the sofa. She took his hand. 'You look dreadful. Your face is paper-white, my dear. You need to retire and get some rest. We can discuss it all in the morning. I must admit I'm exhausted.' But Phin didn't appear to be listening. He was staring off into the distance. 'What is it?'

Slowly, he turned to her. 'I have a horrible feeling that we must have passed his killer. Kincaid can't have been in the water long. In fact, he was still warm to touch.' Lucy shivered as

Kincaid's staring eyes filled her mind. 'Did you see anyone you recognised as we walked to the lake? That man from Argegno, for instance?'

'No, but he could have come by water and escaped the same way.'

'That's true,' he replied.

'And don't forget, we met Giuseppe entering the hotel this evening as we were leaving,' Lucy replied.

'Hmm, so we did.'

THIRTY-ONE

Grand Hotel Bellagio, the next morning

The hotel gardens were beautifully kept and the ideal place to have a quiet conversation with Mary after breakfast. As they rounded the corner of the building, the heavenly scent of late roses, honeysuckle, and lavender wafted around them. After the previous evening's events, it was somewhat soothing to Lucy's ragged nerves. They strolled past the elaborate fountain, its jets of water catching the light as they fell into a marble basin. A gardener, working nearby, looked up and doffed his cap as they walked past. Lucy walked on, hoping there would be a secluded part of the garden where they wouldn't be disturbed by any of the other guests or staff.

When she spied a bench under a pergola in a remote corner, she pointed it out to Mary. 'Shall we? That looks ideal.' Once they were settled and she was sure no one was within earshot, Lucy asked the maid, 'Were you able to find anything out about Fiorella?'

'Well, ma'am, she had something of a checkered history, poor cratur. Caught stealing from guests' rooms and all!

Everyone was shocked. Said she was a lovely woman and couldn't understand it. But that didn't save 'er.'

Lucy frowned. 'Was she caught in the act by a guest or a member of staff?'

'No, ma'am, and that's what bothered 'em. Turns out her quarters were searched, and they found stolen items of jewellery and money hidden there. She claimed someone was setting her up, but the conte fired her on the spot.'

'I knew most of this, Mary,' Lucy said.

'Ah, but you may not know what happened next,' said Mary, looking rather pleased with herself.

'Go on!'

'The next day her father turns up here and there's a right to-do in the conte's office. That manager chap had to step in and calm things down. The conte was extremely angry and threatened to call the police in. Somehow, he was persuaded not to do that, which surprised a lot of people. But not if you think about it.'

'What do you mean?' Lucy asked.

'Well, ma'am, that wouldn't have gone down well. Everyone says you don't mess around with the Armano family, and you certainly don't make an enemy of 'em.'

But Luca was unlikely to think like that. Lucy had a feeling where this was leading, but had to ask. 'Why?'

Mary tilted her head and lowered her voice. 'Bruno Armano, Fiorella's da, 'eads up the biggest criminal family in the district.'

'The contessa implied something similar, saying the family wasn't respectable. But I had no idea that it was that bad.'

'Oh, it is, ma'am. Into all sorts, people say. Smuggling, thieving, the lot. Some of her friends said Fiorella is deeply ashamed and wants nothing to do with it. Was trying to become respectable by taking the job at the hotel.'

'Don't tell me. The family is based in Argegno, and we walked straight into the lion's den.'

Mary nodded. 'Yes, though by all accounts it's a huge family. One valet here described them as... now what was the word he used? Oh yes! A network, a spider's web. Said they can be found in every town and village in the region. Clever, that father of hers is. Works as a fisherman and owns a couple of businesses, too. To most people, he seems quite the business-man. All to cover up his less than legal carry-on. Most nights he's over the border, up to no good. Must be worth it, because seemingly those mountain passes are deadly at night.'

Lucy digested all of this for a few moments. 'I imagine they are treacherous! If it's common knowledge, the police must know about him.'

'That's just it, ma'am. It's said he has them in his pocket,' Mary replied.

'This gets worse and worse, Mary. I wonder if he was suspected of organising the diamond theft here at the hotel. The conte must have considered the possibility.'

Mary shrugged. 'No one said anything about that incident, ma'am.'

'Do you know, it would make sense if her father was the man in the cafe that day and why he followed us,' Lucy mused. She brought the waiter's image to mind. His appearance had been so ordinary. But then, his actions had been otherwise. An image of the cafe flashed into her mind. Lucy gave her maid a sheepish smile. 'Cafè Armano. That was the name of the place we met her.'

'Ah!'

'Dear Lord, Mary! What's wrong with me of late? I should have made that connection sooner.'

Mary gave her a knowing look. 'Can you not guess?'

Lucy's stomach flipped, for she knew what the maid was implying, but it was something she could not, nor would not, give credence to. She ignored the remark. 'This is all very useful, Mary,' she said. 'Thank you. If you hear anything else about her—'

Mary grinned. 'I'll let you know straightaway, ma'am.'

Lucy watched the maid depart and remained sitting in the shade, her mind in turmoil. She should have known Mary would guess. The early signs were there. Or was it wishful thinking? If Phin even suspected the truth, he would send her home. It was far too early to be sure. Besides, it was only a suspicion...

To Lucy's surprise, she found Phineas watching George put his clothes into a carpetbag when she returned to their suite. When Phin turned to her, he gave her a bleak smile and handed her a telegram. 'This arrived a short while ago. Progress at last!'

It was from Matteo.

Come to Milan immediately. Milan police officer has contacted me. Luca met him to discuss robberies at Bellagio. Matteo.

'I must go, Lucy. This could be the breakthrough we have been hoping for.'

'Of course you must,' she replied.

'And alone.' Phin exchanged a glance with George before taking her hand and drawing her over to the window and out onto the balcony. 'The situation is becoming extremely dangerous. Will you please consider leaving for England? It isn't safe to take you to Milan, and it certainly isn't safe to leave you here on your own. You do understand, don't you? Particularly after Kincaid's murder yesterday evening.'

Lucy pulled her hand out of his grasp. 'I do, but if you're that concerned for my safety, leave George with me for I wish to stay in Bellagio.'

His reaction was a sharp intake of breath, quickly followed by a look of resignation. 'Is there nothing I can say to change your mind?' he asked, but he was frowning down at her. Angry even. His cheeks flooded with colour.

Out of the corner of her eye, Lucy saw George slip out of the room. When the door shut, she turned away from Phin, trying to compose her jumbled thoughts.

'No. We're in this together,' she said at last. 'Otherwise, what's the point... of us?'

'Lucy!'

All colour had now drained from his face and she felt awful, but if she didn't stand her ground, their marriage would be a sham. 'You knew who I was when you married me. I'm impetuous, curious, and stubborn, often at the same time, but I can't change.'

Phin let out a long, slow breath. In all likelihood, he wanted to throttle her. 'Very well. I can't force you to go. Promise me this: do not leave the hotel without George.'

It was an olive branch.

She'd be a fool not to accept it.

THIRTY-TWO

Grand Hotel Bellagio

An hour later, Lucy leaned against the balcony rail and watched Phin stride down the path, her heart full of misgivings. The temptation to call him back was strong. To apologise for being such a termagant, as her father used to call her. Would he stay cross with her for long? At the gate, Phin turned and looked up. With a wave, he headed out the gate. He hadn't smiled. Blast! Lucy waited until his retreating form disappeared through the trees towards the town. Should she go after him? It was horrible parting this way.

Their lack of progress on the case weighed heavily on her. Whatever their differences, right now, what was more important was that his trip would be productive. The Milan police might have something significant to reveal. Above all, Kincaid's murder had to be the last. But what was she to do while Phin was away? She hated being idle. In what way could she help? With a groan, she turned away and walked back inside.

The worrying notion that Fiorella might be in danger was foremost in her mind. But Phin had shot down her idea of going back to Argegno with some force. Which, if she thought about it, wasn't that surprising. Indeed, it was sensible, but it was also frustrating. How could she speed up the investigation stuck in the hotel?

She paced the length of the suite in the hope her exasperation would evaporate.

It brought no relief.

Fiorella had to be an important link, especially with Kincaid dead. What if she had more information? Her relationship with Kincaid, whatever its nature, needed to be investigated. Could she have given Kincaid information which helped him solve the robbery of the diamonds? Information Kincaid then passed on to Luca. Which, inevitably, led to the conte's murder and Kincaid's as well, when the first attack in Como had failed.

Lucy paced once more.

Could her analysis be faulty? With a bit of luck, Matteo's enquiries might also help to fill in the gaps. Who had planted that newspaper article? It nearly drove her mad not knowing, and having to wait. But she'd just have to be patient. Damnation! This was going to be hard.

The restlessness would not ease. Her eyes fell on the novel she had been reading. That would pass a few hours. Lucy took the book out onto the balcony, sat down, and stared at a page for several minutes. It might as well have been in Chinese; nothing registered. Her gaze kept straying to the west. Argegno was calling to her, siren-like. She snapped the book shut with a grunt, only to allow the guilt she had suppressed bubble up. *How inconvenient it was to have a conscience!* Some devil within had stopped her from sharing Mary's information with Phin about Fiorella, and her father's row with Luca. But, she reasoned, she didn't know how it fitted into the bigger picture, anyway. It was something she could turn her mind to in Phin's absence. Could Signor Armano be angry enough to kill Luca if he felt the family honour had been challenged by Fiorella's dismissal? Hmm, that didn't really work, for by all accounts, the man hadn't wanted Fiorella to work at the hotel, anyway. But it could still be a motive. One that opened up a whole world of new possibilities. Someone should investigate further.

It would be criminal not to.

She paced the rooms of the suite yet again. What harm could come to her if she went? Argegno wasn't that far away. She could take both George and Mary...

George chose that moment to slip into the room to enquire if she needed anything. Again. Lucy didn't reply, but narrowed her eyes at him, and he scurried back out the door. Since Phin's departure, George and Mary were loitering. Not something either of them usually did. It was extremely irritating. Lucy detected Phin's hand in it and simmered. Popping in and out of the suite on the smallest of pretexts; did they think she was oblivious as to why? Phin's concern for her safety was touching and lovely, but it didn't sit well with her. Was she not more than capable of recognising danger? She was on the point of taking her chances and slipping downstairs when Mary appeared once more. Lucy smothered a sigh, but Mary's face was animated. She had news.

'Ma'am, have you heard?' the maid said.

'Pray tell! I hope it's something interesting, Mary, for I'm sure I shall expire from boredom. I need to be occupied.'

'Signor Carmosino, the conte's uncle, had a bad turn during the night.'

'Good Lord!'

'I heard it talked about below stairs and thought you'd want to know,' Mary said.

'Yes, indeed. Thank you. I wonder what brought that on?' Some exertion, perhaps, like killing a young man? 'How is he now?'

'They say he was lucky. It's his heart, ma'am. He's had

attacks before. The doctor has ordered him to rest in bed for a few days.'

Lucy's mind whirred. This was a golden opportunity and something she could do without leaving the hotel. Even Phin would have to approve. After all, before the summons to Milan, he had intended to question Giuseppe. 'Do you know where his suite is situated?'

With a tilt of her head, and a worried frown, Mary asked, 'Why? You're not thinking of visiting 'im?'

'But, Mary, it's an ideal opportunity. He's still a suspect in the conte's death as far as I'm concerned, and he would not tell Mr Stone where he was and what he was doing the day the conte disappeared. Furthermore, he was out yesterday evening around the time Kincaid was murdered. I think he has questions to answer about both deaths.'

Mary sniffed and gave her one of her sceptical looks. 'Did you not learn your lesson that time in Egypt? Confronting murderers is a dangerous business.'

'He's only a suspect. Besides, what can he do if he's bedridden, pray?'

'That depends. He might be malingering.' Mary's gaze grew cunning. 'I might have known you'd get up to mischief as soon as poor Mr Stone left.'

'I can't ignore this chance, Mary,' Lucy said. 'You must see that.'

'What I see, ma'am, is that the man will be at your mercy.'

Lucy's lips twitched. 'In a way, yes, I suppose he will.'

'I don't think it's a good idea, ma'am. Too dangerous! The master wouldn't like it,' Mary said.

'He doesn't need to worry about it... unless, of course, you and George are telling tales behind my back.'

Mary had the good grace to blush. 'We have our orders, ma'am. Mr Stone was adamant.'

'Do I need to remind you who it is you work for?'

Mary huffed. 'Mr Stone pays me wages these days. Begging your pardon, ma'am.'

A fair point, but Lucy was determined. 'After all we have been through together, Mary, where should your loyalty lie?' Lucy hoped a good glower at her maid would do the trick.

Mary muttered something under her breath. Then she shrugged. 'I should go with you, ma'am.'

For the first time that day, Lucy smiled.

Giuseppe Carmosino's suite of rooms took up a fair proportion of the upper floor of the central block of the hotel. Armed with some flowers procured hastily by George in the town, and with Mary in tow, Lucy knocked on his door. To her surprise, it was Luca's old valet who answered her knock.

'Oh! Enzo,' Lucy said. 'Is Signor Carmosino receiving visitors?'

The valet gave her a curt nod. 'I'm sure he would be delighted to see you, signora.' He stood back and ushered them into the opulent hallway. He waved towards a sofa. 'If you care to wait here a moment, I'll make sure he is comfortable.'

'Giving 'im warning, no doubt!' Mary whispered, as the valet tapped on a door further down and disappeared inside.

'Hush!' Lucy said. Now that she was here, her anxiety was growing. Perhaps this wasn't such a great idea.

Enzo returned. 'Signore is happy to see you.' He hesitated, his features full of concern. 'May I ask, madam, that you do not stay long? He is... how you say... weak. The doctor, he say, signore must be quiet.'

'Of course,' Lucy replied with a nod before sweeping past the valet, who was holding the door open for her. As prearranged, albeit reluctantly on the maid's part, Mary remained on the sofa in the hallway.

At the sight of Giuseppe propped up in bed, resting back

against a bank of pillows, Lucy was overcome with pity. The man had aged overnight. Lucy suspected the attack had been severe. He was pale, Lucy noted, and it was with a wary expression that he watched her approach the bed.

'Signora Stone,' he said, 'this is a surprise. And flowers, too. I'm honoured.' He waved to a chair pulled up by the side of his bed. 'Enzo!' he called out.

'Yes, signore,' the valet said, floating back into the bedroom.

'We're not to be disturbed. You may come back in half an hour.' The door closed and Giuseppe cleared his throat, his expression dour. 'It's very inconvenient not to have one's own staff around. That fellow has some strange ways about him. He fusses too much, and he is clumsy. I don't know how Luca tolerated the man.'

'As far as I'm aware, Luca was fond of him,' Lucy replied.

'Pah!'

'Where is your own man?'

Giuseppe gave her a sour look. 'Attending his sister's wedding.'

'I'm sure Revello could organise someone else if you wish,' Lucy remarked. 'When one is ill, it's comforting to have one's own staff around. Would you like me to talk to Revello?'

Giuseppe's lip curled. 'No! Leave it be. My own fellow will be back tomorrow.'

He's not in the best of moods, Lucy thought with a sinking feeling. *Nor is he the best of patients, like most men. Enzo is probably an excellent valet.* She dropped the flowers on a nearby table, then sat down, doing her best to ignore the patient's disposition. It would take a great deal of effort to be pleasant to the man. But she had to try if she were to get anything useful from him.

'I'm sorry to hear you're ill, signore. The contessa would never forgive me for not making sure that you're being well looked after.'

His brows shot up at that and he half-smiled. 'Forgive *me*, but I doubt she cares one way or the other, now she is back where she belongs. Her behaviour is a disgrace.'

'What do you mean?'

'Running away like that. What kind of example is that for little Salvo? The poor child needs to be here, at home. How can I mentor him if he is in England?' He sniffed. 'That mother of his wants to undermine me. She cannot bear to think of me having any influence. But I ask you, who else can teach him what he needs to know to become the next conte?'

Lucy suppressed a biting retort and tried to smile. If she took the bait and let fly, he'd probably ask her to leave, and she would find out nothing.

'On the contrary, you do Elvira a great disservice. I'm sure that she would welcome any help you can give... when the time is right. Despite your nastiness, let me tell you that she defended you before she left.'

'I'm flattered!' he said with a nasty side-eyed look.

'And I sent her a telegram to inform her you were unwell. I've no doubt you will hear from her directly.'

'You are *too* kind,' he said with a heavenward roll of his eyes. 'No doubt she will dash back to be by my bedside.'

He's testing me. Don't react.

'The contessa would be concerned for any of Luca's family. If she were in Bellagio, she would be visiting you, not I.'

Giuseppe spluttered with laughter. 'Nice words. You do her proud, but I care not for token gestures.'

'You really are the most disagreeable man,' Lucy said, now exasperated beyond endurance.

He cocked a brow, his eyes lighting up. 'And you are an annoying female who should know her place.' Then he grinned, a wicked glint in his eye. 'Now, we know where we stand.'

'Yes, indeed,' Lucy said, sucking in a breath. 'Luckily, I believe in plain-speaking, too.'

This time, he laughed heartily. 'So, tell me why you're really here? Was it curiosity? Or was it to speed me on my way to the cemetery in Milan to join my ancestors?'

'You do have a lovely opinion of me, sir,' she replied with a raised brow. 'But it was boredom, pure and simple, which drew me here. My husband has been called away to Milan.'

'Has he now? No doubt poking his nose in where it isn't wanted,' Giuseppe said, his tone as dry as dust. 'Why can he not accept that Luca's death was an accident and let my poor nephew rest in peace?'

'Oh, really? You had a very different suggestion before,' she replied.

Giuseppe grunted and threw her an angry glance.

'His death was no accident or suicide. Whatever befell him had something to do with those diamonds... and this hotel.'

'Nonsense! If it had, I would know about it,' he snarled. 'I would have done something.'

'Is that so? Perhaps you did do something about it. Luca's death may even be down to *you*.' Giuseppe made an angry gesture with his hands, apparently speechless. Had she gone too far? Lucy drove on. 'Then pray tell why a woman, who used to work here, intimated that the hotel was at the centre of it all.'

Giuseppe flinched and his face drained of what little colour was left in it. 'You speak of Fiorella Armano, no doubt.'

'I do!'

Giuseppe frowned and looked towards the window with a sigh. If Lucy didn't know better, he was attempting to compose himself. How strange!

'I have no idea what she meant by that, but I can tell you she is a kind-hearted young woman, much maligned. Efficient, too. I was sorry to see her go.' He turned back to her. 'She was certainly no thief. I never accepted that nonsense.'

'If she wasn't the thief, do you know who was?' she asked.

'No. It was no longer my place to interfere in such a matter. Luca had it in hand... he was adamant.'

'Have you seen Fiorella of late?' she asked.

'Do you think I associate with servants, dismissed or otherwise?' he growled.

'Your defence of her suggests—'

'What?' he almost shouted.

'I'm not trying to suggest anything untoward,' Lucy replied.

Giuseppe's head snapped back. 'I hope not!'

Lucy reckoned he knew more and was reluctant to say. 'Why do *you* believe she was innocent?'

'Because I knew her. I was the one who hired her originally, and it wasn't an easy decision, for her family are notorious. I was advised not to risk it, but I liked her and took a chance. But unfortunately, when the accusations began to fly, I could do nothing for her. Revello searched her room and found jewellery missing from a guest's room. There had been a spate of robberies over the previous months. Luca's only concern was the reputation of the hotel. He dismissed her, despite her claims of innocence.'

'As far as I understand, no one saw her steal. Someone could have left those items in her room to make her look guilty,' Lucy said. 'I mean, it would be a silly place to leave them if she were the thief. There must be far better hiding places in a hotel this large.'

'Exactly! That's the most intelligent utterance I've ever heard from your lips.'

Lucy spluttered. 'I suppose I should thank you for that.'

His answer was yet another scowl. 'Fiorella is a good and devout woman, but she is timid. She wouldn't stand up for herself. And it was a strange coincidence, the whole affair,' he said, his brows drawing together.

'How so?'

'The previous day, I overheard her and Revello arguing. I

don't know what it was about, but she rushed out of Revello's office in floods of tears and ran past me. She isn't one of those highly strung women who cries at the merest inconvenience. Whatever passed between them was serious. I was curious and when I went into his office to question him, I found him pacing and furious. He refused to tell me what the argument was about. And then, the very next day, she was dismissed.'

'She must have been angry and devastated. I understand her father wasn't too pleased about it either.'

'You heard about that?' he asked. Lucy just raised her brows. 'Yes. There was an unfortunate scene the following day. He arrived, all bluster, demanding to see Luca. The row was spectacular. The entire incident was peculiar because even I was aware how much Armano hated Fiorella having a job here. He should have been pleased she would have to go back to her old life.'

'It was a matter of honour, perhaps,' Lucy said.

Giuseppe's response was a grunt. 'And Luca, of course, was equally angry. The robberies were damaging the hotel's reputation. The confrontation was volcanic. Luckily, Revello intervened, and Armano left. I saw Luca afterwards. He was badly shaken.'

'And that was the end of it?'

Giuseppe gave her a funny look. 'What do you mean?'

'Well, if a notorious criminal like Bruno Armano wanted satisfaction, who knows what he might do? He may have had a hand in Luca's disappearance.' Giuseppe stared back at her as if she were mad. 'I met him,' Lucy continued.

'How? Why?'

'Not on purpose. I was looking for Fiorella. On first acquaintance, he seemed a benign sort of man.'

'The man's a scoundrel,' Giuseppe scoffed. 'A smuggler by night, an innocent cafe owner by day. He is untouchable. He pays off the police to turn a blind eye. His sons are thugs. Some

say they are worse than him.' Giuseppe pulled himself up into a
more comfortable position.

'Can you tell me anything about the diamond robbery?' she
asked, thinking a change of topic might be strategic at this point.

'No.'

'No?'

'I wasn't here when it happened,' he ground out.

'Do you know any of the details?'

'Only what Luca told me. The jewels were taken while the
Wallaces were at dinner in the hotel,' he said.

'And the insurance investigator, Mr Kincaid, did you have
any dealings with him?'

'Is that the fellow who drowned yesterday evening?'

'Yes.'

'He had no interest in me. As I said, I was away when the
theft occurred.'

'Yesterday evening, Phineas and I met you at the gates when
we were leaving the hotel. We were on our way to meet
Kincaid. And you were coming back from... somewhere.'

Giuseppe treated her to a withering glance. 'Yes. I was
coming back from *somewhere*. What I do and where I go is none
of your business.'

'Normally, I would agree, sir. But a young man is dead.'

He scowled. 'Perhaps *you* killed him.'

'No! Of course we didn't!' Lucy was appalled. 'We *found*
him. Floating just offshore. It was horrible,' she replied, doing
her best to block out the image of the poor man on the beach;
Phin pushing the strands of hair from his white face and those
staring eyes. Lucy's stomach flipped with nausea.

'You've gone very pale. Are you unwell?' Giuseppe asked,
narrowing his eyes. 'Don't be ill in my room. I have enough to
contend with.'

Lucy swallowed a couple of times, hoping to settle her stomach. 'May I have some of your water, please?'

He nodded towards the carafe and glasses on his bedside table. 'There's stronger stuff on the sideboard in the salon,' he said, waving across to a door on the other side of the room.

'No, no, water would be fine. Would you like a glass?' Lucy asked as she poured.

'No, thank you.'

Lucy sipped the water, and the sensation eased. 'You didn't answer my question. Where were you yesterday evening before seven o'clock?'

'That's straight talking indeed. You sound like a policeman, madam.'

'I'll take that as a compliment,' Lucy quipped.

Giuseppe's eyes burned in response. 'If you must know, I was taking my usual evening walk. Ask anyone who works here at the hotel. I stroll into Bellagio and back before dinner, weather permitting. It gives me an appetite.' He gave her a grim smile. 'It, however, doesn't appear to have helped me avoid a heart spasm. Dr Spina tells me I must eat a simpler diet and drink less from now on.'

'Not bad advice for a man of your age,' Lucy replied.

'Oho! Signora, you pull no punches – isn't that the English expression? Well, Spina may go to the devil! What's the point of being alive if you can't enjoy it!' He cocked his head, eyes glinting. 'Did you have me down as a murderer? I'm sure that notion gave you great pleasure. What a thrill it must be to enter my den!'

His remark was so close to her own thoughts, only minutes before while waiting to be announced, that it took the wind out of her sails for a moment. 'As I said, I don't like coincidences,' Lucy muttered. Dare she admit this exchange was proving enjoyable.

To her surprise, the fire died in his eyes. 'I didn't harm him or anyone else in any way, signora,' he said, a little above a whisper. Something in his tone convinced Lucy he was telling the truth. Perhaps she had been wrong about this man. He was no saint, certainly, but perhaps Phin was right. Life had dealt him difficult cards. Every setback in his life had added to a pool of bitterness in his soul. Had she judged him too quickly?

'Will you answer one question for me about Luca's death?' she asked after a few moments, when he looked as if he had recovered his composure.

Giuseppe stiffened. 'What about it?' he snapped. 'Can't you leave well enough alone, woman!'

Lucy ignored this, determined to get something useful from him. 'Where were you on the day he disappeared? Phineas said you refused to answer when he asked you.'

'Such impertinence!' he exclaimed, but Lucy threw him a quizzing look. He glared back. 'All I'm willing to say is that a lady's reputation is at stake,' he growled, his gaze slipping away.

A mistress! Now, I hadn't expected that! Lucy mulled this over for a moment. 'She's married?' she asked, and he gave her a curt nod and an icy stare. 'Why did you not tell Phineas this? He is a man of the world.'

'I didn't like his tone,' replied Giuseppe.

'Is that so? Enough to do something about it? Did you have anything to do with my husband being followed the day he met you? Someone attempted to shoot him, except they targeted the wrong person.'

'Absolutely not! I take exception to such a suggestion, madam. He's as annoying as you, but he was, I must admit, enjoyable company over lunch. If I recall, I took a nap when he left. You may ask my personal valet when he returns to the hotel tomorrow.' Then he glowered at her. 'Have you nothing sensible to ask me?'

'For now, no,' she said, getting to her feet.

'Thank goodness for that,' he sniped. 'Close the door on your way out.'

. . .

Lucy headed back towards her suite, so caught up in what Giuseppe had revealed that it took her a moment to realise that Mary was trying to get her attention.

'Sorry, Mary. What is it?' Lucy asked, just as they reached the suite.

Once the door was closed, Mary stood, hopping from one foot to the other. 'It was that Enzo, ma'am. Well, you know how the signore dismissed him when you went in?'

'Yes, I do.'

'He ignored him. He didn't leave the suite. Instead, he went into the room next door and closed over the door. I could hear your conversation with the signore. Mind, not that I was eavesdropping, ma'am.'

'Of course not, Mary. But you think Enzo was listening in, too?'

'Why else did he stay? Seems to me he's nosy,' the maid said with a curt nod of her head.

'Hmm, the question is why. Was he eavesdropping for his own benefit, or is he working for someone else? Lord, Mary! I'm beginning to think everyone in this hotel is hiding something.'

'It's these foreigners, ma'am. There's no trustin' 'em!'

THIRTY-THREE

Grand Hotel Bellagio, early afternoon, the following day

I think I'm going mad, Lucy thought, as she sipped her tea and resumed her bored surveillance of the outside world from her balcony. She had heard nothing from Phin since he had departed. What was happening in Milan? Was Phineas safe? It wasn't beyond the bounds of possibility that another attempt could be made on his life. She cringed. He had left George behind to protect her. If anything happened to him, it would be her fault for being so stubborn. She would drive herself insane, thinking like that. Phin knew how to defend himself. A little calmer, her thoughts turned to more practical matters. What would the police reveal to him? It had to be important; otherwise, why would Matteo have insisted that Phineas travel to hear it in person?

Lucy heard the door of the suite open and seconds later, Mary's face appeared at the balcony door. 'There you are, ma'am.'

'Where else would I be, Mary?' Lucy sighed. Then she

spied the note clutched in the maid's hand. Hopefully, it was news from Milan. 'What do you have there?'

Mary handed it to her. 'This was hand-delivered to reception.' The maid turned to leave.

'Hold on, Mary. I may need to send a reply.'

Much to Lucy's astonishment, the message was from Esposito from Villa Carmosino. The contents made her smile.

'Fetch my coat and hat, Mary. We're going on a little excursion.'

Hands on hips, the maid stared at her. 'The master said we weren't to leave the hotel. Too dangerous. And George ain't here. He's gone to the post office to check if there's any news from the master. He was afraid anything delivered here would be interfered with.'

'That's good thinking, certainly. But we're only going back to the villa. We don't need George for that. We can take a cab. Now, hurry. Someone is waiting to see me.'

Esposito was all apologies when Lucy arrived at Villa Carmosino. 'She was most insistent, ma'am, even though I explained you had moved to the hotel and she should seek you there.'

'Don't concern yourself. She has her reasons.' Esposito didn't look convinced, but Lucy smiled. 'Take me to her, please.' She turned to Mary, who still wore a look of disapproval. 'I won't be long.'

'I should go with you, ma'am,' the maid replied.

'There is no need. She means me no harm, and I want her to talk freely.'

The butler led the way to one of the small reception rooms at the rear of the house. Sitting on the edge of her seat, looking uncomfortable, was Fiorella Armano. She jumped to her feet as Lucy entered the room.

Lucy smiled and waved for the young woman to sit down. 'I understand you wish to speak to me. May I call you Fiorella?'

The woman blinked at her, much like a scared rabbit, then nodded and sank back down onto the edge of the seat.

Lucy settled herself and smiled again, hoping to reassure her. But the woman before her was a bag of nerves, constantly lacing her fingers in her lap.

Fiorella threw a nervous glance at the door. 'I'm sorry you had to come here,' she began. 'I thought you would be here... ma'am. I can't enter the hotel. It's too dangerous.'

Lucy's heart skipped a beat. 'I understand. It's not an issue,' she answered, anxious to reassure her. 'I was happy to come. Senor Carmosino, Giuseppe, spoke highly of you. He doesn't believe that you were stealing at the hotel. I share that belief.'

Fiorella exhaled, her eyes bright with tears. 'I am no thief.'

'I believe you. The evidence against you was far too convenient.' Fiorella clamped her mouth and slowly nodded. 'My impression of you is that you are a decent person, and you want to help. You want the truth to be known. Am I right?'

Fiorella nodded once more.

'Good. Now, what did you wish to tell me?'

The young woman chewed her bottom lip before she asked, 'Is it true that Mr Kincaid is dead?'

'Yes.'

The poor woman stiffened, her eyes widening in fear. 'How did he die?' It was almost a whisper.

'My husband and I are sure he was murdered,' Lucy said, 'possibly because he wished to speak to us. It's my belief that he was going to reveal who the diamond thief was, or a possible connection to the murder of the conte.'

Fiorella's hand flew up to her mouth. '*Mio Dio!*'

Lucy sat forward. 'I saw you with Kincaid. Outside the hotel. Your conversation... well, it appeared to me that you were arguing.'

'He took advantage,' Fiorella said.

Lucy's brow shot up. 'Good grief!'

'No, not like that. I explained to him that I needed money to get away. I told him... what he wanted to know, but then he refused to pay. Said I must wait until the case was closed.'

'Hmm.' Lucy blew out her cheeks. Typical Kincaid. He had never been the most honourable. It was unlikely that he would have shared his reward with the unfortunate woman. 'Did you tell anyone about your arrangement with Kincaid?'

'No, no,' she replied, her eyes popping.

Lucy wondered if the woman in front of her realised the true nature of her predicament. Whoever had killed Luca and Kincaid would have no qualms about killing Fiorella. 'You do realise you're in danger, Fiorella? You need protection.' Lucy asked.

'This is my fault,' Fiorella replied as she sank in on herself. 'My fault.'

'No! Someone evil is behind all of this. All you did was tell the truth. So, if you told Kincaid the truth, you did a good thing.' Lucy let her words sink in. 'What did you tell him?'

Fear flashed in Fiorella's eyes. 'I can't tell you. You will die, too!'

Lucy pushed down her frustration. 'No, I won't. I'm careful. Now, you must trust me. Do you know who stole the diamonds?'

A wary expression settled on Fiorella's features. 'I... I will not say.'

'Then why have you brought me here?' Lucy said, unable to quell her irritation. 'Why are you wasting my time? If you know anything about the conte's death or Kincaid's, you must tell me.'

Fiorella sat immobile, not meeting Lucy's gaze. At last, she looked up. 'I came to tell you that my father' – her voice cracked – 'my father is not a good man. The hotel manager, he comes to my father and they do business together.'

It was as if the temperature in the room had suddenly dropped. 'What? Revello?'

Fiorella jumped up as if to leave. 'I have said enough. Too much.'

'Wait!' Lucy cried, rising off her chair, her heart pounding in her chest as the implications crystallised in her head. She grabbed Fiorella's arm. 'You must be careful. You could be in danger, too. Revello! I can't believe it. Are you sure?' Lucy was aghast. Revello and Luca had been close friends. 'Did you see them together?'

'Many times,' Fiorella said. 'Revello brought stolen items to my father to dispose of.'

Lucy was horrified, but confused, too. 'Was he the thief at the hotel? It doesn't make a lot of sense.'

Fiorella shrugged. 'This, I don't know. He come to my father, my father give him money for the trinkets. That is all I know.'

'Did Revello find out that you knew what was going on?'

Fiorella blushed. 'He must have guessed.'

'Yes, he must. And then he set you up as a scapegoat. I'm so sorry, Fiorella. You didn't deserve that. What will you do now? What if your father finds out?'

The young woman gave her a sad smile and pulled away. Then she stooped down and picked up a large carpetbag from the floor. 'I'm leaving Laglio di Como. For good.'

Lucy was relieved to hear it. 'Where will you go?'

Fiorella's eyes widened. 'As far away from here as possible. Please, I must go. I will pray for you,' was her parting and rather ominous remark as she fled out the door.

THIRTY-FOUR

Once back at the hotel, Lucy summoned George and Mary for a council of war, and quickly explained what Fiorella had revealed. Her servants exchanged a worried glance, which did nothing for Lucy's peace of mind; her heart hadn't stopped racing since her conversation with Fiorella.

'Ma'am, we should leave immediately. We cannot be safe here,' George said.

His words increased her sense of panic, and she began to pace. 'You are right, George. But if we run, Armano and Revello may suspect we know of their association.' She wrung her hands. 'This is so frustrating. We have no proof, only hearsay, yet I doubt Fiorella would have risked so much to tell me a lie. The woman is terrified and has made her escape. But I'm struggling to believe what she said. Revello was the conte's closest friend. Why would he betray him? He's a respectable man. Why would he associate with a criminal?' Lucy ran her hand across her forehead. Her head was thumping. 'Could Fiorella be mistaken? Could there have been another more innocent reason for Revello to associate with Armano?'

George mulled this over for a moment or two. 'I doubt there

is anything innocent about it, ma'am. Armano is a criminal. Fencing stolen items would be easy for him.'

'For a cut of the proceeds. Yes, that makes sense,' Lucy said. 'But could Revello be a petty thief?'

'I'd hazard he had someone doing it for him, ma'am,' George replied.

'Yes, he'd hardly risk doing it himself. And he would have known about the diamonds. It would be a bold move, but perhaps they had grown overconfident and couldn't resist the opportunity.'

'It still doesn't explain how the gems came to be in the pocket of the conte, ma'am,' he replied.

'There could be countless reasons for that. The jewels were well known, so would have been difficult to sell. The thieves may have wanted to get rid of them, thinking the body would not be found. Or, as Mr Stone suggested, it was a way of besmirching the Carmosino name in retaliation for... something. My firm belief is that Fiorella gave Kincaid the relevant information, which he then shared with the conte. Luca must have decided to pursue it himself: hence, the trip to Milan and his visit to his solicitor and the police. Somehow, our suspects discovered this and felt threatened and decided to take action.'

'Your theory is sound, ma'am,' George said, which pleased Lucy.

'The poor conte,' Mary said with a sigh. 'He was doomed.'

'Yes, I fear you are right. And do you know what worries me? The night Kincaid was attacked in Como, Revello was there, too, as part of the search party. Could he have slipped away and done the deed?'

George's demeanour was grave. 'Yes, we were all working alone to cover as many hostelries as we could that evening. If Revello spotted Kincaid in the street, he may have decided to silence him. Once and for all.'

'And now Kincaid is dead, so we will never know for sure,'

Lucy said. 'Is there any other way we can tie Revello to all of this?'

'From what we have heard, Armano's main business is smuggling,' George replied. 'It wouldn't surprise me to learn that he is supplying smuggled items to Revello for the hotel. One of Revello's duties is purchasing supplies.'

'Ah! You think he is buying smuggled goods from Armano, and pocketing the difference?'

'That would seem feasible, and I imagine highly lucrative,' he replied. 'The conte wouldn't have bothered with such day-to-day matters if he trusted Revello.'

'Unfortunately, the conte did trust him. However, we would need to find proof. I can't confront Revello without it.'

George sucked in a breath and Mary's eyes popped. Then he cleared his throat. 'Ma'am, I would respectfully suggest you leave any confrontation to Mr Stone.'

Much as she hated to admit it, she knew that would be a wiser course of action. Treading carefully had to be the order of the day. 'Oh, very well. Still, in the meantime, as we're here in the thick of it, so to speak, we could at least try to find some evidence.'

'I've an idea about that. Leave it to me, ma'am,' George replied. 'I have access to places you do not.'

Lucy smiled back at him. 'I'll concede that point. I wouldn't have any idea where to start to prove any of it, anyway. Let us hope we are successful. Fiorella has probably disappeared already, and she'll not want to testify against Revello or her father, nor do I blame her. I wish she hadn't rushed off like that. It can't be safe for her. But I can't go to the police to help her. It sounds very much as if they are in the pay of her father, from what Giuseppe Carmosino said.'

'We must warn Mr Stone about both men,' George said.

'Would you send him a telegram? But not from here, George. From the post office in town.'

· · ·

It was two hours later when George entered the suite, a spring in his step. Lucy guessed he had made some progress.

'Well?' she asked. 'Have you news? Did you find anything?'

George smiled. 'It was easier than I thought, ma'am. I was passing the gentlemen's smoking room and saw one of the hotel staff refilling the enamel boxes of cigars on the tables. I went in with the excuse that I needed to replenish Mr Stone's supply.'

'And?'

'The man held out the box from which he was replenishing the stock, so that I could take some. It was a Swiss brand, not Italian. Naturally, I made no comment to him and took a few of the cigars,' George said, pulling several cigars out of his pocket to show her.

'I waited outside the room and then followed the fellow back downstairs. My luck was in, as he led me to the stockroom in the basement. Once he had taken himself off, I had a look inside.'

'It was unlocked?' she asked.

'Eh, no, ma'am,' George said, the colour rising in his face. 'Mr Stone...'

'You can pick a lock, too,' Lucy cut in with a grin.

'Only when strictly necessary,' he replied.

'Don't worry, I won't reveal your secret.'

'Thank you, ma'am.' He cleared his throat. 'Sure enough, hidden at the back there were sacks of salt with *Suisse* on the side, and many boxes of cigars, all the same Swiss brand as I had seen in the smoking room. I took a box and hid it in my room to show Mr Stone on his return.'

'Well done, George. Excellent work,' Lucy said. 'It would appear Fiorella was telling us the truth and your theory is correct. Revello and Armano must be working together, possibly for years, with Revello pocketing the difference.'

'Is it possible that the conte had discovered this?' George asked.

'I don't think so. If he had, he would have dismissed Revello on the spot. Unless, of course, his investigations had uncovered something even more sinister, more serious, and he was biding his time.'

'The diamonds? The conte was searching for evidence,' George said.

Lucy nodded. 'I think so. Poor Luca. He must have been devastated to learn of his friend's betrayal.'

'Perhaps there was more than one,' George said, his tone grim. 'The valet.'

Lucy sucked in her breath. 'Yes! He could have been feeding back information to Revello. Luca must have realised and that's why he left him behind in Milan. That's the only explanation that makes sense.' And Revello had specifically asked Elvira if he could employ Enzo. Was that some kind of payback for the valet's help?

But then she followed her train of thought to its logical conclusion. If Mary was right, Enzo had been eavesdropping on her conversation with Giuseppe. If he had gone running to Revello about it, was she in danger? Now, that was an uncomfortable notion, especially with Phin so far away.

Lucy was sitting at the desk writing a letter to Lady Sarah when she heard voices drifting up from the front courtyard of the hotel. Lucy walked out onto the balcony and leaned over the balustrade. It was Revello, chatting to a couple of guests. She pulled back slightly, afraid he would see her, but he bid the guests good day and strolled off down towards the entrance. Where was he off to? Lucy wondered. It might be important now they knew he was not quite as benign a character as they had previously thought. This was too good an opportunity to miss. She'd have to follow to see what he was up to. Lucy grabbed a jacket, shoved her hat on, almost stabbing herself in the head with the hatpin, and scooted out the door.

Lucy received a few dubious stares as she flew down the main staircase. But she had no time to be ladylike, she had to hurry. At the front gate, however, she had to pause. Firstly, to catch her breath, but also to discover which direction Revello had taken. This was silly. She should have waited on the balcony to see where he went. However, it was probable Revello was headed into the town. She'd have to take a chance.

That's what you get for being impetuous, my girl! She could almost hear Phin's reprimand and hesitated. But what harm could it do to follow and observe? It was broad daylight. Even if Revello spotted her, it was perfectly normal for ladies to wander around the shops. But, to Lucy's consternation, as she entered the Piazzale Imbarcadero, she had to stop once more, overcome with dizziness. The bones in her corset were pressing against her stomach, making it difficult to breathe. Mary had tightened her stays too much. Or could there be another reason? She dismissed that train of thought with a shake of her head. No, it must be the heat.

As Lucy waited, breathing as shallowly as she could manage, she searched the crowd. Then, she spotted Revello coming out of the chemist shop in the arcade, a parcel under his arm. What luck! She hadn't lost him, after all. Crossing her fingers he wouldn't come back towards her, she paused, shielding behind a group of tourists examining the ferry timetable. With relief, she saw Revello turn right and almost immediately he turned up into one of the side streets. After a moment or two, Lucy followed.

But at the turn, she stopped, muttering under her breath as she surveyed the flight of steps before her. He would have to choose such a steep route. Just wonderful! But Revello was nearly out of sight. She had to decide. Follow or not? Sucking in a deep breath, she began the climb. The only saving grace was that the laneway, for that was all you could describe it as, was in the shade of the bordering buildings. But for all that, she was only halfway up when she had to stop and lean against the wall. This was ludicrous! What was wrong with her? Worst still, Revello was too far ahead. A bend in the laneway, as it meandered uphill, meant he was now out of sight. Still, she had come this far. No point in backing out now.

Moments later, she restarted her ascent. As she rounded the corner, Lucy was astonished to see a tunnel ahead where the lane continued under a building. A church tower dominated the skyline directly above, and as she approached, she realised the tunnel was only a few yards long and that a street ran perpendicular to it. Lucy hurried through, but stalled at the opening. Anxious not to be spotted, she slowly peered out. The street was almost deserted. Bother! There was no sign of Revello. *All that effort for nothing*, she thought, her fists curling. He could have gone in either direction. Maybe it was a shortcut, and he had gone home to Maria. That would serve her right for disobeying Phin!

Disappointed, Lucy leaned against the cool wall of the tunnel, berating herself for not being quick enough. Phin wouldn't have failed like this. Drat the man! Perhaps Revello would come back the same way. But how long might he be? And she couldn't risk being seen loitering around here. How could she explain lingering in the passageway? It might be better to wait down at the piazalle, where she could lose herself in the crowds. Her presence there would look innocent enough.

Not without regret, Lucy straightened and turned to head back down the steps. But she drew up short. That sounded like raised voices close by and one was a deep baritone. A familiar one. It was Revello; she would swear to it. Her mood vastly improved, Lucy went back to the entrance of the tunnel and stepped out onto the street, turning to look at the building.

Where were the voices coming from? As she strained to hear, the voices rose in volume. They were coming from a doorway to her left. It was a tiny church, with a plaque on the wall proclaiming it to be Chiesa di San Giorgio. The wooden door was shut, so Lucy followed a path down the side of the church. There were two windows in the side wall, but they were up too high for her to see inside. Besides, the conversation inside was in Italian. She could have cried with frustration. Eavesdropping was pointless. Even if one man was Revello, she had no way of knowing what they were discussing. But Lucy's curiosity as to the identity of the other man was raging. She had to find out who it was. What she needed was a safe place to observe the door without being seen.

Across the road was a high wall, and further down the street were steps leading into what appeared to be a house and garden. Thankfully, the road was quiet, with only a few people about. Lucy waited for a man with a horse and cart to pass by, then she ran across to the steps, hitched up her skirts and climbed. Fortunately, the garden she entered was steep. The wall was high with a hollow at the base, not overlooked by the house above. Lucy crouched down and waited. Hopefully, she would hear the church door open and have time to spy on whoever emerged.

They are an awfully long time in there, Lucy thought some ten minutes later, as she winced at the cramp in her leg. *What could they be arguing about?* She stretched out her leg and rubbed the back. Then it struck her how incongruous her situation was. It would be highly embarrassing if anyone spotted her. Then she smiled at the thought of her mother's horrified face if she could see her now, huddled behind a wall, spying on strangers.

The sound of wood scraping on stone broke into Lucy's thoughts. At last! There was more conversation, more civilised now though, and she was sure it was the same voices. As she heard footsteps on the cobbles, walking away from her, she took a chance and peeped over the wall in time to see Revello retracing his steps down into the tunnel. The other man was walking back along the road towards the town centre.

It was Bruno Armano, and he was now carrying Revello's parcel.

THIRTY-FIVE

Grand Hotel Bellagio

Curiosity won over prudence, and Lucy followed Bruno Armano back through the streets of Bellagio. Where was he off to and what had Revello given him? Much to her disappointment, Armano neither stopped nor spoke to anyone of interest. However, it was obvious he was well known as he was frequently greeted by passersby. Lucy wondered if she imagined the hasty greetings from the locals, the unsmiling faces, and the reluctance of people to linger and chat to him. If he was as bad a rogue as Giuseppe made out, it wasn't too surprising. Though why he did a circuit of the town before ending up at the pier was a bit of a mystery. Was he afraid of being followed, or making his presence felt? Lucy hung around the shops in the arcade until she had seen him board the steamer. She had learned little, but at least she had proof that Revello and Armano knew each other well. Tired and now fed up, she made her way slowly back to the hotel.

On entering the suite, a squeak greeted Lucy, Mary rushing towards her, wide-eyed and pale. George appeared from the adjoining bedroom. He, too, wore a worried expression. As soon as she was inside, he rushed to the door, peering out into the corridor before closing and locking it.

'Oh, ma'am, where have you been? We've been frantic,' Mary said, wringing her hands. 'We thought you were in trouble and someone had run off with you.'

'I'm sorry. I didn't mean to worry you, but an opportunity arose to see what Revello was up to, and I took it,' Lucy said, removing her hatpin and hat and handing them to Mary. The maid took the items in silence, her expression grim.

'Ma'am,' George began, then stalled, clamping his lips. 'We didn't know what had happened. If you were in trouble. Where you could be.'

Lucy's conscience prickled. 'Yes, I can see how that might be. You're quite right. I shouldn't have rushed off like that without telling you or leaving a note.'

George frowned. 'Or on your own.'

'The master would have our hides if anything happened to you,' Mary said in a wagging-of-a-finger tone.

Lucy plonked down onto a chair and drew a hand over her brow. 'He would, of course. You're right. It was foolish of me. I won't do it again. I promise.' She glanced up at the two anxious faces and gave them an apologetic smile.

George cleared his throat before walking over to the sideboard just inside the door and picking up an envelope from a letter salver. 'While I was at the post office sending the telegram to Mr Stone, the postmaster handed me this. It's from Mr Stone. I imagine it's urgent.' He handed her a letter.

Lucy gasped and tore the envelope open.

Dearest Lucy,

I have learned much since arriving in Milan. Firstly, Matteo has spoken to the editor of the newspaper. The man was reluctant at

first to reveal the source of the article, and it was only when
Matteo threatened to withdraw the hotel's advertising that the
man gave him the name. It was Francesco Revello. Worrying as
this information is, it's nothing compared to what we learned
from the Milan police inspector. Commissario Falcone only
learned of Luca's death a few days ago on his return from Sicily,
where he attended the funeral of his mother. He was shocked, for
as we had speculated, Luca had indeed contacted the police
during those missing hours. Falcone had been stationed briefly at
Como, where Luca had met him over some local matter. Luca
turned up unannounced at Falcone's station, asking to speak
to him.

During their meeting, Luca told the commissario that he could
not trust the local police, as they were in the pocket of the local
criminal gang. Luca told Falcone he suspected his manager was
facilitating the theft of jewellery from guests and taking a cut
from the criminals. The issue, from Falcone's point of view, was
that Luca had no evidence, only suspicion, but he had promised
Luca he would investigate. Unfortunately, Falcone's mother
passed away, and he had to travel south. It was the commissario's
intention to begin the investigation on his return.

My dear, I do not know if Revello found out about Luca's suspicions and decided to kill him. As I said before, the valet's part in
this could well be informant, which would explain Luca leaving
him behind that day in his dash back to Como. However, we
must assume Revello had some part to play in Luca's disappearance and death.

Matteo, the commissario and I are leaving for Como immediately. However, for your own safety, I implore you to remove
yourself from Grand Hotel Bellagio as quickly as possible.
George will make the arrangements. I beg of you, do not investi-

*gate anything. I would suggest you go to Menaggio. George can
leave your direction for me at the post office in Bellagio.*

Yours, Phineas.

'Well!' Lucy exclaimed, not sure whether to be alarmed at
the content of the letter or pleased that it confirmed what she
had figured out herself.

'Ma'am?' George asked.

'Best you read this, George,' she said, handing it to him. She
watched as he scanned the page.

'Very good, ma'am. I shall return to the post office and
arrange accommodation and transport as soon as possible.'

'Do be careful, George,' Lucy said. With a nod and a plea to
keep the door locked until his return, George left the room.
Lucy turned to Mary. 'We need to pack and be ready to leave
when George returns.'

Mary nodded. 'Don't you fret, ma'am. It won't take me
long.'

'Thank goodness. I don't know what's wrong with me,
Mary. I'm at sixes and sevens these last few days.'

'I think you do know, ma'am,' Mary said with a twinkle in
her eye. 'No monthlies,' she whispered. 'And you are as regular
as clock-work, normally.'

Lucy stared at her. Counted back the weeks.

Then inhaled an unsteady breath.

She didn't dare hope. It had to be a false alarm; she was just
late. She couldn't be pregnant. After all, she was thirty years
old, besides the fact that there had been so many miscarriages
when she had been married to Charlie.

'It's likely the heat,' Lucy answered, jumping up and
instantly regretting it as her head swam.

Mary pressed her back down into the seat and pursed her
lips. 'We'll see. You sit tight, ma'am. You've overdone it today

with all that gadding about. In your condition, you must be more careful.'

Mary poured her a glass of water and handed it to her. Lucy couldn't help but smile at her maid; there was no point in arguing. Mary was far too wily. The maid disappeared back into the bedroom, leaving Lucy to some very incoherent thoughts. Could Mary be right? After all, she had been feeling a bit off. And her corset had been noticeably tighter of late. The suspicion had been rattling around in her head for days, of course. And, only the other morning, she had cried in the bath for absolutely no reason.

A child! Was it possible?

How did she feel? She had no idea how Phin would react. Should she even tell him? He'd send her home, she was sure of it. A thought she could not bear. Besides, it would only end in disappointment like all the other times.

But what if it *was* different this time?

Lucy placed a hand on her stomach and dared to dream.

THIRTY-SIX

Lucy's eyes flew up from her book to the window as the thunderstorm raged. They had been so lucky to make their escape from Bellagio before the storm broke. Rumblings of thunder sounded right overhead, startling in their intensity, quickly followed by bright flashes of lightning illuminating her sitting room. Mary sat across from her, sewing, unperturbed by the activity outside. It wasn't the first storm Lucy had experienced at Lake Como, but it was certainly the most violent.

Between her fears about Revello and what he might be involved in, and Mary's hints as to her state of health, she had much to mull over. She felt a little safer now there was some distance between them and the hotel, but their hasty departure could not have gone unnoticed. She had never felt so vulnerable or so tense. Was Phin really on his way? What if they were intercepted and attacked? There was no way she would be able to get to sleep tonight until she knew he was safe. If only she could think about something else.

Lucy glanced over at Mary, who happened to look up and

smile. How astute of Mary to guess her condition. It was very early days, but the familiar queasiness had started a few days ago, and she could no longer put down the bloating of her stomach to her appetite for Italian desserts and ice cream. It was six years since her last brush with motherhood and that had ended in excruciating pain and devastating grief. An experience she had pushed to the back of her mind. Was that what awaited her? Hope raised, only to be dashed? The idea of being with child was overwhelming. And so soon into their marriage. But that wasn't the real issue. Every other time she had conceived, she had lost the child. Phin had so much on his mind at the moment. She didn't want to add to his worries. She would wait. If it were true, the signs would increase in the weeks to come. Time enough to hope. But it was difficult to dismiss the idea. The notion was tantalising but also terrifying. She had given up hope of ever being a mother.

There was a knock on the door. Mary made to get up, but Lucy held up her hand and called out to George, who she could hear pottering about in the adjoining bedroom. 'George, that will be the maid to collect the tray.' Mary smiled her thanks and took up her work once more.

'Very good, ma'am,' George said, picking up Lucy's dinner tray and heading for the door.

'Who is it?' George called out.

'Room service,' was the reply.

Seconds after George turned the key, the door burst open. George staggered backwards, the tray slipping from his hands and crashing to the floor. Lucy jumped to her feet only to see Revello stride into the room and make for George. He lashed out, striking George on the head with the butt of his pistol. Aghast, Lucy could only watch as the valet dropped to the floor, unconscious. She cried out in alarm and Mary, who had her back to the door, twisted around in her seat and let out a shout.

It was all happening so fast. Two more men entered the

room, one of whom slammed the door shut. One Lucy recognised as Bruno Armano. The other was younger and very similar in appearance. It must be his son, Lucy thought, recalling Giuseppe talking about Fiorella's brothers. How was it he had described them? Thugs?

So, it was true. Revello was in league with Armano.

'What do you think you're doing?' Lucy demanded, recovering her composure and doing her best to sound authoritative, although her voice shook.

Revello raised the gun, waving it at her. 'Be quiet!' Mary started towards George. Revello stepped in front of her. 'Sit down if you don't want to meet the same fate.' Mary backed away and returned to her chair, but her eyes never left George.

'How dare you threaten us. Get out!' Lucy cried, growing frantic. The expression in Revello's eyes worried her. Gone was the fawning hotel manager. His true nature was revealed. How clever he had been. He had hoodwinked them all for so long. Now, the question was, how desperate was he? The fact he had followed them here to Menaggio didn't auger well. Was he reckless enough to do them real harm? Even here, in this hotel? Lucy's blood ran cold. If he had killed Luca and Kincaid, it was unlikely he would baulk at finishing her and her servants off as well.

'I don't think so, madam. You and your damned husband have caused far too much trouble for us,' Revello said. He gestured to the younger Armano to come forward. 'Let's get on with this. Guido, put the blindfold on her. We don't have a lot of time.'

Lucy backed away but came up against a console table. Her mouth was dry, her senses on high alert, but she was trapped.

The young man gestured for her to turn around, a piece of black cloth in his hand. She had little choice.

Her heartbeat was roaring in her ears as the man roughly wound the cloth round her head. Then he pulled her back and pushed her into a chair. Lucy could hear Mary struggling. 'Don't, Mary. Do as they say.'

'Ha! The first sensible thing I've heard from you,' Revello said with a mocking laugh. He spoke rapidly in Italian, and the other men laughed.

'Now what?' Lucy asked, sounding more confident than she felt. This was bad, very bad. Phin would be so cross with her. They should have been more cautious.

'Now, we're going on a little trip, madam.' Something about the way he said it made her stomach churn.

'Are we to meet the same fate as the conte?' she asked.

'Tempting as that might be, no... at least, not yet. You're far more useful to us alive, at present. Go ahead, Bruno. Let's get on with it.'

Lucy heard footsteps approach. Someone went behind her chair and hovered there, making the hairs on the back of her neck stand up. What was he going to do?

There was the pop of a cork and a sickly-sweet smell filled the air. Before she could react, her head was pulled back, and a cloth was put over her nose and mouth.

Amid Mary's screams, Lucy gagged and struggled, but to no avail. Slowly, her senses dimmed until all was black.

THIRTY-SEVEN

Close to dawn, Molzanno, a hamlet in the mountains above
Lake Como

Lucy emerged from a deep dreamless sleep, disorientated, and
with a dry mouth and a horrible taste lingering on her tongue.
Her back ached. The mattress hadn't felt so uncomfortable
before. The bedroom was dark and smelled of damp soil. How
strange! Lucy shifted position only to realise something was
cutting into her wrists... She stretched out her arms to discover
she could not move her hands – they were tied together. What?

For several moments, she remained still, desperate for clues
as to what was going on. A moan broke the silence, sending her
heart pounding. It had come from nearby and had sounded like
Mary. Was she having a nightmare? Lucy's insides turned to
jelly. No, something was wrong. She tried to lift her head only
for pain to slice through it, making her wince. Where on earth
was she? The last thing she remembered was sitting with her
book, the storm raging outside. There had been a knock at the
door...

Someone was close by. Lucy could hear their deep breath-

ing. Might it be George or Mary? She tried to stay calm. Obviously, something had happened the night before, but what?
That nasty taste in her mouth and that strange smell in her
nostrils; they were curiously familiar. Where had she come
across them before? Lucy squeezed her eyes shut, hoping the
fog in her brain would clear. Chloroform: that's what it was. A
dentist had used it on Charlie once when he had to have a
rotten tooth removed.

Lucy tried to relax. There was no point in panicking. She
was alive. That was all that mattered. Whatever situation she
was in, she needed a clear head if she were to find a solution. At
least she wasn't alone.

A vision of a man waving a gun popped into her head...
Revello! He had something to do with this, but what? But her
mind wouldn't cooperate. All was fuzzy, like a dream. If only
she could remember. Then more images began to flash into her
mind, and she groaned. Revello and his cohorts had abducted
them.

Were they still at the lake? She had no memory of the
journey to this place. All Lucy did know was that they were in
trouble, but alive. The silence suggested they were alone.
Where were Revello and his comrades? Had they been abandoned somewhere? Would their assailants return to finish
them off? The latter thought sent her heart galloping once
more.

She needed to think. Moreso, she needed to move. Lying on
her back made her feel vulnerable.

'Mmmm.'

There it was again, that low moan, like an animal in pain.
Who was it? If only she could sit up. But the thought of moving
made her squirm, as she knew her stomach would object.

Take it slow!

The pain in her head was almost unbearable as she shifted
position onto her side. She stretched out her hands and touched

the unyielding earth beneath her fingers. She was lying on soil. Definitely not the hotel, then!

She pushed over onto her back once more and tilted her head up to look behind her. Only blackness. She reached out and felt cold stone. Digging her heels in, she wiggled backwards, and her head touched the wall. She took a gulp of air and pushed herself up. The rough stone caught at her hair, but slowly, slowly, she made it up into a sitting position. Her head throbbed, but she wasn't sick. This was progress.

From her new position, the room slowly came into focus, but it was still too dim to make out much, other than two dark shapes in human form on the floor to her left. Somewhat relieved, she guessed it was Mary and George. Thankfully, her senses were waking up. Now, she just needed to wake her companions.

The nearest shape was the bigger of the two. Lucy nudged what she hoped was George's arm with her foot. The shape grunted and moved, groaned, then went still once more. It *was* George. He must have been given more of the vile stuff than she had been. He was in a deep sleep. Or was his head injury so bad he was still unconscious? *Oh God! If anything happens to him, Phin will never forgive me.*

And Mary, on the other side of the valet, was far too still. 'Mary!' she called out. A whimper was the only response.

For now, Lucy had only her own wits to call upon. It might be ages before either of them came round. It was times like these that Lucy wished she had read more of those Gothic romances where the heroine escapes despite the odds. Or the handsome hero turns up and... oh dear! That wasn't a helpful line of thought. God only knew where her hero of a husband was at this moment. It was likely he was at Bellagio by now and regretting the day he married such a nincompoop. Lucy made a face into the darkness, then shuffled on her backside to lean against the stone wall. She closed her eyes and said a prayer.

There was little else she could do until there was daylight and the others awoke.

Voices. Angry voices woke Lucy. A squeal of ancient hinges and light flooded the room, blinding her. The dark shape of a man was silhouetted against the outside world.

'Good. You're awake. Get up!' It was Revello. To Lucy's disgust, he kicked at George's inert form.

'Don't do that!' she cried.

Revello turned to her. 'Wake up your servants or I will, in a manner they will not enjoy. We have a long way to go yet.'

Lucy glared back at him. 'Where are we? Where are we going?'

'It's always questions with you, signora. Too many questions. It does not matter where we are or our final destination. Just do as you're told.' Revello crouched down on his hunkers and placed a canteen on the floor beside her. He screwed off the top. 'Water.'

Lucy gave him an impatient glance and lifted her tied hands. 'And how do you propose I drink from that?'

With a grunt, Revello held the canteen up to her mouth, and she drank as much as she could.

'That will do,' he said, pulling the vessel away.

'If you have harmed them,' Lucy said, glancing at George and Mary still unmoving, 'I warn you, I'll not rest until you're hunted down and thrown in prison.'

Revello raised a brow and laughed. 'Save your threats. For someone in your position, you have a lot to say.' Then he stood. 'I told you. Get ready. We leave now.'

Two men passed in front of the doorway and Lucy recognised Bruno Armano. 'Your partner?' she asked.

Revello glanced around and grimaced. 'Needs must,' he replied.

'It's true then; you and the smugglers.'

'I saw an opportunity and took it. I have spent my working life kowtowing to the Carmosinos. Well, no more.'

'Don't play that card with me, sir. I'm aware of your history,' Lucy said, as her anger grew. 'The conte's father gave you employment when your family disowned you. And how did you repay the family? You stole from them and tried to ruin their business.'

Revello scoffed. 'What do you know, with your privileged background and your servants? Have you ever worked to pay your bills? Had to demean yourself before people who were your equal?'

'I help my husband with his work,' she replied.

Her captor gave a mocking laugh. 'I don't consider being a busybody as work, signora,' he replied with a sneer before striding out the door.

With daylight streaming in, Lucy could see that they were in a small house or hut, the walls bare stone with an earthen floor. Above her head were rafters, matted with cobwebs. There was a fireplace, empty, in one corner and a single shuttered window. Only one door. Escape didn't look possible. As yet. Hopefully, the journey ahead would provide an opportunity.

Beside her, George groaned. Lucy almost wept with relief as his eyes flickered open. But then he flinched as if in pain. There was a nasty gash on his temple and there was blood matted in his hair.

'George! George, wake up,' Lucy hissed. 'Are you hurt?'

'What—?'

'Revello and Armano have taken us captive,' she whispered.

George groaned, his gaze clouded. Then he made a face as if there was a sour taste in his mouth.

'That horrible taste is chloroform,' she said. 'That's how they got us here.' George clamped his mouth. Whether in anger or pain, she wasn't sure. 'I don't know where we are or where we are going. Revello won't tell me, but they want to take us somewhere. We must get up.'

George blinked at her, but slowly her words sank in, and cursing under his breath, he tried to sit up.

'Take your time,' Lucy said, giving him a sympathetic look. She held up her hands. 'Mine are tied, too. It's best to wriggle into a sitting position.'

As George struggled to sit up, Revello entered the room once more. He stared at Mary, who let out a gentle snore. 'You,' Revello said to George. 'Get up. We can't wait any longer.'

Then he stepped between George and Lucy and hauled Lucy to her feet. The sudden movement made her light-headed, and she almost fell back. Revello grabbed her under her arm and dragged her outside, none too gently.

Lucy looked around, trying to get her bearings. Before her, to the east, the sun had barely risen above the mountain peaks. Lucy reckoned it was just past dawn. Looking back over her shoulder, she could see that their prison the previous night had been a solitary stone hut on a rocky plateau, fringed by tall trees. Nicely isolated, she thought, and probably used by the smugglers as a hideout from the police. Armano and another man were hunched over the remains of a fire, close to the shelter of the house wall. Guido. Wasn't that what Revello had called the younger man? The memory of what they had done returned to her, and she shivered.

From their campfire, the tantalising scent of coffee wafted Lucy's way, and her stomach lurched. She had to turn away. Revello pulled her forward, and she caught a glimpse of the lake between a gap in the trees. It was clear they were high in the mountains and far away from any of the lakeside towns or villages.

A pathetic looking pony, attached to a farm cart, stood before them. Under a tree were two more ponies, nibbling grass. Without a word of warning, Revello picked her up and dumped her onto the cart, much to the amusement of the other two men. Then he marched back inside the house, emerging seconds later with George by the arm, who he pushed up into the cart to sit with his back to Lucy.

'What about Mary, my maid?' she called out to Revello. 'You can't leave her here.'

'I don't see why not. She sleeps like a baby,' he replied with a smirk. 'Two hostages should be sufficient.' Lucy exchanged a worried glance with George, but he could only shrug. Then he flinched. Even that slight movement appeared to cause him pain. Lucy suspected he was still coming round. Panic rose in Lucy's throat. They couldn't leave Mary behind. Anything could happen to her. Mary would be so frightened when she came around and found she was alone, but Lucy knew her appeals to Revello would go unheeded. She could only hope that someone would find the maid and set her free. Mary could raise the alarm. But what if that was too late? It might be days before anyone found Mary up here in the mountains.

She had to make one last appeal. 'Revello! Please don't leave her like that. At least untie her.' But Revello just smirked and turned away.

'Try not to worry, ma'am. Mary's resilient and resourceful,' George said after a moment, licking his lips and clearing his throat. George raised his tied hands to his temple and felt his injury with tentative fingers. He winced, sucking in his breath.

'Is it bad?' she asked.

'I've had worse, ma'am,' George said with the ghost of a smile.

'Have you any idea where we are?' she asked, eyeing up the Armano men who were now on their feet, pulling sacks onto their backs. Bruno cast her a scowling glance before kicking the fire to douse it.

'Unfortunately, no. But my guess is they are making for the border with Switzerland. They must know the master and the police are on their way. Mr Stone's letter could have been intercepted.'

'Or our sudden departure alerted Revello.'

George lowered his voice. 'I'm sorry, ma'am. We would have been safer getting a steamer and heading for Como.'

'Don't, George. There's no point in brooding over it. We must focus on how to get ourselves out of this situation... alive.'

'They have the advantage, though. As smugglers, they know these mountains well. The locals tell them where the police patrols are. Everyone is involved in it, as far as I can tell.'

'But Switzerland!' Lucy exclaimed in dismay. 'How will Phin find us? There must be multiple places to cross.'

'That is correct, however, my guess is they'll take the shortest route.'

'Hence their haste. Why are they taking us with them, though?' she asked.

'They'll hold us hostage until they are safely over the border. Hopefully, they'll free us once they cross,' George said.

Revello was a man who didn't like loose ends, so Lucy didn't share George's optimism. Doing her best to push down panic, she watched as Bruno and Guido clambered onto their ponies and Revello climbed onto the cart and took up the reins. With a jolt, the cart moved forward, taking them towards their fate, whatever that might be.

Lucy kept her eyes on the hut until it was lost to sight and whispered a prayer that Mary would survive.

THIRTY-EIGHT

Val Rezzo, Como

With Bruno riding ahead, and Guido following the cart, they lumbered along the rutted dirt track. The lad to the rear was constantly scanning the trees, sitting upright and alert in his saddle. Lucy figured the Armanos were acting as lookouts, which in a way gave her hope. She guessed these men knew the tracks and paths well, but were also aware of the dangers of coming across custom officials and police who patrolled these hills. If their luck held, the police might intercept them. Hopefully, police who weren't in Bruno's pay.

Lucy and George sat with their backs to each other on either side of the cart, and she felt every jolt, every bump, her stomach objecting, and her head pounding. Amidst the trees, the air was still and the thick forest on both sides gave shelter from the sun, but it also kept them hidden from the view of any potential rescuers. Here and there were hints of autumn orange and gold, but the undergrowth was dense. There was no way through it, even if she was quick enough to reach it. It would be pointless to jump from the cart, as she could not save herself with bound hands and Bruno's son was close enough behind to intervene. Besides, she had no doubt her captors would have no compunction in disposing of her if she were troublesome. One hostage would be sufficient to get them over the border. Every now and then, Lucy glared at Revello's back, out of frustration. There was little else she could do.

George was quiet, and she suspected he was suffering badly from that head wound of his. If there was anyone other than Phin that she would want to be with in this situation, it was George. His army training had been invaluable before. He was sensible, quick-witted and had proven himself an asset on more than one occasion, but she could tell he was struggling. It was disheartening to realise it was down to her to get them out of this mess. She almost laughed aloud, for she could think of nothing. It was as if her senses had been dulled. Perhaps she, too, was still experiencing the aftereffects of the chloroform. Her only hope was that Phin was in pursuit. Without question, he would try his hardest. But would it be enough?

Wherever they were headed, the track was getting steadily steeper. A pass high up in the mountains into Switzerland, as George had speculated, was the most logical destination. Were the passes patrolled? Would there be manned customs stations? She had no idea how many passes there might be. How did Revello plan to evade detection? Ah, of course! He didn't need to. Revello would use them as human shields. But could they risk depending on the kindness of Revello and Armano to just let them go when they got across the border? Lucy was certain they knew too much by now to be spared. Somehow, they had to prevent Revello and Armano from making it to the crossing. If she stayed alert, an idea might come to her, but her throbbing temples made it difficult to concentrate.

Some ten minutes later, hearing a low moan from George, Lucy twisted around. 'What's wrong?' she asked. But she didn't need to wait for an answer. A fresh trickle of blood was coming from the gash on his temple. 'Revello! Stop, please.'

Revello hunched his shoulders and ignored her, laying the whip onto the pony's side.

'Revello!' This time she shouted.

With a snarl, he turned. Lucy jerked her head towards George, who was now half slumped forward, almost in danger of falling off the cart. Revello cursed and pulled on the reins. Guido rode past, smirking, to join his father ahead.

Lucy twisted so that she could get her fingers into the pocket of her skirt. 'Here, use this,' she said, pulling out one of her lace-edged handkerchiefs. Revello snatched it from her and pushed it into George's hand. 'Press that against your head,' he snapped, his eyes flicking towards his companions, who were now disappearing around a bend in the track. He picked up the reins once more, urging the pony to move.

George dabbed at the blood. 'Thank you, ma'am.'

'Give it back to me,' she whispered, as an idea formed in her head.

George wiggled, twisting his body so that he could give her the now bloodstained handkerchief.

Their fingers touched and Lucy squeezed his thumb, trying to communicate... well, she wasn't sure what exactly. An idea... perhaps a silly one. It wasn't much, but it was something.

A clue to follow.

But then, as luck would have it, Guido rode past and took up sentry position to the rear once more. Lucy could have cried in frustration. She hadn't been quick enough. But she had to do something. Ensuring Revello was concentrating on the path ahead, Lucy let the handkerchief slip from her fingers and down onto the side of the track.

'What's that?' she called out, gesturing towards the tops of the trees. Would it be enough of a distraction so that Guido wouldn't notice the handkerchief? To her delight, he took the bait, glancing up as he rode past it. Even in the dimness of the forest, as they turned a corner, the white fabric appeared to glow like a beacon.

Half an hour later, and they were still amongst the trees. Lucy was losing hope. It was probably her last chance to get information from Revello. If she was going to die up here, she deserved to know why.

'How much further?' Lucy asked Revello.

'Not long now,' he muttered in response.

'Why did you have to kill Luca?' she asked.

Revello stiffened. 'There is no blood on my hands,' he replied, rolling his shoulders.

'Then who did?'

Revello whipped the pony. 'My obliging partner.'

'On your instruction?' she asked.

'Luca should have known his place. Should have stayed out of the business. He was never content to be just a conte. He was always meddling with his great plans.'

'What made him suspicious? Was it the robberies?'

'Yes. He knew it had to be someone working in the hotel and guessed the Armano family was involved. They are behind all the criminal activity in the region. My error of judgement was the Fitzwilliam Diamonds. They were too high profile. It cost me a fortune to pay off Marinelli only to find that Bruno could not dispose of them, as they were too recognisable. And then Luca blamed me for the fire.'

'How so?'

'He trusted me with the electricity project. I saw an opportunity to make some money, so I chose the cheapest quote. When Luca challenged my decision, I produced forged references for the company which he appeared to accept. He knew something wasn't right, but he had no evidence. All was well in the end. The contractor paid me handsomely for securing the work for him.'

Was there nothing this man wouldn't do? Lucy asked herself, exchanging a glance with George.

'And who carried out the robberies? Was it you?' she asked.

Revello gave a shout of laughter. 'Lord! No! I had a selection of staff, only too happy to earn extra money. Guests are so careless; it was easy.'

'And Fiorella found out?' Lucy asked.

'She guessed and had the effrontery to challenge me. Of course, she had figured out that her family had to be involved. Silly girl! Bruno didn't want her at the hotel, anyway. And we needed a scapegoat to placate Luca.'

'So, you ruined her life. That poor girl.'

'Fiorella was foolish. Didn't know when to keep her mouth shut and gave information to that insurance investigator. Another mess that had to be cleared up.' Revello sighed. 'Her father will deal with her in due course,' he said, so matter of fact that Lucy was appalled. She could only hope Fiorella had made good her escape.

'Was Enzo working for you?'

'Ah! You guessed. Yes. He was very useful, placed right in the heart of the family. That enabled me to be one step ahead. He warned me that Luca was going to the police in Milan with his suspicions. I instructed him to ensure Luca met with an accident while there, but Luca must have suspected something. He returned without Enzo and threw our plans into disarray. Thankfully, the weather came to our rescue. Luca, desperate to get home, travelled up the shore, trying to find someone to take him across to Bellagio. Unfortunately for him, he ended up in Argegno.'

'And Armano stepped in to silence him.'

Revello shrugged his shoulders. 'We had everyone watching

out for him. It was imperative he didn't make it back to
Bellagio.'

'What happened to him?' she asked, thinking of poor Elvira.

'Bruno was tipped off that he was staying at a lodging house
in the town, where he was waiting for the morning steamer. It
was easy enough. He killed him and a few days later, when the
first wave of panic had subsided, the body was transported up to
San Siro and hidden in a shepherd's hut up in the mountains.
We discussed what to do and as Bruno still had those diamonds,
I came up with the idea of planting them on the body and
throwing the corpse into the lake. It would have been a shame to
miss out on such a golden opportunity. Everyone would assume
Luca had risked sailing across and met with an accident. And
the best part was that he would be implicated in the theft of the
diamonds.'

'All to create a scandal. To make people believe Luca was
the thief,' Lucy said in disgust.

'Yes. Rather clever, don't you think? The more scandal, the
better. I want... wanted to buy the hotel. And what better way
to devalue it? I would buy it for half its value and build it up
once more, except the profits would be going into my bank
account, not the Carmosinos.'

'Matteo and Giuseppe would never have sold to you.'

'We had plans for them.' He shrugged.

Lucy gasped as a sneaking suspicion entered her head. Had
he used Enzo to put something in Giuseppe's food or drink to
cause his seizure? The depths of his depravity were boundless.
If he was prepared to do these things to his friends, there was
little hope for her or George.

'I don't understand you, Revello. Luca was your friend. His
father had helped you when you were in trouble. Gave you
employment,' she said.

'And I was reminded of that every day. There's only so
much gratitude you can proclaim before it turns sour. Luca's

father thought he owned me,' Revello growled. 'When you're treated like that, you want to hit back.' Revello turned and smiled. 'It was so easy for me when Luca took over. He trusted me implicitly.' Then his mouth twisted. 'And now, thanks to you and your meddling husband, I have lost it all.'

'Was it you who tried to shoot my husband?' she asked.

Revello sniggered. 'It was an impulse and I rushed it. I regret another opportunity never arose.'

'And Kincaid?'

'I can't take credit for that one. Bruno obliged.'

Ahead, Armano halted, jumped down from his pony and walked back to the cart. Lucy was relieved. The direction of her conversation with Revello had been worrying.

The two men spoke, then Revello turned to them. 'We will stop here to rest the ponies,' Revello said. 'Stay where you are.'

Revello walked a little distance away with Armano. They shared a canteen and Lucy looked on with longing. She was parched.

'Ma'am?'

'Yes, George.'

'We need to stall them. It's our only chance. I don't doubt Mr Stone is in pursuit, but he could be hours behind.'

'That's not very comforting!' she said, then relented when she saw how crestfallen the valet was. 'Sorry, George. Very well. What do you suggest?'

'I was rather hoping you had an idea,' he replied, his tone echoing her own despair.

'Oh! Me?' But her mind was still blank. 'I'm sorry. I'm at a loss. Other than to recommend we start praying,' she said, fighting a wave of hopelessness.

THIRTY-NINE

Val Rezzo, Como

At this point, every muscle in Lucy's body was objecting to the journey and her head still hurt. Nausea threatened as they jolted over ruts in the track. If she was with child, this journey wasn't doing her any favours. The irony wasn't lost on her. It had been stupid to hope that motherhood lay in her future. And if Revello killed her, Phin might never know. But perhaps that would be for the best...

Just as she was thinking the journey would never end, she heard Revello mutter under his breath, before pulling on the reins and slowing down the cart. A tiny spark of hope ignited. Was something wrong? Peering past him, she could see Bruno up ahead near a bend in the track. He had halted and was standing up in his saddle, his hand raised. Then around the bend ahead of him came Guido, gesticulating wildly as he galloped towards his father. Whatever he said next had Bruno turning his horse and charging up to Revello. Armano was flustered as he dismounted, and Revello jumped down to join him. When Guido caught up, they huddled together. There were some frantic hand gestures and rapid Italian spoken, none of which Lucy could understand. However, there was one word she recognised: *polizia*. She nudged George.

'I heard,' he whispered. 'Your prayers may have worked.'

The conferring concluded, Revello hurried back to the cart. 'You, get down, now!'

Guido jogged past, leading the ponies back down the track, the way they had come.

Lucy made a show of trying to get down, doing her best to delay. George was also taking his time. With an expletive, Revello rushed around the cart, and none too gently pulled George to the ground. George landed with a grunt. Then Revello came for her. One tug, and she landed gracelessly on her feet and promptly fell over. She'd have a lovely bruise on her thigh, but it might be worth it if she could stall for a few minutes. The police must be close by and might rescue them. Cursing once more, Revello drew out his gun, waving it towards the trees.

'Move now!' he snarled. 'Or we can end it here.'

With that, he grabbed her arm and jerked her to her feet, gesturing for George to precede them. Revello marched her off the track and down into the thick undergrowth. Lucy could almost feel the anger emanating from the man. Her heart pounding, she stumbled along as best she could. This could be it. If he were cornered, he would be capable of anything.

After a couple of hundred yards, Revello stopped and held the gun to her head. 'On your knees, both of you, and not one word,' he whispered, his gaze locked with hers.

Despite the heat, Lucy shivered. How had she never noticed how dead the man's eyes were? Lucy did as she was told, dropping to her knees. George followed suit. However, through a gap in the trees, she could see out towards the track. Bruno was now up in the cart, sitting with the reins on his lap, smoking, as nonchalant as you please. Guido was nowhere to be seen and Lucy guessed he had gone into the trees with the ponies further down the track to keep out of sight.

It wasn't long before the sound of hooves could be heard and two riders in uniform came into view. For an instant, Lucy knew relief, but it was soon quashed. Revello must have sensed her mood and pressed the gun against her temple, a warning clear in the intense stare he gave her. It nearly killed her not to cry out. They were so close. A similar thought was going through George's mind, she could tell by the sympathetic look he gave her.

The men's voices drifted across to where they were crouched in the brushwood. Were the police looking for her, or was it a routine patrol looking for smugglers and contraband? The only good thing was that the police appeared not to be in a hurry, which would buy Lucy and George more time. The local police would know Armano. It was common knowledge he was a smuggler. But could she be that unlucky – that these policemen were the ones in Armano's pocket? If they were, they would move on, do nothing. However, when Lucy glanced at Revello, she noted his creased and damp brow. He was worried. Good, she thought. Was it the policemen that worried him, or was he anxious that Phineas and the Milan police would catch up? But perhaps that wasn't a good thing. If he panicked, might he kill them on the spot?

Unfortunately, at that point, the police continued on their way. '*Buongiorno a te*,' the older officer said, and with a nod, they disappeared down the track. Lucy could have cried. Revello, breathing heavily, gestured for Lucy and George to keep still. He wasn't taking any chances.

Out on the track, Armano was still smoking, looking neither left nor right. After what seemed an eternity, Guido appeared and gave a low whistle. Beside her, Revello relaxed and stood.

'Back on the cart, you two,' he said, tugging Lucy to her feet and pushing her in the small of her back. 'Get moving.'

As Revello lifted her up onto the cart once more, Lucy was disheartened. The incident could only have lasted ten minutes at most; it would hardly make a difference and allow any rescuers to catch up. A sense of foreboding crept up on her and she had to swallow back some tears. To her disgust, as she looked on, the men joked among themselves, looking very pleased to have evaded capture.

In Lucy's mind, at that moment, the hope of rescue was as fleeting as the morning mist on Como.

San Lucio Pass, on the Italian/Swiss border

As they emerged above the treeline, about an hour later, Lucy was caught off-guard by the stunning views in all directions. She sat up straight, in awe of her surroundings. It was a beautiful place, with mountain peaks and steep valleys, cloaked in autumn colours wherever you looked. Far off in the distance, she could make out a snow-covered peak. If only she were seeing this scenery under different circumstances. With Phin. Lucy sucked in a breath. Thinking about him was too painful. Would she ever see him again? They had only been together for such a short time. And their parting had been so cool, neither of them willing to back down. How she regretted her hasty words. That would be his last memory of her. How cruel life could be!

Ahead, the dirt track continued in sweeping bends, climbing ever higher up the slope. Then, as they reached the brow of the hill, Lucy was astonished to see a small stone church, Romanesque in style, sitting in a hollow just below them. A stone marker at the side of the track named it as 'Chiesa di San Lucio'. The location of the church surprised Lucy. Who would come all the way up here to attend mass? Could there be a hamlet or settlement close by? Unfortunately, she realised within minutes that the place was deserted and any hope of rescue from a stranger soon died. Lucy guessed they were near the border now. Their fate was sealed.

Bruno and Guido rode up to the church, dismounted, and tied up their ponies. Revello followed, steering the cart over to the side of the building, then ordered Lucy and George to get off. Lucy wiggled her way off, unaided. But as her feet touched the ground, Revello whipped the pony around and took off, back down the hill. She stared after him. Was the crossing down there? Were they free? Lucy's delight was short-lived, however, when she spotted Bruno and his son advancing on them.

'Where has he gone?' Lucy asked Bruno.

'We do not need the cart now,' he replied. 'At dusk, we cross the border. We will wait inside,' he continued, pushing against the side door of the church.

Bruno held the door open, smirking, and George walked ahead of Lucy into the church. However, as Lucy crossed the threshold, she heard a shout in the distance and stalled. It had sounded like Revello shouting a warning. Bruno let out a curse and pushed her inside, slamming the door shut. Lucy and George stared at each other.

What was going on?

'Quickly,' George said. 'There may be another door to the outside.' He took off down the aisle towards the main door.

'George! We can't go out that way. They'll see us.'

A noise behind her made Lucy swivel around. Out of a door, close to the altar, a head popped out. Someone in uniform. Lucy gasped. A policeman! And he was armed. She thought she would faint with relief. The man emerged, followed by two others.

'George!' she called softly. He swung around just as he was about to open the main door. Shock registered on his face, closely followed by relief.

'Signora,' the first officer said, beckoning to her. 'Come!' He pointed at the door the men had just come out of. 'Safe in there,' he said.

Lucy realised it must be the church vestry. George hurried towards her and had just drawn level when the main door of the church burst open amid a volley of gunshots. Guido appeared, gun in hand. One of the policemen flew past Lucy, firing his gun at Guido, while the other two dashed out the side door. Guido fell and lay still.

Lucy stood transfixed. Terrified. Where was safe? What should she do?

The main door stood open, Guido's body half blocking it. From outside, Lucy could hear many voices and several more gunshots.

And then, suddenly, Revello appeared in the doorway. The remaining officer challenged him. Revello merely smiled, raised his gun, and shot him, whilst stepping over his dead comrade, Guido. The policeman fell to the floor, groaning and clutching his leg.

Lucy grabbed George's arm. They were defenceless.

Revello, eyes blazing, advanced towards them, the gun raised.

George stepped in front of Lucy, trying to shield her. Lucy squeezed her eyes shut, bracing herself, and began to pray.

A shot rang out and Lucy slid into oblivion.

FORTY

San Lucio Pass, on the Italian/Swiss border

Lucy came round, groggy and nauseous. The first thing she noticed was that her wrists were free of constraint. Puzzled, she stretched out one hand. Tentatively, she opened her eyes, only to see ruddy welts on her wrist where the rope had cut into it. She was lying down, but not on a floor as she had expected, but on a bench, staring up at the most amazing frescos on the ceiling. It was then she realised where she was and that she wasn't alone. She turned her head only to find Phin, white-faced, kneeling before her. Phin!

He helped her into a sitting position, then cradled her face. 'Are you hurt?' he asked, his voice hoarse with emotion. 'You've been unconscious for several minutes.'

'Was I? No, no. I'm fine. A few bruises, perhaps. That is all. I must have fainted.'

Phin kissed her. 'You never faint,' he teased.

'My only excuse is that it has been a very long day,' she replied, her voice shaking.

He kissed her again.

As pleasant as that was, Lucy pulled away. Everything that had happened came flooding back. Lucy looked about, frantic to find her fellow captive. 'Where is George? Is he injured? Oh, Phin, I think he was shot! I'm so sorry. This is all my fault!'

Phineas jumped to his feet, then sat beside her, putting his arm around her shoulder and pulling her close. 'No, no. Calm down, my dear. George wasn't shot. He's a little shaken, but he will be fine.'

'Thank heaven! But are you sure? The last thing I remember was Revello pointing his gun at us.'

'You chose that moment to absent yourself,' Phin said with a hint of a grin.

'Oh, yes, I see... I think.' Lucy was confused, however. 'But what happened? I'm certain I heard a shot.'

'You did. But it was mine. I had no choice.' Phin gulped and his jaw clenched. 'I had to kill Revello before he could harm either you or George.'

'Oh, no, Phin.' And she burst into tears, the build-up of a day full of stress. After a few minutes, she grew calm. 'You're telling me the truth about George, aren't you?'

'Yes, I promise. He is fine. Nothing that a few days' rest won't cure.'

'I think he deserves more than a few days. He was marvellous, Phin. How will we ever thank him? I would have been so lost without him on that awful journey up here.'

'I don't doubt it; he is always a good man to have around in a crisis,' he replied, swallowing back emotion.

'He kept me sane, and he would have taken that bullet if you hadn't...'

'Yes, he would, and I'll be forever grateful to him.'

'And Revello; where is he?' she asked, looking at the bloodstains on the floor a few yards away.

'He and his cohorts are dead. You have nothing to fear. It's over.'

'Thank God!' Lucy clutched his arm. 'But what about Mary? Revello left her in that awful hut. There was nothing we could do to help her. Was she found?'

Phineas smiled. 'Yes, we found her outside the hut, sitting in the shade, cursing all mankind. As you can probably guess, she wasn't terribly happy about being abducted and then abandoned. However, her only concern was your safety. Don't worry about her. One of the officers escorted her back down the mountain on horseback. Quite a sight, I can tell you.'

'I can imagine. She hates riding. But I feel terrible. We had no choice but to leave her. Revello wouldn't wait for her to come round. But she is unharmed?' she asked.

'Yes! She was well enough to harangue me for leaving you alone and, as she put it, scampering off to Milan without a care in the world.'

Lucy giggled. 'If she said that, she's fine, then. But I'm confused. How did you get here so quickly?'

'We – that is Matteo, Commissario Falcone and I – arrived back in Bellagio to discover you had left. I was relieved at first that you had done as I'd asked. But when we searched for Revello, we discovered he was missing. I could only conclude that he had followed you. Luckily, George had left a message for us at the post office, so we took the next steamer to Menaggio. But when we arrived at the Hotel Victoria, all was in disarray. Fortunately, a guest had made a complaint about the noise from your suite and the duty manager had come up to check. When he found the door wide open and saw signs of a struggle, he contacted the local police.'

'We arrived just as they were about to comb the grounds. Then, by chance, one of the night porters told us he had seen Bruno Armano acting strangely at the rear of the hotel earlier in the evening. Half an hour later, he saw him leave with two other men and they had a heavily laden cart. He assumed it was smuggler activity and wanted to keep out of it. However, he did note the direction they took.'

'Thank goodness! So, you followed.'

'Matteo and I, with a group of police, set off immediately. Falcone stayed in Menaggio to orchestrate things from there, just in case we were on a wild goose chase and Revello was spotted somewhere else. Unfortunately, at that stage, Revello and Armano had at least an hour on us. By now it was dark, so we hoped Revello's little cavalcade would stop somewhere for a few hours. He had the advantage because Armano knows these hills well, knows where every shelter is, where to hide. We guessed Armano would most likely make for the border and that San Lucio was the quickest route.'

'That was lucky,' Lucy said.

'Yes, and we knew we were on the right path when we found Mary this morning. She couldn't tell us much, but there were signs of a hasty camp. About halfway up the mountain, I spotted this,' he said, pulling Lucy's bloodstained lace handkerchief out of his pocket, his finger tapping her embroidered initials. 'It worried me a little, but it convinced the police we were heading in the right direction. Half an hour later, we met a patrol coming down the track who confirmed they had met Armano. We speeded up, then, I can tell you. Luckily, one of the young local officers knew of a shortcut, a track through the trees. It was a tough ride, very steep, but it meant we could get ahead of you. As soon as we got here, we hid. Matteo and I were outside just at the tree-line keeping watch, and some officers were in here in the church. We didn't have long to wait before your party arrived.'

'Thank God you got here! I thought it was the end, Phin. I truly did. He would have finished us off after he crossed the border. We knew too much.'

Phin hugged her tightly. 'I can imagine how terrified you were. This is my fault.'

'No! It's mine. You see, I disobeyed you.'

Phineas chuckled. 'I'd have been more surprised if you hadn't!'

'Well, you see, it was too good an opportunity to miss. I saw Revello leave the hotel, so I had to follow. He met up with Armano in Bellagio, but by the time I got back to the hotel and read your letter, we had lost a lot of time.'

With a frown, Phin looked at her. 'You're such a handful, Lucy.' Then he broke into a grin. 'Just as well I love you so much.'

Somewhat relieved, Lucy leaned over and kissed his cheek. 'But I am sorry. Truly. It was a stupid impulse which cost us dearly. Poor George and Mary were frantic by the time I showed up.'

'Ah, you didn't tell them you were haring off?'

'No,' she replied meekly. 'There wasn't time.'

'I'm not surprised they were upset. It was a little foolish of you in the circumstances.'

'I agree and I did apologise to them,' she replied.

'Well, if it's any consolation, you aren't the only one with regrets. I was halfway to Milan when I began to worry that I shouldn't have left you alone. But of course, it was only when Falcone told us about Luca's visit to his station that I knew the full extent of Revello's actions and how dangerous a man he could be.'

'Please don't blame yourself.' She waved her hand around the church. 'This could have been avoided if I hadn't succumbed to my... impulse to investigate.' She gave him a self-effacing smile. 'Do you think there's a cure for it?'

Phin laughed. 'I doubt it. You're a terminal case, my love.'

They sat for a few moments in silence.

'Is that the first time you have shot someone?' she asked.

To her astonishment, his eyes were bright with tears. 'It was,' he replied. 'When we ambushed him, he turned and fled back towards the church. I knew what he'd try to do. His target would be you, and I had to stop him.'

'Oh, Phin!'

'I hope I never have to do it again,' he said simply. 'But I would! You're too precious.'

Lucy squeezed his hand. 'Thank you – I hope you're never in that position again. But you must realise he had no compunction about killing. And he admitted to me he had orchestrated Luca's death. I suspect Enzo, the valet, sent him a telegram to say Luca was on his way to Como. Revello had Armano and his gang lying in wait for Luca when he arrived. They must have followed him, waiting for an opportunity. They attacked him at a lodging house in Argegno. And... and it was Revello's idea to plant those diamonds on Luca. So, you see. He was a cold-blooded man, and he would have shot George and then me, purely out of revenge for you foiling his escape.'

Phin shifted his position. 'Let's say no more about it, my dear.' He stood and held out his hand. 'Let's get you home.'

Lucy knew it was time. 'Before we do, there's something I need to say.'

Phin gave her a concerned look. 'What is it?'

'You were right. I should have left when you told me to. All of this could have been avoided. I'm sorry.'

A slow smile spread across his face. 'My dear! I know how much it costs you to say that. I'm sorry, too. I didn't want to force you. I only said it because I feared the worst.' He sighed. 'Can I dare to hope that if a similar situation should occur—'

'Yes! I'll trust your judgement,' she said, trying to smile in return. 'If it's a reasonable request, of course.'

'You're incorrigible, Lucy!' But his chuckle belied his words. 'Now, please, can we leave?'

'Certainly, but first, would you mind if I say a prayer of thanks?' she asked, pointing to the top of the church.

'This is a Catholic church,' he replied.

'I don't think God will mind,' she said.

Ten minutes later, they went back out into the sunshine. At the edge of the plateau, the policeman who had been shot was being attended to by a colleague and a little distance away, Matteo and George were talking quietly. Both men turned around and smiled as she and Phin walked towards them.

Overcome with emotion, Lucy rushed up to George and gave him a huge hug. 'Thank you,' she whispered. 'I'm forever in your debt.'

'You're welcome, ma'am,' he replied, his voice a little shaky.

'That wound is nasty. We must get it seen to as soon as possible,' she said, eyeing the blood encrusted on his temple.

'The doctor in Menaggio will attend to him,' Matteo said, giving George a gentle pat on the shoulder. 'A brave man, to do what you did.'

'Hear, hear,' said Phin, extending his hand to his valet. 'Thank you.'

George went bright red as they shook hands. 'It was nothing, sir.'

'On the contrary, George, I think you're courageous, too,' Lucy said. 'Thanks also to you, Matteo.'

'I was only too glad to help, Lucy, and I'm delighted to see you're unharmed,' Matteo said, holding out his hand but instead of shaking her hand when she did the same, he raised it to his lips and kissed it.

Lucy was rather taken by his gallantry but didn't dare look at Phin. Instead, she scanned the surrounding area, almost fearful she might see Armano or Revello still. A couple of policemen were patrolling the area, whilst another two stood aside at a distance, something on the ground between them. As Lucy watched, another policeman appeared over the brow of the hill with Revello's pony and cart. He steered it up to his comrades, which was when Lucy realised the large bulky object on the grass was, in fact, the corpses of her kidnappers. Unable to look away, she watched as the bodies of Armano, Revello and Guido were lifted onto the cart. A blanket was then thrown on top of them, and the cart was led away.

FORTY-ONE

Grand Hotel Bellagio, the next afternoon

Dr Spina pushed his spectacles up his nose, staring down at her with a frown. 'You've had a lucky escape, signora.' Lucy gazed up at him, tempted to laugh at his underwhelming summation of the previous day's events. She still couldn't quite believe she was alive, unscathed, apart from a few bruises and welts on her wrists. It was wonderful to be back safely with Phin in Bellagio.

'But no long-term effects, doctor?' Phin asked, coming in the door at that moment.

'I'm fine,' Lucy said with impatience. 'There's no need to fuss.'

'I advise bed rest for a few days,' Spina said to Phin, as if she had not spoken. 'In her condition, at her age, there's no knowing what might happen if you attempt to travel home in the near future.'

Lucy seethed. She had hoped the doctor would treat her revelation of a possible pregnancy in confidence. Phin gave the doctor a funny look, then raised his brows at Lucy, who just shrugged.

'Thank you, doctor,' Phin replied, still looking confused. He walked the medic to the door and shook his hand. After closing the door, Phin paused, shoving his hands into his trouser pockets; something Phineas never did. He stood for several moments, staring at the carpet. Then he quirked a brow, an expression in his eyes she had never seen before. However, as he came back across the room, he was frowning at her.

'Is there something I should know?' he asked.

Lucy patted the side of the bed. There was no way out. She'd have to tell him. 'Possibly. Sit down and stop looking so worried.' How to find the words to reveal she might be pregnant, but that it was likely it would end in the coming weeks. It almost seemed cruel to get his hopes up. Drat that stupid doctor for blabbing!

'Do you know,' she said, 'I've had the most marvellous idea.'

'Oh, yes?' However, he looked suspicious; diverting his attention was probably pointless, but she had to try.

'Now that Luca's murder and the theft of the diamonds is cleared up, and I must rest up anyway, why don't we stay on here for a few more days? We never had a honeymoon. I'd love to explore more of the lake.'

Phin took up her hand from where it lay on the cover and brought it to his lips. 'An excellent idea, my dear' – he gave her one of *those* looks – 'but before we firm up on a travel itinerary, you might like to tell me what's going on. What did Spina mean by *condition*?'

There was no way out. She'd have to tell him. 'I was going to tell you, soon, but I wanted to be sure,' she said, staring down at the bedcover. 'It's possible that I am with child.'

His hand clenched around hers. Silence.

Lucy looked up and was shocked to see Phin had tears in his eyes. 'But... but you're not sure?' he asked.

'It's only a few weeks and I have an unfortunate history, I'm afraid, as I told you. I'm so sorry. This is so cruel; to give you hope and then snatch it away. That's why I was reluctant to tell you. I was waiting... hoping.'

Phin put his arm around her shoulder and pulled her close, resting his chin on her head. 'But luck might be on our side. And if the worse should happen, it won't change how I feel about you, about us.' He kissed her head. 'Ah, Lucy, don't cry. We will get through this.'

'Thank you,' she said, her voice muffled by a handkerchief. She hated being this emotional. They had so much to be grateful for. A change of subject was required.

'Did you write to Elvira?' she asked after a few moments. 'She will be very shocked, but at least she will know what happened. That Luca had been trying to do the right thing.'

'Yes, I wrote a letter last night while you slept. I hope it gives her some comfort. Such a pity Luca didn't realise how dangerous a man he was dealing with, *and* that he was in above his head,' Phin said.

'Do you know, I think we all were?' she replied.

Phin gasped, then a slow smile appeared, and he nodded. 'I hate to admit it, but you may be right.'

Lucy snuggled back against him as the evening shadows crept into the room, the sound of children playing in the grounds below drifting up through their open window. It was the sound of hope. And Lucy suddenly realised that where in the world they were didn't matter. Home was where Phin was. The man she loved to distraction.

The next afternoon

'Mary! Stop fussing. You're worse than my husband!' Lucy took a deep breath and immediately regretted her words as she turned to face the maid. Mary's face had fallen.

Lucy stepped forward and took the maid's hands in her

own. 'I'm sorry. We're all at sea at the moment. I'm so happy but also terrified.'

'You told 'im, then?'

'Yes.'

Mary grinned. 'I'm that happy for you!'

Lucy found her throat was tight. 'Thank you. But let's be cautious. No one else must know.'

'Not even George?'

Lucy smiled. 'George has been giving me some concerned looks. I suspect Phineas may have told him or George may have guessed; I've never seen Phin grin so much.'

'Good, because we must all look after you now,' Mary replied in a determined tone.

Lucy didn't know how to respond and blinked back some tears. 'Right! Well, what were we talking about? Oh yes! You're right, of course.' She patted the half-done corset around her waist. 'This corset will no longer do. You may order a larger size.'

Mary grinned and flicked a glance at Lucy's stomach. 'I told you so! You're getting bigger.'

Lucy smiled and turned away quickly. The slightest twinge, anything unusual at all, and Lucy was panicking, desperate to hold on to the dream. A child would make their life complete. There! She had admitted it to herself.

You're destined for a fall, Lucy, my girl!

Why were the dire warnings in her head always in her mother's voice?

Lucy shook herself free of her scolding mother. Most of all, she dreaded the look on Phin's face if she had to tell him that dream was over. Best to shove it to the back of her mind and concentrate on the here and now.

'We're lunching with the Carmosinos. Could we try on the lighter of those mourning dresses? I think it's more forgiving around the waist.'

'Yes, ma'am,' Mary said. 'The very thing, for I suspect it will be hot again today.' Mary scooted over to the armoire and pulled out the dress. 'I won't miss this here heat when we get home.' Mary stood, with the dress draped over her arm, her face taking on a dreamy quality. 'Cor, a bit of London mist and drizzle would do me heart good. We will leave soon, won't we, ma'am?'

'My understanding is that we will depart for London at the end of the week, Mary,' Lucy said. And although she had advocated for a honeymoon here on Como, she suddenly wanted nothing more than her maid wanted: the comforting surroundings of home and the sooner the better.

Lunch was a pleasant affair, out on the hotel terrace, in the shade. Matteo was in excellent form and Lucy suspected he had thoroughly enjoyed the hunt for Revello and Armano and seemed determined to dissect every minute of it with Phin.

Lucy smiled at Giuseppe, who was sitting beside her. His answering smile was tempered with sadness as he observed his nephew.

'Are you feeling better, Signor Carmosino?' she asked.

'Giuseppe, please. There's no need for formality,' he said, to her utter surprise. 'We're family now, after all.'

Taken aback, all Lucy could do was blink at him. 'Tha... thank you, Giuseppe. What has the doctor said?' she asked because the grey hue to his face worried her. 'I know he went to see you after me yesterday.'

'Pah! Rest, eat less... blah, blah. I'll do as I please!' Giuseppe said. But there was a glint in his eye as he lifted his wine glass. '*Saluti!*'

'*Saluti!* Giuseppe, you're a rogue!' she answered, clinking his glass. 'It's amazing how a brush with death makes you appreciate every little thing. Of course, we may never be able to prove that he had Enzo tamper with your meals.'

'That scoundrel Revello! I will not have his name mentioned again in my hearing,' he replied.

'Phineas tells me that Commissario Marinelli has been arrested,' Lucy said. 'It would appear that he made a lot of money from Armano and Revello.'

Giuseppe quirked his mouth. 'Little good it will do him now.' With a sigh, he twirled the stem of his glass. Then he gave her a strange look. 'I don't suppose you'd consider staying longer?'

Lucy was astonished and then burst out laughing. 'Are you trying to tell me that you will miss me?'

'Yes, indeed.' He leaned in closer. 'It's not often I find a decent sparring partner.'

Lucy beamed. 'Don't worry. I'm sure we will come back to visit Elvira.'

'Good,' Giuseppe grunted. 'Although Luca and I were constantly at loggerheads, I was very fond of him. He stood up to me and I admired him for it. I miss him.' He took a sip of wine. 'Matteo, however, agrees with me far too readily.'

'He is young and in awe of you, perhaps,' Lucy said, glancing across at the young man who was still in transports about his adventure.

'The business needs a firm hand at the helm until such time as Salvo can take over. Matteo can't manage all of this alone,' he said, glancing around. 'He must stay in Milan, and I will have to take a more active role here until such time as I'm sure Salvo is ready.' The old man sighed, but Lucy suspected he relished the idea. 'And now we have the added responsibility of Elvira and the children.'

'Elvira is stronger than you think. She is very much like Phineas, you know. At the moment, she is grieving and needs the comfort of her family at home. When she comes back, you will see.'

'Are we not also her family?' he demanded, a brow raised.

'Yes, but you must admit you haven't been... the most supportive,' Lucy said.

His eyes flashed. 'Ah! We're back to plain speaking.'

Lucy touched his sleeve. 'You will always get that from me. Isn't that why you like me so much?'

Giuseppe roared with laughter and Matteo stopped mid-sentence and stared. Phin gave her an encouraging glance, tinged with amusement.

'Then, Lucy, she will return?' Giuseppe asked. 'With the children?'

'Absolutely.'

Giuseppe looked relieved as he nodded. Perhaps there was hope of some kind of reconciliation between him and Elvira. 'I'm delighted to hear it. Little Salvo must learn how to be a Carmosino, and a proud Italian.'

'Of course,' Lucy said, hiding a smile. 'But Elvira will need to know she can rely on you and Matteo. The future will not be easy. Of course, Phin and I and all the family will help in any way that we can.'

'I suppose that means you will plague us with visits at least once a year?'

It almost sounded like an invitation. Lucy could only nod.

Giuseppe grunted once more, and Lucy felt that was as good an acceptance of exterior influence and help he would ever accept.

After a moment or two, Giuseppe reached once more for his glass and raised it. 'To Luca!'

They each raised their glass, as their personal memories of the conte filled their minds. However, Lucy's thoughts were firmly fixed on her grieving sister-in-law.

'To Luca!'

EPILOGUE

Phillimore Gardens, London, July 1889

Lucy sat curled up on the window seat in her bedroom. Outside, the world still slumbered and across the room, gentle snores told her Phin slept soundly. To the east, there was a glimmer of early morning pink above the rooftops. But it was a watery pink, not the magnificent hue she would always associate with dawn on Lake Como. It was odd. For some reason, in the last few days, Luca Carmosino had been in her thoughts. Was her own recent near-death experience the explanation? Of course, she could remember little of that time. Faces had swum before her, as she had been ravaged by an infection and a high temperature. Phin, Lady Sarah and even her own mother had been at her bedside. Lucy's mouth twitched. That really had been a shock. Perhaps seeing *Mother's* face had been enough to jolt her back; to fight against the tide of heat that consumed her body. After all, the last thing Lucy wanted was for her mother to step in... No. That was unfair. Charlotte Somerville wasn't the worst mother to grace this earth, just a very neglectful one. Lucy sighed. They were back on speaking terms, but God only knew how long that would last.

Phin muttered something in his sleep and turned over, his face now resting on the palm of his hand. It made him look almost childlike, and she swelled with love. How lucky she was! What would her life have been if she had not met him that day at the mortuary? If her first husband Charlie had lived, would they still be cooped up in that cheerless house in St. John's Wood, him with his secrets, lies and mistresses, and her dreams merely splinters piercing her soul? Poor Charlie. He hadn't set out to hurt her, but he had been a weak man whose moral compass was always pointed due south. She'd had a lucky escape, and it was always best not to question fate too closely.

The last nine months had tested them to their limits, but through it all, Phineas had been her rock. Always supportive, always loving and, most important of all, always understanding. They had grown so close during her pregnancy. Sometimes he drove her mad when the kid gloves were on, and although there had been terrifying moments, they had come through. At times, she worried about what toll it had had on him. Yesterday, she had noticed a few grey hairs at his temples. Once she had reassured him it was distinguished, he had sighed with relief. George, who had been helping him into a jacket, had almost burst out laughing. *Dear George!*

Lucy looked out once more. She had promised herself she would wait until dawn. Self-discipline was not her strong point – as dear Phin often pointed out – but she was learning to curb her impulsiveness or at least to give that impression. Still, what harm could it do? Phin was sound asleep. If she was quick, he'd never know. She slid off the seat and padded across the floor to the door. As she pulled on the door handle and the door eased open, the hinges squeaked. Phin mumbled something, then rubbed at his nose. Lucy froze, the urge to giggle almost overwhelming. Seconds later, he was snoring again. The coast was clear.

She'd have to be fast.

Lucy skipped up the stairs, careful to avoid the step that creaked. She tiptoed along the top-floor hallway, past the servants' bedrooms until she reached the door at the end. For a moment, she rested her head against the door, listening. Not a peep.

Smiling broadly – she couldn't help it – she opened the door.

And drew up short.

'Mary!'

'Morning, ma'am,' the maid whispered with a grin. She was sitting between the two cots, her hand resting on the wooden rail of one of them, rocking it back and forth. 'I thought I heard a cry and should check.'

'Liar!' Lucy exclaimed with a grin. 'You can't stay away, either.'

Mary stood and gestured for Lucy to take her place. 'I'll bring you a cup of tea, ma'am.'

Lucy stared down at the tiny miracles: her son and daughter. 'I keep having to pinch myself.'

Mary stalled at the door and turned around. 'Good things come to good folk, as me mother always says.' The maid was suspiciously teary-eyed.

'Thank you,' Lucy replied, wishing she had a handkerchief.

'I won't be long. Don't go spoilin' 'em while I'm gone.'

'Mary?'

'Yes?'

'You're far too familiar!'

'I know!' Mary said with a wink and was gone.

Dear Mary. They had been through so much over the years. Anyone else would have left long ago, appalled at the situations she had been dropped into, the brushes with villains, the proximity of death. Mind you, the maid frequently gave voice to her complaints, and at length. But Lucy suspected, deep down, Mary loved every minute of it. Just as well, for Phin was in such demand of late. So much so that he had agreed to take his brother Seb on to help at the agency. Now that the children were safely delivered and thriving, Lucy looked forward to helping Phin with his investigations. Well, perhaps in a couple of months...

Too late to escape, she heard the creaking of a floorboard out in the hall.

'I thought as much!' Phin walked in, shaking his head.

'I thought I heard one of them cry,' she replied, Mary's excuse coming to mind.

Phin peered into each cot in turn. Then gave her a knowing look. 'They look sound asleep to me. Just as well, with such a momentous day ahead.' He held out his hand and drew her to her feet. 'You are well enough for us to go ahead, aren't you? We could postpone the christening—'

'Absolutely not. Besides, Elvira and the children have come all the way for the occasion. I can't wait to meet baby Luca. And your father has travelled up from Kent.'

Phin grinned. 'It's all a bit of a circus.'

'Nonsense. Everyone is happy for us,' Lucy replied. 'Did I tell you my friend Judith is coming and my Uncle Giles?'

'You did. And with his new wife, too. That will be jolly interesting,' Phin replied with a chuckle.

'Mother will hate it, of course,' Lucy said, 'for you know what a snob she can be. Him marrying a former servant is unthinkable in her eyes. She's still reeling from Richard's conviction, and my exploits haven't helped matters.'

'I'm well aware of your mother's foibles. I had daily confirmation of her intolerance and snobbishness while she stayed when you were ill.' Was it her imagination or did Phin just shudder?

'Poor Phin! Was it very dreadful?' she asked, but she was laughing up at him.

'Yes, though I handled it with stoicism.'

'Of course you did!'

'I was very hard put-upon.' He pouted. But then drew her into his arms. 'But anything for you, my dear. I couldn't love you more.'

'I'm glad to hear it,' she said with a cheeky smile. Then she turned in his arms to look down at her children. 'Are we agreed on the names?'

'Definitely,' he replied. 'Harold Sebastian, and Eleanor Sarah.'

With a contented sigh, Lucy reached up and kissed his cheek. 'He has your eyes.'

'And Eleanor has your nose,' he replied. 'I only hope she has your spirit, too, my love.'

A LETTER FROM THE AUTHOR

Dear reader,

Many thanks for reading *A Pocketful of Diamonds*, Book 4 in The Lucy Lawrence Mystery series. I hope you enjoyed Lucy and Phin's Italian adventure. If you would like to hear more about new books, you can sign up here:

www.stormpublishing.co/pam-lecky

For news about my writing, upcoming deals and recommendations, you can check out my author newsletter:

subscribepage.io/jf9sWM

If you enjoyed this book and could spare a few moments to leave a review, that would be hugely appreciated. Even a short review can make all the difference in encouraging a reader to discover my books for the first time. Thanks so much!

This story was partly inspired by a holiday spent on magnificent Lake Como. As I delved into the history of the lake, and in particular the popularity of the area in Victorian times as a tourist destination, I couldn't resist setting a Lucy story there. I was further inspired by the derelict shell of Hotel Grande Bretagne, a relic of the golden age of Victorian tourism. It now sits sad and desolate on the outskirts of the town of Bellagio, with tantalising glimpses through the trees of how glorious it must have been in its heyday. Then I couldn't believe my luck when I learned that smuggling had been a huge issue in the area, right up to WW2. It's wonderful when research yields so much material for intrigue! Let's face it, Lucy and Phin's honeymoon was never going to be a quiet affair!

If this story inspires you to visit this incredible region of Italy, even better. Please stay in touch on social media or sign up to my newsletter to find out what happens next...

Thanks again for being part of my writing journey.

Pam Lecky

ACKNOWLEDGMENTS

Without the support of family and friends, this book, and indeed my entire writing journey, would not have been possible. My heartfelt thanks to you all, especially my husband, Conor, and my children, Stephen, Hazel and Adam. I am very grateful to my chief beta readers, Lorna and Terry O'Callaghan, who have read every draft and given me invaluable feedback.

Special gratitude is owed to my agent, Thérèse Coen, at Susanna Lea & Associates, London, whose belief in me, along with her sage advice, helped to bring Lucy Lawrence to life.

Producing a novel is a collaborative process, and I have been fortunate to have wonderful editors, copyeditors, proofreaders, and graphic designers working on this series. To Kathryn Taussig, my editor, and all the team at Storm Publishing, thanks for believing in this series and taking it to the next level. A massive thank you to Bernadette Kearns, my original editor – all the books in the Lucy Lawrence series benefited hugely from your input.

I am extremely grateful to have such loyal readers. For those of you who take the time to leave reviews, please know that I appreciate them beyond words. To the amazing book bloggers, book tour hosts and reviewers who have hosted me and my books over the years – thank you.

Special thanks are owed to my friend Sheila O'Connor who did some digging on my behalf regarding police forces, police procedures and legal issues in Italy at the time the novel is set. I was also very fortunate to find the Museo Barca Lariana, located on Lake Como. My thanks to Emanuele Seghetti, who works there, for kindly providing me with details and photographs of the various types of boats found on the lake in the late Victorian era.

Last, but certainly not least, I am incredibly lucky to have a network of writer friends who keep me motivated, especially Valerie Keogh, Fiona Cooke, Catherine Kullmann, Suzanne Hull, Jenny O'Brien, Brook Allen and Tonya Murphy Mitchell. Special thanks to the members of the Crime Writers' Association, the Historical Novel Society Irish Chapter, and all the gang at the Coffee Pot Book Club.

Go raibh míle maith agat!

Pam Lecky
September 2024

Made in the USA
Las Vegas, NV
14 March 2025

19572614R00187